Responsible Men

Responsible Men

a novel by

EDWARD SCHWARZSCHILD

ALGONQUIN BOOKS
OF CHAPEL HILL
2005

Published by
ALGONQUIN BOOKS OF CHAPEL HILL
Post Office Box 2225
Chapel Hill, North Carolina 27515-2225

a division of
Workman Publishing
708 Broadway
New York, New York 10003

Five opening lines from Psalm 1 from *A Book of Psalms: Selected and Adapted from the Hebrew* by Stephen Mitchell. Copyright © 1993 by Stephen Mitchell. Reprinted by permission of HarperCollins Publishers Inc.

Portions of this novel first appeared, in very different form, in *StoryQuarterly* and *Moment* magazine.

Library of Congress Cataloging-in-Publication Data
Schwarzschild, Edward, 1964–
    Responsible men : a novel / by Edward Schwarzschild.—1st ed.
    p. cm.
    ISBN-13: 978-1-56512-409-7; ISBN-10: 1-56512-409-X
    1. Philadelphia (Pa.)—Fiction. 2. Fathers and sons—Fiction.
3. Divorced fathers—Fiction. 4. Jewish families—Fiction. 5. Sales
personnel—Fiction. 6. Family reunions—Fiction. 7. Bar mitzvah—Fiction.
I. Title.
PS3619.C489R47 2005
813'.6—dc22   2004059780

10 9 8 7 6 5 4 3 2 1
First Edition

For my father and his father.
And in memory of Mildred D. Merin.

◆

A salesman is got to dream, boy. It comes with the territory.

—Arthur Miller

Responsible Men

ONE MID-JUNE MORNING, Max Wolinsky sat in his LeSabre, getting ready to sell what would never exist. He was back in Philadelphia, visiting from Key Largo for his son's bar mitzvah, and while he was in town he'd decided to raise some much-needed cash for his aging father, Caleb, and his stroke-slowed uncle, Abraham. Max didn't like running a new scam so close to his family. Don't shit in your own backyard, as the old commandment goes. It hadn't been his backyard for months, but still, for his father's sake, the last thing he wanted was a mess.

He reviewed the information he'd jotted on a three-by-five card. He had more than enough to work with. *Gail and David Gould. In their seventies. Talked to agents about selling their house. Already visited Breyer's Run and Curtis Estates. Love the New Jersey shore and used to summer at the Ventnor Motel.*

He wasn't going to use his real name. He rarely did in business anymore. For the Goulds he planned to be Larry Zevin, nephew of one of their dead, distant friends. He plugged his razor into the Buick's cigarette lighter and ran the buzzing blades over his face. He wondered if his son, Nathan, was shaving yet. Probably not, though how could he be sure? It had been six months since they'd seen each other, and back then some peach fuzz had begun to appear on Nathan's upper lip and chin.

Max checked his work in the rearview mirror, trying to decide if he looked like someone who had a thirteen-year-old kid. He tended to think of himself as a youthful forty-one, a man who resembled his son more than his father. He kept himself in decent shape; he had his hair, and it was dark brown, without gray. His whiskers, however, were tinged with silver.

Before climbing out of the car, he slapped on aftershave, packed away his latest cell phone, and fingered through a folder of well-made documents: map, floor plans, artist's rendering, miniature blueprint, and glossy pamphlets. Large teal letters headlined each piece of paper: OCEANVIEW GARDENS — THE RETIREMENT RESORT.

I have what they want, he told himself as he walked up the winding flagstone path, swinging his briefcase. *I hold the key to their future.* It was a big front yard and there was more land around back, full of fruit trees, flowers, and green freshly cut grass. A Honda and a Volvo waited in the driveway.

Max straightened his tan linen sport coat and rang the bell. When the door opened, he started pitching to the elderly couple before him. The only word he wanted to hear from them was *yes.*

"My name is Larry Zevin," he said. "I'm Stuart Fox's nephew. Are you Mr. and Mrs. Gould?"

"Yes," said Gail.

"I understand that you want to live near Atlantic City some-day. You want a retirement community by the ocean. On the boardwalk. Far from the casinos. Affordable. Also at least partially Jewish. Am I right?"

"Yes," said David.

"I have a few things I'd like to show you," Max said. "May I come in?"

"Yes," they both answered. David opened the front door all the way.

Max stepped in, moving at their pace. It was ten thirty in the morning and Gail looked like she intended to work in her garden before the weather became too hot; she wore faded blue jeans and a gray T-shirt that matched the wiry hair she'd done up in a red bandanna. David, in his white polo shirt and khaki slacks, could have been on his way to meet a few friends at the golf course. Max glanced around at their nice things and decided where he wanted to sit: on the couch, in front of the large window. Get them on either side of him. Let the sun shine on his back and give him an aura of gold. From where he stood by the baby grand piano, he could see the stately dining room, a crystal chandelier dangling down. The kitchen was back and away to the left. At the far end of the dining room, there was a sliding glass door that opened onto a screened-in porch. "This is a wonderful house," Max said. "A real estate agent's dream. Probably sell in a flash."

"We were very sorry to hear about Stuart's passing," David said.

"It took us all by surprise, Mr. Goul—"

"David, please."

"Well, David, it's like this. Age did not come gradually to

Uncle Stuart. He woke up one morning and it knocked him down and it kept on knocking."

"I still have some coffee in the pot," Gail said. "Can I get you a cup?"

"No coffee for me, thanks, Mrs. Gould. But I'd take a glass of water, if that's not too much trouble."

"No trouble," she said. "And it's Gail."

Following the Goulds to the kitchen, Max noticed the paintings on the walls and the antiques that decorated the dining room—candlesticks, vases, salt and pepper mills, a tea set on a wooden cart. He also noticed how closely David watched his wife, as if she were in constant danger of falling.

"Yes," Max said, "Uncle Stuart was thrilled with how things were going and he tried to share that. He was the first salesman in the family. Loved the business and taught me quite a bit over the years."

"What exactly happened to him?"

"There was one stroke and then there was another. Near the end, he struggled to speak." Max paused and thought that if he changed the names, it would be completely true. He rubbed one of his eyes with his palm. Exhaled. Then he went on. "The words he said were not the sort you and I could understand. He was deep in conversation with himself. But I didn't come here to depress you. I'll tell you this, though. The whole situation led me into this new project. It suddenly made sense to me."

"Let's sit down," David said. "Then you'll show us what you've got."

Gail handed out the drinks and the three of them walked back into the living room. Max took his place on the couch. He set his glass on the coffee table, pulled out his folder, and put the case down at his feet.

"Tell me this doesn't happen to you," he said. "People call you on the phone. They don't even know who you are. You say 'Hello?' three times before they realize there's a voice they can talk to. They want to tell you about a deal, an opportunity. It takes five minutes just to get them to stop talking. It takes another five minutes to end the conversation politely. I get those calls myself. 'I'm busy,' I tell them. They offer to call back at a more convenient hour. 'No, no,' I say. 'There will be no convenient hour.' Now, up front, here's what I'm emphasizing: You want me to be quiet, you don't want me to go further, just say so. I'll stop right away and I'll disappear. Your time is too precious."

"The phone companies are the worst," David said. "I like telling them I don't have a phone while I'm talking to them, just to hear what they say."

"I bet they keep right on going, don't they? Not me. I'll listen. That's what I want you to know."

As if on cue, Max's cell phone rang, a muffled beeping from his case. "I should answer it," he said. "Do you mind?"

"Not at all," Gail said. "You can go out onto the porch."

Carrying his case and folder with him, Max stepped through the house. He didn't close the glass door behind him, but he spoke quietly. He paced the porch as he talked, admiring the view and the furnishings. The floor was made of red cedar, like a giant picnic table.

"Is this the right time?" his father asked.

"Perfect, Dad."

"Is everything okay? You're not having any problems, are you?"

"No problems," Max answered. "I'm getting them. Thanks for the call."

In a louder voice, close to the door, Max said, "We don't have many left. Tell her I'll do what I can. I'll look on the list." Then he hung up and hurried to rejoin the Goulds.

"Sorry about that," he said, sitting between them. "Just the office, checking in. So, let me show you what I've got in this folder. You know the Jersey shore pretty well, right?"

"We used to stay in Ventnor for weeks at a time," David said.

"And we ride a bus to the casinos every now and then," Gail added.

"Ventnor is where we intend to be. We're closing on the land. We've got the designs together. The zoning hearings are almost finished. And, with what the office just told me, we've already reached 87 percent occupancy. But there's still space available for couples. This is a two-bedroom, third-floor, ocean-view unit I thought might interest you. Here's what the building itself will look like."

Max drank his water and watched the Goulds study the documents. They hunched over to get a good look. They handed the papers back and forth to each other. Max waited for questions, smiling at the floor plan as it passed before him. It had small pieces of cutout furniture placed in each room, like a child's pop-up book. Each little chair and table was taped to the page so clients could try their own arrangements. The piece that represented the living room's sofa bed actually unfolded, just to show there would still be plenty of space when guests spent the night.

David sat up, leaned back into the couch, rested his hands on his stomach, and slowly rubbed one thumb around the other. "When will you start building?" he asked.

"That's an excellent question," Max said. "We want to break ground this summer. Finish construction by the end of the year. Then be ready to open the doors at the start of spring. Eleven months from now, give or take a few weeks. That's our aggressive time line."

Max was well prepared for the questions that followed, about facilities, meal plans, and health care. He answered in detail, quoting extremely competitive numbers.

"It seems too good to be true," Gail said.

"Tell us about the down payment," said David.

Max sipped his water. He didn't speak until he had set the glass back on the table. "Look," he said. "People have worries. Uncle Stuart, for instance, he used to worry about what sort of neighbors he'd have. My father, he doesn't want to be trapped in the middle of nowhere with nothing to do. So, instead of rushing to down payments, I'd like you to do this. Take some time and make a list of concerns. Write down what you want and what you don't want. Imagine the place of your dreams. Everything that comes to mind. Then we can get together again and see if our retirement resort is the right place for you. How does that sound?"

"Sounds sensible," David said.

"I'll leave you these copies of our materials and one of my cards," Max said. "Just give me a call when you've finished your list and we'll set up an appointment. Maybe I'll be able to bring the director with me. In the meantime, if anything new develops on my end, I'll let you know."

"Thanks for coming by," Gail said.

Max closed his case and stood up. "My pleasure," he said.

AFTER PARKING NEAR Fifth and Cheltenham Avenue, Max walked into the basement apartment where his father and uncle had lived together ever since the strokes. The smell in that small space carried more than mere below-ground dampness.

Caleb and Abe sat in easy chairs and they looked as if they were in the process of becoming moss. They could see fragments of legs move past their sidewalk-level windows. Judge the weather by the footwear.

When Max entered the living room, Abe called out, "Maxie!"

Max turned to his father. "Looks like we'll be needing the voice, Dad. A few days and it will be time to make the call. I'll be counting on you."

"I'll do the best I can. What were the Goulds like?"

"They wanted to talk about down payments. They're making their list. What's been happening here?"

"Abe thought Nathan's bar mitzvah was today, so he bothered me about that. When I convinced him it was tomorrow, he went back to bothering me about the scooter."

The last time Max had come to town, Abe was still in the hospital. Back then, there'd been talk of rehabilitation. Recovery. But Max didn't see any evidence of that now. If anything, Abe was worse, his speech stranger and more sporadic than it had been six months ago. His body was betraying him and his mind was wandering further and further afield. Occasionally his obsessions would help him focus on the real world, but those moments were brief and, in some ways, at least as difficult as the silences.

During his last checkup, a nurse had let him try a scooter—one of those battery-powered chairs that he could drive around on his own. Maybe she just wanted to see if he could handle it. Apparently, he enjoyed the sensation. Ever since then he'd been fixated on having a scooter of his own. Max had heard about it on the phone. "He can still nag," Caleb had said. "I'll give him that. But those things cost a few thousand bucks. It's not in the budget, no matter how much he badgers me. Plus the doctors say he should be more active, not less."

Max glanced over at Abe, who was silent now, staring at the TV, which was not on. He looked like he was waiting for something to start. "Did you tell him I was working on scooter money?" Max asked.

"I told him that," Caleb said. "That and many other things."

"It seemed almost too easy today," Max said. "Even easier than down in Florida."

"The Goulds will be all right, won't they? You're sure they can afford this?"

"Don't start with the second thoughts, Dad. The Goulds will be fine."

Caleb pushed himself out of his chair, stood, and shook his head. "I know," he said. "But imagine if someone did it to us."

"It's been done to you already, just in a different way. Look at this place."

Caleb didn't bother to look around. "If we ever get enough money," he said, "we'll move somewhere better." He stretched out his thinning arms. "Right now, however, it's time to take a stroll." He walked over to Abe's chair and knelt on the carpet like a shoe salesman. He helped his older brother change from slippers to sneakers. Abe stared at his feet and said, "My territory was not always so small."

"Where is there money to be made?" Caleb asked, loosening the laces.

"Try Singapore," said Abe. "Asia. Try Seoul. Try Tokyo."

Max watched the two of them. He imagined them going through this same routine day after day. An older brother fading fast, dragging the younger down with him. Max didn't want to think about it.

"Hey," Caleb said. "Don't just stand there staring. Ask your uncle about Alaska."

Max played his part. He tried to put some vigor in his voice. "How about Alaska?" he asked.

"Alaska never fails," Abe answered. "I knew people."

Caleb started to ease Abe up from the chair. Max grabbed one of his uncle's arms to help. "We're walking," Caleb said. "Here we go."

Abe reached for the black cane that was leaning against the wall. Then he shook free of his family's hands. "Don't touch me," he said, stepping out the front door. "Always be closing," he added, as Caleb and Max followed behind.

2

IT WAS HOT, but Caleb still felt glad to be outside. He was in the mood for a long walk, the kind of walk he used to take with his brother and his son. The three of them could stroll up Cheltenham Avenue, make their way to the original Lee's Hoagie House for lunch. After some exercise, in weather like this, a cheesesteak with onions, hot peppers, and sauce would hit the spot. He'd wash it down with an ice-cold vanilla cream soda.

But Abe would want to cut the walk short. Maybe he'd last one lap around the block. Then he'd refuse to go farther. And Caleb was tired of fighting him.

He told himself to focus on the positive. Max looked good. Florida didn't seem to have done him any harm. His tan skin made his teeth seem whiter. He had his bounce back—he pushed himself up on his toes as he moved forward, the way he'd walked when he was a little kid.

They passed Lamont's Dry Cleaners, the run-down Executive Office Plaza, and the new Asian market, which had recently appeared right where Seymour's Deli used to be. The road widened to four lanes, the traffic grew louder and picked up speed, and still they walked. This was good news. Abe had his hand on Max's arm and Max was talking, saying something about Key Largo. "People don't think of it this way, but the place is claustrophobic. There's not much land and it's incredibly flat. If you're not out on the water, you can't see past the mangroves. It's like living surrounded by tall hedges. You get no view at all."

Caleb smiled as he listened. It wasn't his image of the Keys, but he wasn't thinking about Florida. He was thinking about how everything was easier with Max around. Just look at them go. Who knew what Abe could really take in anymore, but his mouth was shut, and he seemed to be concentrating, looking Max in the eyes, leaning close. Maybe they'd actually make it to Lee's. Caleb was tempted to point out they were more than halfway there, but he didn't want to break the spell.

"You're fine if you've got a boat," Max said. "Divers, fishermen, smugglers—they're happy on the Keys. I'm not sure it's for me, though. I'm not convinced it's the right location for my future."

Caleb wiped the sweat off his forehead. He should have worn a hat. Still, he felt strong. He could pick up the pace. The people in the passing cars, if they happened to glance out their windows, wouldn't see him as an old man. He carried himself well. He stood up straighter to prove it. He was a fit father with a handsome son, taking an aging brother for a walk. Anyone could see that.

Then Abe stopped walking. "Enough," he said, abruptly turning around.

"Wait a second, Abe," Max said.

Caleb turned, too. "It's not worth it," he said. "He won't budge. I'm surprised we made it this far."

There was a Wawa minimarket at the next corner and Max pointed to it. "Well, let me jump in there for a second. I need to pick up a few things."

Abe was already heading back the way they'd come, his cane tapping against the sidewalk.

"He won't wait," Caleb said. "I'll stay with him. You shouldn't have any trouble catching up to us."

Caleb watched Max jog down the street. Then he walked after his brother and tried to take his arm.

"Quit it," Abe said, moving away.

Caleb wondered how the same old thing could still make him so angry. He wanted to help, wanted their days to be busy and full, but Abe just wanted to get back to his Barcalounger, where he could sit and stare from morning to night. Not the future Caleb dreamed of, not the future he deserved. But who gets the future they deserve?

"You know something, Abe?" Caleb said. "I liked our old walks a hell of a lot better than this. It doesn't have to be this way. It would be good for you to keep walking. It's not that hot out."

Abe moved faster, swinging his cane, as if there were now a rush to get home.

Caleb followed along. "Who knows what you remember in that head of yours?" he said. "I wonder if you even remember the old days anymore."

As HE WALKED, Caleb let himself drift back to those old days. Or maybe it would be better to call them the young days. He was a new father then, often on the road, driving through his territory. He looked to sell all over Pennsylvania, Maryland, New Jersey, and New York. He and Abe sold textiles. They were manufacturers' representatives, working for the mills, selling to the garment makers. They did their traveling, but there was also plenty of business right in their hometown. Three hundred fifty potential clients in the Philly metro area alone. That's how it used to be, not so very long ago, him and Abe hustling in and out of their small downtown office. They called themselves Wolinsky Brothers and Associates. Sounds like a circus high-wire act, and sometimes it felt like one, but they were just simple middlemen, moving goods, yard by yard. No one paid them a salary. They made their money on commission—1 percent, occasionally 2—or they didn't make money at all.

Sometimes people asked Caleb who his associates were. They heard him laugh. "Ha! We never had any goddamn associates! And we never will!"

He'd done better than his Russian father, and his son would do better yet. From the bottom to the middle to the top! School was a ladder, good grades were the rungs. He used to imagine Max climbing through college, up into medical school, but after that his vision went cloudy.

"What if I don't want to be a doctor?" Max asked every now and then.

"Ha! You can be any kind of doctor you want. You can be a surgeon. You can have a family practice. Make X-rays. Work with kids. Fix emergencies."

"Did you hear my question?"

"Yes, I heard your question. Hear my answer. If you don't like being a doctor, you can become something else. You will have plenty of opportunities."

Through good times and bad, Caleb was an early riser. "I got it from my father," he'd say. Years ago, when all was well and getting better, he liked the quiet of the mornings. Bathrobed and barefoot, he padded downstairs, switched on the kitchen lights, stepped out to bring in the paper. After he showered, he listened to the radio, the volume low, as he shaved. Breakfast was Shredded Wheat, and then he put the coffee on. If it wasn't a travel day, at just after six he would wake his wife, Naomi. He'd kiss her, tell her how it looked outside, and say, "I'm off to sell." Before he went back downstairs, he'd stop in Max's room and nudge him awake. "Be good to your mother," he'd say.

It was different on travel days because he had to leave the house long before sunrise. Once a week he drove to Baltimore or Scranton or Harrisburg. Twice a week he rode the train to Trenton and New York City. On those mornings he settled for notes, scribbled on loose-leaf paper, dropped silently onto the bedspreads of his wife and his son, close to their pillows. *Clear and sunny,* he might write. *I'll drive with the windows down. You were in the middle of a good dream when I left.* Then he headed for the car.

He used to buy cars based on their trunk size because he needed room for his bulky binders and his briefcases full of samples. For almost a decade, he chose Chrysler New Yorkers. They rode like luxury liners. And starting early meant no traffic in his way. He had a jump on the whole city, unguarded in the dawn light, and, to him, during those hours, the world was a broad ocean, calm, before the wind picked up. He could cruise downtown, out Roosevelt Expressway and then up along the Schuylkill. The skyscrapers were battleships, his allies, powerful and majestic on the brightening horizon. He steered toward them. Off to starboard he could see smaller boats on the water, scullers practicing, rowing up and back near the art museum. By six thirty he could be in his office or in Trenton or forty minutes outside of Baltimore.

He was good at what he did and he had his goals. He wanted to sell more. Make more money. Not the most original objectives, it's true. Did he love his work? Well, he never felt that, but he loved his wife and he loved his son. They were all on their way up together.

Back in 1963, Caleb and Naomi bought a small brick house in Cheltenham, outside of northeast Philly. They'd been married only a year and already they had their own backyard, with a patio and a stone barbecue. They bought a red picnic table and benches. They hung a tire swing from their oak tree. They had an oak tree! Then they learned they would have a baby, too. After work, Caleb puttered in the yard, putting in a garden, while Naomi sat dangling on the swing, more and more pregnant. Everywhere he dug, Caleb found amazing things. Mostly old glass bottles, marbles, pieces of china. A thin silver ring. They lined up the objects above the kitchen sink, treasure to study while they washed their dishes and their hands.

In the house, out in the yard, wherever they walked, Caleb gazed at his wife. He could barely say anything about her. He talked for a living, but he couldn't talk about her. If anyone asked, he said they had to meet her. He'd first met her in Wanamaker's. He was checking to see what the store was stocking, something he did from time to time, in Philadelphia and New York, just to make sure he was up-to-date. He saw a young woman getting bad advice from a salesman. She was trying on a pantsuit with a Nehru jacket. The material was a decent double-knit, but the sewing was shoddy, all single-needle work, so he pulled a few better pieces off the racks and walked over.

The salesman took Caleb for the woman's husband; the woman took Caleb for another salesman. He showed her why the clothes in his hand would last longer. He ran his fingers along the seams. "This cut is better for you," he said. "It's a better garment. And these colors are better for you. Turquoise, umber, rose." She stepped into the fitting room. When she came back out, anyone could see that Caleb had been right. "What else are you looking for today?" he asked. And they went on from there.

Years passed by. Caleb still didn't love his work, but nothing made him happier than providing. To celebrate how happy he was after seven years of marriage, he arranged for Abe to stay with Max, and he took Naomi on the train to Atlantic City. He'd booked a weekend at the Marlborough-Blenheim Hotel, high above the boardwalk. In addition to the normal amenities, every bathroom had hot and cold running salt water. Who needed the ocean? You could make waves in the tub and adjust the temperature yourself! They did both of those things in their tenth-floor room, and they strolled the boardwalk in the evenings. Even then Atlantic City wasn't what it used to be; it was losing out to Florida, but it was still a fine place to feel young and in love and on your way up. It was a fine place, late at night, to walk across the beach, down to the surf, hand in hand, talking and talking, all about having another child, and maybe it would be a daughter this time.

Caleb had arranged a surprise to end the weekend: They wouldn't ride the train home. Instead, he gave Naomi the keys to a baby blue Datsun Fairlady. When she climbed in, she gripped the steering wheel and leaned forward. "Will I fit here when I'm pregnant?" she asked.

They roared back inland with the top down and they had to shout to be heard. Naomi drove them through the salt air, racing toward the Pine Barrens. Some people called the Fairlady a stubby car. The windshield was too high, they said, and Datsun skimped on the chrome. But it thrummed along, fast. Caleb felt the adrenaline rushing through him and he wasn't even driving. Just holding on tight. Just grinning like mad. They'd park this pretty speedboat right beside his luxury liner. Yes, they were a two-car family now, with a son, a house, and excellent prospects.

He didn't have to reach far to massage the back of his wife's neck. She slowly tilted her head up and down, stretching into his touch, and then she turned to face him. He wasn't the only one grinning.

THREE MONTHS LATER, Naomi smashed that new car into an embankment on Lincoln Drive. She hung on in critical condition for sixteen hours before passing away.

AFTER THAT, WHAT was left? For a long time, Caleb had no answer. He had his son, his brother, his friends. He had routine. Memories. He started getting up earlier and earlier. Why stay in bed when he couldn't sleep? Hours would go by before he could wake Max. They were not productive hours. He tried to focus on being a father. People would have understood if he'd started drinking. Months passed. He did not drink. People told him he was still a young man. He talked for a living, but he said a lot less.

What did he want? He made a list. That age-old salesman's tool.

> *I want never to have bought that car.*
> *I want to have been in that car with her.*
> *I want to recover.*

Abe lived with Caleb and Max in the house for a year. Abe, the older brother, was a lifesaver back then. "Go on," he said. "That's what we have to do. I'll stay with you for a while."

So Caleb worked. He drove his big car. He watched his son grow and he tried to help.

Of course, if she hadn't died. At first, that's what Caleb thought about constantly. If she were somewhere waiting to be found. If she just needed some peace and quiet for a while, some healing time to herself.

What exactly would have been different? Well, who can begin to say? Those left behind become who they become.

Max did not become a doctor. He did not go to medical school. He spent a year in college before dropping out and joining the family business. That was supposed to be a temporary arrangement. He was supposed to get his feet back on the ground and then move on to bigger and better things. He was supposed to go back to school, but he didn't. Instead, he moved on to trickier kinds of business. He traveled on his own and more years passed by.

Then Max found Sandy. They met at a bar in Chestnut Hill, the courtship steamed along, and in less than four months they were engaged to be married. Caleb wasn't even tempted to complain about how quickly they'd decided. He knew it could happen that way. Plus, he'd believed his son was sinking, drifting down instead of rising up. It was easy enough to see Sandy as a savior, and that was before she was pregnant, before she delivered Nathan into the world.

How could he not have hope again? He saw his son become a husband and a father, he saw his son supporting a family, providing, and he remembered what it felt like to come home after a full day's work to his wife and his baby boy. He'd pull into the driveway, trying to guess where they were and what they were doing; he'd picture them playing out in the yard by the swing, reading together in the living room, working on dinner in the kitchen, sewing something down in the basement. He was often right, though more often wrong, but, really, it didn't matter since either way he'd walk in and call out to them and Naomi would call back, and once he was old enough Max would call back, too, and sometimes they'd rush to him and sometimes he'd rush to them, and that would be the beginning of the best part of the day.

He'd thought Max was in the middle of that kind of happiness. Even though they didn't talk about it, Caleb believed he could see it. It was difficult to describe. There was the bounce to Max's step, but it was more than that. After Naomi died, Max seemed to grow quieter and quicker—you couldn't get a word out of him and he was always leaving the room so he could be somewhere by himself, his feet hardly making any noise at all as he slipped out the door. It was as if he were becoming less visible, almost disappearing, for weeks and months at a time. At first, Caleb assumed he was at fault—he'd lost sight of so many things and now he had to add his own son to the list. When he began to pay closer attention, he noticed more about how hidden Max was—hands in pockets, shoulders tensed, head down, sleepy eyes. Then Abe started talking about it, too. "We need to look out for Max," he'd said. "I don't like the way he's leaning."

Abe made the bigger effort, taking Max along on business trips, telling him stories as they drove from client to client. Abe even took Max on a Florida vacation. Max improved, but never completely, at least not until Sandy. She brought back the Max who'd been around when Naomi was alive. Once again, you couldn't miss him in a room. He was taking on weight. Not growing heavier but becoming more solid. And, to top it off, his smile returned. Though it was bigger now, it was still the same smile Caleb used to see when his son was shouting "Dad!" and running right to him.

MORE YEARS PASSED and, for many of them, Caleb almost forgot about worrying. He wanted to tell Max to appreciate everything, savor it, but he held back, afraid of crowding his son, and, besides, he figured Max had worked that out on his own.

Then, one day, Sandy was moving on. There was no accident. No car, no crash, no death, thank God. Sandy simply took the steps she needed to take in order to live more fully, or so she said.

Max drifted further away this time, disappearing all over again. Caleb watched and listened. "Nathan will be better off growing up without me," Max said. To his credit, Max acknowledged the irresponsibility of it, the shallow self-pity involved, but he insisted he was just being realistic. He claimed to be learning about gaining and losing confidence, and he had no confidence in his ability to be a decent parent. "I can't be a good influence," he said, more than once.

Caleb let his son go. He couldn't have stopped him if he'd tried, and he knew that certain things took time, and even time was no guarantee. He saw through the corroded credo, the excuses and rationalizations, that Max tried to stitch together: Where had ethical behavior ever gotten the family business? Most everyone takes advantage when they can; why should I be different? Who in this world goes twenty-four hours without deceiving someone?

Months went by, and now it was almost a year, and Caleb

kept hoping Max's life would change back again, return to solid ground. He wanted to believe that despite everything, Max desired to be good. He wanted to believe that Max was telling the truth when he said that Abe's stroke had made him decide to become a better son and a better father.

That's what Caleb was thinking when he heard his son's voice again, heard the lively footsteps, and turned to see his bouncing boy approach. "Hey, you two," Max called out. "I have brought sustenance for our journey."

Max waved a brown paper bag when he caught up. He pulled out three packages of Tastykakes. Butterscotch Krimpets. The light brown frosting already melting in the heat. They weren't cheesesteaks, but they looked good to Caleb. Even Abe was smiling. So they stopped, leaned against a brick wall in front of a dentist's office, and ate.

"Thirsty?" Max asked.

Before either Caleb or Abe could answer, Max lifted a bottle of cream soda out of the bag. He twisted off the top and passed it around.

At such moments, Caleb could almost understand how he'd managed to hold on to the dreams he'd had for his son. It still surprised him, that hope. It didn't feel very strong when Max was a thousand miles away. But when Max came to town, there was possibility. Caleb could feel it again as he drank down the soda, so cool and refreshing.

3

WHEN MAX VISITED Philadelphia, he would often take a morning walk with his father and uncle, and then, in the evenings, he would walk by himself. The night before Nathan's bar mitzvah, he turned down New Second Street and headed into the suburbs. There were few streetlights, as if the residents didn't fear the darkness. He strolled by quiet parks and the word that passed through his mind was *pure*. It was more than the tennis courts, the fields, the ponds, the landscaped lawns. *I could still fit here,* he thought. *I could be another well-dressed man, a homeowner, a friend of the family.*

Gradually, the houses gave way to minimalls. Max enjoyed stopping in at open businesses — a bar, a pool hall, a Laundromat. He drank a beer, shot a rack, watched a bundle of whites tumble in a dryer. He sat silently and no one bothered him.

He ended up in Rockledge. When he saw the neon red sign for Del Ennis Bowling Lanes, he thought it might be relaxing to bowl a game or two. The building resembled an airplane hangar, placed at the end of a parking lot, next to a supermarket. It was an old-style alley, where you kept score yourself with paper and pencil. There were locker rooms for men and women. A pro shop. Fifty-four lanes. Machines that looked like ovens from the sixties would wash your ball for a quarter. The main counter had a small bar attached, and there you could buy beer, hot dogs, potato chips. The hot dogs sizzled as they rotated on metal rollers. They smelled fine. Max sat on a stool and decided to start with a beer.

The bartender seemed to be the only one working the night shift. He was a round young man, with a body like three stacked bowling balls. His shirt had the name Shelly sewn into it in gold. "You need shoes?" he asked.

"Just beer for now. Might roll a game later."

"Might be room for you," Shelly said, puffing on a cigarette and looking out over the many darkened lanes.

Max smiled and sipped the beer set before him. He watched a couple teenagers who weren't taking their games seriously, just hanging out together. Several lanes down, four large-bellied guys got a little loft on each shot. Beyond them, two men who looked about Max's age had leather wraps for their wrists, one towel to dry their hands, another towel to wipe the oil from the ball. They were on separate lanes, practicing. They followed through and struck often. But Max looked longest at two women he saw as mother and daughter. For a moment, he caught the daughter's eye.

Shelly stepped away from the desk to check on a pin-setting machine, and Max wondered how much he could take if that were the way he worked.

Eventually, the daughter came over to buy a beer. While she

waited for Shelly to get back behind the counter, she lit a cigarette. Max liked the black hair that hung halfway down her
neck. She was trim. She was a few years younger than he was, a
few years older than the woman he'd been seeing in Florida.
"Couldn't help noticing," he said. "You throw a mean hook."

"Thanks."

"But it looks like your mother's the real bowler in the family."

"How'd you know she was my mother?"

"It's what I saw. Used to go to a place like this with my father.
My name's Max."

"Estelle," she said.

They shook hands. She had a strong grip. "Why isn't your father here?" she asked.

"He's too far away. You mind if I tell you something corny?"

"Tell me."

"I hear him bowling when it thunders," Max said. He looked
down at his hands and then he looked into her eyes. Sometimes
the words that came out of his mouth surprised even him. But
the key, as always, was to remain light on his feet. "Let me get
you that beer," he said.

"You waiting for someone?"

"I'm drinking a beer."

"You want to roll a game or two with me and my mother? It
would be good for us to slow down a little."

"I wouldn't want to impose."

"No one's asking you to impose. Bowl with us if you want to
bowl. You can bring your beer. To even things up, I'll buy your
next round."

"Let the buyer beware," Max said, getting up off his stool.

"What?"

"I'll get some shoes and come over."

ESTELLE'S MOTHER, JANET, reminded him a bit of Gail Gould, silver-haired and hardworking. Estelle watched her mother closely and Max could see why. Janet had classic form. She had her own tan shoes, a monogrammed ten-pound ball, robin's-egg blue, and a compact three-step approach. No wasted motion. No immediate power, either. She couldn't bend herself down low, so the ball dropped from her hand at the line, plunking hard onto the lane, almost into the right gutter. But she'd been at it for years and she had the perfect follow-through. Even as the ball banged against the shiny wood, her arm rose straight up and extended forward, out toward the head pin, as if she were somehow going to grab that pin with her hand.

When the ball hit the white pins, it barely made a sound. If you closed your eyes for a moment and then opened them again, you'd wonder how all the pins had been knocked over. Each time, after she struck or spared, she'd clap her hands together, like a child ready to play patty-cake. Then she'd give Estelle a soft high-five.

It took Max a little while to settle down, but he found his mark in the fourth frame. Struck then and again in the fifth. "You look all right," Janet said to him.

"I wouldn't say that," Max said.

"You don't have to," said Estelle.

AT THE END of the first game, Max missed a spare on purpose. It seemed like the right move. Janet finished with 184, Estelle with 161, and then there was Max's 153. "Loser buys," he said.

"No," said Estelle. "It's my turn."

Max smiled at her. "Don't worry," he said. "You'll lose the next game."

"We'll see. I'm just getting warmed up."

Janet sat in the scorer's chair and laughed. "Sounds like we've got some competition now," she said.

Max walked back to the counter. He waited as Shelly poured the beer. "The old woman can bowl," Max said.

"You should have seen her ten years ago," Shelly said. "Back before she broke her hip."

Max took the three cold mugs carefully and said, "Let me ask you this. Any chance that Estelle's boyfriend or husband is going to come through the front door with a tire iron?"

Shelly said nothing.

"I wouldn't want any kind of ruckus to break out here, that's why I'm asking."

Shelly looked Max in the eyes. "She got divorced a few years ago," he said. "As far as I know, she only bowls with her mother."

"Thanks," said Max.

THE SECOND GAME took longer. In between shots, they chatted together around the scorer's table. Then someone would say, "I guess it's my turn."

In the sixth frame, while Janet stood at the line, Estelle said to Max, "Tell me about your father."

"You're just trying to distract me. And I am already distracted."

"Tell me."

"He threw a backup ball," he said. "Tough on the wrist. He was away too often, driving all over for his job."

"What kind of work?"

"He sold textiles from mills to clothing manufacturers. Slammed into an embankment one night outside of New York City. My father was a salesman killed on the road."

Estelle lit a cigarette. After another strike, Janet came back to the table, clapping. "I guess it's my turn," Max said. As he stepped past Estelle, he felt her hand brush his shoulder.

ONCE AGAIN, JANET had moved far ahead. Once again, Max was neck and neck with Estelle. During the eighth frame, the two of them stood side by side and he asked her, "Where's your husband?"

"Now *that's* distracting."

"It's not like I'm telling you how badly you need to strike in the ninth," Max said. "But you don't have to tell me if you don't want to. I can understand your need to concentrate." He reached up and tucked a strand of her hair behind her ear.

She put her hair back where it had been. Max saw a wince in her smile when she said, "Ask my mother or ask me. We'll tell you about husbands who ran off."

"Ran off or kicked out?"

"A little of both," she said.

Janet picked up her spare.

"Watch me," Max said. "Here comes a big strike."

Janet chuckled. "No taunting," she said.

JANET 191, ESTELLE 165, 172 for Max.

"That's enough for tonight," Janet said. "But we should have a rematch sometime soon."

"Well," Estelle said.

"That could be arranged," Max said.

He walked them to their car and Estelle wrote her phone number on a napkin for him. They made tentative plans for sometime later in the week. Max didn't tell them that he might already have left town by then. He didn't mention his thirteen-year-old son. And he didn't let them know that he was on foot, about to stroll back to the apartment of his seventy-two-year-old father, who was alive and more or less well. Instead, he said, "I look forward to seeing you again. I'll be practicing these next few days. I'll be ready for you." He watched them laugh. He waved as they drove off.

IT WAS LATE, after midnight; it had been a long day, and Max knew a tougher day was coming. He'd be attending a party in his ex-house, his first time there since he'd stormed out almost a year ago. And then there would be the actual time with Sandy, whom he'd seen for a grand total of fifteen or twenty minutes since they'd finalized the divorce and left the courtroom. It would be some sort of test and he didn't feel prepared.

But for now, he was alone on the quiet streets. Occasionally, a cool evening breeze brushed by, rustling the trees, pushing faint clouds past the bright, almost-full moon. It felt good to stretch his legs, swing his arms, flex his sore right hand. The buzz from the beer and the echo of Estelle's laugh made him smile as he retraced his steps.

He wondered why he'd lied to Estelle about his father. No clear reason for that, but plenty of foggy possibilities. He'd won sympathy from the start. Also asserted independence. And the car crash detail was true enough in its way, marking one end of his father's life.

He kept walking through the suburbs, but he rose out of his thoughts long enough to realize he'd turned in the direction of his ex-house. An old habit? Slightly drunk, wandering home? As he turned the corner onto the familiar street, he reminded himself to guard against nostalgia.

These days, he didn't blame Sandy, at least not too much.

When he'd been with her, his ventures had failed for several years in a row and then along came a younger, lively man of the earth who could turn mud flats into beds full of blossoms. Max was doing a stint as a cabdriver at the time. Just a temporary gig, part of a larger plan, and he kept trying to explain that to Sandy, but she stopped sharing his vision. What she saw was a yellow cab parked in her driveway. She saw her husband backing the cab out onto the street. Then the new gardener, Hiram Wilson, pulled in with his red pickup.

Perhaps she was helpless. She couldn't stop herself. Still, her methodology was less than admirable. She could have been more courageous and actually talked to him about what was happening. There are things, after all, that no man should have to see, and his shirtless wife in the kitchen kneeling before a naked, smirking orange-haired gardener is surely one of those things.

But in the world of business, Max wasn't always known for his appropriate tactics. In other words, he had his punishment coming. He didn't like the form it took; he didn't think it was particularly just, but he accepted it as best he could.

He tried to make the whole sordid affair easy, signing away pieces of his life. He made a simple agreement. He gave her everything that he could give at that moment, and in return she promised not to ask him for anything later. She and Hiram kept both the house and the dog. Max wound up with the car and he eventually drove as far south as he could drive, all the way to the Florida Keys.

The southern location was one of the factors that caused his relationship with Nathan to deteriorate. Nathan lived with Sandy during the school year. Max was supposed to have custody for the summer vacation, but this first summer he'd arranged for Nathan to stay with Caleb. Max had explained that there wasn't enough room in Florida, and, more important, his life down there wasn't set up for children. Nathan insisted that he didn't need much. He promised not to get in the way, but he was too young to understand and then he seemed to lose interest.

When Max reached his ex-house, he stopped and stared. Where there had once been some grass and a patch of pachysandra, there were now fountains doubling as sprinklers, irrigating all the available earth. Colored lights illuminated the water; it glimmered red, blue, green, and purple as it arced down to the ground.

Most of the flowers he couldn't have named if he'd tried. He picked out the obvious ones—roses, lilies, tulips. He spotted birds of paradise and dahlias. Then there were some sort of dwarfish palm trees. It didn't seem natural. It could have been a nursery, a small park, a florid exhibition for all to see. Clear proof set before the world that Hiram had improved Sandy's life, made it bloom.

Back when they'd first met, Max had recognized that his would-be gardener had aspirations. He saw it in the way Hiram carried himself, excellent posture, backbone as straight as a hoe handle. Hiram spoke of his dream of becoming a painter. "There's painting involved in any true gardening," he'd said, gazing up at the sky. "Let me show you something."

That's when Hiram had opened the door of his truck and reached behind the seat. Rolled up back there he had dozens of abstract color fields he'd painted. Some were brown. Others were blue. At the time, Max wasn't sure what was being sold, but he always enjoyed seeing someone selling. He wasn't buying, though, and he told Hiram he wasn't in the market for artwork.

"That's all right," Hiram said. "I'll give you a good deal on the landscaping anyhow. I'd like to make some connections in your neighborhood." Clearly, Max didn't know enough about the nature of those desired connections until it was too late.

The windows of his ex-house were dark. He didn't want to wake the dog—a Siberian husky named Natascha who had a loud, high-pitched bark and sometimes howled. But Max couldn't resist taking a few cautious steps up the driveway. Next to the mailbox was one of the few things he'd successfully planted on his own, a small oak that was making real progress. Years ago, he'd pushed a wispy seedling into a shallow hole. The leaves had reached a few inches above his ankle. Now the young tree towered over him. He stepped closer to the surprisingly substantial trunk. He could hear water droplets from the fountain hitting the leaves, like rain. The sound, insistent, gave him the urge and then the need to take a piss. It wouldn't hurt anything, just a few extra nutrients, and it was his tree, after all. He hadn't signed it away, as far as he could remember.

He stood there pissing in front of his ex-house, thinking that the more time passed, the more amusing it all seemed. He wasn't laughing yet, but he was learning where his father got his "Ha!" It was a sound of surrender. It rose up from the bottom of your chest, just below your heart. It couldn't be held back. You had to let it go.

4

ABE IS BAFFLED and astounded by his aging, stroke-stricken body. He seems to hear more than ever before and he believes his vision is improving. His mind moves so quickly it makes his head spin, blurring together all he hears and all he sees and all he remembers. He rarely sleeps.

He's on his back in bed, wide awake. For hours he's been listening to his brother's breathing, that rhythmic sigh he's heard for years. Sometimes, if he focuses exclusively on one thing, he can drift into sleep. It's late, well after midnight, and the city is almost quiet. Occasionally, a bus rumbles downtown. A dog barks. A woman shouts, "Give it!" A man says, "Shush." Are they talking about sex or robbery? There's the echo and then they're gone. In the next room, Caleb inhales, exhales, and Abe tries again to hear only that soothing sound.

He's still awake, listening, when the front door opens and softly shuts. He knows it's Max from the footsteps, how they go into the living room, then to the bathroom, the refrigerator, and the sofa. Abe wants to walk out there and have a conversation. He has plenty that he needs to tell his nephew. It would be good for the whole family if the two of them could have at least one more talk. But the stroke has done its strange damage, removing his power of coherent speech at a critical time, leaving him with his higher hearing, his sharpening sight.

And the memory of the stroke keeps coming back, taking him to that moment at the Country Club Diner, out on Cottman Avenue, their office away from the office, where, at first, he feels no more anxious than usual; he's sitting counter side with his brother, waiting on breakfast, hoping for a good day. There's a deal to close with Federman's Coats. There's Lasky, over in Trenton, who needs a nudge to bump up the yardage on a woolens order. Why not feel confident? His hand is wrapped around a mug of fresh coffee. It's high-test and hot and it tastes like ambrosia. He could sip the stuff all day, what a life that would be, like an opium den, but the opposite, making him ready to charge through the hours, rocket fueled, and it's as if he can almost see the coffee churning down there in his stomach, giving off a powerful gas that rises up from his belly, ascending, bringing a flush to his face, a cloud to his brain, and somewhere outside of his body his brother has something to say. The topic is bankruptcy, the subject is Easternland, Inc., the question is rhetorical: *Who ever thought we'd be around to see that mill go under?* If Abe could speak, he'd remind his brother that everyone's going under all the time. There used to be hundreds of clients around Philly and now there are seventeen. Pretty soon there won't be anyone left. And Abe would also like to point out that pretty soon the cloud in his brain is going to make it impossible for him to see the hand in front of his face. Where is this pressure from, in his jaw, his forehead, his chest? Why does it press down so hard? He blinks and blinks, but only with his left eye. Caleb is waiting for a response he can understand. *What is it, Abe?* An interesting question. *Swing* is a word he seems able to say. *Crawl* comes next, but that's as close as he can get to *stroke.* Then there is movement. He feels the stool sliding out from under him and he holds on to the counter with both hands and Caleb is cursing now, wrapping an arm around his shoulder, and the waitress wants to help, but Caleb has everything under control, more or less, saying, *I've got him, I'll take him in,* and that sounds fine to Abe, and *fine* is another word he seems able to say, so he repeats it again, biting into his lip with each *f,* listening carefully to himself and tasting blood and longing for more of that damn coffee.

In the hospital, for hour after hour, he is slack-faced and stuttering, and it's terrifying to think that he has arrived at this point in his life. Just when he starts to imagine how limited his future might be, the cloud within him begins to disperse, slowly and then quickly evaporating, and the doctors run their tests and decide to call this whole episode a mild stroke, something that can be addressed with medication, though his lip needs three stitches, the only visible scar. Those stitches can't keep him from smiling. Yes, he'd thought he was a goner there for a little while, he'd thought he'd reached the end of the road, where his game was over, his book closed, his gig and number up, bye-bye, but he'd survived, fought back hard and won. Maybe, for once and at last, everything will work out and he'll get to finish what he's started, especially his most recent, truly international venture, a well-made, handwoven plan, his best business ever, all set up and ready to go.

How can he not keep returning to those hours in the hospital bed, where he somehow improves by the second, watching, amazed, as the world drifts back to him? How it shimmers! It looks almost new and he swears there are halos hovering above even the most ordinary objects, the green plastic chair, the off-white curtain, his silly blue johnny, all suddenly gorgeous, and he vows not to jinx anything or make any last-minute mistakes, which means, since he's okay, he should keep the business plan to himself, so he spends those hours looking at the startling world around him, flirting with the nurse, joking with his brother, and he's laughing when the second stroke hits, and this one's not mild at all.

The months pass, the rehab is no help, and the plan starts rolling without him. The days make him miserable, the nights go on forever, walking scares him because his balance comes and goes, and too often he feels as if he's about to fall. He hopes, when he remembers to hope, for something small, something simple. He's not greedy, never has been, even though he's always been a dreamer. At this point, he'd settle for one more lucid moment. Such things are not impossible. Even the comatose are sometimes granted a burst of clarity and he just wants to get out a few sentences and, okay, it's true, he also wouldn't mind if he could grab onto those sentences, use them like a rescuer's rope, and climb back up to the world he used to know.

But now there's Max, home for the first time in months, pulling out the sofa bed. The lights go off, the apartment darkens, and it doesn't take long for Max's breathing to slip into its sleep rhythm, another soft and steady sound Abe hears as some kind of hazy lullaby. He wills it to work because he craves sleep, he longs to let his mind rest, gather strength for whatever lies ahead, but one hour leads to another, and once again he's awake to watch the rising sun chase the night from his room.

5

MAX FELT SOMEONE shaking him awake. He looked up from the couch and saw his father standing above him, dressed and ready to leave. Without checking his alarm clock, Max knew it was too early.

"You can still change your mind, Max," Caleb said. "We can all drive over together."

This was a typical ambush. One of his father's old strategies, get him talking before he was thinking clearly. This time, it wasn't going to work. Max had his plan and he wanted to stick to it. He'd agreed to attend the bar mitzvah and the reception, but he'd go on his own terms, by himself, in a separate car. He'd walk in late, slip out early. Give himself a chance to reenter this world slowly. Give people time to adjust to his reappearance.

He rubbed his eyes, sat up, and stretched his back. "This couch really isn't that comfortable," he said.

"We'd be happy to wait for you," Caleb said, glancing over

at Abe, who was standing by the door, leaning on one of his canes.

"Thanks, Dad, but I'll meet up with you later, as planned."

"All right. I tried. You know your way to the temple?"

"Has it moved since I got married there?"

Caleb sighed. "This is Nathan's day," he said. "Just remember that. Try not to live in the past."

Excellent advice, Max thought, but he knew that neither one of them could point to much success in following it. You didn't have to look very hard to see that the past decorated this apartment. An old map of Pennsylvania hung on the wall above the couch. To the right of the TV, at eye level, Caleb had nailed a pair of plaques from Uprich Textile Mills, tarnished bronze thank-yous for two lifetimes of service at almost zero commission. There was also a framed black-and-white photograph from a long-ago trip to Atlantic City. Caleb and Abe, tuxed and bow-tied on the boardwalk, backs to the ocean, toothy smiles, heads touching, temple to temple.

His father and uncle weren't tuxed for this occasion. They were each wearing lightweight spring business suits. Pin-striped blue. They'd probably bought the suits at the same time, at the same place, but Abe still looked more stylish and elegant, from a distance. Clothes had always fit him perfectly. In his heyday, he was a perfect 44 regular. He could pick a jacket off the rack, slip it on, and it would look hand tailored. People who didn't know better would go out and buy something they saw on Abe. It would never look as good when they put it on.

Max could see that Abe was down to a 42 or a 40 now, but if he wasn't trying to speak, and if you didn't look too closely at his stroke-stunned gaze, you'd think the years had been kind to him. The Atlantic City photo was from the late sixties or early seventies, and Abe's appearance hadn't changed all that much. A little thinner in the face, a little more skin on his neck, but nothing like a seventy-eight-year-old man.

Caleb, however, showed all of his seventy-two years, and then some. Max knew his father would do anything for Abe. That had been clear long before the strokes. These days, Caleb tried to conceal his fear of what loomed ahead, but it creased his skin, hunched his back, slowed his step. At least his voice, the hope and force of it, remained unchanged, and it worked on others, in person and over the phone. It also had a powerful effect on Caleb himself—the act of speaking made him look better, more alive. So Max tried to keep his father talking. "You two make a dapper pair," he said. "You'll look great up on the bimah."

"I hope you don't miss seeing it," Caleb said.

"Closing," Abe said, tapping his cane against the door.

Caleb looked back at his brother and then went on with his own worrying. "Do you think your son will ever get bar mitzvahed again? If you miss this—"

"I'm here, Dad. I've traveled a thousand miles *not* to miss it. I'm through missing things." Max stood up and put his hand on Caleb's shoulder. "I'll see you over there," he said. Then he gently tightened the knot of his father's red paisley tie.

"All right," Caleb said. "Don't be too late." He walked toward the door and reached out for his brother's arm.

Abe slapped the offered hand away. "Quit it," he said. "Scooter."

Max didn't like being alone in the empty apartment, so while he dressed for services he called his latest good friend, Grier Eckerton, down on Key Largo. He wanted to check in, cheer himself up, and beat back his guilt about Estelle. He'd show Grier he was still thinking of her. He also wanted, before seeing Sandy, to remind himself that there were new things in his life, too.

Grier sounded tired when she picked up. "Hey, beautiful," Max said. "You're not sleeping off any trouble down there, are you?"

"The only trouble I have is the goddamn algae ruining my *Syringodium* experiments."

"I love it when you talk dirty."

"Meristematic tissue," she said. "Internodal."

"Stop it, baby. You're making me orthotrophic."

"Hmm," she said. "You're finally learning some of the vocab."

"Say something else."

"Have you seen your lovely ex-wife yet?"

"Not that. Tell me more about your sea grass. Tell me about the manatees."

"Have you?"

Max had been together with Grier for almost four months. He had a dozen years on her and he was in the middle of trying to figure out what that meant, aside from the extremely pleasant physical benefits. He wasn't sure how much he could share with her. That was an enduring difficulty in his current line of work. He couldn't really tell anyone the full shot, though he often longed to. Wouldn't it be liberating, just once, to tell the whole story? If such a thing could even be done. With Grier, he was slowly, cautiously trying. She knew his business hadn't always been on the up-and-up, and she knew a considerable amount about Sandy, Hiram, and Nathan. Still, he wasn't sure he'd ever be able to trust her completely. She tended to make him hesitate. Even before he told her anything, she seemed to know too much.

"I'm off to the ceremony in a minute," Max said. "So I'll see her soon enough. It'll be a long day."

"Wish you were spending it here."

"Me too," Max said. "I'd fight that goddamn algae for you, that's for sure."

"How gallant."

"Have there been any messages for me?"

"Not a word. Is that good or bad?"

"You know what I always say."

"No news is no news," she said.

"That's the way it is."

"Great," she said, "but is there anything I should be on the lookout for?"

"Me," Max said. "Look out for me. I'll be back soon."

WHEN MAX STEPPED onto the sidewalk, he saw something else to look out for. Johnny Sklarman was standing over by the Buick, leaning against the driver's door. He was wearing an odd tennis outfit. His shorts and polo shirt were too tight, his socks didn't cover his ankles, and a Phillies cap hid his eyes. "I heard you were back in town," he said.

Max shook Johnny's hand and said, "I haven't been here long."

Johnny didn't show his teeth when he smiled, he just pursed his lips. "You're all dressed up. What's going on?"

Max had met Johnny during his brief stint at Temple University. They'd both enrolled the same year and become decent friends. Max had admired how graceful the guy was despite being six foot four and matchstick thin. Max rarely played tennis, but he knew a beautiful stroke when he saw one, and Johnny's one-handed backhand was a sweet shot. Then there was the fact that Johnny wasn't afraid to take risks. He was, he liked to say, a true racket man. He came from money and he enjoyed spending it, even when it kept on disappearing.

He should have stuck with serving and volleying, but unfortunately he developed a fondness for betting. First he ran into trouble with his bookie and then with his bookie's boss. There was Sklarman family trouble as well. For a while, Max had been too close to all of that. It had been alluring—not the betting, but the schemes Johnny planned to recover his losses—and it was no coincidence that the two of them dropped out around the same time. Their first project hadn't gone smoothly at all. Then, years later, before he and Sandy split up, Max had tried a second project with Johnny. Another mistake. They'd managed to stay cordial afterward, but Max had vowed never to work with him again.

Standing on the sidewalk, not wanting to be too late, Max reminded himself of that vow and said, "Today's my son's bar mitzvah, so I'm in for a quick visit."

"Hard to believe Nathan's thirteen," Johnny said. "A little man already." He reached into his back pocket, and though the shorts seemed too tight to hold much his hand brought out a plastic bag full of granola, which he offered to Max.

The stuff looked like bird food and Max waved it away.

"Congratulations and all that," Johnny said, crunching on a handful of the nuts and raisins as he spoke. "But I heard that's not the only thing going on. I heard you might be doing a new project on the side."

Max glanced at his watch and then he looked up and down the street, wondering if any other familiar faces lurked in the shadows. Traffic was light on Cheltenham Avenue and the only real noise came from a few women who were pushing their well-stocked shopping carts out of the Asian market. No familiar faces over there. He turned back to Johnny and said, "You better check your source. If I was working, I'd tell you myself. You know that."

Johnny spit some kind of shell onto the sidewalk. "Guy disappears for months without a word. Who knows what he'll tell you and won't tell you."

"I'm here for my son. That's all there is to it."

"Fine, if that's the way you want to play it. Look, we used to be friends, so I decided to stop by this morning and tell you, as a friend, that things are trickier than you think. Now I've told you."

What things? Max almost asked, but he wanted to move on. "It's good to see you, Johnny. It would be nice to catch up, but I need to get going."

"Don't forget you've been gone for a while. It's not all the same in the old neighborhood."

Max remembered his late-night stroll to his ex-house. "I know it," he said. "That's why I won't stay around. That's why I moved to Florida. What do you want me to say?"

Johnny shook his head. "You're not the only one in a rush, Max. I've got a match in five minutes. You know where to find me if you want to talk. For old times' sake. I might be able to help, at least for a little while."

Johnny crossed the street, loping along to a green minivan. To most people, he probably wouldn't have seemed threatening, just a thin guy in shorts off for some Sunday morning tennis. Max knew better. He hadn't been back in Philly long, but he felt almost ready to leave.

IN OTHER PARTS of town, not that far from Temple Beth Israel, there were several ornate synagogues, with enormous

wooden doors and windows of brilliant stained glass. They towered above the houses and strip malls, like the cathedrals of
other neighborhoods, lifting everyone's eyes up toward a holier
world. One of the temples had even been designed by Frank
Lloyd Wright. Supposedly, he'd meant for it to resemble Mount
Sinai. As a kid, Max used to laugh when his uncle would glance
at the tall, pointy building and say, "Looks like a plain old dunce
cap to me."

Beth Israel was different. It had never really recovered from
moving out of its downtown location. The temple used to be an
enormous, deep-red brick building at the corner of Sixty-third
and Market Street. It was a community center as well as a synagogue, complete with an Olympic-sized basement pool, where
Abe and Caleb had learned to swim. But the neighborhood had
changed and the building eventually became a Baptist church.
Money was lost, as it often is, leaving no funds available to make
the newer site glorious. There were committees and pledge
drives and architectural designs, but as far as Max knew there
was no timetable for construction yet.

In the meantime, the congregation gathered in a very modest
temporary temple. Without the blue-and-white sign at the
parking lot entrance, the building could have been mistaken for
doctors' offices or the low-rent headquarters of a humble corpo-
ration. Max walked from his car to the entrance and he noticed
that the grounds — about an acre or so — were covered by thin,
spindly grass. The lobby's linoleum floors had yellowed like
bad teeth. The sanctuary was as bland as a junior high school
auditorium, with a stage, rows of folding bridge chairs, and a
flimsy ark that looked like a home for cheap blazers, not ancient
Torahs.

Still, it was a house of God, and Max felt hushed once he was inside. He tried to breathe quietly. Walk without a sound. He was glad to see that everyone else was already in the sanctuary. He could hear the service beginning, the call and response of prayer, full of praise for the Lord.

When he'd last spoken with Sandy, she'd called to make sure he'd be attending and then she offered him an aliyah. Max told her no, thank you. He didn't want to have a role in the service and he made her promise not to surprise him. "I'm not going to make you do anything, Max," she said. "That's no longer one of my ambitions."

Max didn't completely believe her. He knew she'd want everyone to see the contrast between him and her younger man. She'd want Max to be visible so those who hadn't yet seen her lawn could still appreciate the difference in her life.

But Max was keeping his low profile. He put on a black *kippah* and made his way to the back rows while the congregation was rising to face the opening ark. The smell hit him immediately. He should have been prepared for it. The sanctuary had been landscaped. Yellow lilies in vases lined the walls. Some sort of small, well-trimmed trees in gilded pots decorated the edge of the bimah. Only the burning bush was missing. Hiram certainly knew how to bend occasions to his advantage. Here was free advertising to a bunch of potential clients, mostly parents with their children, parents looking forward to lives full of festive events. They'd all need florists in the times to come. Max scanned the rows and guessed there were close to a hundred people in the temple. Then his eyes found Sandy. Above her heart, she'd pinned a billowing cream-colored corsage.

Rabbi Weinberg, gray-bearded and pudgier than he'd been at Max's wedding, stood at the rickety podium, leading the service. He called Nathan up to the bimah. Max turned away from the

flowers and focused on his son. Nathan was as thin as he remembered, still waiting for his body to catch up to his broad
back, though he was a few inches taller now. A great-looking
kid, suave, dressed in a black suit, carrying it off with something
of Abe's former grace, and he was about to become a man of
responsibility.

From where Max stood, his son didn't look like a trouble-
maker. He hadn't heard many details about the recent problems.
A teacher had called Nathan sullen and there'd been some bad
grades. Caleb hadn't seemed alarmed on the phone, but Sandy
had emphasized that she was *concerned*.

Max told himself again that Florida probably would have
been worse for Nathan. Someday, though, there might be other
possibilities. He and Nathan would start anew, grow closer. He
didn't yet know exactly how to make this happen, but the thought
of it made him smile, hopeful.

As he tried to turn to the right prayer, he discovered that he
hadn't been the last one to enter the sanctuary after all. An older,
bald man came in and stood next to him. The man picked up
the prayer book that was on the chair, paged through it, and
dropped it. He kissed its spine with a loud smack when he lifted
it off the floor. Then he stared at the side of Max's face. "Looks
like your boy up there," he said.

"Excuse me?"

"I'm good with profiles," the man said. "Plus your smile is putting out heat."

A woman turned around to shush them. Then she noticed
Max. He recognized her as a friend of his father's from one of
the old downtown factories. He couldn't remember her name.
"Nice to see you, Max," she said. "Why are you all the way back
here?"

"It's complicated," he said.

She nodded, turned away, and whispered to her husband.

"There's also the nose," said the old man next to Max. "And the forehead. And the photograph I saw. He'll wind up taller than you, I bet. Might even be taller than I am. But I've heard he hasn't been a stellar kid lately."

Max introduced himself, holding out his hand. "And you are?"

"Mervyn Spiller," the man said, taking Max's hand and squeezing hard. Then he held up a three-fingered salute. "Scoutmaster," he explained. "Troop 158."

Max had heard Spiller's name in conversation before. Caleb had been talking for a while about getting Nathan to join the temple's new Boy Scout troop for the summer. And Abe, before the strokes, had mentioned Spiller together with some sort of possible big business, but there had never been any more information. Max was interested in big business, of course. He also had no objections to Nathan's becoming a scout, but as he watched his son reciting prayers, looking so calm and confident, it was hard to picture him in a drab olive uniform. He knew his son wanted to pitch curveballs, not tents.

For a moment, Max worried that Spiller was about to launch into a pitch of his own, but the scoutmaster was more respectful than that, and they both settled into silence. Caleb and Abe were sitting up in the front row and all Max could see of them was the backs of their heads. Still, he knew they'd be smiling proudly, "kvelling," as his father would say. There'd also be sadness in their eyes. Who could know what was going on in Abe's mind, but Max felt sure his father was thinking about how much time had passed, and so quickly. How could Nathan already be up there, the baby grandson, now a bar mitzvah?

When Max had last spoken to his son on the phone, Nathan had talked a bit about his Torah portion. Rabbi Weinberg had arranged the date so the reading would feature the biblical Caleb, the same Torah portion Max had studied for his bar mitzvah, almost thirty years ago. He was curious to learn what Nathan thought of the verses. He'd asked to hear some of the lines interpreted and chanted over the phone, but Nathan had refused, saying, "You'll have to wait."

It was worth waiting for. Nathan began to chant and his voice, still young and delicate, carried well, filling the temple. Max couldn't remember all the Hebrew, but he knew the story by heart.

Caleb appears in the book of Numbers, one of twelve spies chosen by Moses, sent from the post-Egypt wilderness to explore the Promised Land. Max had heard the story so often he'd come to picture his father scrambling over an enormous desert dune, peering off into the distance. Parched, his skin burning, he looks down into a new valley. He wipes the sand from his eyes and sees the answer to his prayers. Fertile fields, a crystal-clear river, hillsides thick with trees. A breeze caresses the lush leaves and they glisten like a green ocean. He finds grapes as large as apples, figs sweeter than honey, pomegranates as round and bright as the setting sun.

He gathers an abundance of evidence and carries as much as he can. He can barely hold it all in his arms. He is a walking cornucopia.

When he returns from his mission, he feels triumphant, ready to put an end to all the wandering, but his fellow spies are frightened. They report that the Promised Land is hostile, full of giant, unmovable foes. *We looked like grasshoppers to ourselves,* they say, *and so we must have looked to them.* Shocked and furious,

Caleb tears at his robe. *We should go there at once!* he shouts. *It's a fantastic place, overflowing with riches. The Lord delights in us. He will bring us into this land and it will be ours!*

Caleb keeps shouting, but the people do not believe him. They'd rather remain terrified, stuck in the wilderness, blaming everything on God. They're accustomed to complaining. For months they've been complaining about the weather, about the food, about their loneliness, about how long they've had to wait and wait. They scream for Caleb to be quiet. They pick up stones and they start throwing.

Their aim is good, but Caleb is not hurt, for God approves of him. Even as the stones fly at his face, he continues to shout. He will not keep quiet. He yells about the beauty that stretched out to the horizon. How sparkling fish arced out of the clear water. How the gentle sun kissed his forehead.

The people refuse to listen and for their doubt they are punished by God. They are destined to perish in the wilderness. And their punishment will go on after that. Their children are condemned to decades of wandering.

Caleb, however, is allowed to go forward and his descendants are promised the Promised Land.

NATURALLY, CALEB LOVED the story, the heroism of it, the dedication, the sense of destiny, but Max tended to focus more on God and the nature of his character. This biblical Caleb acted courageously, Max never disputed that. But what of this Lord and the land he keeps promising? Thousands of people left to wander in the wilderness? The occasional glimpse of the gorgeous country that's waiting, always waiting? It's just around the corner, over the next hill. Or a little ways up the sleeve, under the shell you didn't pick. Poor Moses on the mountaintop, abandoned with these words: *This is the land which I swore unto Abraham, unto Isaac, and unto Jacob, saying: I will give it unto thy seed; I have caused thee to see it with thine eyes, but thou shalt not go over thither.*

The old bait and switch. The prize is there for the taking, but in the end you're the one taken, left in the lurch, bled dry as the desert itself. Caleb didn't like to hear that God conned with the best of them. He preferred to argue that mistakes were made, that Moses shouldn't have done this, shouldn't have said that. It all could have been different, Caleb argued, if Moses had just followed the directions exactly. "Spoken like a true mark," Max would say, and that usually ended, or at least postponed, the argument.

IN THE TEMPLE, as the bar mitzvah continued, Max saw nothing to make him alter his interpretation. Nathan stood at the podium, the Torah unrolled before him. He held a long silver pointer in his hand and he moved it slowly back and forth across the sheepskin scroll until he reached the end of his verses. By his side stood his mother and his potential stepfather. They were beaming, proud and prosperous. Betrayal battered some and brought beauty to others, as was so often the case. Sandy and Hiram offered the blessing after the reading and their voices rang out.

But Max wasn't going to be bitter. He wasn't going to worry about how his Promised Land was being watered by someone else. Instead, he focused back on his son, thinking about his success and his possibility.

Spiller poked his arm and said, "Don't you have an aliyah?"

"I'm just a bystander today."

"That's odd."

Max shrugged and kept his eyes on his son. That was the best thing for him to do, but then Nathan turned around and sat behind the rabbi, out of sight. To keep his bitterness at bay, Max tried thinking of Grier and what a future with her might promise, a life lived out on the Keys, a place some called paradise. Maybe there would be kids, siblings for Nathan, more grandchildren for Caleb, nieces and nephews for Abe, and those Wolinsky brothers could find a good, legitimate retirement community right nearby, free forever from winter. Plenty of their friends had already made that Florida pilgrimage.

But Max couldn't get that southern vision to hold. It slipped further away as the rabbi spoke. Then the memories started coming, and once they began it was hard to pick and choose. He thought he might revisit his own bar mitzvah, see his own proud young self standing on the bimah, but that was at the downtown temple, with a long-dead rabbi leading him through the service. It was his wedding that had been in this particular space, with Weinberg presiding, and that voice, its smooth cadence, carried back the memory of one of the poems Sandy had picked out for their ceremony. Max could almost hear himself reciting the psalm, at least the lines he still recalled:

> *Blessed are the man and the woman*
> *who have grown beyond themselves*
> *and have seen through their separations.*
> *They delight in the way things are*
> *and keep their hearts open, day and night.*

Fortunately, Nathan returned to the podium. He began speaking, thanking his teachers, his family and friends. Max could barely follow the words because he was staring so hard at his son. In Nathan's voice he could hear Caleb and Sandy and himself. "Most of you know that this has been a tough year for me," Nathan said. "It was a good time for me to study and think and wonder."

Max watched his son's mouth move. If he paid attention, Nathan could fill his mind and everything would be all right. The speech shifted toward the Torah portion and its mystery. "I began asking myself questions," Nathan said, "like what kind of person can be a hero? Or how can a spy become a leader? We don't usually think of spies as trustworthy or upstanding." He rested his hands on the podium and said that it was probably better to think of Caleb as a scout, not a spy.

Spiller tapped Max's shoulder and whispered into his ear. His breath smelled of butterscotch. "A wise boy," he said.

"Shh," said Max.

Nathan wasn't reading. He hardly glanced down at all and Max marveled at his son, the public speaker. Nathan appeared somehow relaxed, casual. He said that the name Caleb seemed to bring together the names of Cain and Abel, at least in English. He wasn't sure what that might mean, but it could be a sign of possible healing. "Really," he said, "in the end, no matter how many questions you ask and answer, it's a confusing story. People go somewhere and they look at the same place and see different things, and how do we know what to believe if we haven't been there ourselves? And why is it that one day you can be a chosen person and the next day you can be condemned to a lifetime of wandering? The child of a stone thrower, sitting at home, unable even to lift a stone, is punished in the same way as the parent who did the throwing. Why? What kind of justice is that?" Nathan paused briefly, looking up toward the heavens, as if waiting for an explanation. There was silence and he continued. "Well, I decided there were more questions than answers. Understanding that fact must be part of what it means to become an adult. Still, we have to be careful about the people we choose to listen to. There are people, like that clear-minded scout, who have the right answers. But how can we tell which voices are right and which are wrong? How can we know which voice to follow?"

Nathan paused again and this time he looked over at the rabbi, at Sandy and Hiram. He gazed into the audience and, for a moment, Max thought he was being sought out. Then Nathan went on with his speech. "This is where the biblical story becomes true," he said, "because the person I always listen to is my grandfather, my *zayde*, Caleb Wolinsky."

Nathan stepped down from the bimah and hugged Caleb. Max could see people bringing their hands together, holding them quiet in their laps. They wanted to clap, even though no clapping was permitted in the sanctuary.

The rabbi returned to the podium briefly before yielding it to the leaders of the temple's brotherhood and sisterhood. There were announcements to be made, about meetings and other events, and then there would be a final prayer. Max stood up and walked out. He heard Spiller call his name, but he kept on walking.

OUTSIDE, MAX WAS standing by the LeSabre when he saw Spiller jogging toward him. The guy moved quickly for an old man. He had a good gait, a serious rhythm to his swinging arms, and he didn't seem winded when he stopped and said, "We should talk."

"This is my son's day," Max said. "I don't have a lot of time."

Spiller smiled. "The way I figure it, you probably don't want to be the first one at the reception, welcoming the guests with Sandy and Hiram. No need to rush away. We'll sit in my office for a few minutes. We'll talk there."

Max wondered how this man knew so much. He wasn't feeling particularly trusting, especially after that brief chat with Johnny Sklarman. Was there a connection between Sklarman and this Spiller guy? It was something to think more about. In the meantime, he might as well gather information.

"We should go in before the crowd starts coming," Spiller said.

"Okay," said Max, and he followed the scoutmaster around to the back of the synagogue. The building looked even less distinguished and sacred from the rear. They walked up to a concrete loading dock that was cracked all over, spotted with weeds and a few very tall dandelions.

Spiller unlocked a green metal door and they took the stairs to the basement. The office down there was windowless, like a bunker. Cinder-block walls, painted the off-brown of root-beer foam. A large oak desk, immaculate. A half-dozen file cabinets. Crates of what appeared to be French kitchenware, LE CREUSET stamped in black on each box. Max shifted one and it was extremely heavy. There were stacks of eight and there were at least twenty stacks. Cookware for a battalion of scouts. Those pots would weigh down a backpack fast.

After handing Max a folding chair, Spiller walked behind the desk and eased himself into his burgundy CEO's seat. He looked comfortable. The CEO's seat had wheels. Spiller put his black wingtips up on the desk and slid his chair back and forth.

"What's with the kitchenware?" Max asked.

Spiller clasped his hands behind his neck and leaned back a bit. "What have you heard about me?"

"Not much," said Max. "My father's interested in having Nathan join your troop. I've also heard about some sort of business possibility. That's the extent of my knowledge."

Spiller nodded. "You're right," he said, "it's not much, but all true, though 'some sort of business possibility' doesn't really capture the grandeur of what I've been working on with your uncle."

Max knew that if this scoutmaster was any kind of salesman, it was going to take time to hear more about that grandeur. And it was going to require real effort to find out about the crates of pots and pans, if that's what they were. "I see," he said.

"Do you want to hear what I know about you?"

"Sure," Max said. "Why not."

Spiller leaned forward, pulled open a desk drawer, and fished out a spiral-bound composition book. He flipped quickly through the pages and then held the book close to his face for a moment. When he was finished, he tossed the book back into the desk and shut the drawer. "Well," he began, "there's more than we have time for. I know your family could use considerably more money than you have. I know your tactics over the last few years, and especially since your divorce, have been less than admirable and often less than legal. And I know the Goulds are a mistake."

Max was listening carefully. "That's it?" he asked.

"You dream of going back to college. You've got a woman in Florida. She's too young."

"I guess my father trusts you."

"Your father a little, but mostly your uncle. It's terrible what's happened to Abraham. He's been a friend for decades."

"I don't remember my uncle mentioning you that often."

"Well, sometimes it's best not to mention our friends."

"I imagine there's something you want."

"I already told you. I want to talk."

"You don't strike me as the Boy Scout type. We could talk about that."

Spiller stood, walked over to a closet, and pulled out a Boy Scout uniform on a suit hanger. The slacks and shirt were cleaned, starched, and pressed. There was a maroon-and-silver neckerchief draped around the neck, a green sash full of bright merit badges slung across the chest. "Look at this uniform," Spiller said. "What do you see?"

"A pretty bizarre outfit. Militaristic. Nothing I'd want to wear."

"No," Spiller said. "Look harder. Every outfit's bizarre, if you think about it. Try thinking like your uncle."

"Something about how sharp Nathan would look in the uniform? How well it would fit? What he could achieve as a scout?"

Spiller shook his head. "You're a father, I know that, but you're also a businessman, aren't you?" He looked at his watch. "Think about textiles, all right? I didn't think I'd have to spell it out for you. I heard you were good at what you do."

"You'd need serious connections to get involved in Boy Scout sales."

Spiller grinned and looked down at the floor for a second, almost shyly, as if he were trying to dodge the compliment. Then he said, "Extremely serious."

Max watched the scoutmaster return the uniform to the closet. He could feel himself reaching for more, with caution. "And?" he asked.

"That's enough for today," Spiller said. "I was hoping to go along to the reception with you, but I have another pressing engagement. I'll walk you to your car."

"I'll be all right," Max said.

"I'm on my way out," said Spiller. "It's no trouble."

Back in front of the synagogue, all the other cars were gone. They'd moved on to the next event of the day. It was good weather for a reception, blue sky, not too hot or humid. More fine fortune for Sandy and Hiram.

When they were a few steps from the LeSabre, a black convertible BMW pulled up in front of them and stopped. Sitting behind the wheel was a young, very attractive Asian woman, her hair cut short and close to her face. She could have been a flapper from the 1920s.

Spiller put a hand on Max's shoulder. "I absolutely trust your father," he said, "but with Abe in his condition, I'm going to require your help as well. We'll keep talking."

Max had more questions to ask, but Spiller was climbing into the BMW. There was a long kiss on the lips and then the woman raced the engine, ready to take off. Spiller kissed her, smiled, and waved farewell. "By the way, Max," he shouted, "mazel tov!"

6

NATHAN WALKED OUT of the synagogue knowing he'd done a good job. During the last year, he'd attended many bar and bat mitzvahs and he'd seen how easily the ceremonies could go wrong. None of his friends had completely failed, no one had ever been booted off the bimah, but Nathan had witnessed his share of awkward moments. It was easy to remember, for instance, how Rich Silver spilled the wine he'd been blessing or how Eric Robbins hadn't been able to keep his voice from cracking. Then there was Jeff Gluck, who froze after losing his place in the middle of his Torah portion. He went wide-eyed, staring at the congregation as if he were suddenly comatose, and he didn't snap out of it until his rabbi banged a hand against the podium and said, loudly, "Come on, boy, be a man."

But, for Nathan, everything had gone smoothly. He was grinning as he followed his mother and Hiram out to their

Chevy Suburban. He climbed in and went directly to his seat of choice these days, in the way-back, near the spare tire.

His mother offered her praise from the front. "I can't get over how wonderful that was," she said.

He said nothing in response. He'd been giving her the silent treatment for almost a week now.

"I wish you'd sit up here, closer to us," she said.

He shook his head and looked out the tinted window at the beautiful day, a perfect afternoon for stickball. It didn't take much to get him thinking again about the unfair circumstances that surrounded him. And yet, despite the unfairness, he'd done his part, he'd done all he'd agreed to, and he'd done it well, in front of everyone. He hadn't let anyone down.

"Look, Nathan," his mother said, "I really hope we can talk before Hiram and I go away on our trip."

She didn't care about his hopes, so why should he care about hers? Why should she always get exactly what she wanted? He didn't get what he wanted.

She started whispering to Hiram, which meant Hiram was probably about to speak to him.

"Hey buddy, you hear your mama?"

Nathan kept silent, thinking that Hiram's voice sounded more stupid than ever. Had it always sounded so stupid? Nathan remembered back when everything was starting to change, his mother telling him to "give the guy a chance." "He's nervous," she'd said. "Even if he doesn't look it." She'd smiled then and mussed his hair. They were in the living room, looking out the front window, watching as Hiram began to move in, pulling his bags from his truck and swaggering up the driveway.

Hiram had been born and raised near Princeton, New Jersey, but he seemed to like pretending he was from Texas. He often dressed the part. For the bar mitzvah, he was wearing a dark green suit, a white cuff-linked shirt, silvery snakeskin boots, and a gold bolo tie. Cowboy formal, or something like that, but usually he resembled a hardworking ranch hand or rodeo star—tight blue jeans, beat-up boots, brocaded shirts, and a wide-brimmed cream-colored hat. When people asked him where the hat came from, he'd say, in a slow drawl, "Stetson's a Philadelphia company, partner, always has been." Nathan knew his mother wasn't the only woman in the neighborhood who liked watching Hiram work around the house.

"Why not start the silent treatment after we leave?" his mother asked.

Nathan kept looking outside. They were almost home, passing Shoemaker Park, right by the high school. He could see the summer leaguers out in the fields. Four teams were practicing, everyone wearing their matching T-shirts and caps. Nathan knew his friends Rich, Eric, and Jeff were in that crowd. He wanted to be on the field with them, but instead of playing in the league he was being forced to join a Boy Scout troop. He didn't have any friends in Boy Scouts.

"You'll have the whole summer not to talk to us," his mother said.

If he were speaking, Nathan would have said, *The whole summer, the whole summer, the whole goddamn summer!*

It was hard to believe now, but back on that move-in day, he'd felt hopeful. He'd stood close to his mother, her hand warm in his hair, and he'd smiled with her, thinking that everything actually might be better from now on. A boyfriend who paid attention might be better than a father who was rarely around. Wouldn't it be an improvement to have someone who made his mother happy and affectionate, instead of someone who made her storm through the house slamming doors? As much as he hated to admit it, he'd looked through the window that day and thought he might be getting, all at once, not only a new dad but also an older brother and, who knew, maybe even a friend.

But that wasn't the way it had worked out. No, what had waltzed into the house that day was competition, and Nathan was smart enough to know he was losing, big time. His father was gone, and his mother was slipping away.

He should have seen the signs from the very start. The first thing Hiram had said to him was, "Do me a favor, buddy. Go out and bring in the painting that's bagged in the flatbed. It's a new one. A gift."

Nathan obeyed. It was a large piece, almost as tall as he was, and it was no picnic carrying it up the steps and into the house. He'd expected Hiram to help, but there was no one waiting to open the door for him. He managed to step inside and lean the painting against the wall. He heard his mother laughing upstairs, then heard the bedroom door close.

He felt left out, but the laughter sounded good. And at least she hadn't slammed the door. He'd torn some of the brown paper that covered the painting and he wanted to make sure he hadn't done any real damage. He also was curious to see what it looked like. It was probably a gift for the house, mostly for his mother, but at least partially for him, too, so he started to remove the rest of the paper.

He heard more laughter from upstairs. He had some idea what they were doing, taking off whatever clothes they still had on, but the precise mechanics of what would follow remained mysterious. He uncovered the painting and found himself looking first at the back of the canvas. It was white, with a few words written lightly in pencil: *Hiram—Self-Portrait #44.*

He turned it around carefully and was glad to see it was unscathed. Nathan didn't know Hiram that well back then; he hadn't paid close attention to the gardener's appearance, so he wasn't the best person to judge a resemblance, but still, he couldn't see any face or body at all in the painting. He saw a hazy rectangle of blue. Much darker than the sky. As blue as his father's aftershave, that's what it reminded him of.

He heard the bedroom door open again and it startled him. He looked up, but no one was coming down. Hiram called out to him. "Buddy," he said. "I left a ten-spot on the kitchen counter. Go out and do something you want to do."

Nathan understood that they wanted time alone. He told himself that he didn't need to feel bought. It wouldn't hurt to feel optimistic. Maybe everyone could have what they wanted. He pocketed the bill and went to find his friends.

As TIME WENT ON, there was more money, and it continued to come his way, and he found himself spending more time with his friends. That seemed normal enough. After all, his friends were spending more time with him. What bothered him was how he started to feel. Guilty about this, guilty about that, guilty about the other thing. During his bar mitzvah study sessions, Rabbi Weinberg had warned him about such feelings. Nathan had never confided in him, but the rabbi gave his advice anyhow, again and again. "Your parents' problems are not your fault," he said. "You need to remember that. You are not to blame."

Nathan believed him. It was obvious, really. He knew that things didn't always work out in this world. Why should a mar-

riage be different? Not every family could be happy. And yet,
when he was angry with his mother or jealous of Hiram or sad
about his father, he usually couldn't help feeling that he'd done
something wrong.

But now, as they pulled into their driveway, parking behind
the caterer's red van, his anger seemed completely justifiable to
him. The guilt would come later. He knew how this reception
was going to go. His best friends wouldn't be there because they
were playing baseball. He'd keep an eye out for Jennifer Ostrow,
just in case. He had a serious crush on her, but she probably
wouldn't come, either. He hadn't said many words to her since
she'd moved to town a year ago. He'd handed her an invitation,
watched the smile on her freckled face. She was a new kid,
though, which meant she had to be nice to everyone. He could
tell she was only being polite.

So, most likely, he'd spend the reception searching for her,
missing his friends, chatting with some distant cousins. He'd see
his father dart in and dart out, like he'd done at the temple.
Maybe they'd talk for a minute or two. Then he'd wind up
spending the rest of the afternoon with his grandfather and his
uncle Abe. They'd hide out somewhere and watch the Phillies
on TV while everyone else ate and drank. The whole event,
which must have cost a small fortune, was mostly for his mother
and Hiram anyhow. They were three days away from a summer
in Hawaii. They weren't married yet, but the reception seemed
like it was really for their wedding, a big party before the bigger
party of a long practice honeymoon.

As Nathan opened his door, ready to face what was coming,
his mother and Hiram fired out their parting shots, a quick one-
two combo.

"Now," Hiram said, "I work with my plants and my dirt, so

I'm used to being around things that don't talk to me. But you should talk to your mother."

"Who knows, honey," she said. "We'll be gone for so long. Maybe this is just Nathan's small way of preparing himself."

Hiram laughed his cowboy laugh. It sounded almost like yee-haw. "That's right," he said. "A Boy Scout has to be prepared."

People didn't know how difficult the silent treatment could be to enforce, how alone it could make you feel, but Nathan stayed with it. He was a man of responsibility now. It was easier than ever to rise above the childish and immature. He walked calmly up to the house, reminding himself that he had legitimate reasons for being angry. If his mother and her stupid boyfriend couldn't engage in a real discussion about the summer, there was no reason to speak to them. No reason to say even one word.

7

MAX HAD TO drive a few blocks from the house before he could park, nosing the LeSabre in at the end of a long line of shiny minivans and SUVs. He had plenty to mull over as he strolled down Marvin Road. What would he say to Sandy? And to Nathan? And to good old Hiram? He dodged those questions for the moment. Instead, he flashed back to the sight of Spiller in the BMW's passenger seat, speeding away with that gorgeous woman. Who was this guy? What kind of scoutmaster could he be? And who was he to say that Grier was too young?

Ah, Grier. At a time like this, it was a pleasure to think about her. A surprising wisdom was one of the many qualities Max had come to admire in his Florida woman. There was her intense attention to her science, her practical, mathematical mind, and then there was her talk about detachment. Sometimes she could sound hokey, but she could also make fun of herself, and a lot of what she said seemed true or, at least, vaguely helpful.

Grier gave more manageable advice than his father, for instance. Before Max had left Florida, she'd told him to avoid judging the people of his past. "Watch your thoughts as if they're a passing train," she'd said. "Note the familiar cars. You can study the train, but don't jump in front of it."

And then, of course, it didn't hurt that she was fit and shapely, with her soft lips, her blue eyes, her long, strong swimmer's legs.

For better or worse, Max had the memory of her body and her words on his mind as he walked quickly up his former drive- way. He didn't want to dwell on the landscape again, but he paused to glance at his tree, and when he did that he recognized a man standing amid the flowers. It was Harrison Phelps, an- other ex-owner of the house. Harrison had been the one living there when Max and Sandy came in for a tour. Harrison had done the selling himself, and a few years after that he'd given them Natascha — one of his husky's puppies. Max remembered him as a beefy man who lumbered around like a proud bouncer, ready to boot you out onto the streets if you couldn't appreciate the shine of the hardwood floors, the exposed brick in the living room, the kitchen cabinets he'd designed himself. Now he was slighter, older, crouching beneath a giant fern, rubbing fronds between his fingers.

"Hello, Max," he said. "This place sure has changed."

"Tell me about it," Max said as they shook hands. It didn't seem natural to see Harrison without a dog. It made him look weak and lonely. "I'm glad you're here," Max said. "I was just thinking about Natascha."

"I already asked about her. She's in a kennel for the party."

"That's a shame. That's a reunion I was looking forward to. I wanted to find out if she'd remember me."

"Of course she would. She'd be happy to see you."

"A rarity around here," Max said. "But tell me where you're living these days. You still in the neighborhood?"

"I'm over in one of those retirement communities. Curtis Estates. They're treating me all right." He turned to reexamine the fern and pushed some of it toward Max. "Smell this," he said.

Max worried that he might somehow catch a whiff of last night's piss, but he took a deep breath through his nose. The plant smelled like peat moss, which was probably what they were standing in.

"It's not a native species," Harrison said. "I never planted anything like this. Even the roses smell funny. They must be hoping to sell high someday. But who's going to be able to maintain this yard?"

"You can buy the house, but you never stop paying the gardener."

"So that's how it works," Harrison said, shaking his head and stepping back onto the black asphalt of the driveway.

Max followed along. "Did you keep any of Natascha's siblings for yourself?" he asked.

"You're allowed to bring a pet with you to Curtis Estates," Harrison said, "but once it dies you can't get another. That's one of the rights they make you sign away."

"I'm sorry to hear that."

Max remembered how Harrison would visit during those early years, after the sale, after the moving out and the moving in. He'd bring by Natascha's mother, Laska, and the dogs would dash around in the backyard. Spring, summer, and fall, they would meet for walks through the neighborhood. In the winters, they'd wait for the snow and then laugh at how much the huskies loved it. Max would hold Sandy close, and together they'd thank Harrison again and again for the puppy. It was almost unbelievable, even then. He and Sandy had their young lives in a new home with new friends, a puppy, and a healthy son. Months passed that way, a whole decade went by, and maybe he wasn't appropriately amazed or appreciative, though God knows he was happy. He didn't see why everything couldn't just keep improving.

Harrison cleared his throat. "All my kids have dogs," he said, "so at least I've got that. If I were you, though, I wouldn't get old."

Some klezmer music kicked in around back, the reedy wail of a clarinet leading the band into their first song. Max smiled and looked up at the house. "Going inside there is bound to make me older," he said.

"Well," Harrison said, "I'm heading home."

"Don't leave yet."

"I already said hello to your father and your uncle. I don't know anybody else here."

"Come on," Max said, putting a hand on the man's still solid shoulder. "Who knows anybody, really?"

Harrison turned to walk down the driveway. "I haven't got time for philosophy, Max."

"We haven't seen each other in a long time. At least let me ask you something before you go."

"I'm listening."

"What did you think back when you used to visit us?"

Instead of answering right away, Harrison closed his eyes and kept them squeezed shut for a few seconds. His brow furrowed, as if he were concentrating, reviewing the past in his private dark. When he opened his eyes, he said, "You know the answer to that. Those were good years. We all knew it."

Max didn't want to get maudlin, but he kept his hand on Harrison's shoulder. "You're right," he said.

"Now I've got to go," Harrison said, "but drop by my place sometime when you get a chance. Bring Caleb and Abe if you want. We'll go see some of Natascha's brothers and sisters. Maybe some of her nieces and nephews, too."

"I'll take you up on that," Max said.

"Don't wait too long."

As Max watched his fellow ex-owner lumber back to the street, he reviewed his simple plan: step inside, congratulate Nathan, congratulate Sandy, and then, very soon after that, move on. He'd have time to visit with Nathan later, in more comfortable surroundings.

The front door—teak he'd stripped and stained with Sandy, brass handle and knocker they'd picked up at a flea market near New Hope—was open. There at the threshold, he paused and looked over the party, which was in full swing, mostly on the back deck, spilling out into the yard, where well-set tables waited on the green grass. A buffet line was forming on the red-brick patio, off to the side of the band. White-shirted caterers worked the kitchen, and Max could smell blintzes cooking in buttery pans, knishes warming in the oven, sliced onions, smoked fish, and more. A few kids milled around near the bathroom. They looked like they wanted to stay out of sight. He could sympathize. Something about them made him think they weren't Nathan's friends. Their designer clothes were a few notches too fine. They were probably related to the trendier clients and potential clients Sandy and Hiram had invited.

Max didn't see those two or Nathan or Caleb and Abe. Instead, he saw a bunch of old acquaintances who'd chosen Sandy over him. He didn't hold it against them, but he wanted to steer clear of as many awkward conversations as possible, so he looked in another direction. Rabbi Weinberg smiled at him from across the

living room. The rabbi always liked to see people overcoming conflict, and that must have been what he thought was happening.

Years ago, Max had put in a few cork panels at the bottom of
the staircase, making a place for him and Sandy to thumbtack
up some of their favorite photographs. Most of the old photos
were gone, of course. Near the cork hung two printers' trays
they'd once filled with trinkets, totems of their time together.
Those objects had been swapped out, too. What had Sandy
done with the old photos, the postcards, ticket stubs, key chains,
toy rings, and cheap plastic prizes? Trash? Or was it all in a box
somewhere in the attic? Max hadn't carried much with him
when he'd driven south, but even in that short time he'd found
plenty to throw out.

Hiram's paintings covered the rest of the walls. He was working in a deep, bright green now, with faint black charcoal traces
in the background, like branches almost completely hidden by
leaves. Some of the old blues and browns were also on display.
Max had liked them when he'd first seen them and he couldn't
help admiring them still. They looked better on the walls than
they'd looked in the back of the truck. He leaned closer to one
that had *Natascha* written in the lower left corner—Hiram had
sketched the outline of the dog's whiskered face near the center
of the vibrant green field.

When Max stepped back from the painting, Sandy was by his
side. She seemed too thin, almost fragile. Dressed, she could
look bony, like her narrow, knuckly hands, but naked she was another story. He kissed her cheek. The corsage kept her distant.
Maybe not just the corsage. He looked for strands of gray in her
short black hair. He saw none.

He wanted to be polite, but as soon as she started speaking he
knew he'd have to struggle.

"I didn't think you'd make it," she said.

Well, he almost said, *I knew I'd make it.* He stopped himself and instead of saying anything right away, he caught her light brown eyes for a second and remembered one of the many things that had first drawn him to her. Sandy was five four, a little shorter than she wanted to be, and early on she'd told him how as a high schooler she used to stretch herself out in bed almost every night. She'd grab on to the headboard and point her toes, counting to three hundred while she extended her whole body, trying to lengthen herself, hoping for at least five six. It didn't work. That had always been fine with Max. He liked her height, and when they made love he liked noticing how often she held on to the headboard, as if maybe he could help her get what she'd wanted for so long.

He knew he should think about different memories. He searched for them. "You've done wonders with the place," he said.

"You haven't been here in a while."

"That's the way it worked out."

"I'm glad you're here now," she said. "I know it can't be easy."

Max shrugged his shoulders.

Sometimes Sandy would whisper when she didn't know what to say. She was whispering now. "We've got bigger plans for the house," she said.

"I'm sure you do."

"That's what's behind our trip to Hawaii, after all."

There was no end to their good fortune, or so it seemed to him. Of course, he'd heard about this upcoming trip. Their luxurious post–bar mitzvah practice honeymoon. On several occasions, Sandy had made it clear that they wouldn't be around at all this summer. They'd be thousands of miles away, unable to help with Nathan if there was any trouble.

Max inhaled and returned to Grier's idea of the train. Choo, choo, choo. He saw the envy car right in front of his eyes, the jealousy car chugging up close behind. And there was anger coming on around the mountain.

"You should take Nathan with you," Max said. "I'm sure he'd love some time on the islands."

"Not possible," she said. "Besides, your father would be upset, even if you wouldn't. And we'll be very busy over there. It's not a pleasure trip, you know. Well, not entirely. Hiram's going to learn more about Hawaiian landscape science, and we'll both be taking intensive Japanese classes."

"It all sounds wonderful," Max said. "The rewards of prosperity, long overdue."

"And what are your big plans?"

Suddenly the conversation started to feel familiar, just like old times, and Max caught himself slipping back into his customary role from their bad years. She wanted to know what he was working on and he wouldn't tell her and that confirmed her worst assumptions: he was irresponsible, a fool, shortsighted, selfish, and so on.

She was simply asking about him, about his life, he knew that. She was trying to be friendly, but it was difficult to let her be friendly, and the fact that it was difficult made him feel as if he hadn't yet traveled far or long enough to get beyond her. "Did I say I had big plans?" he asked.

Her voice grew a little louder, rising away from her whisper. "You're still not telling anyone what you do, I guess."

"I tell people what they need to know."

"I see," she said. "And what do I need to know?"

He tried not to take the bait but failed. He looked at his watch. "I wish I had the time, Sandy. I'd need hours."

"You had years," she said, glancing over his shoulder. "Hey, here comes my future husband."

Max turned to see Hiram approaching, and instead of trains, he thought first of his father and cars. Caleb occasionally dispensed life lessons based on driving. Naturally, they had a bleak backdrop. There were the obvious lessons, like "Get the big picture" or "Aim high in steering" or "Leave yourself an out." But there were also more complicated teachings. A story he shared several times had to do with the crazy tailgating driver who roars up behind you on a narrow road. You accelerate, out of common courtesy. But this driver stays right on your tail, as if he wants nothing more than to drive directly into your trunk. He flashes his high beams at you, leans on his horn, performs various gestures with his hands. Then he starts weaving back and forth, looking for room to pass on the left, on the right, either one, and he doesn't care how narrow or windy the road might be. "In that situation," Caleb would ask, "what do you do?"

"I don't know," you're supposed to say. "You tell me."

"Pull over," he says. "Let them pass. That's what you do. Who knows where they're going or why. Who knows what they're capable of. You don't get to know and probably don't want to know. Forget your ego. Forget how at fault they are. Just pull over and let them race on by."

Caleb had brought that chestnut out when Max first told him what was going on between Sandy and Hiram. Well, actually, first Caleb had said, "I never liked her." Then Max said, "Oh yes you did." And then the advice came, not all that different from Grier's, now that he thought about it.

So Hiram closed in like a tailgater. His anger, seething, always marked him. It was part of what made him attractive to women, Max believed, even though he'd never learned exactly what the guy had to be so angry about. What didn't he have? What was he missing? Sandy used to be fascinated by the fact that Hiram had spent a night in jail, turned in by his own parents. "My father felt threatened," Hiram had said. "Saw me as a stallion in need of breaking." The injustice of it made Hiram furious. Basically, as far as Max could tell, Hiram was always innocent and often irate. Max used to believe he'd be safe from that righteous anger. He thought it all got channeled into the work, the gardens, the canvases. He didn't see why it would ever be channeled his way. Count that as another one of his many mistakes.

In any case, Sandy looked happy to find Hiram by her side, happy, again, to be rescued. "You got here just in time," she said. "Max is about to tell me what I need to know."

Hiram's green suit matched his paintings and his eyes. He surveyed the bustling room, smiling like a tall leprechaun. "I remember the first time I came to this house," he said. "It's amazing how much has changed since then. I remember thinking there were things *you* needed to know, Max. But then I figured you'd discover everything on your own. After all, I've heard you're such a smart and cunning man. You had that year or two of college."

Max managed to let it go, thinking instead how it was something to see them both together again, up close like this, without all the shock and nakedness. He prided himself on his ability to read people, his ability to detect their desires, but he couldn't really read these two, even though he'd married one and hired the other. He wanted to watch them go on by, watch them shrink smaller and smaller into the distance, like the train, like the speeding car, but the joint custody of Nathan meant he'd see what happened to them down the road. Unless this Hawaiian vacation turned out to be permanent, a way for them to sail out of sight forever.

"We're waiting," Sandy said. "What do I need to know?"

Hiram wrapped an arm around her and pulled her closer. "Go ahead, Max. Enlighten us."

It wasn't easy, but he held himself back. "Maybe some other time," he said. "For now, I want to pay my respects to the bar mitzvah boy. Congratulations to you both."

When he turned to go, he saw the rabbi approaching. "It's good to see the three of you together," Weinberg said. "This is exactly what we discussed. How time would pass. Yes, how time must always pass."

"Have you seen Nathan?" Max asked.

The rabbi nodded. "I saw him going upstairs with Caleb a little while ago."

"Thanks," Max said, "and shalom to all of you."

THE BATHROOM AT the top of the stairs was where Sandy had gone into labor when Nathan was about to be born, those thirteen years ago. They'd been in the house for six months. Harrison was a good man, he'd given them a fair price, and he'd had his reasons for feeling proud of the place, but it was a mess back then, everywhere a project. "It's full of potential," Sandy often said, an open hand on her big belly. "Just like me."

That birth-night, Max was kneeling on the tiled floor, re-caulking around the tub while Sandy worked at the sink. Whenever he looked at her, he wanted to tell her to sit down. She'd finally stretched out, that was for sure, but the extra inches gave her width, not height, and her balance seemed so precarious. Her swollen ankles seemed too delicate to support her front-heavy body. How could she not tip over? He wouldn't be able to get to her quickly enough. But if he told her to be careful, she'd tell him to relax. Then she'd be more reckless. She'd decide to climb a ladder and clear cobwebs from the ceiling.

She paused at her work, gazed into the mirror, and watched herself as she reached her arms straight up into the air, tilting her head right then left. She lowered her arms and rolled her shoulders. Then she turned around, leaning back against the sink. She took a deep breath. "I think it's time to go," she said. "Can you get my bag?"

Max dropped the caulking gun and it banged against the floor, cracking one of the tiles. "It's already in the trunk," he said. He helped her downstairs and they raced to the hospital.

The tug of nostalgia almost pulled him into the bathroom to look for the cracked tile. The whole house was an express train into the past and he could have spent hours wandering the second floor, remembering too much, but then he heard the voices of his father, uncle, and son. It sounded as if they were in Nathan's room, so that's where he went.

The door was closed. Max stood quietly and listened for a moment. "Give," Abe was saying. "Let me."

Max knocked. "Who's there?" asked Nathan.

"Another Nijinsky," Max said. "Stravinsky. Jet-ski."

Max walked through opened doors all the time; he tried to walk through them confidently, ready to accomplish what he needed to accomplish. But stepping into his son's room for the first time in a year made him nervous. It was hard enough to know what to say downstairs. It didn't feel any easier on the second floor. He wasn't even sure whether he should reach out for a handshake or a hug.

Before he could decide, Nathan was walking away from the door, back to the center of his room, where he sat cross-legged on the rug.

Max couldn't recall what he'd said and done the last time he'd stood in this room. Was this where he and Sandy had told Nathan about their decision to separate? That didn't seem right. Nathan wasn't even home that day; otherwise the kitchen love scene would probably have occurred elsewhere. No, Max had already been gone for a few days, packed and moved out, before he told Nathan he was leaving. There was a phone conversation and then a long walk by Tookany Creek, Max trying as best he could to explain what he barely understood himself.

Now Max could notice that at least this room hadn't changed much. It was still blue, as Nathan had wanted. Bunk beds with blue covers, blue wallpaper with streaks of silver. The curtains and window shades were also blue, which could darken the sunlight and make the place feel like a B-movie hideout. Almost like another basement. Without looking too hard, Max saw traces of himself that hadn't been swept away. A few father-son photographs were pinned to the bulletin board. Two airplane models they'd built together hung from hooks they'd screwed into the ceiling. He'd sent some cheesy souvenirs back from Florida — a treasure-chest bank, a plastic manatee, a rubber alligator — and they were lined up on one of the bookshelves.

The only glaringly obvious change to the room had to do with all the new bar mitzvah gifts. They were in a pile on the rug, a stack of boxes and a bunch of envelopes, some attached to the boxes, some separate. Pens and kiddush cups seemed to be the most popular presents so far. Caleb perched on the bottom bunk, leaning out so he'd have less chance of bumping his head, a pad of legal paper balanced on his lap. Nathan was opening the envelopes and boxes, handing the cards up to Abe, who sat at the desk, arranging and rearranging the rectangles of colorful paper. It was something of an assembly line, Max thought, with well-dressed workers, their jackets off, ties loosened, sleeves rolled up. Leave it to Caleb to organize an inventory in the middle of a celebration.

Still standing by the doorway, Max said, "You know there's a party going on downstairs."

"Is that what you came up to tell us, Dad?" asked Nathan.

Max didn't want to have another lousy, all-too-familiar conversation. He wanted this upstairs room to be a refuge. "No," he said, "what I came to tell you is that I thought you did a great job today. I felt proud watching and listening to you in the temple."

Nathan looked down at the rug, his ears and cheeks blushing pink.

Meanwhile, Caleb was doing calculations on the legal pad. "There's significant money coming in here," he said. "I'm thinking I should get bar mitzvahed again. Don't people do that?"

"People do lots of things," Max said.

Nathan opened the next package and found another pen-and-pencil set. "Does being an adult mean you get the same gift over and over?" he asked.

"There's an excellent question," said Max.

"Who's that set from?" Caleb asked, his own pen poised and ready.

The inventory continued. Nathan read out a name, Caleb made a note, Abe demanded the card. Whether or not Abe could really read anymore was a mystery, but he kept reaching out and saying, "Give." Then he opened one of the desk drawers and suddenly there was a cigarette lighter in his hand and he was trying to get it going.

Max walked over and took the lighter away. It was a nice, heavy, silver-plated piece, unengraved, with a smooth flip top. "Hmm," he said to his son. "Was this one of your gifts?"

"No," Nathan said.

"I heard you were doing some troublemaking, but I didn't know you were smoking."

"I just like having a lighter," he said. "Is there anything wrong with that?"

"No," said Max. "As a matter of fact, I like having one, too." He flicked the top open and shut, then slipped the lighter into his pocket.

Nathan was about to protest, but a young girl poked her head into the room. "Hi, Nathan," she said.

"Hey," Nathan replied. "Is Jennifer here yet?"

"I haven't seen her. Where's the bathroom?"

"Back by the top of the stairs."

The young girl walked away. Max sat down on the bed beside his father. "Who's Jennifer?" he asked.

"Listen to you," said Caleb. "Maybe if you started spending more time around here you'd have a better idea about the major players. You could hear all about Jennifer if you took your son to Florida for a few weeks this summer. I'm sure he'd happily talk your ear off about her."

"I don't talk about her that much," said Nathan, reaching for another box.

"I don't yawn much," said Caleb, yawning. Then he smiled. "I also don't fart much," he added, leaning slightly to roll out a three-beater.

"Anyhow," Nathan said, "I might not even want to go to Florida."

"What do you want to do?" Max asked. "Sit around and smoke?"

"Baseball camp."

"I heard you were doing Boy Scouts. They play baseball, don't they?"

"They play softball, maybe once a month. I want to play the

real thing every day, with my friends. I should be playing right now. That's where Rich, Jeff, and Eric are. My friends aren't even here. They're practicing for their game this afternoon."

"The scouts will surprise you," Caleb said. "You'll thank us eventually."

Max turned to his father and said, "I need to know more about this Spiller guy, by the way. I ran into him this morning. And he wasn't the only person I ran into."

Abe was opening and closing a few more drawers, putting some of the cards inside the desk.

Caleb looked across the room at his brother before answering. "Abe's the one who's always thought highly of Spiller, but the man's made a good impression on me, too. So far, at least. Who else did you see?"

"I'll tell you later."

"I think I've got the scoutmaster's gift here," Nathan said, holding up a small box.

Max eyed it suspiciously, wondering about the contents — the box was almost the same size as a pack of cigarettes — but also wondering how Spiller's present had made it to the house.

"Doesn't look like cash," Caleb said. "And a pen set wouldn't fit in there."

"Let me," said Abe.

"I bet it's another mezuzah," Caleb said.

"Kiddush cup," Max guessed.

Nathan read the card aloud. "Congratulations, Nathan. May you keep yourself physically strong, mentally awake, and morally straight, like all true scouts. May this gift help you to be prepared." He quickly opened the box. "It's a Swiss Army knife," he said, "in a leather pouch. And there's another note in here."

"What's it say?"

"P.S.," Nathan read. "This is a dairy knife."

"Is he serious?" Max asked.

Caleb nodded. "Of course he's serious, Max. It's a kosher troop. Two sets of dishes, fleishig and milchig, and so on."

"That will help make backpacking interesting. No wonder Nathan isn't thrilled about joining. Who ever heard of kosher Boy Scouts?"

"Exactly," said Nathan. "That's what I've been saying."

"It's not such a bad thing," Caleb said.

Max shook his head, hunched forward a little more, and looked around the room. They weren't agreeing about much. Just bickering and teasing and chatting and getting more or less nowhere, but he didn't feel unhappy.

When Abe stood up and started walking toward the door, Caleb pushed himself carefully off the bed. He handed the legal pad to Max. "You two could use some father-son time," he said, "though you probably won't be able to hide here much longer. We'll see you downstairs."

As soon as they were out of the room, Nathan got up and closed the door. Max looked at his son. Somehow, it had been easier to talk with Caleb and Abe around. Now he didn't know what to say. Nathan seemed to be expecting something, standing there, quiet and waiting. Max searched his mind for the right way to start in again, but he found himself thinking about how there were a bunch of people who would have paid real money to see him so tongue-tied. Finally, he opened his mouth, wondering what would come out. "So," he said.

Nathan grinned. "You're lucky I'm not giving you the silent treatment, too."

"What do you mean?"

Max sat and hunched again on the lower bunk. Nathan returned to his spot on the rug, stretching his legs and leaning back against his desk. "I haven't talked to Mom and Hiram in almost a week," he said.

"Hmm."

"I just really, really, really don't want to join this troop," he said. "I'm a man of responsibility now, right? That's what the rabbi said. That's what all these cards say. It's my decision and I've decided."

"You'll have to work this out with your mother. And your grandfather. Sounds like he feels pretty strongly about it. You're the one who said he was worth listening to."

"I know," Nathan said. "I have to give it a shot, but if I don't like it, I'm quitting, and I mean it."

"Whatever you say. Right now, I'll just enjoy thinking of my son as a Boy Scout. Who would have guessed? But tell me about the silent treatment."

"It's not working, if that's what you want to know."

"Tell me this then. Do you have to do a lot of gardening to get your allowance?"

"Hiram says I don't have the flair for it. He says gardening's not for everyone."

"The two of you get along all right?"

"What do you want to hear, Dad? He's okay. He tries, in his stupid way. Back when we were speaking, he kept asking me if I wanted a baby brother or sister. It was driving Mom crazy."

Once they were talking, it wasn't bad. Nathan didn't seem resentful and that let Max begin to relax. Florida felt far away from this room. It was hard to believe he'd been living down there for most of a year and it was even harder to believe that he hadn't missed his son every single day. Why did he miss him more than ever when they were closer than they'd been in months? He didn't know the answer to that one, but it made him wonder if Nathan had missed him or was missing him now.

Nathan had a question of his own. "Can I have my lighter back?"

Max brought the lighter out of his pocket. It was heavy in his hand. "Smoking's not good for you," he said. "It's idiotic."

"I don't smoke," Nathan said, "but I think Jennifer does. I want to be able to light her cigarette for her sometime."

"You should tell her to quit."

"I will, after I get to know her better. I don't think it would be good to start out as a nag."

"What if she wants you to smoke a cigarette with her?"

"I'm an athlete, Dad. I'll say no, thank you."

"Is there anything else you want to tell me about this girl? Does she have any other destructive habits?"

Nathan shook his head. "She's new in town, that's all. I think that's the only reason she smokes. She wants to look cool."

Max flicked the lighter open and closed before handing it back. "All right," he said, "but what's so special about Jennifer?"

Nathan took the lighter and smiled. "That's what I'm trying to figure out," he said.

"Fair enough, I suppose, but I'd love to hear more about her."

"When are you going back to Florida?"

Sometimes Nathan looked older than he was. Sometimes he sounded older. And sometimes he sounded just like Sandy. Max decided he should probably continue with his plan, though he was in no rush to leave. "I'm not sure yet," he said "I'll keep you posted." Then he stood up and glanced around the room again. All those gifts, and he realized he hadn't brought one with him. "What do you like these days, besides Jennifer and baseball?"

"You don't have to get me anything, Dad."

"What you said about your grandfather was very nice, by the way. Did you really mean it?"

"Yes."

"Good," Max said, moving closer to the door. "He needs all the help he can get." He reached out for the knob and then he thought better of it. Maybe now they should have that hug, or at least a handshake, but this time his thinking was interrupted by Sandy's voice, calling from the bottom of the stairs. "Nathan? Are you up there?"

"Your grandfather was right again," Max said, opening the door. "Can't hide up here forever. You going to answer her?"

"No. That's not how the silent treatment works. But I guess I should go down."

"We'll spend more time together soon," Max said.

"Sure we will," Nathan said, and then he was gone.

BEFORE MAX FOLLOWED his son back downstairs, he looked around the room. He didn't want to snoop, but he wondered what else, besides the lighter, was hiding in those desk drawers. It was time for him to go, he knew that. Nothing good was going to come from hanging around longer. He was lifting up the books by the foot of the bunk bed—a Boy Scout handbook and a history of the Philadelphia Phillies—when Caleb came back in. Max was glad to see him.

"Where's Abe?" he asked.

"Sometimes I need a break. You know, like a parent who needs his kid to nap. He's watching some baseball."

"I need to get out of this house," Max said. "It's not healthy for me here."

"You'll do better than this someday. Though maybe you should have taken better care of her."

"Maybe this, maybe that, and maybe the other thing. Speaking of which, let's hear more about Spiller."

Just then Max's cell phone rang. He answered it and recognized David Gould's voice, full of excitement. "Larry? Gail and I have made our list. We'd like to schedule another appointment."

Max motioned for Caleb to close the door. "It's good to hear from you, David. I was just thinking of you."

"We've been looking over all the material you left us."

"Great," Max said. "Things have been moving along here, even in the middle of the weekend. In fact, I may have more information for you tomorrow. I think we should try to meet sometime this week. But let me have until tomorrow before we set a date."

"So things are progressing?"

"Well, as my father likes to say, 'There's always some kind of good news coming around the bend.'" Max grinned and gave Caleb the thumbs-up.

"Here," David said, and Max heard the sound of rustling paper over the phone. "Gail wrote down a top-three wish list. I'll read it to you: 'I want to walk on the beach in the mornings. I want to hear the sound of the waves as I fall asleep. I want to live someplace people will love to visit.'"

"That's wonderful, David. You two have been doing some work!"

"For me, just the boardwalk's enough."

"Excellent," Max said. "I look forward to seeing the whole list in the next couple days. Please give Gail my best, and we'll hopefully talk again tomorrow."

Max switched the phone off and put it back in his pocket.

"I miss working," Caleb said.

"You're working all the time, Dad. All you do is work."

"But I miss how it used to be. The three of us, together and legitimate."

"We're together this weekend," Max said. "And in a day or two, you'll need to make the call."

"It's not the same."

"Let me hear the voice," Max said. "You'll still do it, won't you?"

Caleb cleared his throat. "I'm calling from Larry Zevin's office," he said. "I have an urgent message for Mr. and Mrs. Gould."

"That's it, Dad," Max said. "Perfect."

8

THE NEXT MORNING, Caleb woke up early, but not as early as his son. When he walked into the living room, the linens were already off the sofa, folded underneath the endtable, and Max was dressed in dry-cleaned black slacks and a gray polo shirt, looking like a sharp, respectable businessman. Caleb rubbed his forehead and wished he'd stopped at two glasses of the bar mitzvah wine. "Let's have a cup of coffee before you go," he said.

"Can't do it, Dad," Max said, shuffling through the papers in his briefcase. "I've got to be downtown and then maybe Atlantic City and then back downtown. I'll call in from the road if there's any news."

"Yesterday was a good day, wasn't it? Easier than you expected, I bet."

"Could have been worse."

Caleb padded around the kitchen in his sweats and T-shirt.

He poured himself a glass of water and opened a bottle of aspirin. "I was wondering," he said, "what do these Goulds look like?"

"Don't think about that, Dad. They're part of my day, not yours. What are you and Abe doing this morning?"

"I'll drop him at rehab, then I'll have a little peace and quiet."

"Sounds good," Max said, slapping his case shut. "Don't get into any trouble while I'm gone, okay? Things go right, we'll do some more celebrating soon."

"I'll be fine here, but you be careful. Remember we're not desperate and you don't have to—"

"Don't worry, Dad. This one's a snap. We'll get Abe what he wants. And there should be plenty left over to get some of the things you want, too, so you'd better start figuring that out."

Caleb nodded and took his pills. "All right, son," he said. "Just keep me posted."

He watched Max high-step out the door, then got the coffee going, listening for the Buick, the sound of the engine revving up and fading away.

Though he hadn't heard the details, exactly, he had some idea what his son would be doing all day. Max would be out there making arrangements, negotiating tasks and percentages during his meetings with a few schemers and dreamers. The people involved would have their reasons for doing what they were going to do. Some would tell themselves they had no choice. Others would know they'd made their choice long ago. They'd have their own wish lists in mind, debts they had to pay, things they believed they couldn't do without, trips they needed to take.

Max used to mention trips often. They were the gifts he'd give as soon as he was flush. For a while, after driving to the very bottom of the continent, Max would call and talk about a family reunion in Florida. But so far it was only talk. The three or four times Caleb had tried to pin something down, Max was too busy or heading out of town, or money was tight, or the weather was terrible. Eventually, Caleb stopped asking about it.

He couldn't stop thinking about it so easily. It was on his mind as he waited for the coffee to finish brewing. He'd never been to Florida. Abe, always more of a traveler, had flown there a few times, and once he'd tried to get Caleb to go, too. He had been in no condition to travel then, but now it was certainly possible. Now he would enjoy a change of scene. He didn't want to visit Tampa or Fort Lauderdale or any of those other places where everyone retired—he did enough of that kind of visiting right here at home. The Keys, though, they would be beautiful. In his imagination, they were always much more striking than the towns along the Jersey shore. He pictured Max driving him, Abe, and Nathan down the coast from Miami. There would be beach, then marsh, then more and more water until the car cruised high up on a long white bridge connecting ever-smaller pieces of earth. Abe would love it. The sunlight, splendid. The ocean, brilliant. Through their open windows, salt air would blow, strong and healthy and good for them.

The percolator banged and hissed at him. "All right, all right," he whispered. "I'm coming."

ON REHAB MORNINGS (Mondays, Tuesdays, and Thursdays), he had to take Abe to Rosentown Community Center, which used to be Rosentown Elementary School, where Max had gone for K through 6. The center didn't really offer rehab; it was more like day care, with lunch provided. Abe would spend the hours from ten to two staring at the TV or looking at a card game or sitting outside. He never complained about going and he always seemed relatively content there, so Caleb figured the place wasn't doing him any harm.

Still, he felt guilty about how much he looked forward to being free of his brother for part of the morning and afternoon. Usually, the extra time let him visit friends, go out for coffee, lunch, a stroll, often in retirement communities or, worse, in hospitals. He also occasionally had business to do, since, over the years, he'd managed to retain a few loyal clients. On a good day, Caleb and Abe were remembered in a handful of small Pennsylvania towns—Ephrata, Altoona, Scranton—and every now and then he'd get a mercy order from Baltimore or New York City.

Whether he was visiting or working, though, wasn't really the point. It was easy enough to explain what he did and why. He knew his desire for time alone was understandable and he didn't think anyone would blame him for how he spent those hours, but that didn't make the guilt disappear. Since when was guilt logical?

FOR A FEW months after the strokes, there'd been a volunteer speech specialist at the community center. Like several of the doctors, she'd been optimistic at first. She'd told Caleb that Abe's brain might "adopt compensatory strategies." It could "develop new plasticity, create alternate pathways." "I wouldn't mind some alternate pathways myself," Caleb liked to say. For a long time, he'd tried to have faith in recovery. He noticed that Abe was most lucid in the moments between sleeping and waking, as if the neural network needed a few minutes to recall the strokes and the damage done. So, in the mornings, Caleb would sit by his dreaming brother and search for the words that would stretch those minutes into days and weeks. He felt like a boy, like

Nathan, who used to believe the baseball cards in each new pack kept changing until the very instant he ripped the wrapper open. Caleb would stare at his sleeping brother and wait for the right split-second, his fingers fluttering in the dawn air.

But it hadn't been that way for a while. Now he simply shook Abe awake. "Come on," he'd say. "Let's wake up. Let's get this day started."

Then they went through their morning rituals, their daily give and take, Abe offering his sporadic monologue: *Quit it, don't touch me, quit it, don't touch me.* Some days Caleb talked back, but today he just pushed Abe gently along, oblivious to the words that did or didn't come, keeping quiet until they arrived at the center and he said, "See you soon," as he watched Abe slowly walk down the hallway that led toward the TV lounge.

He didn't find any messages about the Goulds waiting for him when he got home. He hadn't counted on Max being busy for the whole day and now, trying to plan the rest of his morning, he couldn't get past thinking how fuzzy his brain still felt from the bar mitzvah wine. He showered, hoping the hot water would clear his head. It didn't. He dressed, poured mug number two, and unfolded the paper, but he wasn't ready for the news. Instead, he walked over to the coffee table and picked up some of the scooter pamphlets and advertisements Abe had stacked by his Barcalounger. He flipped through the bright pages that promised "more active and rewarding lifestyles," mobility, independence, comfort and ease.

In Abe's favorite catalog, for Viva Deluxe Scooters, the slick color photos showed a man and a woman driving their matching blue scooters, videotaping each other in a garden by a clear stream. One couple, dressed to the nines, had parked side by side

on a wooden bridge at sunrise, the man leaning across to present a freshly cut red rose. Then there were the two scooter fishermen, casting from their seats into a rushing river. Nearby, a
woman, pad and paper in hand, sat on her silver scooter in front
of a rhododendron, sketching a butterfly she must have
stalked—her twenty-four-volt transaxle motor was that quiet,
that responsive.

These men and women were probably his age or older, but
they looked younger, healthier, giddy yet dignified. To Caleb,
they appeared ridiculous, and yet they were still, somehow, in
the prime of their lives. None of them was alone. None of them
felt embarrassed by the shiny scooters. The endorsements offered more proof of that. A gigantic defensive line coach with
gimpy knees swore by his Viva Deluxe. Who would argue with
him? Not the arthritic gold-medal weight lifter. Not the bull
rider with a busted back.

Just last night, before they'd all turned in, Max had spent two
hours by Abe's side. Together they'd gone over those glossy
pages and they'd eventually managed to pick out the model Abe
seemed to want. It had a champagne-colored chassis, a heated
hunter green seat, and the sport package: four all-terrain tires;
the biggest motor available, with a top speed of ten miles per
hour; two cup holders, one attached to the side of each armrest;
halogen lights, front and back; heavy-duty suspension for a
smooth ride. All rock solid, and yet the whole thing came apart
into five easy-to-transport pieces. The warranties guaranteed
years of driving pleasure.

For this they would fleece the Goulds? Caleb shook his head,
took another sip of coffee, and looked at his watch. He didn't
know the Goulds, but he could picture them, and if he sat down
with them, it probably wouldn't take long to discover that they

had friends in common. Philadelphia was a big city, but it wasn't that big.

He picked up the phone book for a reason, telling himself he wanted to check in at Cheltenham Medical Supplies, find out how long it would take to get delivery on the type of Viva Deluxe they wanted. But even as he made that call, he was flipping through the pages, looking to see how many Goulds there were. He spotted a David and Gail out near the Main Line. He was going to need the number anyhow. Soon enough, Max would ask him to call and he'd have to call. Might as well write down the address, too.

He didn't want trouble, he just wanted to take a look at their house, make sure they had plenty of money. Before he knew it, he was outside again, climbing back into his car.

His last New Yorker had been junked years ago. He was down to a Taurus now and it was full of plastic, not at all elegant. The only thing shiplike about this car was the way it seemed to shudder and shift in a strong wind. Still, as long as he stayed off the highways and took roads he knew well and avoided rush hour and the dark, driving could be like walking, a good way to clear his mind. His thoughts wandered and he relaxed and somehow it wasn't dangerous. He reacted instinctively to any trouble he encountered. How else to explain the fact that he'd driven hundreds of thousands of miles, over a million probably, without a serious accident.

Naomi hadn't driven nearly as much. Had she been daydreaming? Was that what had happened? Those sixteen hours, she hadn't said a word. He'd tried to lure her back, sitting by her the whole time. Doctors and nurses bustled in and out. "I'm here," he kept saying. "Lift your arm. Squeeze my hand. Open your eyes." He asked Abe to stop at the house and bring her alarm clock over. He made it ring for her. "Time to wake up, Naomi," he told her. "Time to wake up now."

It was all supposed to make him stronger. Which meant he should have the strength to get through whatever was going to happen with Abe. His parents, his wife, and, soon, his brother. More silence, more slipping away.

He'd never understood why Naomi had loved him, though he had his guesses. Where did something so absolute come from? Where had it gone?

At the bar mitzvah, during the service and the reception, he'd looked at Sandy, seen her standing beside her new man, and he couldn't help wondering if he was seeing love. Would this last for her? He simply didn't know Hiram, but he used to be able to talk to Sandy. Still could. She was the one who'd pushed him toward that third glass of wine. This was after Max had gone. Abe was napping in front of the ball game. Caleb went outside and wandered to the farthest corner of the yard, where the music didn't sound too loud. There was a stone bench beneath a white trellis and he sat there. He gazed out over the party, watched the people dancing and eating and talking. The family had been rearranged, but these friends and relatives seemed happy. They were moving on, enjoying their day. Even Nathan wound up amid the dancers, smiling, waving his arms in the air.

Caleb was watching his grandson when Sandy came over and sat down beside him. For a few minutes, they made polite conversation, as if they were two distant acquaintances, not once father-in-law and daughter-in-law. They praised the happiness of the occasion, Nathan's wonderful performance, the success of the party. Then Caleb reached the limits of his small talk and he didn't know what to say next.

Sandy put an arm around him and kissed his cheek. "Oh, Caleb," she said. "I'm sorry."

He did like her; Max was on the money there. She wasn't someone who'd wanted to do anything wrong. She believed in family, in good business, in moving ahead. She'd worked hard with Max and then she'd given up. He could understand that. "It's all right," he said. "I'm sure, in the end, it's for the best."

"You probably don't want to talk to me much."

"I'm no judge, Sandy. I'm happy to see you happy."

"You're being nice, but okay. I appreciate it."

Caleb sensed that in her own way, she was still reeling. She appeared strong and content, but he couldn't help suspecting that part of it was some sort of facade, as if she believed that acting happy would eventually make her happy. And, who knows, maybe she was right. Maybe that was how it worked. Maybe it was that simple.

"I realize this isn't what you wanted," she said.

"I don't think it's what you wanted, either."

She rested her hands in her lap. Whenever she moved, Caleb caught a whiff of lavender. "We did very well for a while," she said. "Then I started worrying about Max and what he was going to do next. Every time I saw him I was worrying. Now I see him and I can't do it anymore. The worry doesn't come. I just wind up angry."

Caleb smiled. "I can't say that my worrying has gone away. But he's still my son. He's not your husband anymore."

She stood up and looked back at the house. The band had given way to a disc jockey, who was playing something new and slow. Caleb couldn't make out most of the lyrics, but he heard the word *baby* several times. Sandy swayed her hips and held out her hand. "I couldn't persuade you to dance with me, could I?" she asked.

It wasn't easy to refuse. He could have taken her hand, closed his eyes, and pretended for a while that the family was all together again. But he said no and shook his head. "Not today, but thanks for asking."

"We'll still talk, won't we? You're Nathan's only grandparent."

"Of course we'll talk."

"You can be angry at me. I won't mind."

"It's okay," he said. "I'm not angry."

He stayed on the bench, waved good-bye to her, and tried to figure out what he was if he wasn't angry. Puzzled? Miserable? Or was this just the latest variation on his everyday melancholy? He watched his ex-daughter-in-law dance closer and closer to Hiram. From where he sat, how could he know if it was love or not? The two of them had something, though, that much was certain.

When he finally walked in to check on Abe, he paused at the bar long enough to drink another glass of red wine.

CALEB STOPPED DAYDREAMING when he pulled up across the street from the Goulds' house. He didn't plan to stay long. He didn't want this impromptu spying expedition to be remarkable in any way.

He turned off the car and looked over at what was a perfectly nice home. It radiated prosperity on this warm, almost summer day. The sun and the clear blue sky seemed to brighten all the colors—green shutters, white siding, black shingles, silver Volvo, red Honda. He glanced up and down the street and decided that no one driving by would worry about the people who lived here. Everyone in this neighborhood appeared to have plenty. He noticed that the Goulds kept their windows clean. Their blinds were up, but he couldn't see any movement inside. He was too far away.

He looked next at their small garden, fenced off just beyond the screened-in porch. Tomato plants dominated the tilled space, but he also saw some basil and a handful of sunflowers.

A couple walked by with a slow-moving dachshund on a long leash. He didn't want to appear suspicious, didn't want them thinking he was casing the place, so he got out of his car and walked away from them, down to the end of the block, giving them enough time to turn the corner. Then he strolled back toward the Goulds'. As he approached, a woman came out of the house and walked toward the garden. She was smiling, a bandanna in her hair, pruning shears in one hand, a basket in the other. He would have guessed late sixties, but it was hard to tell. She knelt down to work and he couldn't get a good look at her.

Max was right about something else: there was no need to worry about these people. Still, he wanted to wave to the woman, walk across the street and tell her to be careful. It was hard to resist the impulse. But how would the conversation go? What could he really say without getting himself and whatever remained of his family in serious trouble?

So he climbed back into his car. He noticed that a green minivan had pulled in behind him. Then he saw the husband come out of the house. He was a tall, fragile man, bald, with a bit of a belly, who put on a khaki fishing hat and went to work alongside his wife. These were the Goulds, kneeling on the ground on a Monday morning, fussing with tomato plants.

For some reason, watching them work was much more difficult than watching Sandy and Hiram dance. Caleb started the car and drove off too quickly, wondering why those people in that simple garden couldn't have been Max and Sandy in, say, thirty years? Why, for that matter, couldn't they have been him and Naomi, right now, and yesterday, and tomorrow?

9

THAT NIGHT, MAX had a good time bowling again with Estelle and her mother. It might have been the perfect way to round out a tough two days. Roll the ball, think about the pins, feel Estelle growing closer and closer. After their third game, Max floated the idea of a late-night snack at the diner, but it was almost eleven and Janet said she was too tired. So he dropped her off and waited in the car while Estelle walked her inside. Then he drove Estelle the three blocks to her place. When he stopped the car, she said, "I think I still owe you a beer."

"What if I've had enough beer?"

"You can come in anyhow," she said, and Max turned off the engine.

They stood in the kitchen. Estelle opened a bottle of beer and handed it to him. He didn't take a drink. She opened one for herself. Then she wrapped her arms around him and they kissed, her full lips pressing hard. There was some awkwardness with the bottles they had in their hands, but they managed to set the beer back down without spilling. Max began to remember his last kiss. A thousand miles south. Had he and Grier ever done anything in the kitchen? He remembered being out on the boat near Islamorada, under the stars, just before sunrise. But he stopped those thoughts. You never knew what life would give you and what it would take away. He held Estelle close and wondered where her bedroom was.

SOON THEY WERE stretched out on top of her comforter, and Max watched Estelle reach into her night table for a cigarette. For a moment, he thought of Nathan and the lighter. Might have used it if he'd kept it, but Estelle had no trouble lighting her own. She lay on her back and set a glass ashtray on her stomach. It rose and fell with each breath. "Do you have to smoke those?" Max asked.

"It's what comes after," she said. "Can't have the before without the after."

"In that case—"

"That's what I thought. You want one?"

"No, thanks. But I'm hoping you'll need another in a little while."

"I'm glad you're an optimist," she said. "And I'm glad you're looking ahead."

"Are you looking ahead?" he asked. "What do you see in your future?"

"I think about a lot of things," she said. "I'm a legal secretary now, but I think about nursing school. My mother would love that. But the truth is I don't like sick people. You're not sick, are you?"

Max stood up. "Do I look sick? Don't feel sick." He walked naked to the bathroom and left the door open so he could hear her if she kept talking. But she waited for him to come back. She returned the ashtray to her night table and rolled up against him, resting her head on his chest. He ran a hand through her hair.

"I figure there are nurses who don't have to deal with sick people," she said. "Some of them work for insurance companies, but they're on the phone all the time, and I wouldn't like that, either. Then there are the nurses who put people to sleep. The anesthetists. They don't have to listen to much complaining. That's a scary job, though. What if someone doesn't wake up?"

"If you were a nurse, you could take care of your mother."

"I know," she said. "I like that part of it. But what about you? What do you see ahead?"

"I've been selling," Max said. "Now I'm finishing up with selling and I'm not sure what's next. There's the need to make money, of course, but it's amazing the ways people find to do that. I can give you an example. It's one of the things I've been thinking about. You ever hear of James Lake Young?"

"No. Who's he?"

"My uncle used to talk about him. For me, he's a model. Even his name. Lake Young. Like the fountain of youth."

"What did he do?"

"He was born a while ago, back in 1853. He had an oysterman for a father. When he was three, his father left. So he was alone with his mother and they lived in what would become Atlantic City. When he was old enough to work, he did, and he took care of his mother until she passed away. Lake Young was a carpenter and he got a job patching up the boardwalk and the new pavilions. Then one day, while he was pounding nails, he met a baker from Philadelphia. They talked and the subject turned to investments. Are you still awake?"

"I'm awake," she said. "I'm listening. But I'm also thinking about the more recent past and the not-so-distant future." She moved her hand over his chest, over his stomach, up and down the inside of his thigh. "Go on."

"To make a long story short," he said.

"Make it long," she said.

"They opened a roller-skating rink and the money poured in. Then a carousel. And in 1891, they bought a pier. The baker made enough money and went back to Philadelphia, but Lake Young was just getting started."

"Getting started," Estelle said, lifting her head from his chest and pushing his legs apart with her hands.

"And then he lived happily ever after."

"No, no," she said. "Tell me."

"Tell you," he said. "I'm trying."

"I can stop," she said.

"Don't." He looked up at the ceiling. "In 1906 he opens Million Dollar Pier. Full of rides, shows, exhibits. Harry Houdini. Teddy Roosevelt. Miss America. The kind of place people dream of. And to top it all off. You listening?"

"Yes," she said, pausing for a moment.

Max exhaled and then went on. "To top it all off, he builds his home right on the pier—his own personal concrete Italian villa. Three stories, twelve rooms, a conservatory, a garden, electric lighting designed by Thomas Edison. Eventually, he owns ten miles of beachfront property, acres of land in Florida. He owns steam yachts, a fleet of sailboats, hotels, cottages. He hosts presidents and stars. The leaders of the world. And he always makes sure that everyone knows his address. Do you know what his address was?"

"No," Estelle said, pausing again. "What was his address?"

Max reached down and brought her up to him. He kissed her forehead. "Number One, Atlantic Ocean," he said.

"That would be an excellent address," she said.

He rolled her onto her back. "I agree."

MAX COULDN'T SLEEP in Estelle's four-poster bed, even though it was comfortable and queen-sized, a far cry better than the basement couch awaiting him. It was a nice apartment, too, from what he could see: high ceilings, wide-board hardwood floors, a marble mantel over the fireplace, and a spacious master bedroom. She had some money, or her mother did, but he wasn't going to think about her like that. He was thinking about having a cup of coffee together in the morning. He'd noticed a tall window in the kitchen. It would catch the light from the rising sun.

He wanted to sleep and wake in a few hours to that sun, but when he closed his eyes, his mind raced faster. This is the way it was before a deal closed, before a project finished, before a scam slammed shut like a trap sprung just right. The Goulds would never feel a thing, or so he liked to think. He'd feel it for a while, though, churning in his stomach, beating in his heart.

Estelle moved beside him and he wondered if she was awake, too. He wouldn't mind talking more. Then her leg twitched, a dream reflex. He tried to make out the stars through the gauzy white curtains, but all he could see out there was the waning moon, not far from full. Its ghostly light grayed the dark of the room. The pieces of furniture looked like solid shadows pushed up against the walls. It was easier and more comforting to look over at Estelle. She reminded him of someone, but he couldn't yet say whom. She didn't have the body of a bowler, though she looked strong. Sturdy. Warm. Naked, she didn't look that much older than Grier. Maybe early thirties. Being around her made him feel almost understood. It was late and he'd been busy these last few days, so he knew better than to trust his thoughts, especially not the corny ones, but when he tried to pinpoint what was drawing him in, he remembered the way she was with her mother. Just what he needed in his life, another aging senior citizen, and yet, he could still picture Estelle slowly walking Janet to her front door. It had looked like real kindness to him, and he'd sensed something gentle in those soft high-fives by the scorer's table. Whatever it was between the two of them, it had made him smile throughout the evening.

He told himself to simply enjoy the night for what it was. A peaceful, pleasurable moment. A gift amid some chaos. A taste of the new amid too much that was old and fading away. He moved closer to her, put an arm around her surprisingly slender waist. She was sleeping so soundly and he wanted to join her. He closed his eyes again.

It was no use. He listened to Estelle breathe and he knew he should stay, even if it meant being awake all night. He'd heard the way she talked about those husbands who somehow both ran off and got kicked out, the hurt still there in her voice. Leaving in the middle of the night couldn't be the right thing to do. But part of him didn't want to stay too long. He didn't want anything awkward in the morning. Why overreach? Be satisfied with the evening, the closeness and the warmth. Leaving early, he told himself, was actually a way of moving slowly, cautiously.

He devised a test. He knew it was childish. He'd stand up and walk to the window and look out at the sky. He'd count to ten and if she didn't wake up, he'd write her a note and go. Climbing out of bed, he wasn't as quiet as he could have been, and he took his time counting, but she didn't stir. He dressed and went back to the kitchen, where he found a pen and a legal pad. *Had to get to work*, he wrote. *I want to be in touch again soon.* He reminded himself of his father. For once, that felt all right, and he wrote another line: *You looked like you were having good dreams.* He slipped back into the bedroom and left the note on the pillow.

HE DIDN'T EXPECT anyone to be awake when he walked into the basement apartment. Then he heard, "Maxie!" and it startled him. Abe was reclining in his easy chair, wearing his terry-cloth bathrobe and slippers, eyes wide open to face the early morning light.

"Shh," Max said. "Dad's sleeping."

"Talk," Abe said.

Sometimes he did seem suddenly lucid. He'd make sense and you'd think he was back to normal, ready to make sense from moment to moment. "Okay," Max said, hoping, even though he knew how he replied wouldn't really matter. Abe would say what he would say. Max would follow if he could. "Let's talk," Max added. "Tell me whatever you want."

"Cowardly," Abe said.

Make conversation, Max thought. *See where he manages to go.* "You'd like the woman I met," he said. "You and Dad both."

Abe said nothing. He put his index finger into his ear and wiggled it for almost a minute.

To get him to leave his ear alone, Max said, "That scooter's coming soon."

Abe set his hands in his lap. "The jungle," he said. "Diamonds."

Max sat in his father's chair, next to Abe. They both leaned back and looked out toward the sidewalk. "Aren't you glad your brother is with you?" Max asked. "Aren't you glad he doesn't leave you somewhere and go away?"

"I'm busy. Don't bother me."

"I wonder if you would have stayed with him," Max said. "I wonder if I would. If I will."

"A man goes out," Abe said, and he started to stand up.

Max stood and put his hand around his uncle's gaunt right bicep, helping him to his feet. "Here we go," Max said, as they shuffled to the bedroom, where Abe curled up on the mattress, still in his bathrobe. Max took off Abe's slippers and adjusted his blanket. Then he stood by the door for a little while. He was watching everyone sleep tonight. Before Abe drifted off, or maybe it was after, Max could hear him say, "He was a happy man with a ton of concrete."

IN THE MORNING, Max woke up to find a phone close to his face. "It's Sandy," Caleb said. "She wants to talk to you."

Max squinted at his watch. He'd managed to get a few hours in, at least, though it wasn't yet nine. "You told her I was sleeping?"

"I told her."

Max took the phone. "Good morning," he said.

"Max," she said, "as I was telling your father, I have my doubts about this Boy Scout troop working out. I don't know if Nathan will cooperate. We're not communicating well these days."

"Did something happen?"

"I'm not getting involved in this one," she said. "I can't. We're off for Hawaii in two days. You'll have to work it out with him yourself."

"Fine. No problem. How was the rest of the party?"

"The rest of the party was fantastic, Max. Sorry you had to leave so soon."

"Just keeping busy," he said.

"Aren't we all," she said, and then she hung up.

10

ABE'S ON HIS back in bed, awake, as usual, though his eyes are closed. He hears Max talking on the phone and he catches a few words: *something, fine, problem, busy.* Then there are the typical morning noises, like a tide rushing in, pouring into the sinks, the toilet, the shower, the pipes behind the walls. Footsteps scurry fast and slow, the movement sending slight vibrations across the floor, up through his mattress. Again, the start of the day shivers into his spine.

He inhales the damp smell of the steam, the sharp aftershave, the strong Maxwell House, the bagels toasting. He breathes deeply, focusing on that simple sensation, so crucial and calming. If he can't sleep, he can at least make every effort to enjoy this peace and relative quiet, this nearly gentle beginning. His brother will be in for him soon enough.

Or maybe this morning he'll beat Caleb to it and walk into the living room on his own. He has things to say. He tried last night with Max, but it hadn't worked out. Still, he'll keep trying. He's been dreaming or remembering for hours, days, weeks now. It won't be easy to know where to begin. Plus he's never been known for his brevity. Explanations, especially his, take time. Somehow, though, he has to mention Mervyn. Has to spill about Spiller.

What he wouldn't give to walk right out of the bedroom, stand before his brother and his nephew, and talk the way he used to talk! He can almost see their shocked faces. For a moment, he thinks he hears his old voice, as if in a dream, already speaking, or about to speak.

Listen, he'll say. *Listen to this.*

11

AFTER SANDY HUNG UP, Max stayed stretched out on the sofa, trying to recapture and connect the unsettling images from his quickly fading dream. He'd been trapped in a room filled with trash bags, each one stuffed, shiny, and seaweed green. He was dressed in white, struggling to move, but the trash bags kept accumulating, taking up more and more space, blocking out all available light. An older woman appeared with a small husky that roared like a lion. Then they both vanished, leaving him alone, unable to breathe.

He was glad to look across the apartment and see his father preparing to take Abe to rehab. "I'll be back soon," Caleb said. "Then we'll do some visits together. You'll be ready?"

"And waiting."

Once they left, Max showered, shaved, and dressed, puzzling over the dream. Sandy was only thirty-five, hardly an older woman, at least not to him. Still, it would probably be safe to say it was yet another divorce dream.

Max poured himself a cup of coffee, ready to jump-start his day, but then he wandered back into the living room and sat down in Abe's Barcalounger. His thoughts turned to Grier. Maybe the dream came out of his guilt. He was trashing himself for his infidelity.

He picked up the phone and called her. He listened to the ringing, imagining Grier out on the boat, pulling her wet suit over her bikini, brightly dressed for another day of research in Florida Bay. The last time he'd been onboard with her, she'd taken him snorkeling. She'd led him under a mangrove island. Another murky, almost nightmarish space, light occasionally slicing through the foliage and roots to reveal hundreds of fish, from tiny anchovies to sinister barracudas. It was easy to feel trapped and vulnerable and short of breath down there, but Grier moved with calm and grace, adjusting her position with a flick of her flippers, pointing out the sparkly, vibrant sights she wanted him to see.

When the answering machine came on, Max hung up. Grier lived with a bunch of fellow researchers she didn't like all that much, and he didn't want to share his message with them. Also, he didn't know exactly what he wanted to say.

On the kitchen table, there was a Bible open to the book of Numbers. Caleb must have been reviewing the family Torah portion. Max turned a few pages as he sipped his second cup of coffee, his mind flashing from graceful Grier to those ungrateful Israelites. Then Caleb came in, moving faster without Abe.

Max kept looking at the Bible. "Are you studying Scripture these days, Dad?"

"Oh, that," Caleb said, waiting just inside the door. "I had a tough time paying attention at the service. I wanted to reread those verses."

"I'd forgotten this part with all the quail."

"You can remind me about it in the car," Caleb said. "Let's hit the road."

IT WAS EASY for Max to remember how, out in the wilderness, the Israelites grew tired of eating manna. Always the same thing, morning, noon, and night. They moaned and kvetched, even though the manna tasted like cake. *Would that we were given flesh to eat,* they whined. *We remember the fish, which we were wont to eat in Egypt, the cucumbers, and the melons, and the leeks, and the onions, and the garlic, but now our souls are dried away, there is nothing at all, we have nought save this manna to look to—*

Those poor fools. So quickly they forget. How could they long for Egypt? Back to slavery and bondage? What were they thinking? Could they really have been surprised by God's response?

The Lord will give you flesh, He declared, *and ye shall eat. Ye shall not eat one day, nor two days, nor five days, neither ten days, nor twenty days; but a whole month, until it come out at your nostrils, and it be loathsome unto you; because you have rejected the Lord who is among you, and have troubled Him with weeping, saying: Why, now came we forth out of Egypt?*

Quail soon fell from the sky, whole flocks dropping down all around the camp. The people gathered up the birds, heaps of them, more than enough for anyone who wanted to eat. The greedy began immediately to feast, but while the flesh was still in their mouths, God smote them with a deadly plague, thereby weeding the lustful out of the multitude. Or so the story goes.

MAX COULDN'T RESIST a little needling as he drove his father to their first stop. "What do you think about that God, delivering the food, letting them put it in their mouths, then bringing down more obliteration. What kind of lesson do you see in that?"

"I'm not in the mood, Max."

"There you are, out wandering around the desert day after day. You just want a little variety, you're not asking for a miracle necessarily. The birds appear and maybe you think things are looking up. You're chewing away, happy for a moment, your faith restored. You smile at how delicious the quail tastes. You've got your menu planned for the next week. Barbecued quail. Fried quail. Maybe some roast quail with manna stuffing. Then the plague blasts you."

"Well, sounds like you're feeling good this morning. Were you this happy in Florida? I'd do Bible study with you every morning if you'd move back up here."

"Wouldn't that make me as stupid as the Israelites, lured back by the place I fled not that long ago? You can't go home again, that's what I've heard."

Caleb kept quiet until they reached Rolling Hill Hospital. "Nathan's birthplace," Max said as he parked the car. "More memory lane for me."

"I like to do the hospitals first," said Caleb. "That way things seem like they're improving as we go along."

Max watched his father pause in the lobby and pull a list from his pocket. "Who will we see here?" he asked.

"Joe Lonzinger just got out of the ICU. You remember him, he repped with Ralph Solomon. And, let's see, we might run into Ruth Hornig. She's a volunteer. Rabbi Weinberg also stops by a lot."

Caleb clearly knew his way around Rolling Hill and Max followed behind, noticing how his father didn't need to glance at the signs. He also noticed that the buildings had been extensively remodeled since his last visit, thirteen years ago. The hospital used to resemble an old hilltop mansion, a luxury hotel that had seen better days. Max remembered there being an eerie connection between the building's fading grandeur and the patients' declining health. The circular driveway and Doric columns were gone now. The place was more modern, brighter, sleeker, and cleaner, but as far as he could tell the people in the elevator and the hallways and the waiting rooms hadn't become healthier or happier.

Max listened for the sound of babies crying. He knew there was a nursery somewhere on one of the floors, but he didn't see it.

Then they were in Joe's room, a small, sterile single, with the narrow bed pushed close to the window. Caleb didn't sit down. He stood by the foot of the bed and spoke like a doctor who'd stopped by to check the chart and assess the treatment. "How you doing, young man?"

"You brought your boy with you," Joe said. "That's nice."

"I've got him in town and I'm hoping to make him stay. Figured the sight of your beautiful face would be the convincer."

To Max, Joe's face looked pale and papery, the skin far too thin. He couldn't remember the last time they'd met. There might have been a train ride to New York years ago. Or maybe they'd sat together in the waiting room at Katz Underwear. In any case, Max stepped over to shake his hand.

"I heard about that woman of yours," Joe said. "What comes around, goes around, that's what I believe. I bet she's not so happy now."

"She's off to Hawaii in two days. She's absolutely miserable about it. Smiling so much her lips hurt."

"Slowly turns the wheel of fortune," said Joe, patting the back of Max's hand. "Sit down, you two. Take a load off."

"Been sitting all day," Caleb said. "But thanks. We can't stay too long anyhow."

"Since you're here," Joe said, "I'm going to give you a tip. A little thank-you from me to you. I've been chatting with some of the nurses and I've got a real moneymaker." He flipped the blanket and sheets off his body. "Look at this," he said.

Caleb didn't flinch, but Max had no idea what he was supposed to see. The bony, toothpick legs? The knobby knees? The clear tube that snaked down one thigh to a plastic bag suspended beside the bed? Max saw a man wasting away. Maybe Joe's mind was going along with everything else.

"This cheap johnny," Joe went on, fingering the thin blue material that barely covered him. "It's lightweight and it's ugly. One thing I've learned from all my tests these last few days is that most of these rooms here are awfully goddamn cold."

"Any news from those tests?" Caleb asked.

Joe covered himself back up. "Don't try to change the subject," he said. "Here's my gift to you: corduroy johnnies. Or how about flannel? Flannel sheets, too. Now that would make a patient feel more at home. Think about it. Who wouldn't pay extra for a thing like that?"

"Flannel holds too much dust," said Caleb. "And I don't think all the static electricity would be welcome here. But corduroy. You might have something there."

"Of course I've got something. And that's just the beginning. Look at all the sewing they do in hospitals. Sheets, pillowcases, scrubs. Abe would love this idea."

"What about those surgical masks?" Max asked, trying to get into the spirit.

"Woven paper," Joe said. "I thought of that, but it would be a whole separate business."

Caleb was pacing back and forth, making himself a moving target for whatever diseases might be lurking in the room. He kept his arms crossed, as if he wanted to avoid getting anything on his hands. "You sound all right, Joe," he said. "You sound better."

"I'll be walking out of here in no time. But enough about me. Let's hear what you got going on. How's business? What's hot these days?"

"We're not here to talk shop. Besides, business stinks, same as ever. You don't need news like that."

"How is Abe?"

"More blessed than us in some ways. Doesn't seem to worry about much."

"Give him my best."

Max was waiting for the conversation to sink down deeper, to drop below the superficial, stiff-upper-lip banter. That glimpse of Joe's body made him think he'd never see this man alive again, and that thought made him watch his father more closely, and then, before long, they were shaking hands, saying good-bye, sorry to leave so soon, thanks for stopping in, don't be a stranger.

Back in the lobby, Caleb said, "Lonzinger hasn't got a prayer. He's worse than he looks, believe me."

"He looks pretty bad."

Caleb checked the time and glanced around. "No sign of Ruth or Weinberg. Let's move on."

They continued with their rounds, appointment by appointment, like clockwork, not all that different from a day spent calling on clients. Max remembered those days, following his father around, lugging the sample cases from the car to the office and back to the car. When he was a kid, there was something exciting about traveling on a Wolinsky Brothers trip. Even though he didn't do very much, he was somehow good for business. He tended to put everyone in a better mood. He felt older and important, and people paid attention to him, touring him around the factories and the mills, floors of looms, floors of dye, floors of sewing machines, the dust like brightly colored snow, the smell like paint and sweat and laundry, the noise an endless train running over his head.

It was different during those years before Sandy and Nathan, when Max was past being a kid, when he came back from college and tried to work as the first and only associate. People wondered how soon he'd be taking over and no one was at ease, including his father. Max felt as if he were in the way, useless, or worse, bad for business. Caleb wanted company, needed company, Max knew that, but he also knew that Caleb longed for him to have a better career. In his father's mind, there would always be time for Dr. Wolinsky to appear. And that was only part of the problem. The other part had to do with how bored Max was. So many of those calls were almost exactly the same, one basic formula, traveling all those miles for fifteen minutes here, twenty minutes there. The brief meetings weren't really about selling but about showing your face, being respectful and punctual, staying in touch, making yourself available. Then, when it came time to place an order, you got the call because you were the one they remembered; out in Altoona, Scranton, Ephrata, Baltimore, and Trenton, you were the one who leaped to mind. "Old school," Caleb would say. "Take care of the little things and the bigger things are bound to come your way."

Now the territory was smaller, as Abe liked to point out. And nobody was going to phone in from the hospitals or retirement communities asking how long it would take to ship fifty thousand yards of this or a hundred thousand yards of that. These visits wouldn't bring in any commissions. There were no new lines to push. No deals to pursue. But that didn't matter today. For a few hours at least, Max trailed his father again. In and out of the car, up and down the walkways, working one room after another. They went from Rolling Hill to Spring Garden to Chestnut Circle to Breyer's Run. They saw Milly and Charlie, Edith and Meyer, Sidney and Reva. They saw Pauline, Herb, Sam, and Helene. Shaking hands, kissing cheeks, hello, good-bye, nice to see you, sorry to leave so soon, thanks for stopping in, don't be a stranger.

Max began to understand each visit as a kind of closing. Caleb, dedicated to the end, would keep making his rounds until everyone signed off. The talk might sound like banter, idle chitchat, but that was merely the code. Taken together, after years and years, these words added up to the final negotiations, the last old school lessons.

When they reached the end of the day's list, they did what they used to do. "Let's stop at the diner," Caleb said. "We can grab a cup of coffee before we pick up Abe."

They slid into a booth. It was after the lunch rush so they had the place almost to themselves. They'd been offered food at almost every stop, but Max had eaten nothing and now he was hungry. "Do we have time for pie?" he asked.

"Sure, son. It's the least I could do. It felt good to have company today."

A waitress poured their coffee and recommended the peach pie. Max saw her as too old for the son and too young for the father. A northeast Philly woman, big-haired and long-nailed, probably wife or girlfriend to one of the cooks. Her name tag said Missy. Max leaned back against the red vinyl, exhausted, and he watched as his father kept talking to her, asking after her two daughters, her mother out in Harrisburg. She smiled and touched Caleb's arm before she went to plate up their pie.

For so long, Max had dreaded becoming like his father. He was frustrated by what he saw as his father's refusal to heal. Why did he stay so alone? Why wouldn't he take any more risks? Max still didn't want to wind up that way, but he realized it was more complicated than he'd previously thought. The divorce, the flight, the return—it was making everything look and feel very different. "I don't know how you do it, Dad," he said.

Caleb shrugged, stirring his black coffee. "Do what?"

"All this visiting, for one thing," Max said. "I've only been here a few days, and I'm pretty turned around. I guess I don't know how people drop in on their old lives."

"You wind up grateful that you have an old life to drop in on. Think of it that way."

Missy brought over the pie. Max noticed his piece was by far the smaller of the two.

"Thanks, honey," Caleb said, and then he turned back to Max. "Give it time," he said. "You'll see."

Max often felt as if he'd heard everything his father had to say at least a million times. Usually, this was annoying, but every now and then it was comforting. He focused on his pie. It was warm and fresh.

"Enough about old lives," Caleb said. "Let's hear about the new life. Tell me more about your Key Largo girl."

"I dreamed about her last night, I think."

"Before you tell her that, make sure. But what else?"

"She's smart, she's young." He searched for more to say. Then he remembered the bar mitzvah, how her advice matched up with Caleb's. "Sometimes," he said, "she reminds me of you."

"Ha," Caleb said, forking off another piece of pie. "That's a little scary, actually. Where do you think it's heading?"

"Don't know yet. There's too much else going on right now. Speaking of which, why don't you tell me more about Spiller."

Caleb looked at his watch and reached for his wallet. "I like what I've heard. Boy Scout uniforms, China, he lets us work as representatives for a mill he has an interest in. It's simple, legitimate. The old-fashioned way. Might not even have to bother with the Goulds."

"Stop worrying about that, Dad. It's almost over. It won't get in the way of anything else."

Caleb was silent for too long. After he cleaned the crumbs from his plate, he sat still, drumming his fingertips against the tabletop.

"What is it?" Max asked.

"We should go get Abe, but first I've got a confession to make."

Max could see it coming. "You talked to the Goulds? Tell me you didn't talk to them."

"I just drove by, Max. I wanted to see their house."

Max needed to stay calm. He was in a good mood. He was feeling closer to his father. Everything would be fine. No problem. He inhaled before he spoke. "What are you planning, Dad? Tell me now so I can take care of it. If you're going to torpedo the whole setup, let me know so I can make sure no one gets hurt."

"I kept thinking they could have been my friends. Whatever you've done in Florida, that's different. I don't know those people. I don't respect the people who retire down there."

"Let's not talk about Florida right now."

"Could we really get out of it?"

"It might be possible, but this is nothing to fiddle around with. If you want me to let it go, I need to know now."

"I don't think it's worth the risk, especially with Spiller and what he may have for us. I want to feel good about the money I make up here."

Max said what he needed to say. "Okay, Dad. Okay. But you have to promise me something."

"I will."

"You know I was working yesterday. I'll do what I can to call it off, but I can't guarantee it. Meanwhile, you can't do anything else. No more drive-bys, all right? No more interference."

"All right."

"I have your word on that?"

"Yes," Caleb said. "You have my word."

Max left a few bills under his coffee cup. Then they said good-bye to Missy and walked out to the car. On the way, to lighten the mood, to bring back the closeness he'd felt moments ago, Max said, "I have a confession, too," and he told Caleb about Estelle, how much he liked her, how surprised he was. "So maybe you're right about all of this," he said. "Maybe I shouldn't be doing anything in our backyard."

"What about the Florida woman?"

Max laughed. "You're always looking out for someone, aren't you, Dad? I thought you might like the idea of someone local."

"I might," Caleb said, "but first I'd have to meet her."

Max wondered, again, why he'd told Estelle that story about his father's fatal crash. "It's a little early for an introduction," he said. "But we'll see how it goes."

12

NATHAN WAS WALKING, down Marvin Road, High Street, Ashferry Avenue, closing in on Temple Beth Israel. He was taking his time because he wanted to be doing something else, almost anything else. But he was going to the scout meeting, as promised.

Off in the distance, the sun was setting like a golden home-run ball, dropping in slow motion behind the city's jagged sky-line. If he could have decided for himself, Nathan would have been blocks away, over at Maisel Elementary, playing stickball with Rich, Jeff, and Eric. The three of them had signed on to the Rosentown Sunoco team and their parents had already taken them shopping for pinstripes and cleats. They'd worn their new caps the last week of school, carrying their gloves everywhere, breaking them in, giving off the lush smells of linseed oil and leather.

He didn't know much about Troop 158 yet, but he knew

there were no teams and only two patrols: the Cobras and the Owls. The uniform was an embarrassment. The shorts were made for old men and Nathan wanted nothing to do with a red neckerchief. He couldn't believe that instead of getting his first cup, he'd be getting garters to hold his green kneesocks in place.

He was always hoping to run into Jennifer. Now he'd have to hope she never saw him in uniform.

And then there was this kosher business. Just thinking about it made him want to keep walking forever.

He turned another corner and tried to cheer himself up by visualizing his swing. He was a line-drive hitter with decent form, but he wanted more power. He needed to practice stepping into the pitch, turning his hips, snapping his wrists; then he'd be able to drill the ball over the chain-link fence again and again. Like Rich and Jeff and Eric, he could play for hours. They played until the sun went down, but even then some light always hazed out the windows of nearby houses. Their eyes adjusted. When he was pitching, he didn't need to see the strike zone chalked onto the redbrick wall. He knew where it was. Batting, he learned to sense the ball, hear it speeding closer, feel the pulse it pushed through the air.

Each one of their stickball evenings ended the same way. Rich's mother would begin by shouting from behind her screen door, up at the corner: "Richard! Richard!"

Her high, strong voice carried well, echoing off the brick and concrete. That didn't stop them from ignoring her. She would open the door, continue to shout, and come closer. Her silver hair caught the dim light. Her heels tip-tapped against the sidewalk. Her husband followed quietly alongside.

Even though Nathan wanted to keep playing, he smiled as they approached. He would have denied it, but he was always glad to see them. They looked sharp in their work clothes and he liked how undaunted they seemed, clearly taking pleasure in their part of the game. The voice grew louder, but it hit him full of kindness, not anger: "Richard! I know you can hear me!"

If Nathan was batting, he swung harder. If he was fielding, he hoped to make an astounding bare-handed grab. They'd have to be impressed.

Eventually, their presence became impossible to ignore. He could hear them breathing, and that was when Rich would begin to bargain. "One more out, Mom," he would plead. "We're almost done."

But Rich's mother would allow no bargaining. Once she was standing there, she would not be denied, not for a moment. "You come home with us now, mister," she'd say. "Right now!"

WHEN NATHAN WALKED into the synagogue, he could hear the evening service in progress. *Barkhu et Adonai ha-mevorakh. Barukh Adonai ha-mevorakh l'olam vayed.* Praise the Lord, to whom our praise is due. He peered through the sanctuary's glass doors and saw Rabbi Weinberg up on the bimah. He remembered those months of lessons, chanting his Torah portion, the rabbi by his side. Weinberg always followed along letter by letter, breathing out his cinnamon breath, his deep voice, chiding, "Don't squawk and parrot. Cherish these words. Let each one rise up. Feel its spirit."

He moved away from the doors. He was supposed to meet the scoutmaster, so he walked down the stairs to the basement office. The door was wide open and Spiller was pacing behind the desk, talking on the phone. He looked creased, from his starched and pressed uniform to the straight lines on his forehead. There was order in his voice and in his office. Nathan noticed imposing stacks of crates along the walls. Cartons of canned food, enough to feed dozens of scouts for weeks. Powdered eggs. Powdered milk. Peaches in heavy syrup. Peas and baby onions. Not the sort of food he associated with camping. Cans like that wouldn't be fun to carry.

Spiller seemed to grow angrier at the person on the other end of the line. "Absolutely no less than twenty-five thousand," he was saying. "That was the arrangement." He walked around the desk and slapped the back of a plastic bridge chair, nearly knocking it over. He waved Nathan toward the chair. "Don't give me that garbage," Spiller said into the phone. "I'll cold-ass those fools if that's what they want."

Cold-ass? What sort of threat was that? This was how his would-be leader spoke?

And this was how he looked? His spring uniform was slightly modified—with the shirt, shorts, and kneesocks, he sported shiny black wingtips. The shoes went with the double-breasted business suit that hung from the back of the door. He kept pacing and the pointy toes of the wingtips looked like they could do damage, especially in motion. Black hair covered his arms, in contrast to his completely bald scalp. Bulky gold-framed bifocals showcased his big eyes and bushy eyebrows. A smaller man might have appeared weak and uncommanding in such an outfit, but Spiller looked tough. Only his knobby knees seemed vulnerable.

Nathan remembered his grandfather praising Spiller. "I was impressed by him, Nathan," he'd said. "I heard him speak. He had a vision I could see."

"If Atlantic City's your idea of a small town," Spiller shouted, "you're useless to me." He slammed the receiver down. He sat in the desk chair, leaned back, clasped his hands behind his neck.

Nathan crossed his arms, bracing himself for whatever was

coming next. He felt targeted. The scoutmaster's elbows pointed at him, like range finders for those big, gold-framed eyes.

"Nathan Wolinsky," Spiller said. "Congratulations on your bar mitzvah. You did a fine job."

"Thanks. And thank you for your gift."

"It was nothing," Spiller said. "I hope you'll find it useful. Now, your grandfather has spoken with me. A nice man. How are you feeling about scouting today?"

"I'm giving it a lot of thought."

"Just give me the straight talk, kid. I'm not a man who has time for bullshit. I see you're not in uniform."

Nathan's heart was beating faster, but he held his ground. "The truth is I'd rather play baseball."

"Is that so?" Spiller leaned forward and flicked a hand in front of his face, as if he were shooing away a fly. "Well, we'll see about that. In the meantime, let me tell you a few of the qualities that distinguish the boys of Troop 158. We don't play games. We believe in service to the community. We uphold our moral standards. We are prepared and we will be prepared for today, tomorrow, and the days that follow on into the future. And, as you may have heard, we keep kosher. Many of the boys don't realize what that means at first. They don't appreciate the day-to-day ramifications. Your mother doesn't run a kosher house, does she?"

"She lights the candles on Shabbat sometimes. That's about it."

"It's work for a troop to keep kosher in the wilderness. I'm not saying it isn't. But our ancestors did it, and they were far worse off than we are. It will be an education for you, I can promise that. I believe Troop 158 makes boys better leaders and tougher spirits. We discipline the mind and the body. Do you feel your mind and body are disciplined?"

"Baseball takes discipline," Nathan said.

"I'll let you in on a little secret. Your grandfather will not go for baseball. It's a pitch you can't make. A strikeout, kid."

What could he say? When in doubt, be polite. "Thank you for taking the time to meet with me."

"Your grandfather told me you were a go-getter, on your way up. Maybe he was just dreaming. As grandfathers do. You understand there's nothing like being an Eagle Scout? Not only in this country, but throughout the world. Instant respect. That's what it amounts to. People listen when you speak. They fall quiet and attend to your words. Doors open."

Nathan looked at the office door. He smelled mildew and wondered if some of the airtight food had begun to rot.

"Don't sit there in silence," Spiller said. "Ask me something. It's an opportunity to be in my office, though you might not believe it. Don't leave without taking advantage. Hasn't your grandfather taught you anything?"

"What does 'cold-ass' mean?"

Spiller barked out a laugh. "At least you're listening," he said. "It's my own vitriol. Not Yiddishkeit, if that's what you're thinking. It comes from Samson, that poor sap. Packs a real wallop. Ask me something else."

"How long does it take to become an Eagle Scout?"

"Your grandfather told me he bought you a handbook. Read it. Make a plan. See if you can stick to it. It takes as long as it takes you to meet all the requirements, which are clearly described for anyone to see. You don't have to come in here and ask me a chickenshit question like that. Come in here next time and *tell* me how long it will take you to become an Eagle Scout. Come in here and show me on paper how quickly you can accomplish it. Then I'll ask you a thing or two."

"As I said, I'm hoping to play baseball."

"You're wasting my time. I'll have another conversation with your grandfather about this. Maybe your father, too." Spiller pulled up his sleeve to glance at his watch, a thick bar of shiny metal wrapped around his wrist. He caught Nathan looking at it and held his arm out across the desk, offering a better view. "Platinum," he said. "Now go spend some time with my boys. See what you think."

NATHAN WAS EXPECTING the troop to have at least twenty kids, all Hasidim, in *kippot* rather than caps. He pictured them as a nerdy bunch, with glasses and plenty of pens, carrying around science-fiction paperbacks or comic books or pocket-sized Bibles.

Well, he was wrong about all that. He found Spiller's boys in the center of the parking lot. He counted six of them and they were busy tending two fires that blazed almost side by side. The flames reached up into the darkening sky, like twin trees of flickering orange. A two-piece burning bush, right in front of the temple. There was no God calling out, *Hineni! Here am I!* Just the scouts laughing, one of them shouting, "Burn, baby, burn!" A boy tossed a branch into one fire. Glowing bits of ash shot up to be carried and cooled gray by the breeze. At the other fire, two boys fanned the flames with large squares of cardboard. The fires seemed more or less under control, far away from the parked cars, nowhere near any trees. As Nathan stepped closer, the heat hit his face, tightening his skin, and he wondered if the asphalt would melt back to stone and tar.

The scouts looked older than Nathan had expected. Most of them were probably fifteen or sixteen. Two of them had beards already. And as they moved around the fires, their faces flickering in and out of shadow, they seemed crazed, manic, dangerous.

Not trustworthy, loyal, or helpful. They wore their uniforms, but they still looked like a gang of thugs.

So it made some sense to Nathan that the only person he recognized was Ricky Gersh. Maybe the least likely kid in the world to be a scout. Usually Ricky got a ride to school with a bunch of football players, but occasionally he came out to Nathan's bus stop. He'd smoke and play catch with a crony or two, tossing a tennis ball as close as he could to the windshields of passing cars. "I like to play in traffic," Nathan had heard him say, more than once. On the bus, Ricky would sit back by the emergency door, rubbing his ringed fingers through his buzz-cut red hair, blasting a radio, hawking up something to spit out the window.

Ricky was the loudest of the boys and Nathan watched him circle the fires. "Cobra fire," Ricky shouted. "Go Cobra fire!" A large knife in a leather sheath was attached to his belt. The rest of his belt glittered with skill awards. In one hand he carried a squirt bottle of lighter fluid.

Then Ricky was standing by Nathan's side, slapping his back, saying, "Wolinsky. I heard you might be making an appearance tonight."

"Who told you that?"

"I'm a patrol leader," Ricky said. "I know things. So, you'll be a Cobra, won't you?"

Already this was Nathan's longest conversation with Ricky. What to say next? "I never knew you were a scout, Ricky. Do you like this stuff?"

"It's an opportunity. You'll see."

"Is this a typical meeting?"

Ricky smiled. "Well," he said, "it's important to know how to make a fire before you go camping. It's also important for the Cobras to prove they make better fires than the Owls."

"Aren't there other things you'd rather be doing?"

Ricky gazed into the flames. "I don't know," he said. "I'm liking this just fine."

Each time Ricky opened his mouth, Nathan expected a threat or a curse to come thundering out. But Ricky just kept smiling. Nathan acted differently around different people, he knew that. He wasn't the same when he was playing stickball as when he was with his father or when he was in the classroom or when he was by himself. Maybe Ricky the scout was different from Ricky the bully. Nathan decided to wait and see. "What kind of knife is that?" he asked.

"These knives are not easy to get," Ricky said. "It's a bowie knife. Only for patrol leaders. Spiller sold me two, meat and dairy." He undid a snap on the sheath, and he seemed about to show Nathan the blade, but then they heard the siren and a police car roared into the lot.

"Cops," Ricky said. "Shit."

The car stopped a few feet away. When the officer opened his door, he was still speaking into his radio. He was a very large man who took up most of the front seat. He had no partner. There wouldn't have been enough room. "It's a bunch of Boy Scouts," he said. "I'll handle it. Cancel the fire trucks."

The officer lumbered up to them. His face was flabby-cheeked, shiny, and clean shaven, as if his day had just started. "What the hell's going on here?" he asked.

Nathan was amazed at how quickly Ricky responded. "We're practicing making signal fires, sir," he said, "in case we ever get lost in the wilderness."

"We're a long way from the wilderness. And these fires are sending the wrong signals to the neighborhood. They need to be extinguished. Pronto."

The other boys had gathered around. "Of course," Ricky said. "Whatever you say. But before we put them out, would you mind judging?"

"Judging?"

"Just tell us which fire is larger." Ricky gestured with his right arm, like a game-show host, introducing each fire. "The Cobra fire or the Owl fire?"

The cop hesitated. "All right," he said. "Give me a second." He took the task seriously, eyeballing the fires, walking around them, stepping back, inhaling. There was no obvious answer. The flames danced up and down. The burning wood crackled. The cop squatted, pursed his lips, and stared. He looked like he was trying to get a line on a putt.

Ricky grinned, and then, working for his patrol, he pointed his bottle of lighter fluid at the Cobra fire and squeezed. But his hand was too close to the flames, which shot up higher. There was no time to drop the bottle. A sizzle burst into a boom as the fluid exploded in Ricky's hand. Nathan thought his own hair was on fire, burning up, and yet he froze, shocked, watching the cop pounce like a panther, shouldering Ricky to the ground. The cop tore off his own jacket and smothered the flames with it. Ricky yelled, his voice alarmingly high. "You stupid shit," the cop was saying. "You stupid little shit."

People ran out from the synagogue. Spiller came first, followed by Rabbi Weinberg and the congregants. By the time they reached the fires, the cop had carried Ricky to the car and was carefully buckling him into the backseat. "I'm taking this kid to the emergency room over at Abington Hospital," he said. He pointed at Spiller. "Get those goddamn fires out. I'll be back in touch with you."

"Let me see my boy," Spiller said, striding to the back door and peering in at Ricky. "You'll be fine, son. I'll call your folks and come right over." He mussed up Ricky's singed hair, closed the door, and stepped back. Then the siren was wailing and the car sped out of the lot.

Nathan stood still through it all. At one point, he caught a glimpse of Ricky's burned hand, bloody and blistered. He noticed shining bands of metal and wondered if the rings could have melted. He closed his eyes then, feeling sick to his stomach, breathing in the charred air.

NATHAN WANTED TO leave and not come back, but he also wanted to see what would happen. One of the scouts uncoiled a hose and began dousing the flames. It didn't take long to transform the blazes into scraps of soaked, hissing wood. With a pair of shovels, a few heavy-duty trash bags, and a big broom, the scouts gathered up the remains of the fires. The congregants loitered and murmured for a little while. "Idle hands—," began an old man, leaning into his walker.

"Don't make fun of that poor boy," said his companion.

"Well, when I was his age, I'll tell you—"

They drifted away, back to their cars. Then Nathan heard a familiar voice, rising and resonant. Rabbi Weinberg always sounded as if he were midsermon, circling toward wisdom. He was letting Spiller have it. "How could you allow this to happen, Mervyn? This is terrible. This is not what we want to sponsor. To have this, on our doorstep—" He spread his arms and gazed up at the stars. Then he looked Spiller in the eyes. "In case I'm not being clear, I want you to know I'm furious."

Spiller hung his head. He appeared full of remorse and he put an open hand on the rabbi's back. "I got a good look at him, Herman," he said. "It was mostly first-degree stuff. Except for some of the fingers on that hand. Overall, he's a lucky boy. There must not have been much fluid left in that bottle."

"You were going to bring honor to the temple. Good publicity. Instead we have bonfires in the parking lot? Police?"

"I'll talk to the boys. Nothing like this will happen again. It was a ridiculous accident. Still, there's a lesson here, I feel sure of that."

"Tell me what kind of lesson there is in a boy playing with lighter fluid?"

The rest of the scouts had moved closer to listen and await punishment. Nathan thought they might be embarrassed to watch their leader being scolded, but they seemed calm. Obedient. Almost as if they'd seen this sort of thing before.

"Well," Spiller said, "I'm reminded of something, from the Baal-Shem, I think. How does it go? 'If a man has fulfilled all the commandments, but has not had the rapture and the burning, when he dies and passes beyond, paradise is opened to him, but because he has not felt rapture and burning in the world, he also does not feel it in paradise.'"

Rabbi Weinberg smiled. "This is not that kind of burning, Mervyn."

"The lesson's not finished," Spiller said. "I'll keep working on it."

One of the scouts spoke up. He was the only remotely bookish-looking kid in the group, with horn-rim glasses and big ears. "Does that mean those who burn on earth might not burn in hell when they die?"

Rabbi Weinberg turned to the boy. "What's your name?" he asked.

"Felix."

"Felix," said the rabbi, "you ought to know Jews don't believe in hell."

SPILLER, WEINBERG, AND the five scouts drove off to the hospital to check on Ricky. They invited Nathan along, but he told them he had to meet his mother. Spiller gave him a quick, disapproving stare. Nathan could feel another lecture coming, but there wasn't time, and they sped away, half the troop in the rabbi's green Camry, the other half in Spiller's BMW.

Nathan started walking home. It was going to be difficult not to tell his mother or Hiram about this. Maybe he would tell them. Then, if they still wouldn't let him quit, he'd snap right back into silence. That would show them.

13

MAX DROVE TO Beth Israel, hoping to catch the end of the meeting. He'd see what Troop 158 looked like and he'd offer Nathan a ride home. On the way, they could stop in at Lee's or at the diner. Wherever Nathan wanted. Within reason.

He figured the meeting had at least a half hour left, so he was surprised to find the parking lot empty and the synagogue deserted. It smelled like there'd been a barbecue. Inside, the fluorescent bulbs buzzed and the cooling system hummed away while he looked for someone who could tell him where the troop had gone. He went downstairs and saw light beneath Spiller's office door. No one answered his knock, so he turned the knob. It clicked open.

He couldn't have said what he was looking for, but he wanted to know more about Spiller and this was too good a chance to pass up. He wouldn't stay long. He noticed there were different crates stacked by the walls now; the Le Creuset had become canned food. A scoutmaster moving goods? From where to where? Was the whole basement used for storage or just this one office? He had plenty of questions. He sat down behind the desk in Spiller's comfortable chair and pushed himself back and forth, like a kid. Then he got down to work. The first thing that caught his eye was a photograph wedged into a corner of the blotter. Spiller was barely recognizable in the image—at least fifteen or twenty years younger, a full head of black hair, neatly trimmed beard and mustache, standing on a rocky mountain summit with his arm around a tiny, bent-backed Asian woman. Deep green, rounded peaks rose up in the distance, set against a clear blue sky. Max couldn't tell where they were. Wherever it was, they looked happy to be there, and Max wondered how long it had taken them to climb to the top.

That was the only photograph on the desk. The next thing he noticed was the spiral notebook Spiller had read from. Max paged through it and couldn't read a word. It looked like Chinese or Japanese, so he guessed Chinese. Was this really Spiller's handwriting? A handful of papers on the desk were also in Chinese, though they were more formal documents, typed, and on one of them there were two English words that stood out: Dutchmaker Clothing. Dutchmaker, a factory just outside of Ephrata, used to be, and probably still was, Wolinsky Brothers' biggest buyer. When Max picked up the paper, he saw what was underneath it: a short stack of three rubber-banded passports. Also Chinese. What was Spiller doing with Chinese passports? Max wanted to see the photographs inside and he was undoing the rubberband when he heard footsteps coming toward the office. He was tempted to pocket one of the passports to study later, but he put everything back the way it was and quietly stepped over to the entrance. "Hello?" he said, as if he'd just arrived.

Rabbi Weinberg was strolling down the hallway. "Max," he said, "what are you doing here?"

"I came to pick up Nathan, but everyone was gone. Thought I might find Spiller in his office."

"Your son chose a wild night for his first meeting. The scouts got slightly out of control."

"What happened?"

"Bunch of pyromaniacs," Weinberg said. "They wanted to see who could build the biggest fire. Just fun and games until someone got hurt and the police came and we all rushed to the hospital. Looks like the boy will be okay, thank God."

"Did Nathan go to the hospital, too?"

"No, he stayed behind. He said he had to meet his mother."

"It's true, he didn't know I was planning to pick him up. I thought we might grab some dinner together."

Weinberg said nothing to that, ready to hear more. Max remembered the few awkward meetings he'd had with the rabbi and Sandy right before the divorce. They'd sat together in silence and Weinberg had kept leaning forward, wide-eyed and eager, certain that his unending patience could get wife and husband talking. Max had appreciated the effort, hopeless though it was.

Now he had to speak or Weinberg would just keep on waiting. "You know," he said, "Nathan already had his doubts about this troop."

Weinberg nodded. "I have doubts of my own," he said, "and those bonfires didn't help. Mervyn was trying to put a positive spin on the whole incident, but I wasn't convinced. Still, I have to give those boys credit. They were extremely substantial fires. Impressive, in their way. They brought something to mind."

Max looked into the office. He wanted to get back inside that desk, but he could tell Weinberg wasn't going to leave him alone. And, worse than that, Weinberg was going to make him have a conversation.

First the rabbi took some keys from his pocket and locked Spiller's door. He rattled the knob to check it. Then he said, "Let's go up to my study. It would be good for us to talk."

THE STUDY WASN'T much larger than a coat closet and it was as makeshift as the rest of the temple, the same folding chairs, a metal desk, a worn gray carpet. All the dues and donations must have been invested somewhere else, hopefully performing well, waiting for the day a new temple could arise. At least Weinberg had a large window that looked out toward the street, and books lined the walls, giving the cramped room an air of learning and distinction. Also, something imposing emanated from the framed photographs of past rabbis, solemn in their dark robes and white tallith. The only face Max recognized belonged to Harold Eskin, the man who'd presided over his bar mitzvah.

Max sat down and turned from old Eskin to watch Weinberg, who was searching the shelves, moving a finger through the air. Eventually he pulled down a slim volume and paged through it quickly. "Here's what I was thinking about those fires. Listen: 'For every deed an angel is born, a good angel or a bad one. But from halfhearted and confused deeds which are without meaning or without power, angels are born with twisted limbs or without a head or hands or feet.'"

Max was remembering how solid Nathan's lighter had felt in his palm. "My son didn't have anything to do with starting those fires, did he?"

"No, no, that's not what I'm getting at. It just struck me that there was nothing halfhearted about those flames and there was plenty of power. The boy in the hospital might have a twisted hand for a little while, but the angel should be all right and maybe even good."

"Sure," said Max. "Why not."

Weinberg sat down behind the desk. "It probably sounds strange," he said. "You don't need to hear me talking about angels, but I have high hopes for the troop. It's one of our many initiatives. We have to get out of this building. This place is the opposite of a recruitment tool. People visit and move on."

"I wish I was in a position to help."

"You are helping. A large, successful troop will be a boon for us, and we're thrilled that Nathan will be a part of it."

"Well," Max said, "Nathan's not thrilled, but the summer trip won't hurt him. He needs to get out of the house, meet new people. I'd like to know more about Spiller, though. Where did he come from? How'd he wind up scoutmaster?"

"A New York colleague recommended him very highly. Mervyn's a businessman and a fund-raiser and I know many people who have profited by association with him. I'm not a betting man, of course, and I don't want to be overly optimistic, but I feel almost certain that when this temple recaptures its former splendor, it will have a Mervyn Spiller wing."

"That's great," Max said, wondering how much a Chinese passport would cost. "Do you know what kind of business he's been in? And what drew him to Boy Scouts?"

"You should ask him these questions yourself. He'll be happy to answer. I think you'll like talking to him."

"We spoke for a few minutes after the bar mitzvah," Max said.

Weinberg clapped his hands twice. It was a loud sound in that small space. "That's what I wanted to discuss with you," he said, leaning forward. "The bar mitzvah was better with you here and I'm glad to see you in town, but Nathan needs more from you, Max. Especially now. Sandy's off in her own world, Hiram's no stepfather, who knows if they'll even get married, and your father is overwhelmed with his brother. You know all this. You don't need me to tell you the way things are, but it's my duty. I'd like to see you do more."

Max accepted the scolding. "I want to see myself do more," he said. "I want to help Nathan. And I want to help my father, too. I don't know how he keeps going."

"Your father does good deeds, day in and day out. You should follow his example. You should have accepted the aliyah, for instance. It would have been a mitzvah. That would have been the full-hearted way to be here. Don't be halfhearted, Max. We don't need any more deformed angels in this world."

Max let the angels pass again. "I'm doing the best I can," he said.

Weinberg nodded. "I know you are. I can sense that. And I know this last year hasn't been easy for you, so take this for what it's worth. I have people leave me all the time. The congregation is my family and we're always losing members, more than ever these days. They convert, they intermarry and disappear, they move away, they die. Then there's the temple, my house of worship, and it has been taken from me, and I have wound up here, in this awful building, where I never intended to be."

The rabbi swiveled his chair and looked through his window. A few cars drove out Ashferry Avenue, heading downtown, toward the city and the old temple. The rabbi watched them go and then turned back to face Max. "You and I," he went on, "we have some things in common. I've often felt the desire to leave town, cut my losses. And, really, my leaving wouldn't matter for a moment. I'm not irreplaceable. I'm not some sort of precious prophet, carrying around a special message from God. I could simply be another member of this family who goes his own way. So, you may ask, why am I still here? It's a good question and this is the answer: I'm tired of seeing my family broken and hurt and torn apart. I also happen to believe there are rewards for staying and struggling. It doesn't stop the losses from happening. It doesn't make the hurt disappear, but there are rewards for those who remain."

Now it was Max's turn to wait and gather his thoughts. Let Weinberg say more if there was more to say. But that was the end of the speech. Weinberg moved his head from side to side, like a boxer trying to stay loose. He could outwait anyone.

"Rewards," Max said. "Rewards would be good."

Weinberg laughed and then he stood up. "Okay, Max, that's it for my rabbi talk. We've both got things to do, I'm sure. I've got to get home. I'm starving."

FOLLOWING THE RABBI'S advice immediately would have meant driving right back to the apartment, but Max was thinking about another night on the couch and where he'd rather be, so as he walked to his car, he called Estelle. He was glad when she answered. "Been thinking about you," he said.

"You've been on my mind, too," she said. "But *thinking* isn't what I'd call what I've been doing. I'm not sure I've been thinking all day."

"I want to hear more about that. What are you doing tonight?"

"My mother came by for dinner. Now she's telling me you could be trouble."

"I could be. But I'm not."

"Hold on a second," she said.

Max tried in vain to hear what Estelle was saying to her mother. He thought he heard the word *fantastic*. Wishful thinking. While he was waiting for Estelle to say more, he found a three-by-five card on his windshield. A note from Johnny: *Visit me at the club when you get this.*

"Come on over," Estelle said. "You can show my mom you're all right. If you say no, she'll keep thinking badly of you."

"I wouldn't want that," said Max. "I've got one more errand to run and then I'll be there."

The Sklarman Racquet Club wasn't far from Estelle's, maybe four miles away, on Church Road. Max figured it would be better not to put off seeing Johnny, so he drove over, hoping for a quick and easy meeting.

The Sklarmans had built their no-frills club back in the seventies. It was, essentially, a beige, aluminum-sided barn that contained eight tennis courts, a row of vending machines, two shabby locker rooms, and an office with a racquet-stringing machine. These days, it was the last piece of the once-sizable Sklarman family fortune. Johnny used to talk about improving the club when he took over. That was how he'd begin to recover everything that had been lost. But Max walked in and saw the place hadn't changed at all.

In the office, a kid Nathan's age was stringing a racquet. He had a pile of racquets at his feet. "Have you seen Johnny around?" Max asked, wondering if this kid was happy about his summer plans.

"Court 3," said the kid, keeping his eyes on his work.

On his way downstairs, Max could see that business wasn't bad. The place was full, everyone playing doubles or singles, except Johnny, who was practicing serves by himself. Max stepped through a gap in the green curtain at the back of the court. Johnny, in his tight outfit, stood at the closer baseline with his hopper of balls. He looked over his shoulder at Max and nodded toward a bench by the net. "Have a seat. Give me a minute to finish these up."

Max sat next to the water cooler and watched Johnny toss each ball into the air, a few feet above his head, always to the same spot. For a split second, the ball was almost motionless, at the top of its arc, about to come down, and then Johnny's arm snapped to full extension and his racquet smashed that ball onto a completely different course. He thumped a few into the deuce court, a few into the ad court, and they all landed in. He'd managed to hold on to this gracefulness and skill for at least twenty years now. It remained his gift, something to build a life around, but Johnny had never seen it like that. He was always looking for something else.

"You're getting serious pop on those serves," Max said, as Johnny approached the water cooler.

Johnny had his racquet and the empty hopper with him. He set them down, picked up his racquet cover, reached inside, and pulled out a plastic bag of chocolate chips. After he poured a few into his hand, he offered the bag to Max. Max was hungry, so he took a handful and put them in his mouth. They tasted like chalk. He grabbed a cup of water to wash them down.

Johnny smiled. "They're carob, Max. Better for you than chocolate."

"Better for you, maybe," Max said, refilling his cup. "But look, I'm late for dinner. For real food. I got your note. What's on your mind?"

Johnny started to gather the balls he must have hit into the net earlier. He banged the bottom of the hopper down onto each one of them. "How'd the bar mitzvah go?"

"Nice of you to ask. Nathan did a great job. Made us all proud."

"Must have been fun for you to reconnect with your ex and her new friend."

Max listened to a few more bangs, the metal scraping against the asphalt. "Talk to me if you want to talk to me," he said. "Otherwise I'm out of here."

"I heard you were into something; you said you weren't. Okay, fine. But the bar mitzvah's over and you're still hanging around and now I've got a friend traveling in from out of town and he's *telling* me you're into something. If he's got proof, he won't want to hear about how you told me there was nothing going on. And he's not as nice as I am."

Max thought this whole bit was a bluff. Johnny knew the kind of work he did, so he was trying to weigh in, grab a piece of whatever action there was. Still, Max wanted to hear him out. He sat there like Rabbi Weinberg, waiting.

Johnny gave the hopper a rest and munched more carob chips. Then he went on. "This could be perfect timing for everyone. It would be good for me get in on something new and, right now, I think I can still help you, but that won't be true much longer. I'll lose my ability to step up for you."

Max stood and for a moment considered taking the easy road. Cut the guy in a little on the Goulds and be done with it. But that went against his vow, and really, the Goulds weren't going to yield that much. He wanted his whole share to go to Caleb and Abe. Besides, bluff or no bluff, he'd be back in Florida before too long, out of Johnny's sight. He drank his water, trashed the cup, and stonewalled.

"I'm visiting, Johnny, like I told you. I'll probably be out of town before your friend gets here. Just keep playing tennis. Don't worry about me."

"All right," Johnny said. "You can't say I didn't try." Then hopper and racquet in hand, he walked toward the far side of the court. "I'll see you later."

"Take care," said Max, on his way over to the curtain. Before he stepped through the opening, a tennis ball whizzed by his head.

"You take care yourself," Johnny called out. "And watch your back."

IN HIS CAR, Max fished a breath mint out of the ashtray, still trying to get rid of the chalky taste in his mouth, and as he drove up Church Road he remembered how those small projects with Johnny went wrong. Each time, there were the same two problems: Johnny was too greedy and Johnny didn't tell him everything. During their student days, Johnny used his connection with a printing company to get counterfeit tickets to Temple basketball games at the Palestra. Those were popular events, which made it easy money, and Johnny let Max in on it. They sold the tickets in advance, seats in a row that didn't exist, and the buyers knew they were just supposed to stand or, after the game started, find their way to open seats. As long as they didn't sell too many, the odds of their being caught were slim, and for most of the season they were each pulling in several hundred dollars per game. Then, a few weeks before the NCAA tournament, there was a big matchup with Villanova. Johnny was coming off a streak of bad bets, so they decided to sell more than usual, but Johnny sold far more than they'd planned. They wound up getting caught and expelled. Max might have been able to stay in school; he could have been apologetic, begged for probation, but he was close to failing economics and math, and he felt ready to leave.

The other project was more recent, just two years ago, before the taxicab, back when Max was with Sandy, trying to stay straight, selling hard, helping his father out every now and then, but mostly doing a lot of one-on-one work, pushing vacuum cleaners, telescopes, even aluminum siding. Johnny, under pressure on yet another debt, approached him and asked for some names. Once Johnny explained himself, it seemed simple enough. Max would pass along information about a few of his wealthier clients—where they lived, how one might break in, what sort of valuables seemed easy to grab—and Johnny would take care of the rest. Max would get a cut and Johnny would get rid of his trouble in a night or two.

Max had reservations. Though he couldn't claim any kind of high moral ground—he'd already run his fair share of small cons by then—he prided himself on never really hurting anyone, never taking more than he thought his marks could spare. Also, there was something about the way people stepped into cons on their own that made them easier to excuse than sneaking into someone's house and stealing their belongings. But Johnny asked for old times' sake, for just this once. "Give me the names of the guys you don't like," he said. "The real assholes. Then you won't feel bad."

Max figured that someday Johnny might wind up being a good ally to have, so, against his better judgment, he helped set up three people. He was surprised that the decision didn't haunt him, and maybe everything would have been fine if he hadn't seen one of those names in the local paper a week later. Milton Levy, who lived over in Blue Bell and who'd put in an order for a five-hundred-dollar Optimal home vacuum, had been hit on the side of the head with a VCR. After the burglars left, he'd managed to call 911 just before passing out. He'd needed six hours of surgery.

Johnny said it wasn't his fault. He said he hadn't been on that job, but at that point it didn't matter what he said. Max could still remember delivering the vacuum cleaner and staring at Milton's scar—it ran from the bottom of his jaw to the edge of his eye. Worse than the scar was how scared Milton looked, as if he'd never again feel safe in his own house. Max made his vow about Johnny then and there. He never cashed Milton's check, he told Johnny not to bother cutting him in, and he tried even harder to stay straight.

IT WAS NICE to see Estelle's apartment with the lights on, but he didn't get much time to take it in because Janet started grilling him as soon as he walked through the door. While Estelle worked in the kitchen, her mother fired away from her rocking chair. "I know it's early for an inquisition," she said, "but it's the way I am. I won't stand idly by. Please, sit down."

Max sat in the beige wing chair across from her.

"Now," Janet said, "why have you been living in Florida? I never understood why people moved there."

"I needed to get away. It happened to be chilly when I left. I needed to drive and I had a few friends down there I wanted to see."

"Fine, but there's more I want to know. For example, how long have you—"

Estelle came into the room and stopped the interrogation. "Mom, I think that's enough for now."

"I have a question for you, Janet," Max said, "if that's okay."

"Go right ahead."

"How did you get to be such a good bowler?"

"Practice," she said.

"Did you grow up downtown?"

"It's a nice effort, Max, but it won't work. You won't make me forget my questions. I'll let them go for now, though." She looked from him to Estelle and smiled. "You've got different things to attend to this evening, I imagine. I was actually on my way home when you called."

"I'd be happy to give you a ride."

"The walk's good for me. My daily constitutional. But thank you. It was gentlemanly of you to offer."

"I'd like to insist."

"Even better. Thank you. Let's all go together."

The three of them drove over to Janet's apartment and Max waited in the car again while Estelle walked her mother to the door. He studied how they moved side by side, trying to understand more about why those few steps affected him. He was struck by how sweet Estelle could be, and how tough. Of course he should be doing the same thing for his father, every day. Instead, he was giving a little help to someone he hardly knew. Maybe all the help evened out somewhere, finding its way to those in need, but Max didn't believe that for a second.

When Estelle returned to the car, she suggested they hurry back to her apartment. Max almost agreed, but he hesitated. "Let's go for a drive," he said.

She settled into her seat. "Okay," she said, putting an open hand on his thigh. "There's something I wanted to talk about anyhow. You asked about my husband. I decided I should tell you."

"You don't have to. I don't—"

"It's all right," she said. "We married too young. I was twenty-three, dreaming of being a bride. My mother was already divorced and he was jealous of the time I spent with her. You can see that she might be difficult. Whenever she came over or whenever I went to visit her, he would go out. Sometimes he wouldn't come back for days. Then he didn't come back at all."

"I'm sorry," Max said. "I am."

"Were you ever married?"

"Yes, I've got an ex-wife out there. It might be I wasn't young enough when I married, or it might be I didn't stay young enough long enough."

"What do you mean?"

"It's hard to explain."

They drove in silence through the suburbs. Estelle moved her hand to his neck and played with the hair on the back of his head. His scalp tingled. "Try," she said.

"Maybe later."

At first, Max didn't know where he was going. There wasn't much traffic. The windows of the houses they passed flickered with the blue haze of computer and TV screens. He wondered, again, what Grier was doing down in Florida. He needed to call her, but it wouldn't hurt if she called in once or twice herself.

"In the end," Estelle said, "I don't think my ex knew what he wanted. Even when it was just the two of us, he was restless. Are you restless?"

"Well, I usually don't have trouble sleeping at night."

"You were up pretty early this morning."

"Last night was really something, but a man's still got to make a living."

"A man and a woman both," she said. "You know, I didn't really believe that whole boardwalk story. You want yachts? A concrete villa? You seem more practical than that. More level-headed."

Max shrugged. "It's a kind of success."

"What kind of father was that guy? Did he have kids at all?"

"Kids," Max said. "That's an interesting topic. Do you have any?"

"No, I don't. But it sounds like you do."

"I have a son," Max said, and then he realized where he'd been driving. He didn't know if he was testing her or trying to scare her off or trying to scare himself, but he stopped the car across the street from the Goulds' house. Following in his father's footsteps once again. He kept the motor running. Could he trust this woman? It's the people you trust who most often betray you. People you don't trust you don't give a chance. "Let me show you something," he said, pointing to the house. "Do you see what that is?"

"It's a nice house."

"It *is* a nice house," he said. "And there are two nice old people who live there. Guess what's going to happen to them?"

"I don't know, Max. Is this a joke?"

"No, no. I'll tell you what might happen. One of these days, the owners of this house are going to get a call, and because of what they hear and what they've been told already, they're going to rush to Atlantic City where they will pay twenty-five thousand dollars for a piece of paper. This piece of paper will promise them the right to purchase a particular condominium in a particular building soon to be under construction. To celebrate their transaction, they'll spend the evening in a very posh hotel room. Then, sometime later, maybe the next day or maybe not for weeks, they'll begin to discover the truth. They'll learn their paper is worthless and their money is gone. This is the sort of thing I can arrange. This is the kind of work I've done lately."

Estelle sat quietly with her hands in her lap. She looked at the house and looked back at Max. "I don't know you," she said. "But I know you better than that."

Max studied her face. Now she'd start seeing him with open eyes. Eyes that were long-lashed and light green and uncomprehending. While he turned the car around, she slowly shook her head, frowning, her lips pressed together, and it was clear she was angry. At him and at herself.

"I guess I wanted to tell you the truth," he said. "You're a good person. I can see that. When I leave town, I won't be running off from you. But you might be glad to see me go."

Max remembered how Sandy would shout and slam doors when she was angry. Grier hadn't yet been angry at him, as far as he knew, but he'd seen her rage against her experiments, ripping up graph paper and cursing her supervisor. Estelle just stared out her window, and he wondered what she saw. The Goulds lived near Overbrook Park and the drive back ran along the edge of the Main Line, past Upper Merion and Bala Cynwyd. From the road, it looked as if the fortunes in those havens were extremely safe, guarded by seminaries, Episcopal, Baptist, and Roman Catholic. The seminary of St. Charles Borromeo was the largest of them all, set far back from the street, an enormous stone fortress on several acres of prime real estate.

Max didn't think explaining would help, but he tried. "I know it's not exactly a good deed. Still, no one will be hurt. And I'll use my share of the money to help take care of my sick uncle. Then I'll be able to do things differently. Then I'll be able to make real changes."

Without looking over at him, Estelle said, "I shouldn't even bother to ask this, but what kind of changes do you have in mind?"

"Will you believe me if I tell you?"

"I doubt it," she said, "but tell me anyhow."

"I'll become more like the person my father wanted me to be.

I'm not saying I'll become a doctor, which is what he really wanted, but I'll work hard to be respectable and upright. A decent father, a better son, a good businessman."

"Sure," she said, "I see," but she didn't look or sound convinced at all, and she didn't speak again until they'd passed the Belmont Reservoir. Then she rolled down her window, lit a cigarette, and asked, "By the way, what was the address of that house?"

"Why do you want to know? You're not going to turn me in, are you?"

"No," she said. "I don't think so. It's just that it seems far from Number One, Atlantic Ocean."

Max smiled. "I guess it is."

She left the window down and kept smoking as he merged onto Roosevelt Expressway. He didn't want to stop talking, but the wind was loud, and he didn't know what to say. It wasn't long before he took the Broad Street exit. As they passed through Logan, Olney, and Fern Rock, Max registered some of the familiar landmarks—Albert Einstein Medical Center, the Philadelphia High School for Girls, the old White Castle, the Oak Lane Diner—but mainly he was wondering if he'd ever see Estelle again. He didn't like the idea that he might not. That wasn't what he'd planned for this evening. That wasn't why he'd called her and rushed over to her apartment.

He slowed down and pulled up in front of her building. "I probably told you too much," he said.

Estelle had her hand on the door, but she didn't open it. "Did you have a plan for my mother and me?" she asked.

"I don't work that way. It wasn't like that at all."

"I see," she said again. "For the record, here's what I thought it was like. I was glad to find you over at Del Ennis and I liked the way you bowled with us. You talk a good game, too, and, I admit it, I've been looking for something new. But I don't think I need a con man in my life right now."

At least she was looking at him. She was angry and unsure. He couldn't blame her. Besides, he didn't need to get tangled up in anything here. He was supposed to be getting untangled. Still, he liked that she didn't seem ready to give up on him completely.

When she climbed out of the car, he did the same, and he walked with her to the lobby door. "You could try thinking of me as a salesman," he said.

"I don't know, Max."

He was urging himself to let her go, even as he kept talking. "Look, this might be even more stupid than what I've done already, but I'm going to tell you one more thing. Might as well put everything on the table. How much worse can it get?"

She didn't object, just stood there, her keys in her hand.

"Remember when I told you my father was dead? Well, he's not. He's alive. It's my mother who died in a car wreck."

She waited for more.

He shrugged his shoulders. "You probably want to know why I told you that story in the first place. I wish I could explain it. It's just what came out and then it was too late to say anything else so I kept going. That happens to me sometimes. The truth is my father looks forward to meeting you."

"The truth," she said. "Sure."

"I'm sorry," he said.

"I'm sorry, too, Max, but what am I supposed to say? I mean, what kind of person are you? A crook? A liar? What else?"

When Max didn't answer, Estelle crossed her arms. Then she said, "Maybe."

"Maybe what?"

"A lot of things. Maybe you're a sick person. Maybe you'll change. Maybe you already have."

Max watched her unlock the door.

"Maybe I'll be glad to see you go," she said. Then she kissed his cheek, pulled the door closed behind her, and walked toward the stairs.

ON HIS WAY to the car, Max told himself there was no reason to feel sad. He'd done what had to be done. Now he could finish up his business, spend a little more time with Nathan, Caleb, and Abe, and then drive back down to Florida. Grier would be waiting. Everything was fine.

He was trying to convince himself when he saw Johnny Sklarman and another guy stepping out of a black Explorer that had pulled in right behind his Buick. "You just cost me ten bucks," Johnny said.

"I told you he didn't have a chance," the other guy said.

"I gave you the benefit of the doubt, Max," Johnny said. "I thought you'd be with her all night, or at least a few hours. I thought Dexter here had a stakeout on his hands."

"I saw the failure in his shoulders," Dexter said. "Way too tense." Dexter was a blond, crew-cut thug Max hadn't seen before. He wasn't as tall as Johnny, but he was three times as wide, wearing a thin suede jacket over jeans and a T-shirt, and probably packing something under that jacket.

Johnny had on different tennis gear, a navy blue Fila sweat suit, and he was nibbling at a plum. He didn't look nearly as threatening as Dexter, but he was the one in charge at the moment, so Max spoke to him. "I thought we cleared everything up already."

"I thought we had, too. But I guess you didn't believe me

when I told you the neighborhood had changed. We'll take a ride and I'll tell you more."

Max didn't want to get in the Explorer, but he didn't see any other options. "Fine," he said. "Sorry about that ten bucks, though. I've been telling you to stop betting for years now."

"This bet worked out well for everyone," Dexter said. Then he tilted his bright, big-boned head toward the apartment building. "You're not missing anything, man. That woman's got too much age on her."

Johnny spit his plum pit out toward the center of the street. "Shut up, Dexter," he said. "You don't know what you're talking about. These days, we all need everything we can get."

14

CALEB WONDERED WHERE Max was. He tried the cell phone, but Max didn't pick up. He decided to be positive, for a change, and he told himself that everything was all right. Max was making some minor adjustments, or he was out having fun with that new woman. He might even be spending the night with her. That would probably be good for everyone.

Caleb had cooked an early dinner—a salad, ravioli and tomato sauce—and now Abe was taking his fourth Barcalounger nap of the day. Caleb's energy moved in the opposite direction. He was pacing in the kitchen, waiting for the coffee to finish brewing, hoping the phone would ring, when he heard a knock at the door.

There stood Spiller, and he wasn't alone. He had an Asian entourage with him, a young woman and two older men. Caleb guessed Chinese. Spiller's bald head looked freshly shined, and he was wearing lightweight olive slacks and a short-sleeved, button-down, ivory shirt. Silk. Sharp, stylish garments, the kind Caleb always admired but could never afford. The woman wore an equally fine sundress, flowery, azure, periwinkle, with thin shoulder straps that showed off her neck and shoulders. She had short black hair, as did the two men, whose outfits were less interesting, though they matched—plain khakis and dark brown T-shirts. Together, the four of them looked like an elite gang or a well-to-do international family.

Caleb didn't know exactly what this visit was about, but he told them all to make themselves comfortable. "I've got a fresh pot of coffee almost ready," he said.

Spiller walked into the kitchen, glanced at the percolator, and took a sniff. "We'll have tea," he said.

Caleb found the kettle and opened the cabinet above the stove, searching for the Red Rose or Lipton he knew he had somewhere. "Our tea selection is pretty limited," he said.

"Don't worry," Spiller said. "We brought our own."

The woman took the kettle and filled it at the sink. One of the men reached into his pocket, pulled out two tea bags, and handed them to her.

"I wasn't expecting you," Caleb said. "But it's good to see you and your friends."

"We were in the neighborhood," Spiller said. "We won't stay long. Let me introduce you to everyone. My wife, Anna, is boiling the water. And we're hosting two of her cousins, Ping and Y. Y., both visiting from Hong Kong."

Caleb waved to the wife, wondering how much younger than Spiller she was. When she waved back, she fluttered her fingers, as if to say her age would remain a mystery. Her smile moved quickly, wide and full, then gone.

The two men were both thin, their pants held up by leather

belts that seemed to wrap twice around their waists. Still, they were tall and vaguely imposing. Caleb fought against the stereotype, unsuccessfully. He imagined them as masters of a storklike martial art, all knees and elbows. He wanted real information about them, but they walked through the apartment and then stayed close to the door, saying nothing.

"Of course you can't see the world through another man's eyes," Spiller said, "but I can tell from your face that this all looks more than a bit strange to you."

"I was wishing Max were here."

"That would be nice, but I don't mind having a chance to talk with just you and Abe."

Caleb glanced over at his brother to see how he was responding to this crowd. Abe remained in his chair, oblivious.

"Abraham!" Spiller shouted. "Say something. Surprise us."

Abe didn't stir.

"He's been sleeping more and more," Caleb said. "Sometimes it worries me and other times I'm grateful for the quiet."

Anna poured the tea into five mugs she'd lined up on the counter. It smelled like weak horseradish to Caleb, so he stuck with his coffee. The entourage had some sort of prearranged choreography. Y. Y. and Ping took their mugs and stepped outside while Spiller and Anna sat on the couch. Caleb settled into his chair, hoping Max would walk in.

Spiller sipped his tea and turned again to Abe. "Let me say this," he said. "I believe we should show our friendship for a man when he is alive, not after he is dead. But these strokes make it difficult for me. If I do something for him, will he even know?"

Abe's hand twitched and Caleb wondered what his dreams were like. "What did my brother do for you?"

"You don't completely trust me yet, I can see that. You can't figure out why I want to help and you can't figure out what I would want to take. Is that right?"

"That's the way Max thinks. Myself, I don't see why I shouldn't trust you."

"I'm an open book," Spiller said, spreading his arms wide, careful to keep this mug steady. "Ask me something and I'll answer. That's one reason I'm here."

"It's true," Anna said. "He loves to answer questions." Her voice was deeper than Caleb had expected, husky, with no Chinese accent that he could hear.

"All right," Caleb said. "So tell me why you want to do something for Abe."

Spiller set his mug on the coffee table. "I don't know what you know about quadruple bypass surgery. It's a thing that happens. One moment you're going along, living your life, then some young doctor is holding your heart in his puny rubber-gloved hand. Talk about trust and faith." He squeezed his hand into a tight, boxy fist, crushing whatever imaginary heart he might have held in his palm. Then he unflexed his fist and unbuttoned his shirt, opening it slowly, like a curtain.

Caleb didn't need to see any more damaged bodies. The memory of Joe Lonzinger's withered legs still shadowed his mind, and then there were the daily rituals with Abe. Not to mention the glimpses he couldn't help catching of himself. He saw enough frailty right in his own bathroom. These days, even when he was feeling upbeat and strong, the mirror would mercilessly reveal a body that looked rickety and drained.

Now he was supposed to study Spiller's chest. The tracks of the incision ran down through his belly. Evidence that he was lucky to be alive or that everyone would die no matter what.

Spiller was the tour guide stepping out onto his own stage.

"This is my scar," he said. "It's from back when the technology wasn't what it is today. And there were complications. Not insurmountable, thankfully. My heart stopped and then it started again, and everything was different. Who got me to the hospital when I was collapsing? Who made certain I had a chance at survival? Ask yourself questions like that and then you'll have an idea of what I owe your brother."

Caleb wanted to wake up Abe. Maybe he could at least nod his head, offer a version of his friendship with Spiller. Even if that wasn't possible, it would be nice to have company. Instead, as he watched Spiller rebutton his shirt, Caleb said, "I wonder why Abe never mentioned anything about it."

"You know as well as I do that it's not always a good thing for people to have knowledge of your weaknesses and your debts. I asked him to keep the whole episode to himself." He sipped more from his mug. "Do you have any cookies we could have with our tea?"

"I've got a few bagels we could toast."

Spiller put an arm around Anna and pulled her closer. "Go tell Y. Y. to bring in that box from the car," he said.

Caleb watched her obediently hustle outside and then he went back to asking questions. "Can you explain more about the uniforms to me?"

"It's so simple, really. So easy. So in keeping with the general way of the world, alas. Take the green berets as just one example. The hats of perhaps our most highly decorated military unit. Everyone knows where those hats are made now. Who do you think handles their buying and selling? Did I mention where Y. Y. and Ping work?"

Caleb remembered Abe's attempts to import sweaters from Peru, fur hats from Sweden, pajamas from Taiwan. "Big money,"

Abe promised each time, but those ventures, and others like them, always failed. Why should this one be different? How would Abe have pushed it? "Scouts are a guaranteed clientele," he might have said. "There are millions of them and they have to buy uniforms." Abe would also have pointed to Spiller. "The man knows what he's doing. This time we'll have experience on our side."

Caleb asked Spiller a question he would have asked Abe. "The military is one thing, but do you think the Boy Scouts of America will buy uniforms made in China?"

Spiller nodded, as if he'd been waiting for this question and was glad it had at last arrived. "You're right to express some doubt and your question is nothing if not reasonable. But there are several ways to close in on the answer. You could say that there's too much money to be made for them to say no, especially given their recent trials and tribulations. You could also approach the subject of who exactly 'they' are and how many of 'them' would need to agree before it could be accomplished. And perhaps all of 'them' wouldn't have to know where the uniforms were made. Those opposed to such an idea might be led to believe that their deeply patriotic uniforms were being made in Philadelphia or Scranton or, say, Ephrata. One needs only the proper agreements and understandings."

The door opened and Caleb glanced over, hoping again for Max, but it was Anna, returning with a small plastic container. She went back into the kitchen and brought out a plate with two types of cookies, almond and sesame. "Y. Y. will bring in the rest shortly," she said, sitting beside her husband.

Spiller patted her thigh, then reached forward and held the plate up for Caleb. Caleb took an almond cookie. It went well with the coffee. "I wish Max were here," he said again. "I know he'd like to hear all of this."

"Let me ask *you* something," Spiller said. "How did Max slip?"

"What do you mean?"

"He didn't always run things like this Gould scam."

Caleb didn't know where to begin. How far could he trust Spiller? What difference did it make if Spiller already knew so much? "I'm not happy about it," Caleb said.

"I'm not happy about it, either. I understand it, though. To some extent, at least. What do you think happened?"

"Lousy things happened. If you know Abe, you've heard all about it. Max was always a dreamer, like his uncle. Looking for bigger and easier money. Abe used to say, 'The wing that touched me lightly touched him hard.'"

"I like that," Spiller said. "You and your son, you've both had your share of losses. I've heard how you've struggled, but maybe it was the divorce that pushed him over an edge. It can be such a difficult ordeal. And he's now, what, forty-one?"

Caleb nodded.

"Still so young. Life begins at fifty, right?"

Anna flashed her quickly fading smile. From her purse, she pulled a lump of clay, about the size of her hand, and she started to work it with her thin fingers.

Spiller kept talking. "I know something about scams, I won't deny it. Let me tell you one of the projects I was working on when I was Max's age. Abe's heard about this, as has Anna. I was northeast of here, selling Pine Barrens land. Lots of all sizes, and plenty of them. It was hand over fist for a while. I had the perfect pitch for that place. I talked about the great unbroken city that stretched from Boston to Richmond, the unstoppable, inevitable development that had to continue up and down the northeast corridor, the Pine Barrens smack dab in the center, destined to be more than forest, more than unpopulated wilderness. An airport was coming and it would be the largest airport on earth.

"Exactly how large would this airport be? Put Newark, La-Guardia, and Kennedy together, then multiply by four. And this wasn't just an idea. It was happening. In process. Architects had done the work. The designs were beautiful and they'd already been approved by a dozen commissions and agencies. The FAA had all but promised its support. That's what I was talking about. A new airport and a new, modern city, developing hand in hand. The land values would take off. Like the planes. And did I mention that those planes were going to be supersonic? People-friendly, too, of course. Respectful of the city and the community. The jets would wait until they were over the ocean before they shattered the sound barrier. Then, in record time, they'd be landing in the capitals of Europe. Now, who wouldn't want to get in on that?"

It was easy to see and hear what Abe would have admired in Spiller. Over the years, Caleb had seen many people pitch. He knew his own limitations as a salesman—he was, as Max often reminded him, *old school,* a trudger, steady and reliable. That didn't mean he couldn't appreciate other styles. Spiller practiced a grander approach, relying on his considerable charm and force. He was more than a door-to-door salesman. Let him into a room and he'd go wall to wall, floor to ceiling.

Caleb was happy to listen, and though he vowed never to take out his checkbook for this man, he also found himself trusting—and liking—Spiller more. He'd always enjoyed being sold far more than he ever enjoyed selling. It was one of the reasons he'd never been able to get furious with Abe, no matter what crazy scheme he brought home. It was also why he had such a hard time trying to make Max straighten up and fly right.

He looked over to see how Anna was taking the pitch. She was still concentrating on the lump of clay, pressing into it with her fingers. Who knew what she was making? He wanted Spiller to keep talking so he raised the predictable objection: "But there's no new airport in the Pine Barrens. There's no new city."

"Not yet. A bunch of people are holding on to that land, though, and they're still hoping. They paid money and they received something. Nothing illegal about that. I remember how you could stand out there on Forked River Mountain and see the red lights flashing on top of the Empire State Building. Straight out of *Gatsby,* in its way. All that yearning and dreaming. They wrote their checks and they were thinking about love. They were thinking about money. If you stared long enough, you could see Manhattan creeping closer. It wasn't even a challenge to make people visualize that."

Y. Y. opened the door, stuck his head in, and glanced over to the couch. "Not yet," Spiller said, and then he went on. "I know what you're thinking. 'What does this have to do with Max?' After all, Max hasn't tried to sell any cities. He just peddles his little retirement community. By comparison, it's penny-ante. But I'm trying to illustrate that I can understand the temptation. I can sense where he's coming from. Like you, though, I don't want him to do this thing. It risks too much for insufficient rewards. It's not big enough, and it happens to be illegal, and, most important, it's causing trouble, interfering with the plan that Abe and I put together."

"I already told Max I wanted him to call it off. He said he would try."

"Do you think he'll really try?"

"Probably not."

"Do you know a guy named Johnny Sklarman?"

"I know the name. He and Max were friends, years ago."

"Well, Sklarman hasn't grown into the kindest soul. He's going to be putting some pressure on Max and he'll use the Goulds if he can."

"I did what I could."

"But that's not all we can do."

This was Spiller's closing, Caleb could feel it, the pause and the pressure filling in the empty space. There was no money involved, at least not yet, just the heavy push for approval. He tried to stall. "How do you think Sklarman would use the Goulds?"

Spiller turned to Anna and whispered in her ear. When she stood up, she left the lump of clay behind, except it wasn't a lump anymore. She'd rounded it, made it into something like a head. Caleb wanted to get a closer look at it. He was going to ask if that would be all right, but she was already walking back outside. Spiller waited until the door closed behind her, and then he said, "I'm not asking you to betray your son."

"I promised not to interfere."

"I didn't promise anything like that," Spiller said. He looked longingly over at Abe. "Come on, Abe. Tell him. Tell him he can trust me."

Abe said nothing.

"It makes me so sad to see him like this. Without him available, I really need you to trust me, Caleb. There's nothing for you to lose here. Abe believed in me and I can tell he still does and he's right to. I want to pull the plug on this Gould thing and then get Max to help us all make real, significant money on these silly uniforms."

Caleb could feel how easy it would be to slip under this man's spell. But he resisted a little longer. "You must want something from us," he said.

"I know, I know. How could you not think that, being who you are, having lived as you've lived. But, listen to me, I'm giving back. That's where I am these days. I'm giving back to many people in all kinds of ways. I'm doing service. It's related to that surgery, but not only that. I have my reasons and they're important to me. Maybe you haven't run across too many examples of generosity in your life so far. I can understand that. Maybe I don't fit your image of a philanthropist. I can understand that, too. But I'm using the tools I've got to do the good I can do. That's the way it is and that's where I think Max and you and Abe and I have a lot in common. I'm here to help, Caleb. It's as simple as that. I give and you receive."

Spiller stood up. "Y. Y.," he called.

The door opened and when Y. Y. and Ping came back in they were pushing a shiny, new, champagne-colored Viva Deluxe.

"I heard Abe might be interested in one of these," Spiller said.

Caleb stared at the scooter. There was the hunter green seat, the two cup holders. "We can't accept this," he said.

"We'll leave it with you. You can present it yourself when Abe wakes up, though I'd love to be here to see the look on his face."

Caleb got up and touched the scooter. It seemed surprisingly solid. Sturdy. The seat felt soft and durable. "It's kind of you," he said, "but we can't take this. It's too much."

Anna walked back in, took one of Spiller's hands, and began tugging him toward the door. "There's no obligation," he said. "I promise. This is a gift from me to Abe. It's just the start. But we'll have to stop this Gould business. You can see now that it's unnecessary."

"I'll do what I can," Caleb said, "but I think you should talk to Max."

"I have," said Spiller, "and I will."

AFTER SPILLER AND his entourage left, Caleb noticed that the Viva Deluxe had come complete with a bumper sticker. He'd had no chance to protest the message. It must have been slapped on earlier by Spiller, right below the basket, and it read, in bold, black letters, SALESMEN DO IT ON THE ROAD.

The road, however, no longer seemed to interest Abe. The scooter was fully loaded, ready to roll out the door, up the ramp to the sidewalk, and into the city, but once he woke up Abe would not go outdoors. He acted as if he wanted to discover how much he could do in the apartment without ever standing up again. It was the exact opposite of the doctor's advice. He wasn't going to push himself at all. For the rest of that first night, Caleb watched his brother pull up table side for a snack, then head to the bathroom, where he brushed his teeth on board the scooter. Abe climbed out of the plush seat to use the toilet and to crawl into bed. That was about it. Caleb wondered if Abe was ashamed, now that he actually had the contraption, but he seemed content, at peace, except when Caleb tried some nagging of his own. "Let's go for a walk," he said. "Let's test this new thing outside."

"Don't bother me."

"You're being so lazy, Abe. You've got no excuse now."

Abe motored to his bedroom and stuck his fingers in his ears. "Shut," he said.

CALEB WOUND UP napping on the couch and when he awoke the first thing he saw was the miniature clay sculpture

Spiller's wife had left on the coffee table. It was a spooky object, some kind of Chinese voodoo doll, with its closed eyes and sunken cheeks. It was cool to the touch. He wanted to throw it out, or at least put it in a drawer, but he didn't dare.

Instead, he shuffled to his bedroom. On his way, he stopped at Abe's open door and stared in at the Viva Deluxe, also a spooky object. It glittered in the dark, all wrong for the space. Like a small, evil mower, hiding its blade.

He put the phone right by his bed and he kept hoping for a call from Max. They really needed to talk about Spiller and the Goulds. Caleb wondered exactly what he should say; he wanted to plan it out, get it right, but he couldn't shake off his nap, and he was woolly-headed, and before he slipped back into sleep he found himself remembering a different late-night call, near the middle of Max's second semester at Temple. Caleb had been watching the Flyers and he'd grabbed the phone on the first ring, hoping, then like now, to hear Max's voice.

"Dad?"

"You're not watching the hockey game, are you? We're getting hammered."

"I need to tell you something."

"All right," Caleb said. "Go ahead." He switched off the TV and listened carefully as Max talked about school, about his grades, the professors, the other students, the time he felt he was wasting.

"I hate to say it, Dad," Max said, "but it's just not for me."

Of course it's for you! Caleb wanted to shout. *Who else could it be for?* He tried to stay calm so he could gather more information. "I'm surprised to hear this," he said. "I thought you were happy. Are you okay? Did something happen?"

"I'm fine, but nothing's working out for me here."

A good salesman needs to know when to press and when to hold back, but a father has never been the same thing as a salesman and Caleb, shocked by what he was hearing, didn't know what to say to his son. "What do you want to do?" he asked.

"I'm going to take some time off. Then I can go back later, when I'm ready."

"But what will you do instead?"

"I've been thinking about that," Max said. "I was wondering if I could come home and work with you for a while. I could be an associate."

Of course, Caleb should have said no. Absolutely not. He should have shouted at his son: *We've never had any associates and we never will! Finish the semester. Over the summer, we'll talk and make a real, legitimate plan.*

But he didn't shout and he didn't say no. The house was far too empty; he missed his son, longed for his company, and besides, the arrangement would be temporary, just a leave of absence. Plus, a little sales experience couldn't hurt anyone, and wouldn't it be better to be able to watch over Max, keep him close by, instead of letting him drift off on his own to God knows where?

15

WHEN MAX OPENED his eyes, he saw a dark green curtain before him. He was cold and uncomfortable, sprawled out on a rough, hard surface. There was light, but he couldn't see any windows. From the other side of the curtain, a female voice shouted, "It's about time you showed up!"

He stood and rubbed the back of his head, which was sore and swollen, tender to the touch. He was thirsty and a little dizzy and he needed to take a piss.

Several women were talking now. They didn't seem to be speaking to him.

"It's not our fault you're always early."

"Who picked this god-awful time anyhow?"

"You're lucky I'm here at all. I woke up this morning and couldn't feel my elbow."

Max took a step and almost twisted his ankle on a tennis ball. He began to remember his ride with Johnny and Dexter, how they'd eventually driven over to Johnny's club. They'd gone inside to talk.

He wanted to find the bathroom and then get back to the basement apartment, pop some ibuprofen, shower, and figure out what to do next. He saw that he was on the far side of the club, so he kicked a few balls out of his way and walked carefully through the opening in the curtain. There were four women on the court. They were wearing a lot of white, holding big, bright racquets in their hands, getting set for doubles. The one with the yellow racquet spoke first. "Excuse me," she said.

Max apologized and kept moving.

Blue Racquet must have noticed that he looked a bit disheveled, maybe even hurt. "Are you okay?" she asked.

"Had a rough night," he said, close to the net. "Be out of your way in a second."

He walked past Gold Racquet next. "Are you bleeding?" she asked.

There was the thumping in his head, some dried blood on his hand, but he wasn't bleeding. In fact, he had his balance and his focus back. He could even make out the face of this woman. She reminded him of Janet, Estelle's mother. She squinted at him and he could see more questions coming.

"I'm fine," he said. Then he was beyond her, at the baseline, where the last woman was waiting to start the game, impatiently bouncing a brand new ball. "Serve it up," he told her.

She shook her head, clearly disapproving of whatever she saw in him. Then she turned back to her friends and raised her red racquet. "Love-all," she said.

IN THE EMPTY locker room, Max washed up and assessed the damage. There was the bump on the back of his head and a deep purple bruise by his left temple. The palm of his right hand was scraped and red. Could have been worse. He splashed cold water on his face until he felt fully awake, though even then the women on the court lingered in his mind, four hazy visions of who his mother might have become—up early, trying to wring the most out of the day.

It was just after 6 A.M. when he stepped outside into the humid morning. A Mercedes and a Lexus zipped down Church Road, reminding him that, unfortunately, his car was parked in front of Estelle's building. He could walk that way, but his father's apartment was closer, and he could shower and change there. Each step seemed to bump his brain into his skull, so he tried to hold his head still. That didn't help, so he tried to steady his mind by focusing his thoughts on what had happened.

"This one's just a warning," Dexter had said. "A little taste of our new menu. Think about it next time we ask you a question." Then there'd been the blackjack, its blurry motion, the sharp pain blinding him into darkness.

When they'd picked him up in front of Estelle's, Max had been ready to surrender a reasonable piece of the Goulds. Let them horn in if they wanted in so badly. That's why, at first, he hadn't been worried. He didn't think there'd be any real conflict.

But the first thing Johnny said inside that Explorer was, "Let's hear what you've got going with this Spiller guy."

Max heard that and knew he was going to take a beating. He also knew Spiller was more promising than he'd suspected.

He kept moving slowly, staying near Tookany Creek for a while, going right past Rosentown Junior High School. The place looked deserted, a few redbrick rectangles arranged in a U on a treeless hill. Add a few smokestacks and it could have been an abandoned factory. It was early, of course, but the emptiness had more to do with the season than anything else. The buildings would stay dark and dormant until the students returned in the fall. Still, in the weeks ahead, some kids would probably use the fields and the asphalt basketball courts, and if not for the scouts, Nathan might have been one of those kids. Max could picture his son out on the parking lot, choking up on his broom-handle stickball bat, swinging for the fences. That picture reminded Max of something else Dexter had muttered as they'd walked into Sklarman Racquet Club. "Keep this in mind," he'd said. "You're not the only one you need to worry about."

Later in the day, Max was supposed to take Nathan over to the temple and drop him off with Troop 158. It had been something he'd been willing to do, but now it was getting more complicated. Would his son be in danger? How far could he trust Spiller? How could he return to Florida if his son wasn't safe? He couldn't imagine Johnny harming Nathan, but he didn't know anything about Dexter. Would Johnny be able to control his thug? Once he stepped off a tennis court and put his racquet away, how much control did Johnny ever have over anything?

Those questions circled through Max's thumping head as he walked down New Second Street to Oak Lane Road and then turned onto Cheltenham Avenue. Eventually, he found himself thinking about possibility. Back in college, the Johnny Sklarman he'd first met seemed full of potential, someone well worth knowing. Now look at what he'd become. Max wasn't sure exactly how to label this older, jaded Johnny—fool? flunky? fink? —but whatever he eventually came up with, it wouldn't be good.

He'd vowed to keep himself distant from his ex-friend, but that was quickly becoming impossible. Even worse, as he pushed his key into the lock of the basement apartment, he couldn't help wondering what his father and son would say when they saw his bruised face. Wouldn't they also see possibility lost? Wouldn't they, like so many others, see wasted potential, someone who wouldn't or couldn't be good?

16

ABE SEES HIS beat-up nephew standing by his door, saying something, but he drifts away quickly, and then Abe closes his eyes again, remembering a difficult day, decades ago. He hears his father calling to him. It's early in the morning and he's downtown in the Ellsworth Street apartment, a child again. His father, Solomon, is young, a harried, hustling hero, and Caleb is a baby asleep in a crib on the other side of the room.

"Abraham," his father says, "are you awake?"

He lets the voice lead him to the bathroom. He likes to keep his father company while he shaves. The mirror fogs from the steam and it squeaks when his father wipes it clean. The closed toilet is Abe's chair. He likes the way his father's face comes out from underneath the shaving cream. He looks closely, hoping there will be no nicks and blood today, but if that happens he's ready to hand over a piece of toilet paper.

His father rinses off the razor, then his face, and then he

catches the small towel Abe throws him. "It's time for you to wash up and get dressed, Abe. Your mother is probably waiting for you."

She's in his room. It's early, but she looks wide awake. She speaks quietly so that baby Caleb will stay asleep. "You don't have to go if you don't want to," she says. "We could spend the day together."

"I want to go," Abe says. He puts on the white shirt and buttons it up to the top. Everything else is brown—the woolly pants, vest, and jacket. The tie and shoes and socks. His mother's fingers fuss with them all. "Breathe in," she says, tightening his vest.

She follows them to the front door. On her tiptoes, she reaches up to kiss her husband. Abe waits for her to bend down and get him. "Stand up straight, Abraham," she says. "Obey your father."

They step out of the house and it's before sunrise. They walk together in the dark, up Ellsworth to Sixty-third, then down toward Market Street and Temple Beth Israel. It is one week after Rosh Hashanah. He's been to synagogue before, but these are the High Holidays and this is the first time he's gone with his father for the whole day.

"Father," Abe says, and his voice seems too loud for the quiet streets.

"Shh."

He's only seven, but he knows about the High Holidays. Sometimes people don't behave. They do things that are wrong. God keeps track. Every year, during the ten days between Rosh Hashanah and Yom Kippur, he sits high above with three giant books open on his desk: the Book of Life, the Book of Death, and the Book of Those-Who-Are-in-the-Middle. God writes the names of the people who behaved all year in the Book of Life and they live for another twelve months. He writes the names of the people who misbehaved in the Book of Death and they die, maybe not right then but soon. "Most of us," his father has said, "are in the middle. We have these ten days to repent. God will listen and inscribe us in the Book of Life."

As they walk in silence, Abe thinks about his father in the Old World, where he had an old name. He was Shlomo Woliyniec; he lived near Odessa, and he was going to have an important job. Kosher slaughterer. He would kill animals cleanly so everyone could eat. There were rules to follow and he had to learn them all. He had to practice. Rabbis damaged his knives to see if he could make the blades perfect again. He could. When he passed their tests, the rabbis gave him official letters, written on thick parchment. Then his parents told him to take a boat to America. It was dangerous to stay. He carried his knives and his letters in his coat.

By the time Abe was born, the knives were gone. Sometimes he imagined them, hidden in his father's black overcoat. They were used to kill and kill again, but the blades were so sharp that the cows and chickens did not suffer. That's what his mother said.

His father took the rabbis' letters all over Philadelphia, but no one would hire him. He told people he needed a job to make money because he had no money. He showed them his open hands, turned up in front of him. Empty. He was eighteen. They could see how his fingers bent strangely from holding his knives hour after hour. If they shook hands with him, they could feel how his fingers pressed into their palms at odd angles. Like a fortune-teller.

One morning, a long time ago, his father stopped by a tiny

slaughterhouse he hadn't seen before. The owner almost hired him. They talked about money and time. Then a chicken darted out from a cage. It had only one wing. One huge wing. It zipped past the smocked workers. It was a blur of white that ran toward the street. "Grab that chicken!" the owner shouted, but Abe's father stood still and let the unclean bird go free. Who knew how far a one-winged chicken could run? Would someone else catch it? Would another young slaughterer chase it? His father didn't care. "I suppose I've done enough killing," he said. He went right to a pawnshop to sell his knives. *There must be other ways to make a living,* he told himself. He decided to be someone different.

"Why?" Abe often asked. "Why did you let the chicken go?"

"You want to know why I let the chicken cross the road?"

"No, no. No jokes. Why did you change? Why did you sell your knives? Why did you stop killing?"

His father's only answer was another story, a story about an angel born with one wing. The angel kept trying to fly. He jumped up with all his might. He leaped off of mountaintops. He wanted his wing to lift him high into the air. But he fell and he fell and he fell. He broke his legs. He broke his arms. Some people who found him wondered how an angel could look so terrible. Kind people nursed him back to health and he wandered off to try again. He fell. He hurt himself. He got better.

"But tell me why you changed," Abe would say.

"Imagine that poor angel," his father would answer. "Wandering, falling, hurt, healing. Wandering, falling, hurt again."

THE SUN IS beginning to rise, making the city yellow and orange, but it looks like everyone else is still asleep. "Father," Abe says.

"Shh," his father says. "Think about earning forgiveness."

"Why do we need to be so early?" Abe whispers.

"You want to know about the early bird?"

"No, no."

"All right," he says. "I'll tell you why."

"I'll listen."

"What's my job?"

"You get things for people."

"Yes. People pay me and I get them the things they want. But sometimes they pay me and I can't get them what they want right away. They might want their money back. But I don't keep their money. It does me no good to hold it in my hands. I can't just give it back because I use it to buy other things. Then people can get angry."

Abe has never heard his father talk so much about work. He wants to hear more. He tries to make sure his questions are good questions. "Do you ask them to wait?"

"I ask them, but they usually don't want to wait. And it can take a long time. So I need to pray for forgiveness. It's important to be generous during the High Holidays. Patient, too. It's not a time for meanness. You know we're not the most Jewish family, but everyone wants to be in the Book of Life."

"How angry do people get?"

"That's a good question, Abraham. It depends. There seems to be more anger lately."

At the corner of Sixty-third and Market, the El runs above their heads. They stand still, listening to the thunderous rattle, the high whistle of the brakes. Abe sees two men working in a bakery, carrying trays of dough. An old man pushes a cart full of shiny apples. Some people step off the train, others step on. Abe looks for anger in their faces.

• • •

They're the first to arrive at Temple Beth Israel and they go straight to their seats in the cold sanctuary. The wooden chairs are not comfortable. Abe waits. He likes watching what happens on the bimah. The rabbi will carry the Torah above his head. The cantor will sing. The rabbi will spread his arms wide to welcome everyone.

"You can nap," his father says. "Services won't start for a while."

But Abe fights to stay awake. He wants to remember everything he did wrong. When he was yelled at. When he lied. When he pretended to be asleep. The handful of nickels he took and hid.

His father's eyes close and his head tilts down. He's thinking. When Abe stands up to go use the men's room, his father says, "If anyone bothers you, here's what you tell them. You tell them you are not permitted to make promises for me."

There are people in the lobby. Abe walks quickly past them. In the bathroom, he has his choice of urinals. Then two men come in behind him. They are older than his father, and bigger. They make the room feel crowded.

"There he is," the first one says.

"The little Wolinsky," says the second one, laughing.

Abe inches closer to the white porcelain. He's not completely done, but he stops and zips up. "Good *yontif*," he says, on his way to the sink.

"Yes, yes," the first one says. "A good *yontif* to you, too."

"And to your father," says the man who is no longer laughing.

"Of course," says the first, "if you're going to give him our good wishes, you'll need to know who we are."

They block the door and the first man keeps talking. His voice is almost kind, like a teacher's. "I'm Mr. Phil Lipkin and that's Mr. Ronald Hess. We'd like a chance to speak with your father, but we know from experience that will be difficult. So we're speaking to you. We'd like to ask your father to return something of ours. And we know he'll be generous for the next few days, with so much at stake."

"The Book of Life is open to those who seek forgiveness," says Hess. His voice is not kind. It is rough and strong, like a truck engine.

"What do you say, little man?" asks Lipkin.

"I can't promise you anything."

"You just tell him you saw us," Lipkin says. "We'd speak with him ourselves if he'd step outside the sanctuary."

"He's busy."

"He can't stay in there all day long again," Hess says.

"I hear he has a special diet for the High Holidays," says Lipkin.

"I hear a lot of things," Hess says, stepping closer to Abe at the sink. Abe sees anger in this man's face, especially in the thick, black eyebrows, so heavy that he has to squint. Abe steps back and wonders if he's fast enough to lock himself in one of the stalls. Hess turns on the hot water all the way. "How long do you think he would stay out there if you didn't come back?" he asks.

Abe watches the hot water. It rises up in the sink, but it does not overflow.

"Cut it out, Ron," Lipkin says.

"Thirty minutes? An hour? Eventually, he'd have to come looking. How long has it been?"

"We wouldn't hurt you," Lipkin says. "No one's saying that, so don't worry. We just might make you comfortable somewhere for a while."

"What do you know about your father?" Hess asks.

"I know he's a hero," Abe says.

"Sure he is. If heroes steal. If heroes are weasels. If heroes don't keep their word."

"That's enough, Ron."

"Let me tell you this, little man. Your father—"

"I said that's enough."

"Your father is in trouble. That's all I wanted to say."

"This is a small boy," Lipkin says. "This is two days before Yom Kippur. You decide how far you want to go."

Hess puts his hands up, just above his shoulders, like someone being robbed. "I'm standing here talking," he says. "I'm checking the temple's hot water. I'm not going too far." He drops his hands and picks up a few cloth towels from a pile by the sink.

The bathroom door finally swings open and two more men walk in. Lipkin and Hess give them space, watching Abe closely. Nobody says anything. The new men look away. Abe wonders if it would be better for him to shout or run. He could do both. Then his father comes in. "Let's go, Abraham," he says, holding out his hand.

He's standing between Lipkin and Hess. Lipkin takes a step back. Hess dips his hand, wrapped in the towels, down into the sink and he splashes Abe's father with the hot water. In his face and all over the front of his suit. Abe watches his father reach inside his jacket and he waits for one of the knives to come out. The perfect blade will shine. The men will rush toward the door. But his father pulls out a white handkerchief and dries his face, red now like it is after shaving. He folds the handkerchief carefully before putting it back in his pocket. "Let's go, Abraham," he says again. "We're done in here."

"You may be done in here," Hess says, turning off the water. "But you're not done."

"We're leaving," Abe's father says. "See me after Yom Kippur. You know I run my business alone. My son has no part in this."

"That's one way to look at it," Hess says. "But here's how I see it. You take something of ours. We might take something of yours."

The two men who came in earlier stand with their backs to the urinals. They are ready to leave, but they can't get to the sink or the door. "This is not the time," one of them says. "This is not the place. Services are about to start."

"The Book of Life and the Book of Death," Hess says. "The Book of Pain and the Book of Suffering."

"All right," Lipkin says. "We've made our point."

"For now," Hess says.

"Let's go, Abraham."

"I need to wash my hands," Abe says.

Hess moves toward the door. "Go ahead," he says, and then he turns his back, walking out behind Lipkin.

Abe's father's clothes are still wet when they walk across the lobby a few moments later. They enter the sanctuary. People are quiet when they pass by.

THERE ARE PRAYERS Abe wishes he could sing together with his father. There are prayers that seem to go on forever.

The rabbi tells a long story about a place on the other side of the world. Abe listens as closely as he can. The rabbi says that everything in the world has a heart and the world itself has one very large heart and this large heart beats at the top of a high mountain, near a clear spring that flows from a gigantic rock.

Every night, after the sun sets, the heart beats more slowly and the world starts to die. Then the clear spring sings to the heart. The heart of the world strains to sing back. Their singing echoes, and shining threads grow out of the songs and reach every living thing, connecting one heart with another. And then there is one just man who is chosen by God. He wanders through the world before sunrise, gathering the shining threads from every heart. He weaves the threads into time. When he has woven a full day of time, he gives it to the heart of the world. Then the heart of the world is revived and begins to beat strongly again.

Abe looks at his father. He wants to ask questions. "It shows how fragile we are," his father says.

"How precariously we are balanced," says the rabbi. "Without forgiveness, we cannot last."

The praying continues and Abe stands and sits beside his father. He doesn't see Lipkin and Hess anywhere. Again and again, he tells God he's sorry for not being better. He prays that he'll keep his family away from death. He imagines visiting the other side of the world, the mountain, the rock, and the spring. Would it be different from the world of the Black Sea and Odessa? When he grows up, he wants to be a surgeon, but he'd also like the job of gathering everyone's shining threads. He'd carry each one carefully and people would always be happy to see him.

They don't leave the sanctuary until long after the end of services. The whole temple is empty when they start to walk home in the dark, through backyards and parking lots, avoiding the streets. As soon as he can, Abe's father unzips in a secluded corner, behind a closed pharmacy.

"No rest for the middleman," he says.

Abe pisses, too. He finishes before his father, who goes on for minutes and maybe the sound gives them away. Footsteps and voices come up from behind.

"Good evening, Solomon. We had more to tell you."

Abe's father knows who it is without looking and he does not stop what he's doing. "All right," he says. "My heart is open. I'll have it for you tomorrow, holiday or no holiday."

"I'm glad to hear that," Hess says. "Still, I have to give you this message. Phil asked me not to. But I feel it's necessary. So we reached a compromise. He'll take your son home while you and I have our discussion."

Abe's father has finished at last. He turns to face Hess and Lipkin. He stands up straight and Abe follows his example, pressing his feet into the ground. "Is this the way it has to be?" his father asks.

"It is," Hess answers.

"All right," he says, and then he puts a hand on top of Abe's head. He looks down and says, "You go with Mr. Lipkin, Abraham. He'll take you home and you tell your mother I'll be there soon."

"I can wait," Abe says.

"I know you can, but I want you to go. I'll meet you there. I'll be fine."

Lipkin steps closer to Abe. "Forget those things we told you in the bathroom," he says. "I'll take you right home. I give you my word."

His father pushes him away gently. "Go on," he says.

Abe obeys and walks in front of the store, back to the street. He turns around, just once, and sees his father and Hess standing side by side in the dark, as if they were best friends who wanted to be left alone.

Farther down Sixty-third Street, Lipkin says, "You spent the whole day in the temple, little man. Do you want to be a rabbi when you grow up?"

"I want to be a surgeon."

"I see. Medicine's a good business to be in."

"I'll have a scalpel," Abe says. "I'll keep it sharp."

"You'll be able to make sure your mother and father stay healthy."

"What will happen to my father?"

"He'll be all right today," Lipkin answers. "You know, I have a son, older than you, and I wonder what will happen to him. It's hard for me to be sure. I'll tell you this, a son can do a lot to change a man. Maybe your father will surprise me."

"What will your friend do to him?"

"I'm thinking of getting a different job myself," Lipkin says, as if he didn't hear Abe's question. "It's a bad business we're in, your father and I. It's no way to raise a family."

"Is he hurting my father?"

"I'm not going to lie to you," Lipkin says, putting his hand on Abe's back and giving him a push with his fingers. "There's Ellsworth Street. You can make it home from here. Go on and tell your mother not to worry."

Abe runs the rest of the way. He is faster than ever.

His mother is waiting by the door. "Mr. Lipkin walked me home," he says. "Mr. Hess had a message for Father. I wanted to stay with him, but he told me to go. He said to tell you he'd be home soon."

The two of them eat dinner and hardly talk at all. Abe eats more than she does. They both want to hear the door open.

"Did you like the services?" she asks.

"Yes. I asked for forgiveness and I didn't take a nap."

"Are you tired now?"

"Yes."

"Why don't you get ready for bed. After your father comes home, I'll tell you a story."

In his room, Abe takes off his dress clothes and puts them neatly on his chair. He stretches out in bed and listens. His mother does the dishes. She paces. He fights to stay awake.

When he hears his father's voice, he sneaks out of his room. He stays close to his door and they don't notice him. His father sits by the kitchen table. "That bastard," he says. "He didn't have to do this." Abe's mother is standing behind his father, washing blood from his face and hair. "Shh," she says. "We'll be all right. Don't wake the children." She leans over him and holds him up in the chair with her hand on his shoulder. After the blood is gone, Abe can see the bruises and the cuts. The face is the wrong shape, the skin puffy, red and purple and dark. One eye is black, swelling shut. Abe stops staring and runs toward him. It seems to take a long time. They're growing closer and closer, Abe opens his arms, and he knows his father will never look the same again.

17

WHEN MAX SAW the brand new Viva Deluxe parked right by Abe's bed, he called back to his father, who was sitting on the living room couch. "Spiller said it was a gift? He just brought it in here and *gave* it to you?"

"Shh," said Caleb. "Let Abe sleep. He'll be up soon enough."

"It's strange," Max said, walking over to sit next to his father. "How'd he know which one Abe wanted?"

"He probably checked in at the medical supplies store."

Max felt his father's hand on the back of his head, lightly touching the bump there. Then the fingers moved to his temple and traced the dark violet bruise.

"It looks like a storm cloud," Caleb said. "Does it hurt?"

Max had taken his shower and his ibuprofen and both things had made him feel better, but the bruise was still tender and sore. He brushed his father's hand away. "I'm all right."

"Sure you are. You walk in here before seven, black and blue and absolutely fine. I don't understand why Johnny would do this to you."

"It wasn't Johnny, I told you that. It was one of his thugs."

"Then I don't understand why Johnny has thugs and I don't understand why he'd let one of his thugs do this to you."

Max wanted to stretch out on the couch, close his eyes, and get some sleep. That's what he needed. But his mind was wide awake, working hard. Plus his father was in the way.

"Johnny's always been a punk," Caleb said. "I never understood why you hung around with him."

"You've got a good list going, Dad. Things you don't understand. What else?"

Caleb let out his laugh. "Ha! We could be here all day." Then he leaned forward to rearrange a few objects on the coffee table, stacking the newspaper, pushing aside a tiny, unfamiliar sculpture. "Listen," he went on, "I don't want to argue with you, it's just that I hate seeing you beat up like this. It reminds me too much of your grandfather. And you know what happened to him. That didn't have to be the end, but, in so many ways—"

It was the lead-in to another story Max had heard a million times. He didn't need to hear it now. How Solomon became a broken man, how he gave up when there'd been no reason to give up, how only Abe could remember him as strong and confident. Caleb was born too late. All his memories came after the beating.

"Look, Dad," Max said, "here are a few things I don't understand. Why does Spiller want me to let go of the Goulds? And why is Johnny so interested in Spiller?"

"You and Spiller need to talk. I still don't really know him, but I can tell he's got more class in one earlobe than Johnny has in his whole family."

Max walked over to the freezer to get some ice and remembered how he'd hoped to run a quick scam, easy and shit-free. It hadn't seemed impossible at the time, but now there were complications. Too many unknowns. He wrapped the ice in a dish towel and shifted it back and forth between his bump and his temple. At least that was cool and simple and soothing. Then he heard his cell phone ringing.

When he answered, Grier said, "I hope it's not too early."

Max heard her voice and felt guilty. More complications. "I've been up for hours," he said.

"Why? Is everything all right?"

Max took the phone outside, where he paced the sidewalk and watched the commuter traffic build up as he told Grier everything was fine. Across the street, a few large guys were repaving a driveway and the bitter, tarry smell of the molten asphalt seemed to make the morning air thicker and hotter than usual. Max tried to get out of range, wondering exactly where Grier was at this moment. He pictured her on the dock behind her lab, the palm trees rustling in a fresh Florida Bay breeze, her boat ready and waiting. If he were there, standing beside her, would he tell her more? Would he describe the complications, the ice he'd left in the sink, the pulsing he could feel in the back of his head? Would he mention the Goulds, Spiller, and Sklarman? And what about Estelle?

He let those questions go. Instead, he asked, "What are your plans for the day?"

"I'll be out on the water in a few minutes," she said, "so I can't talk too long. Some jerks need to run across the bay to Flamingo. I'll help with their sites, and then they'll help with mine on the way back. I've set up my *Syringodium* in tubs by Sunset Cove, not too far from the lab. You wouldn't believe how much sand I've had to move out there to fill the tubs; it's all I've been doing these past few days. You could help with the shoveling if you were here. It would be nice to have my favorite nonscientist around."

"Are you trying to tell me you miss me?"

She laughed. "Could be," she said. "And what are you trying to tell me?"

"Remember what you said about those trains? Well, there's more of them than I thought, and some of them are awfully close when they pass by."

"Hmm," she said. "Does that mean your ex is giving you trouble?"

"No, she's off to Hawaii tomorrow. She and her gardener haven't been a problem."

"Who *has* been a problem?"

"I'll tell you when I see you."

"And when will that be, mystery man?"

"I'm not sure yet," Max said. "Soon, I hope."

"I hope so, too."

INSIDE, ABE WAS up and already on the Viva Deluxe, wearing a set of bright green hospital scrubs that clashed with the shiny new hunter green seat. Parked in front of the TV, he was watching an overly tan weather woman promise the city a week of sunny days. The scooter hadn't yet made him more happy and alert. His eyes were glassy, half open, as if he were about to slip back into sleep.

"Hey, Abe," Max said, "you look sharp on that scooter."

"Maxie," said Abe, his voice quiet.

Max turned to Caleb, who was brewing coffee in the kitchen. "Abe doesn't seem too good this morning."

"He's resting. He'll be disruptive in no time. You could wait and see, but you've got to drop Nathan off at the temple soon. Spiller will be waiting over there to talk to you. Who was that on the phone?"

"The woman from Florida, just checking in."

"Did you tell her about getting beat up? Did you tell her about the bowling woman?"

"I told her I was fine, Dad."

Caleb brought out two mugs of coffee, handing one to Abe and one to Max before returning to the kitchen for his own. "Add this to my list," he said. "I don't understand how you live your life."

"Don't start overworrying," Max said. "Let's both be optimistic for a change, what do you say?"

"I'll try to be optimistic, but I don't think it'll work."

Max shook his head and smiled. "That's not a good start." Then he glanced at his watch to see how soon he'd have to leave. He thought he had plenty of time, until he remembered again where his car was. "Shit," he said. "I've got to go."

While he hustled around, getting ready, he could hear Abe loudly sipping his coffee. Then, as if the caffeine were kicking in, Abe started to talk. "Just Japan," he said. Or it might have been "Must demand." Whatever it was, he said it more than once, back in his badgering mode.

Max stopped in front of the mirror by the front door and adjusted a baseball cap so it would fit over his bump. It covered most of his temple, too.

Abe spoke again. This time Max heard, "Dust the man." He looked over to his father. "What's he saying, Dad?"

"It's a new one," Caleb said. "He shouted it a couple times last night. I think it's 'Trust the man.' I told him I did, but that didn't stop him."

"Trust the man," Abe repeated, louder, as Max left the apartment.

AT ESTELLE'S WITH time to spare, Max found himself staring up at her building, trying to pick out her window. He felt like calling her on the intercom. It wasn't yet nine. Maybe he could offer her a ride to work. He knew there was no way he'd do it if he thought about it too much. Even as he pulled open the front door, he could tell it was a bad idea. He was in a rush and how could this help? Still, for reasons he couldn't really explain, he wanted to stay in the picture with her. He didn't want to disappear.

A crackly voice came through the small speaker asking who he was.

"It's Max," he said, "I was in the neighborhood so I—" Before he could finish, the door buzzed and he grabbed it.

Upstairs, someone stepped into the hallway, but it wasn't Estelle. Instead, Janet was standing there, waiting for him. She looked stylish and awake, well dressed in tan linen slacks, a matching jacket, and a loose white blouse.

Max didn't know what to say. "Good morning," he tried. "I was driving by and—"

"We saw your car parked out there all night, Max. We wondered what was going on. Why not just tell me the truth?"

"The truth," he said, rubbing the back of his neck. "Well, I wasn't thrilled with the way Estelle and I said good-bye last night, so I was hoping to give her a ride to work, maybe talk with her some more."

Janet moved closer to him, frowning. "What's that mark on your temple?"

"It's nothing."

Janet shook her head and crossed her arms, like a tough,

disappointed principal, someone who'd seen it all before. "It's difficult to tell the truth, isn't it? Especially when you're so out of practice. Wait here for a second." She went into the apartment, came back with her pocketbook, and pulled the door shut behind her. "This probably isn't the best place for us to talk," she said. "You can give me another ride home."

The elevator was brightly lit and had mirrored walls. Everywhere Max looked, he saw Janet looking at him. In her face, he could see traces of Estelle, in the delicate, barely upturned nose, in the wide-open eyes that didn't seem to do much blinking. As he watched her walk out to the car, he remembered her pure, slow-motion follow-through at Del Ennis Lanes, the smiles after the strikes, the soft high-fives, and he found himself comparing her to Abe and Caleb. She was of the same generation, and yet how much more solid and alive she seemed. How much happier. Had she simply suffered less? Had she made smart investments? Received good fortune instead of bad? Is that all there was to it?

She struck him as too honest and content for any of his tricks. Even if it had been possible, which he seriously doubted, he had no intention of taking advantage of her. Still, he recognized the desire to pluck off a piece of her prosperity. He *deserved* a piece of it. At least that's how it often felt down in Florida. That's how it had felt with the Goulds. Such people wouldn't miss the small portion he wanted. There'd be plenty left over.

In the car, Janet fiddled with the lock on the glove compartment. "Do you keep any weapons in here?" she asked.

"I don't use weapons."

"Looks like you could have used one last night."

"Nothing happened last night."

Janet shook her head again. "Of course not," she said.

As different as she was, Janet talked a little like Caleb, and she seemed to have a similar capacity for worry. But her curiosity and concern didn't bother him the same way. It was almost endearing. Regardless, he'd be dropping her off soon.

She leaned forward and reached under her seat, as if she expected to find a weapon taped to the floor. When she sat up again, her hands were empty, but she had another question. "Isn't there something else you want to tell me?"

"Such as?"

"Such as how much you like my daughter. How highly you think of her."

"I wouldn't have come looking for her if I didn't like her. I guess I want to spend more time with her."

"I guess you do, too," she said. "Now, what really happened last night?"

"You're persistent," Max said, stopping the car in front of her building. "I'll give you that, but there's still nothing to tell. A few impressions were clarified, that's all."

Janet didn't open her door right away. Instead, she kept talking. "Well, I think at least one of us should tell the truth. Estelle wouldn't want me talking to you, I'm certain of that. But she's clearly interested in you and I think she could use a project and I think you might be a good project for her. Or I might be an idiot. I suppose we'll find out. If you really want to spend more time with her, give her a few days and then show her you're making progress."

"What kind of progress?"

"You'll have to figure some things out for yourself," she said, opening the door. Then she glanced back at him. "If I were you, though, I'd wait until that black-and-blue mark goes away."

Max watched her until she was inside the building. Then,

before driving off, he checked his reflection in the rearview mirror. He adjusted the hat so it covered the bruise more completely. He didn't look that bad, considering.

As HE PULLED into his old driveway, he thought of his ex-house empty for the whole summer. One of Hiram's helpers would probably care for the garden, so someone would be around every now and then. Still, what would it be like to move back in? Reoccupy the place. Either that or he could arrange a robbery, some kind of profitable cleansing. Take it back to the way it was when they'd bought it. Loot out everything from the shrubs to the canvases.

He could have just honked and waited for Nathan to emerge, but he parked, walked up to the front door, and rang the bell. He heard the familiar barking, the skittering sound of toenails on the wood floor, and as soon as Nathan opened the door Natascha bolted out. She ran a few quick circles around Max, occasionally jumping up. When he knelt down, she licked his face and almost knocked him over. She was wagging at least half her body.

"Looks like she remembers you," Nathan said.

"Where will she spend the summer? She's not going to Hawaii, is she?"

"She's going to the kennel. But it's supposed to be the fancy kennel."

"The fancy kennel?"

"Mom says she'll be fine."

Sandy appeared at the door and looked at Nathan. "So you won't talk to me, but you've got no problem talking about me?"

Nathan ignored her and she turned her attention to Max. "What happened to your temple?"

"There was a small misunderstanding last night," he said. "Nothing to worry about."

"Who's worrying?"

"Let's take a walk before you drop me off," Nathan said.

"A walk's a great idea," Max said. "Spoken like a true Wolinsky."

"That might be an oxymoron," said Sandy.

Max could feel the easy comeback dropping onto his tongue. *Let's talk about what it is to be true. You'd have some interesting insights, I'm sure.* But he didn't want to get into it. "This is a friendly visit," he said. "I'm saying bon voyage to you. I'm happy to wish you well."

Sandy did a little hula dance, with a shimmy in her hips. She'd look sexy in a grass skirt and a lei. "I *am* well," she said. "Have a nice walk with your silent son. Inside Natascha."

Max thought the dog could have resisted, at least for a second or two, but she ran in right behind Sandy, didn't even look back. He'd been remembered and forgotten, just like that. He brushed off the black and white hairs she'd shed onto his pants.

"Shouldn't you be in uniform?" he asked Nathan, who was wearing a plain white T-shirt and baggy blue shorts that covered his knees.

"I'll change after I get there," Nathan said, lifting up his overstuffed backpack. He wobbled under the weight of it as they walked down to the car. "Some summer I've got coming. You wouldn't have believed the meeting last night."

Max helped guide the pack into the trunk of the LeSabre. "I came by looking for you," he said. "Wound up talking to Rabbi Weinberg. Sounds like things got slightly out of hand."

"I really want to do something else this summer."

"Let's not talk about quitting."

"It's not quitting if I never join."

Max told himself to look more closely at his son and, standing in front of his ex-house, that's what he did. To look was to marvel, and to worry. Here he was, thirteen years old, with his face still smooth, though the lip fuzz was definitely ready for a razor. His eyes were gray blue, a good color for wool, and they were deep set, which could make him seem distant even from close up. His brow should have been smooth and yet it was furrowed. Think of how far he'd traveled already. It wasn't that long ago he was in a stroller. He looked sad and burdened now, in some ways less alive than Janet had appeared when he'd dropped her off. The problem was that all the good times had happened when he was too young. The better memories must have slipped away before they'd managed to take hold.

"Come on, Nathan. We can't decide anything different right now. You'll see how it goes. Let's drive over to Tookany Creek. We can take a walk there."

They climbed into the car, but the argument wasn't finished. "You should have seen Ricky's hand," Nathan said. "I don't understand why this is so important."

Max drove and talked. "There's plenty you don't understand," he said. "Trust me. Plenty I don't understand, too. There doesn't have to be an immediate reason for everything. Listen. I'm not saying you need to stay in the troop forever. I'm not saying Eagle Scout or bust. I'm just saying you need to give it more of a shot."

"Why should I care what you think? I don't even know what you do or where you live these days."

"I'll tell you whatever you want to know."

Nathan turned and stared out the window. He spoke quietly, almost as if he were talking to himself, making simple statements, testing them out loud. "You don't listen. You don't tell anyone anything. It's just like Mom says. You'll go back to Florida. I'll have to work all of this out on my own anyhow. Maybe I should give you the silent treatment, too. If what I say doesn't mean anything, I should stop wasting my time and yours."

"You've got to talk to someone. Might as well be me."

Nathan said nothing more. Max parked in the lot by the playground. Little kids went up and down on swings and slides, supervised by parents and day-care workers. Older kids, just out of school for the summer, packed the basketball court, the tennis courts, the soccer fields. From a distance, these children seemed happy, they'd made it through another year, their faces and voices overflowing with what looked to him like reckless joy. Meanwhile, his son was in a different world, upset and miserable.

A bridle path ran along the far side of the creek, away from the street and the traffic. Some time in the past it must have been a place for horseback riders. Now there were occasional mountain bikers, but the path was only about two miles long, not much of a challenge, so the bikers tended to go elsewhere. Max and Nathan crossed a sagging wooden bridge and started down the path, Nathan walking quickly ahead.

Max called out to his fast-moving son. "You keep quiet as long as you want, Nathan. Just like a child. Seen and not heard."

Nathan kept walking.

"Here I am," Max said. "I'm ready to have a conversation. In person, man to man. Are you going to insist on being a kid? Why not slow down? Ask me a question. I might surprise you."

The last time they'd strolled this path together, they'd discussed Max's moving out. They'd both been shocked, in their different ways, and there'd been a good deal of silence then, too.

"All right," Nathan said, stopping and looking back at him. "Here's a question. What's the worst thing you've ever done?"

For a moment, it was Max's turn to be silent. He caught up to his son, stood by his side, and then, to buy time, he asked, "What do you think?"

"Mom says—"

"Let's leave her out of this for now. It's just you and me here. What do *you* think?"

"I think you lie to people."

"It's true."

"I think you use your lies to get as much money as you can."

"I have done that."

"Have you ever hurt anyone?"

Max gave a knee-jerk answer. "No," he said, but the question sunk down deeper. It was natural for Max to gaze at his son, study his appearance, how he kept changing and growing, moving through puberty, from child to teenager. But as his "no" hung in the air, Max began to wonder more about how he himself was seen. How did he look to Nathan? Did he look like someone who would hurt people? Did he look like a liar in his son's eyes?

He knew men who'd done some hurting, thugs like Dexter, but ever since his last collaboration with Johnny, he'd managed to avoid that sort of work. And it was that kind of difference he'd always been able to keep straight. Do this but not that. Break some rules but not the rules that matter. Sandy had never been able to understand. Neither could Caleb. Now Nathan. Maybe, in the end, the difference was clear only in his own mind.

"I've never hit anyone," he said. "I try to work alone and I've never been involved in violence. Here's what I've done: I've lied to get money from people who have a lot of money."

Nathan was still staring, waiting. Max considered answering

the question again, this time offering a list of people he'd hurt in one way or another, starting with Nathan and moving through his whole family.

"How do you do it?" Nathan asked.

"What do you mean?"

"When you lie," he said. "How do you get them to trust you?"

"That's what you want to know?"

"I'm curious."

There were no benches, but Max saw a nearby oak with thick, gnarled roots. He sat on one and brushed off a space for Nathan. It was cool and comfortable in the shade and he leaned back against the tree trunk. When Nathan was sitting down next to him, Max said, "You start by telling people what they want to hear. So you need to have a good idea of what they want to hear."

"But why do they trust you?"

"Why do you trust me?"

"Because you're my father."

"Well, the people I meet don't think I'm their father, so that's not the answer. If I wasn't your father, would you still trust me?"

"Maybe."

"Why?"

"Because you remind me of my father."

"Ha," Max said. "But what if you didn't know me and I didn't remind you of me?"

"Can you give me answers without asking me questions?"

Max smiled at his son's persistence. "It's hard to talk about trust, Nathan. First, you should know that for a long time, for years and years of my life, I wasn't deceiving anyone, as far as I knew, so I didn't have to worry about whether I seemed trustworthy or not. Looking back, I can see that's probably the best way to be trusted. Get it by not seeking it, if that makes any sense. But, all right, to answer your question, when I got deceptive, when I went after trust and abused it, I tried to offer something in exchange."

"Something in exchange?"

"I didn't ask openly, but I did my best to suggest that if they gave me their trust, they'd get something in return. Not just *some* thing, but the very thing they wanted. If they'd only trust, they could have what they wanted. They could have their dream. Of course, eventually, they'd have to back up their trust with cash, but that was easy, once I had the trust."

"That's what you do in Florida? That's why I can't come visit?"

"I'll tell you another secret. I did less than people think in Florida. I made a little money and I took my time spending it. Nothing extravagant in the making or the spending. I just needed some time to see a future again."

Max wondered what was coming over him. Where would all this openness lead? He hoped he wouldn't find himself in a police station, signing a stack of confessions. For now, as he stood up from the low, makeshift bench, all he knew was that it felt good to answer his son's questions. Maybe it was his version of a present, though he still wanted to find a real gift.

Nathan also got to his feet. "Can you see a future now?" he asked.

Max took his time answering that one. He turned to his son and stared into those gray-blue eyes for a few seconds. "Yes," he finally said. "I can see a future now. I'm looking right at it. Just don't follow in my footsteps, okay?"

DURING THE CAR ride to the temple, Max managed to get in some questions of his own. He heard about Troop 158's summer schedule. For the first month, they'd have a base camp on the lawn by the temple. They'd take some short weekend trips, and then, near the end of July, they'd go away for a month, two weeks in the Poconos and two weeks of scout camp at Treasure Island, up on the Delaware River. It didn't sound ideal to Max, but he hoped it would be all right, and he told Nathan again how proud he was, how he knew none of this could be easy. "Next summer will be different," he said. "I promise."

The car had barely even stopped in the parking lot before one of the scouts sprinted over. Max noticed the bandages on the kid's hand and knew this was the chief pyromaniac. "Nathan," the boy said, "you're a Cobra. Here's your patch."

Nathan wrestled his backpack out of the car and set it down heavily at his feet. Then he took the patch, set it on his palm, and studied it. A black serpent, coiled and hissing on a field of red. It brought out a smile that Max tried to hold on to.

"Is this your dad?" the boy asked.

"My name's Max. You must be Ricky."

He held up his injured hand. "The bandages gave me away," he said. "And they make it tough for me to shake your hand, but I'm Nathan's patrol leader. I promise to look out for him. We're going to have an excellent trek."

"I'm glad to hear that," Max said.

With his left hand, Ricky lifted up Nathan's pack. He made it look light. "I'll take this over to your tent," he said. Then he hustled off with the pack. "Thanks," Nathan called out, and in response Ricky waved his bandaged hand above his head.

Nathan crossed his arms, no-nonsense, all business, as if he wanted to make certain Max understood that Ricky's kindness hadn't changed anything. "If I don't like it after this trip, I can quit, no questions asked, right?"

"Yes, and if you have a great time, I promise not to say I told you so."

Max opened his arms and finally got his hug. He didn't want to embarrass his son in front of his fellow scouts, so he let go sooner than he would have liked. He wanted to say something more, but there wasn't enough time and suddenly Nathan was walking away. Max stood by the car and watched him go. Then he went to look for the scoutmaster.

SPILLER WAS STANDING at his desk, wearing his full summer uniform — shorts, shirt, neckerchief, kneesocks, hiking boots — topped off with a tan, well-ventilated safari hat. Max had wondered, on his way down to the basement office, what sort of inventory would be stacked up in the office this time. What came after cookware and canned food? He saw that the goods had stayed in the *cs* — CUTCORP was stamped all over the new boxes.

"CutCorp?" Max asked.

Spiller was going through a drawer and bringing out folders. He answered without looking up. "They make excellent knives right here in the USA. Chef-tested kitchen cutlery. Ergonomic thermoresin handles and stainless steel blades with a lifetime guarantee. A far better product than those Germans at Henckels and Wüsthof put out."

"I want to thank you for the Viva Deluxe," Max said. "I was surprised to —"

Spiller interrupted. "It was nothing. I don't want to hear another word about it. I'm sorry that's the sort of thing he wants these days. Now, Caleb must have told you we need to talk more. Would you close the door?"

Max did as he was asked. Then Spiller sat down and mo-

tioned for Max to do the same. "Seems like I need some information," Max said, removing his baseball cap.

Spiller leaned across the desk to get a closer look at the bruise
and the bump. "I knew Sklarman was up to something," he said.
"The man's a nuisance. Still, it looks like he went easy on you."

Max laughed. "Didn't feel easy," he said, but then he wondered if getting hit on the head wasn't, in some ways, the easi-
est thing that had happened since he'd come up from Florida.
Nothing this morning had been easy, for example. He'd had his
postbeating time with Caleb, Abe, Grier, Janet, Sandy, and
Nathan, and those conversations had all seemed complicated
and difficult, and now he was meeting with Spiller, hoping
this bald guy in kids' clothing would somehow make sense of
everything.

"Can you speak Chinese?" Spiller asked.

"No. Can you?"

Spiller smiled and spoke words Max couldn't even begin to
understand. He'd eaten his fair share of Chinese food, but all he
really knew about the language was that the letters came from
drawings and that it was tonal, so you could make big mistakes
in pronunciation, accidentally saying "May I kiss you?" when
you meant "May I ask you a question?" or something like that.
In any case, Spiller kept talking, his voice smoothly rising and
falling, and it was odd to hear that mysterious, musical gibber-
ish coming out of his mouth.

"I'm impressed," Max said. "What were you saying?"

Spiller opened one of the files, pulled out two papers, and
held them up. They were similar to what Max had seen when
he'd gone snooping: formal, notarized documents, with imprints
and signatures and bright characters in red and gold. "I'm going to tell you as much as I can right now, but I can't give you

all the details. Abe never even knew all the details. Basically, the borders are the trickiest part, though it's much easier to move the goods out of China than it is to get them into the States, especially these days. We don't want anything getting embargoed at Customs, that's for sure. After that, it gets much simpler. These pieces of paper show we have the quota we need for the shirts, pants, and shorts. They won't look like official uniforms when they come in, of course — no tags or anything like that. The finishing will be done at the manufacturers Abe and I lined up here. We'll transship the neckerchiefs, the patches, the socks, and the caps. That'll have to be a slightly more clandestine process."

Max tried to absorb it all. The money would be in the difference between buying the goods in China and selling them as made in the USA. Nothing too innovative about that. The volume was the key factor, and the steady clientele. No worries about the fashion changing from year to year. But who would be getting a cut? The contacts in China, the contacts at the manufacturers, the Boy Scout contacts who'd need to be paid off to let the deal fly, Spiller, and that was just a start. What kind of numbers were involved? Once again, too many unknowns. "What about the people making the stuff now?" he asked. "Aren't they going to be suspicious when their sales suddenly drop?"

Spiller carefully returned the papers to the folder and put the folder back in the desk. "We phase the goods in slowly over a few years. In the end, it works to our advantage that the BSA is so secretive about their contracts. And, remember, it will look like everything's made in the good old US of A. So, the orders drop because the old guys are being undersold by their competition. Happens all the time, right?"

Max kept trying to get his mind around the setup, but he

could tell that the biggest question would be whether or not he could trust Spiller. After all, if the guy had the connections he seemed to have, why wouldn't it work? Max pushed for more details. "There must be a ton of people in the middle here. How will you keep it quiet?"

"There are no middlemen in this," Spiller said, crossing his arms. "Well, almost none. There's me, my wife, and her extended family. We work direct all the way through. No trading companies, nobody taking their percentages."

The talk was good, but what if it was only talk? In the classic con, Spiller would be the roper, leading the marks in for the slaughter. And yet he hadn't asked for money. He'd done the opposite, somehow getting Abe the exact scooter he'd wanted. "It all sounds good," Max said. "Too good, really. But I guess I don't see what you need us for."

Spiller shook his head. "I share this masterpiece with you and that's the best you can come up with. You're suspicious, just like your father. Still, I would have appreciated a better reaction."

"I didn't mean to—"

Spiller cut him off. "Let me tell you something, Max, and try not to take this the wrong way. You Wolinskys don't dream right. With my help, Abe was learning and he wanted to bring you and your father along. I said okay, I allowed that to happen, but now Abe's where he is and your father's more grief stricken than before and I'm stuck having to teach you."

"Teach me what?"

Spiller took his glasses off and began massaging his temples with his fingertips. The task before him seemed to give him pain. "Forget the petty, penny-ante stuff," he said, "the Goulds, and crap like that."

"Speaking of the Goulds," Max said, "I—"

Spiller stopped his massage and raised his voice. "Forget them, I said!" He smacked his hand against the desk. The sound echoed off the concrete walls like a gunshot. Spiller put his glasses back on, stared at Max, and exhaled. "Listen to what I'm telling you, for God's sake. You need to dream differently. Bigger. So big that no one can see the edges of the dream. That way no one can grab on and fuck it up."

Max touched his own temple. "What about Sklarman? He's trying to grab on."

"Sklarman's a punk," Spiller said. "A particularly stupid punk and one way he'll try to get to you is through the Goulds. That's another reason why you have to call that whole thing off. Today."

Max remembered how, not that long ago, he was telling his father that they should both be optimistic. Well, it would be nice to let the Goulds go, and it would make Caleb happy. It also might give him a good reason to call Estelle. And, who knew, maybe Spiller's scheme was going somewhere. Still, there were other concerns. "Before he blackjacked me," Max said, "Johnny's thug was making threats. Would he do something to Nathan or Caleb?"

Spiller stood up and walked to the door. "You take care of the Goulds and I'll take care of good old Dexter."

Max, following behind Spiller, asked one more question. "What happens next?"

"There's someone else I want you to meet and then I'll need you to make a sales trip to some longtime clients in Ephrata, but I'll be in touch about that. Now I've got to go see to my—I mean, our—boys."

They stepped out into the hallway and, as they went upstairs to the lobby, Max could hear pieces of his morning conversations echoing inside his bruised head. There was Caleb's lack of understanding, Grier's hope, Janet's push for progress, Sandy's oxymoron, Nathan's future. And let's not forget Abe's parting words. "Trust the man," he'd repeated, as if it were the chorus for what was to come. Who could know what Abe really meant, but walking back across the parking lot to his car, Max hoped Spiller was indeed the man.

18

NATHAN HAD HIS emergency plan. A simple, predictable one. The house would be empty for the whole summer, after all. He reached into his pocket to feel the key, just to remind himself that he wasn't completely trapped. He was sitting on the temple's lawn, next to his pack, outside the red tent that had been assigned to him, and he wasn't going to cry. Not a chance. He pulled up a handful of grass instead. Then Ricky and Felix came over and hustled him off to a patrol meeting.

Of course, those blazing signal fires showed that the scouts of Troop 158 might have a few tricks up their drab olive sleeves, but Nathan still expected day after day of dull, conventional camping. Hiking, cooking, cleaning up. He'd have to memorize oaths and pledges, learn to tie knots, make a tourniquet, use a compass, fold a flag, and so on. He'd heard they would visit several historic sites on their hikes. They'd also tackle some community development projects. In other words, as far as he knew, there was nothing about the trek to look forward to.

His nonexpectations were confirmed by the patrol meeting, which seemed to be about assigning chores and scheduling other meetings. Apparently, a lot of time would also be devoted to what Ricky called troop service. Felix tried to chart the week out on a piece of legal-sized paper. They were sitting at a picnic table and the uneven, cracked surface made it difficult to draw the lines straight. "Don't worry about it," Ricky said, but Felix focused on his task. The other kid in the patrol was Scott, a thin, six-foot-five fifteen-year-old who wanted desperately to gain weight. He thought it would help his basketball game. He had a loaf of wheat bread with him, a jar of peanut butter, and a plastic bear filled with honey. While Felix fiddled with his paper and pencil, Scott ate three open-faced sandwiches. He caught Nathan looking and grinned. "In the fall," he said, "I'm going to post up like a motherfucker."

For Nathan, keeping quiet was becoming more and more natural. He let Scott return to his food. He watched Ricky and Felix work, saw them give him easy jobs for the first week. He'd be the wood gatherer and the table setter. Later he'd rotate into cooking, cleaning, and fire making. Nothing very exciting, but he wasn't going to complain. He didn't want to get that kind of reputation. Still, when he glanced at the complete schedule, he was surprised by how early the nights seemed to end. "Taps at eight thirty and then we're in the tents?" he asked, trying to sound curious instead of critical. "Isn't that early?"

Felix glanced over at Ricky. "You haven't told him yet?"

"When was I going to tell him?" He held up his bandaged hand, as if it offered proof that he'd been busy. "*You* were supposed to call him and tell him."

"Tell me what?" Nathan asked.

Ricky picked at some of the tape at the wrist-end of his bandage. "Did you maybe bring any dressier clothes with you?" he asked.

"Dressier clothes?"

"Okay," Ricky said. "It's not really a problem. We can easily work out something for tonight."

"What's tonight?"

Scott cleared his throat. He needed to drink some water before he could speak. "Tonight is Sharon's birthday," he said.

The answer clarified nothing.

"You know," Felix said, winking behind his glasses, "Sharon Kutnack."

Nathan had a ready image of Sharon, a middle school senior and lacrosse star. On game days, during lunch period, her whole team would go to the locker room and change their clothes. They'd come to afternoon classes ready to play, decked out in white polo shirts and red tartan skirts. That was a uniform Nathan didn't mind. He, Rich, Eric, and Jeff had talked more than once about Sharon's legs, and not only her legs.

But the image of her slender calves and thighs didn't explain the early tent time. Nathan looked from Felix to Ricky.

Ricky smiled. "Our troop has been invited," he said.

Nathan was waiting to hear more when Spiller, standing by the temple's door, called out to them. "Fall in!" he shouted.

AFTER LEADING THE two patrols into one of the Hebrew school classrooms, Spiller stood in front of the teacher's table, which could have been a chemistry lab castoff, thick wooden legs supporting a black soapstone top. The Owls took the desks closest to the door. The Cobras headed for the seats near the windows. As Nathan walked across the room, he noticed that spread out on the stone tabletop, there was a full set of knives, from paring knife to bread knife to cleaver, about a dozen in all, including a bulky pair of scissors.

Spiller waited for the troop to settle in. He checked his watch, glanced behind him at the blank blackboard, and then began. "I've promised you an opportunity," he said. "But, first, I'd like to remind you of a few important things. And even before that, let's give a strong 158 welcome to our two newest scouts, Danny Feldman, our most recent Owl, and Nathan Wolinsky, our latest Cobra."

Nathan looked down at his feet as the other kids clapped.

"Hip, hip," Spiller said.

"Hooray!" shouted the Cobras and the Owls. Nathan glanced across at Danny, to see how he was handling the cheer. He was smiling, whispering to Alan, his patrol leader.

"Hip, hip."

"Hooray!"

Nathan wondered how he was supposed to respond. A version of his typical classroom concerns descended on him. He hadn't done his homework. He'd made no scout progress plan and he hadn't memorized the scout law yet. Trustworthy, loyal, helpful, something something something—that was all he could remember.

Spiller went on with his agenda. "Recruitment," he said. "We all know that's the lifeblood of our fledgling troop. We want more Cobras and more Owls. Eventually, we want more patrols—Flying Eagles, Antelopes, Wolverines, to name just a few. Over time, we'll make our own version of Noah's ark here at Beth Israel. So keep your eyes open. Keep looking for boys who could prosper with us."

Nathan remembered how in the basement, during that one-on-one meeting, Spiller had been extremely intimidating. That hadn't really changed. Above ground, he was still intimidating and in charge, no doubt about that. But there was more than intimidation going on, something else, something inspiring, almost. The scouts around him leaned forward to listen. Though Nathan remained skeptical, he also felt himself drawn in, lured closer by a strangely inviting camaraderie. Maybe it was the relief of not being called on. Maybe the tone of voice was friendlier. Maybe it was the way Spiller's silver neckerchief shimmered in the late afternoon sun.

"Now," Spiller said, "there's another form of lifeblood crucial to our troop's survival. We've talked about this before, as most of you will recall. We need to raise funds to strengthen our troop and our home base here at Beth Israel. We all know what Girl Scouts sell, don't we, Felix?"

Felix answered immediately. "Girl Scouts sell cookies."

"They certainly do. Year after year they sell the same cookies and year after year they rake it in. What kind of product do the Boy Scouts sell? Scott?"

"The Boy Scouts have no equivalent of cookies."

"Well put. And sad but true, I'm sorry to say. Troops try lightbulbs, fruit from Florida. Nothing very distinctive about that. No evidence of original thinking there. They also put together recycling initiatives, and I applaud them for it, but alas, that's no way to make money. Fortunately, this state of affairs need not continue. We're a new troop and we have to try new techniques, new products."

At this point, Spiller checked his watch again. Then he was holding the cleaver in his right hand, a long bread knife in his left. "If I had time," he said, "I could speak about this cutlery for hours. Could cutlery be our version of cookies? That's not a question we can answer yet, but it is a part of my vision."

After carefully returning the knives to the table, Spiller walked over and opened the classroom door. A younger man with curly blond hair, a tan linen suit, and a pinkish bow tie stood waiting in the hallway. He stepped in behind Spiller, a soft leather bag over his shoulder. Spiller shook the man's hand and said to the troop, "I'm going to leave you with Mr. Gottlieb for now. I know you'll give him your undivided attention. He'll give you more details and answer any questions you may have."

Nathan still had many of the questions he'd had after his first meeting with Spiller: This was a scoutmaster? Was this what his grandfather expected? What kind of troop was this?

As he watched Spiller walk out of the room, Nathan knew he wasn't going to get answers to any of those questions for a while.

Gottlieb looked like a man on the make, except for the bow tie. "Pull your desks in closer, gentlemen," he said. "I'm going to pass these knives around and I want you to begin by studying the extraordinary handles. They're made out of thermoresin, the same material they use for motorcycle helmets and bowling balls. They're that strong, and yet see how perfectly they fit your hand? These pieces of fine craftsmanship will practically sell themselves. Now, here's a demonstration you'll want to use. These are our kitchen shears. They're truly amazing. If someone will lend me a quarter, I'll show you what these babies can do."

Over among the Owls, Alan convinced Danny to fork over a quarter. Gottlieb took it and placed it in the V of the open shears. "The key here," he said, "is to set the coin at the base of the blades, not out near the tips. Then you just apply a little force."

Gottlieb pressed down for a few seconds, using only one hand. The quarter snapped in two. "Presto!" he said.

CUTTING THE QUARTER was the clear highlight of the presentation. Still, Gottlieb went on for almost two hours. He insisted that salesmen were the wealthiest men in the world. "It all comes down to what you sell," he said, "in what quantity, for how much. Some men sell aluminum foil, other men sell aluminum smelters. Some men sell electrical appliances, others sell nuclear power plants. There are people out there who sell battleships and skyscrapers and space stations. Those people— those *salesmen*— have vision and now they have millions. Troop 158 has vision and we all want to get our share. I am fully committed to that, I can assure you."

Then he passed around glossy brochures. There were price lists and bargain package deals and other handouts full of product specifications. They were told about the illustrious history of the CutCorp company. "Made in America," Gottlieb repeated. "Lifetime guarantee." Nathan wondered how this troop could be so radically different from what he'd imagined. Would they be camping or working? When Rabbi Weinberg walked into the room with boxes of pizzas and bottles of soda, Nathan shook his head in disbelief.

"Well, boys," the rabbi said, "Scoutmaster Spiller tells me that selling these knives will not only be good for the temple. Along the way, you should all earn a handful of merit badges. Salesmanship, Personal Management, Communications, Wood Carving, and I'm sure there are others."

Gottlieb announced that they should pair off and practice making pitches to each other. Felix worked with Scott, Gottlieb himself sat down with Ricky, and that left Nathan without a partner, but Rabbi Weinberg stepped over to help. "Nathan," he said, "I know this can't be easy for you. I know you're a reluctant scout."

Nathan smelled the familiar cinnamon breath. He didn't want to appear weak, especially not with the Owls and the rest of the Cobras all around him. "I wasn't given too many choices," he said.

Gottlieb called out above the chatter. "Make sure you stress the incentives, gentlemen. The free paring knife, the free pizza cutter, the free cutting board."

The rabbi waited for Gottlieb to get back to work with Ricky, then said, "You've heard enough from me these last few months. I'm sure the last thing you want is more of my advice, but it's part of my job and I can't resist. You're a man of responsibility now—"

"Doesn't seem to make much difference," Nathan said.

"That's exactly what I'm getting at," the rabbi said. "You're a man of responsibility now, but that doesn't mean you're suddenly *given* responsibility. It means you have to *take* it. *Take* responsibility, Nathan, for yourself, for your happiness, for the shape of your life."

Gottlieb's voice rose out again. "Tell them that CutCorp sells knives to NASA. This is space-age technology. These are the knives in the kitchens of royal families, in England, Spain, and Sweden. There are two full sets in the White House."

The rabbi picked up a bread knife and looked it over. He brushed his thumb across the serrated blade. "It's a little strange," he said. "I won't argue with you about that. But it's not that bad. I think you can find something good here."

Nathan wasn't in the mood for the rabbi to be right, but he heard the advice. He took it in as best he could. Then he paged through the brochure on his desk. "Am I supposed to practice a pitch on you?" he asked.

Rabbi Weinberg stood up and smiled. "You've done enough practicing with me," he said. "Besides, I don't think you'll have a problem selling. You're a Wolinsky. It's in your blood."

THE EVENING GREW only more mysterious. After the pizza was finished and Gottlieb departed and the rabbi retreated to his study, the scouts left the temple. They were in their tents by eight thirty. Then, at nine, they reemerged and followed Ricky to the parking lot. A van pulled up and they all climbed in.

19

DAVID GOULD WANTED to know what he'd done wrong. "I spoke with our accountant," he said, "and I found out this would be a great time to cash in some of our investments. It would be easy for me to get the money together and—"

Max was sitting next to Caleb on the couch in the basement apartment. He moved the cell phone away from his ear so his father could listen in. Then he kept talking to David. "You don't understand," he said. "What I'm telling you is that *our* funding fell through and we couldn't get capitalized. It turned out there were a few New Jersey forces beyond our control. I wanted to tell you myself because of our personal connection and because I really enjoyed meeting you—"

"I appreciate that," David said. "But how long do you think it will take to find other funding? We're in no rush to move, thank God. I'd still like to reserve that unit you showed us, if that's okay. We'd be happy to make a deposit."

Max shook his head. What a joke. The money was coming right at him and he had to turn it away. "We won't find other funding," he said. "We're not seeking any new investors. The project is over. I'm sorry to say there will be no Oceanview Gardens, not now, not ever."

Max could hear a woman's voice asking questions in the background. "Hold on a second," David said. "Gail wants to talk to you."

"Good morning," she said, a quiver of desperation in her voice. "Can you tell me what's happening?"

During a good, smooth scam, the marks were excited when they gave away their money. They couldn't wait to hand it over. Then, soon after that happy exchange, Max would disappear. If necessary, he'd hire somebody to make sure the marks stayed sewn up, but he didn't need to hang around for that. He liked to be long gone before the disappointment and anger set in. And yet, as he saved the Goulds, he was getting no money and plenty of disappointment. The worst of both worlds. He tried to rise above it. At least his father looked happy.

"It's nice to hear your voice, Gail," Max said. "I'm sorry not to have better news. I explained it all to David. I've got to run, but I'll be in touch if I hear anything else. In the meantime, I wish all the best to both of you."

MAX WAS LOOKING forward to a nap, but he'd promised to go see Joe Lonzinger again with his father, so that meant another pair of ibuprofen, another cup of coffee, and then the two of them were walking out to the LeSabre.

As Max drove to the hospital, Caleb talked about the trouble he'd had taking Abe into rehab. "I don't know if he's getting more stubborn or more lazy, but I almost couldn't pull him out of that damn scooter this morning. I guess I hoped that thing would be an improvement. I hoped it would help him do more, not less."

Max tried to listen carefully, but he was distracted. He could blame it on the aftereffects of his beating, or it could have been the thought of the money he'd just lost, or maybe he was putting all his energy into keeping an eye out for Johnny. Whatever it was, Max kept quiet as they made their way to Rolling Hill.

In the lobby, an older woman rushed over to them, and Max, startled, wondered what was wrong. He was relieved when the woman hugged his father and said, "I heard you were in yesterday. I must have just missed you."

"Ruth," Caleb said, "I'd like you to meet my son."

Max shook her hand, noticing the volunteer's badge pinned to her light blue jacket. She was a youthful sixty-something, with the excellent posture, the toned arms, and the healthy glow of someone who'd been doing yoga for years. She seemed very happy to see Caleb. It was obvious, in her smile, in the way she kept a hand on his bicep. And there was no wedding ring on that hand.

Max used to ask his father about the women in his life. He'd ask about dating and the possibility of someday marrying again, but Caleb never seemed able to handle that kind of conversation. Max would try to get it started and then it was as if he could watch the memory of the accident slip out of his father's brain, down to cover his face. Caleb would frown and say what he always said: "Some things only happen once. Other things happen over and over."

Now Caleb said, "We came to see Joe."

"Of course," Ruth said. "He'd be thrilled to see you and God knows he needs more visitors, but he's been having a bad day.

They put him on some pain medication that's keeping him pretty far out of it."

"Could I look in on him anyhow?" Caleb asked. "You never know what he might notice."

"I guess that would be all right. I'll go up with you."

The news about Joe was depressing, but for Max it was even more depressing to watch as his father barely spoke to Ruth in the elevator. An alive, interesting, energetic woman was standing right there, close by his side, and Caleb all but ignored her. Max knew better than to be surprised; he also knew better than to get angry about it. And yet something about the last few days made this wasted opportunity almost unbearable. He'd come back to help, but what could he accomplish if this was the way it was? What could he do if his father could really only focus on the dead and the dying? Could money fix that? A new apartment? Why should he walk into a Chinese uniform scam he couldn't fully comprehend, let alone control? Why should he bother getting his head bashed in if it was already hopeless?

Max felt too frustrated to speak and he wondered if the silent treatment was contagious. Was this, in a way, how Nathan had been feeling? The two of them could have this in common: They were both sons unable to understand their fathers. And, somehow, at the same time, they were sons who understood their fathers too well.

He followed Caleb and Ruth out of the elevator, down the hall to Joe's room. Along with Ruth, Max stopped just inside the door. From there, Joe looked even less substantial than he had the day before. Hour by hour, he was disappearing. There was his head resting very still on his pillow, his eyes shut, tubes running into his nose, his mouth open, his thin neck, and then everything else was covered by the blanket and the sheets. The only sign that he was alive came from the slow, steady beeping of a machine beside the bed.

Caleb walked over, lifted the sheet away from Joe's right arm, and took his hand. He stood there silently for a few moments, looking down at that hand, as if he were comparing Joe's withered fingers to his own. "Just wanted to let you know I came by to see you, young man," he said. "I'll be back again soon. And I'm warning you, I'll expect a much better welcome next time."

While Caleb was carefully putting Joe's hand back beneath the sheet, Max turned to Ruth. "We'll probably get a bite to eat after we leave. Would you like to join us?"

Her eyes lit up, but she had to get back to work. "I'm on until six," she said. "Maybe another time, though."

"Does my father have your number?"

She stepped back into the hall and smiled. "Yes, he's had it for a while."

Ruth needed to go over to the oncology ward, so they said good-bye to her and then made their way back down to the lobby and out to the car. As Max drove to the diner, he reminded himself that he really didn't know Ruth at all. Maybe he was overreacting. She might simply feel sorry for Caleb. She might not want anything from him. If she did, she was probably more than capable of asking for herself. Max also reminded himself how much he admired his father's dedication to his rounds, his commitment to staying in touch and doing what he could, even and especially when it was difficult.

Still, Max couldn't just let his frustration go. When they slid into their booth, he didn't know what to say, but he knew he had to say something. Missy came over, poured their coffee, and took their order. "You gonna be with your father every day from now on?" she asked.

"I don't think so. I live down in Florida."

"Too bad," she said. "It's nice seeing the two of you together."

He watched her hustle back to the kitchen. "She's sweet," he said, thinking it might be easy to move from her to Ruth.

"I want to tell you something," Caleb said. "I meant to tell you earlier."

"Is this another diner confession?"

"In a way. I just want you to know I'm proud of what you did with the Goulds this morning. I know that wasn't how you wanted it to go, but I'm glad you made that call."

The praise caught Max off-guard. He was also surprised by how it made him feel. Warm in his chest, flushed, proud of himself. He couldn't help smiling. Still hard-wired for his father's approval, after all these years. "I was happy to do it, Dad," he said. "But did you hear how willing they were?"

"I heard."

Max found himself wondering if Estelle would also be proud of what he'd done, and then he realized what he was going to say. Might as well get everything out in the open. "Look," he said, "there's something I wanted to tell you before, too, though it's not as good as what you just told me. Remember that woman I was telling you about?"

"The bowler?"

"Right. Her name's Estelle and that first time I met her, we were talking and I did a stupid thing."

"What?"

"Well, I told her you were dead."

"Dead?"

"In a car crash, I said. A salesman killed on the road."

"You said that?"

"I did," Max admitted. His father stared at him, but not into his eyes. The stare seemed to focus on the side of his face. Max scratched at his cheek.

"I don't need to know this," Caleb said. "You tell people what you need to tell them. That's what you do, I know that. You must have needed to tell her."

"I didn't need to."

Caleb leaned forward, put his elbows on the table, and held his head in his hands. "Dead. 'My father is dead.' You said that?"

Max reached across and took one of his father's hands. He could feel the bones of the knuckles sharp against his palm. "There was no reason, Dad. But it's what I said. It's what I told her."

"We don't need to talk about this. This is not something we need to discuss further."

"I don't know why I said it. I do think you'd like her."

Caleb took his hand away. "I look forward to meeting her. 'I'd like you to meet my dead father. This is the dead dad I told you so much about. Go ahead. Shake his hand.'"

Max had more to say. He hadn't made his point yet. He wanted to talk about how he never would have spoken like that to Estelle if there hadn't been some truth to it. *For instance,* he could have said, *back in the elevator, you acted as if you were dead. Think about it. And, you know, I never saw Mom die, but I've been watching you die for years.*

Maybe he didn't need to get everything out in the open after all. Maybe he'd already said enough, or too much. A moment ago, his father had been proud. He didn't seem proud anymore.

"I'm sorry, Dad."

"Ha," he said. "It's okay. Don't worry about it."

Missy returned with their food. "You two need anything else?" she asked.

"Everything looks fine," said Caleb. "Would you like to know how my son picks up women?"

"Dad," Max said.

Missy, puzzled, glanced at Max. "I guess I wouldn't mind a little more insight into the male brain, but make it fast. I've got an order waiting."

"Dad. I didn't mean to."

Caleb set his napkin on his lap and took a sip of coffee. "I'll tell you some other time, honey. I probably shouldn't embarrass him."

"You guys and your secrets," Missy said, grinning. "So full of mystery."

20

ABE WATCHES HIS younger brother bend down and put his hands on the arms of the Viva Deluxe. "Come on," Caleb says. "This is what you wanted. Let's see you use it out in the world."

Though Abe hears the words, he also smells the diner on Caleb's breath—grilled cheese, he'd bet—and it's easy enough to feel perched on that stool by the counter, waiting to be served. Is the old stroke coming again, or is this a brand-new one, clouding through his mind, drawing him backward? It's difficult to know the difference, but either way he keeps remembering.

Now he's the same age as his jacket size, a perfect 44, and he's the one doing the urging, standing in his brother's place, in what used to be the living room. That room, like the whole house, is full of mourning, dark and hushed. Max is seven and Naomi has been dead for eight months. To start the new year, Abe has planned a one-week vacation to Florida. He's taking Max with him and he wants to take Caleb as well. Caleb sits on the couch while Abe paces in front of him, trying to close a deal at the last second. "Come with us, Caleb," he says. "It'll be good for you."

"I've made my decision."

"Out in the field, you wouldn't let a line like that stop you. What's your decision based on?"

"I already told you."

"Tell me again."

"I've got too much work to do. I'm too busy."

"It's New Year's. Nobody's doing any business. You and I both know you won't miss a thing. Every other office will be closed for the holidays. Might as well close ours, too."

"I'm not ready for a vacation. Maybe you can't understand that."

Abe has been hearing versions of this so-called reasoning for months. Since he's unmarried, since he moves from one woman to another, he's supposedly unable to fathom his brother's loss. Well, who can fully grasp another's loss? It's an impossible task, and yet Abe knew Naomi, loved her for who she was, and loved her even more for how she changed Caleb, how hopeful she made him, how she lifted him up. She wouldn't have wanted to see Caleb this way. She would have wanted Abe to do his best to help. So he keeps trying.

"I understand as much as I can," he says. "I understand this vacation's not only for you. It's also for Max. He needs to see you back out in the world. You both need to get away from this house for a while."

Caleb looks over his shoulder and says, "Shh."

As if he's heard his name, Max is shuffling into the room, leaning backward, carrying a suitcase that he holds with both hands, straining to keep it off the floor. Max has been unnaturally quiet since the death, but it's still amazing to Abe that this seven-year-old kid has managed to get something so heavy down the stairs without making a sound.

"You ready, Maxie?" Abe asks.

Max nods.

"I just want to talk with your father a little longer. Leave the bag there and we'll meet you outside, okay?"

Max sets the suitcase down. Then, before dashing toward the front door, he smiles and says, "Florida, here we come!"

When Abe hears the door close, he claps his hands once. "Come on, Caleb," he says. "It's not too late. I've got a ticket on hold for you. Go up and pack and let's get out of here."

Caleb doesn't move from the couch. He seems to sink deeper into the cushions. "I appreciate what you're doing," he says. "But the two of you go ahead."

"I can't watch you waste away like this. Naomi wouldn't—"

"Would you go already, please. You've made your pitch. You can't make me do this right now."

Abe can't hold himself back any longer. He steps up to the couch, reaches down, and pulls Caleb to his feet. Adrenaline shoots into his blood and he thinks he's about to slap his brother, but it's worse than that. His right hand is balled into a fist.

Caleb, staggering, somehow gets his hands onto Abe's shoulders and steadies himself. "Don't hit me, Abraham," he says, surprisingly calm. "That's not the answer. That won't help either of us. I just need more time."

Abe feels disgusted, with himself and with his brother. "We don't get more time," he says. "You know that by now. We only get less time." Then he shoves Caleb back down onto the couch. His hands are shaking when he grabs Max's suitcase, and he can't get out of the house fast enough. Still, even as he slams the door, he's hoping Caleb will rush after him, ask him to wait, shout, *I've changed my mind, we'll all go together.*

HERE'S WHAT HAPPENS instead: Abe walks to the car, wondering if it's safe to leave his brother behind, and he considers postponing the trip. He and Max could stay downtown in his condominium, take day trips, visit some museums, catch an Eagles game. It could be a Philadelphia vacation. Abe could go to Florida now or three months from now, there's no real difference. It wouldn't hurt him to wait.

Then he sees Max standing by the car. It's supposed to snow later in the week, but today the blue sky is clear and bright. Even in the dark, it would be easy to see how excited Max is. In the winter sunlight, it's unmistakable. He shimmers with eagerness. He can't wait to go.

In the car, Max seems to talk more than he has for months. He wants to remind Abe of all the sights they'll see in Florida. "It'll be so much better than Atlantic City," he says, and then he starts running through his list. They'll go to the beach and the ocean will be warm. They'll visit the Everglades and see birds he's only seen on TV, like flamingos and pelicans. They'll go fishing and who knows what they'll catch, and while they're out on the boat they might see dolphins and sharks and manatees, and when they go snorkeling it'll be like visiting another planet. Then, of course, there's Disney World, with the Matterhorn, the Haunted Mansion, and Captain Nemo's submarine, and as they walk from ride to ride, they'll meet their favorite cartoon characters, every one of them, smiling and alive.

Max pauses and Abe finally gets to speak. "Is that it?" he asks.

"And," Max says, "you never know who else we might get to see."

"Such as?"

"You never know," Max says.

Something in Max's voice makes Abe glance across at him. "Is there anyone you have in mind?" he asks.

An all-too-familiar quiet drops over Max. He turns from Abe and looks out the window. When he speaks again, he's almost whispering. "I've heard that sometimes a lot of people run away to Florida."

Abe is always in favor of dreaming, but there are limits. He needs to make everything clear before they go any farther, so he exits the expressway near the Ben Franklin Bridge and parks in front of a Mobil station. He rests his hand on top of his nephew's head, as if he's about to offer a blessing. "Look, Max," he says. "I don't know exactly what you're thinking, but your mother isn't waiting for you in Florida. You know this. She crashed her car and she died. Don't think you're going to see her. You'll never see her again. No one is ever going to see her again."

Max rubs his eyes with his palms. Then he stares down at his sneakers.

"I'm sorry," Abe says. "She shouldn't be dead, but she is, and none of us can change that. Do you understand?"

"Yes," says Max. "I understand."

21

MAX KNEW IT wouldn't take long to gas up the Buick, merge onto I-95, and start speeding back to Florida. Whenever he climbed into his car, he'd feel the temptation to head south, and then he'd run through his growing list of reasons for driving away. So far, he'd been the only one clobbered by trouble, but if he stayed longer there would be more trouble, he felt certain of that. Leaving would get him out from in between Johnny and Spiller. They'd have to deal with each other directly. And if Spiller truly wished to do something for Abe, he'd do it regardless of who was or wasn't in town. The guy hadn't needed any help getting the Viva Deluxe, so why would he need help with whatever was next? It would be trickier to leave Caleb behind again, but they were already beginning to grate on each other, and if he left now he might at least be able to leave on a good note. He could make a similar argument about Nathan, although there was this significant difference: even if he hung around, he wouldn't really get to see his son for weeks; then the summer would end and school would start and Nathan would be back to living with Sandy and Hiram.

Finally, there was Grier, restless and alone on Key Largo. Or maybe not so alone. They'd talked two days after that visit to Lonzinger and she was the one who'd cut the conversation short. She'd been raving about a new, young professor from the University of North Carolina who would be staying at the lab's house for a few months. He was an expert on *Thalassia*, otherwise known as turtle grass. "He's the first person down here who really understands my research," she'd said. "It's so good to have a faculty member I can connect with."

"You've connected with a faculty member?"

"Don't start, Max. You're not even here and who knows when you will be."

"Still, I'd like to hear more about this connection."

"Stop by sometime and I'll tell you the whole story. Right now, I've got to go."

All in all, it was a compelling list, but it obviously wasn't compelling enough. Max stayed in town. Following his father's example, for better or worse, he tried to be optimistic, even though he didn't think that would work. He was moving forward with Spiller, waiting to hear about the next step, and while he waited he thought he'd get in touch with Estelle. The bump on the back of his head was almost gone and the bruise on his temple was also disappearing, fading from deep violet to a faint reddish shadow. It looked like a small wayward smudge of lipstick, practically invisible.

The first time he called Estelle, no one answered and he didn't leave a message. The second time, no one answered and he left a short message, challenging her to another bowling rematch and telling her he had some news she might be happy to hear. Then another day went by, and when she still hadn't returned his call he drove over to Del Ennis. The place was crowded. Inside, he discovered that it was a seniors league night. The jukebox blared Sinatra, balls rumbled down the lanes, crashed into the pins, and the bowlers shouted to be heard. As the sounds washed over him, Max walked from lane 1 to lane 54 and back. No sign of Janet or Estelle—it had been a long shot—but there were a few open lanes, so he rolled two games, just to keep sharp. Janet would have trounced him.

Right after he dropped off his shoes, someone called his name. He didn't think Johnny or Dexter would bother him with so many people around, but he jumped anyhow. When he glanced back, he saw Harrison Phelps waving from lane 4. Max went over to say hello and noticed that Harrison looked much better than he'd looked at Nathan's reception. He was sporting a satiny red bowling shirt with a picture of a Siberian husky sewn over his heart.

"When are you coming by?" Harrison asked. "We've got some dogs to visit."

"Soon, I hope. I had a brief reunion with Natascha the other day. Her loyalty was elsewhere, but she looked fine. How's your team doing?"

Harrison laughed. "We're the Curtis Estates High-Rollers," he said. "We're old, but we're out in front. Still another game left, though. You want to have a drink and cheer us on for a while?"

Max took a rain check, wished him no open frames, and left through the side door. He thought he'd just go back out front to his car, but it was a nice night; he was in no rush to return to the basement, and a little exercise seemed like a good idea. He looked around until he felt safe; then he stopped worrying and started walking. At first, he didn't know where he was going, but he knew a few places he'd avoid. For instance, he didn't want to do anything foolish, like pass by Estelle's building, so he made sure to head off in the opposite direction. He also had no desire to put himself through another visit to his ex-house.

He cut across Fox Chase Road and passed through a southern California–style development from the fifties, complete with faux-adobe bungalows and streets named after Pasadena, Los Angeles, and San Diego. Then he turned onto Cedar Road and found himself facing, on the right, a small farm and, on the left, a cemetery. The combination made some sense — the ripe smell of manure probably didn't bother the quiet sleepers across the street. Max steered clear of the graveyard; he didn't need to find more ghosts in these neighborhoods. When he crossed Township Line Road, he was back among houses, and as the houses became more grand he realized where he was going.

He knew that the Sklarman family no longer lived near Cedar Road, but he still began to feel like a spy. The houses for the next few blocks were large, dramatic mansions, set far back from the road, veiled by well-trimmed trees. They had U-shaped driveways and column-lined entrances. Max figured each one of these places could hold at least four of his ex-houses or maybe a dozen of his father's apartments.

As he approached the old Sklarman house, Max remembered meeting Johnny in economics class. Max had managed to do well on the first test, and even though that turned out to be a fluke, Johnny was impressed and seemed to identify Max as a potential resource. Around midterms, Johnny planned a party. While his parents were snorkeling in Belize, he invited a bunch of people, including Max, to his family's place. Johnny drove a new silver Camaro back then, so Max had guessed that the Sklarmans had money, but he was unprepared for the rolling lawn, the brightly lit tennis court and swimming pool, not to mention the home itself, the size of a small department store.

The grandeur of the house didn't raise the level of the guests' behavior that night. They wound up staging a simple fraternity party in an upscale setting. Beneath the high ceilings, they danced to the Talking Heads. In the sleek, modern kitchen, a different crowd snorted cocaine off the marble countertops. Eventually, a group of girls stripped down to their underwear to swim in the heated pool. And then, an hour or two before the party broke up, Max was standing in the ornate dining room, fooling around with a sophomore physics major named Brenda. Together, the two of them admired the gleaming mahogany table, but they didn't go that far.

After that night, Max didn't see Brenda again, and in the end there was nothing particularly memorable about the party itself, nothing really remarkable about the college kids and their predictable actions. What Max would remember, as time went on, was the house—how it had awed him. To his mind, the most startling piece of the house was the elevator. He heard later that it wasn't something anyone in the family needed. This shouldn't have been surprising. The machine didn't look like it had been designed for the injured or handicapped. Instead, it looked extravagant, glamorous, a polished brass chamber like a gilded cage that could rise slowly up to the second and third floors. Max didn't spend much time with his host that night—they hardly even spoke with each other—but he did see Johnny riding that elevator, ascending every now and then with one of the smiling, waving girls. Johnny would stand by the lever and the red and green buttons. He stared straight ahead, bored and, it seemed, slightly displeased by the girls' excitement.

Spy or not, Max wasn't going to get too close to the house on this occasion. He'd heard various versions of how, years ago, it had become the Sklarmans' ex-house—bankruptcy, fraud, divorce, gambling debts—but he didn't know who was living there now. Didn't even know if they'd kept the elevator. Someone had bought a few new cars, though—parked by the garage were an Infiniti, a Porsche, and a Jaguar—and they'd installed brighter lighting, not just for the tennis court and the pool but for the whole grounds. They'd also added security fencing, which seemed a bit overboard for the suburbs.

Standing there in front of all that wealth, Max felt the desire for revenge. It didn't make sense—he knew the Sklarmans were gone and none of this property belonged to them—and yet he wanted to damage something, to strike back in answer to the beating he'd received. He shook his head at such stupid, late-night thinking. Then he turned away, ready to begin the walk back to his car. Before he left, however, he did what was, perhaps, becoming a bad habit. He stepped close to a nearby pine tree and took a piss.

When he finally got back to Del Ennis, it was well after midnight and his car was alone in the parking lot. Only when he was right beside the Buick did he notice that the driver's side window had been smashed in. He opened the door carefully and found a Penn tennis ball on his front seat, a bright green message left atop the tiny pieces of glass. He imagined Johnny or Dexter or some other thug watching him go in to bowl and then waiting for him to come out. Whoever it was must have grown impatient. Good thing he'd left through that side door. He owed Harrison Phelps a favor.

MAX DIDN'T WANT to add more worry to his father's life, so he woke up early, kept silent about the broken window, and took the car to be fixed. He planned to track down Spiller as soon as the repairs were done, but while he was waiting at the garage Spiller called and told him to come visit the scout office. "Coat and tie, Max," he added. "You'll be meeting someone."

It was almost ten thirty by the time he walked into Beth Israel. He'd hoped to see Nathan at the temple campsite, but the place was deserted and, once again, he made his way quietly down to the basement. Though Spiller was in the same office, still surrounded by CutCorp crates, he wasn't dressed for scouting this morning. He was wearing a sharp black double-breasted suit, his polished wingtips, and a wide, bright tie. The tie featured rows of small yellow circles that dropped down from his neck like shiny coins. He was typing away on an ultrathin laptop when Max knocked on the open door.

"Sorry the boys aren't here," Spiller said, after briefly looking up from the screen. "They're out doing community service, but you'll be happy to hear that Nathan's adjusting quite well. He's already met almost every requirement for Tenderfoot and he should easily reach Second Class by the fall. Here's something to keep you busy while I finish up with this crap."

Spiller handed across a postcard and a photograph. Max looked at the photo first. It was an evening campfire shot and, thankfully, on this night the flames seemed to be under control. The three scouts pictured were in summer uniform. They were sitting side by side, s'mores in their hands, their faces almost touching. They were enjoying themselves, and somehow they didn't look silly in their outfits. Nathan was the boy in the middle and the sight of him there came as an incredible relief to Max.

The postcard was a prestamped, unlined three-by-five card.

Not much room for writing, especially in Nathan's big scrawl. *Dear Dad—OK, it's better than I expected. There have been some interesting developments, but I still miss baseball, and I still want to visit you in Florida. Love, your son, Nathan.*

Max shuffled the card and the photo in his hands, glancing from one to the other. It felt like the best news in ages.

"It's such a pleasure to see the face of a happy father," Spiller said, shutting down his laptop and getting up to close the door. "Believe it or not, I happen to have more good news."

Max kept studying the photo. "I thought he'd wind up having fun, but I figured it would take longer."

Spiller returned to his seat behind the desk. "Many things happen more quickly than we expect," he said. "There's a person upstairs I need to introduce you to, but we should go over a few details first. Now, when Abe and I first discussed this business venture, his goal was to clear enough money for him and Caleb to move into a retirement community—a real, local one, not a fake like your Oceanview Gardens. That should be possible and I want you to know your family's cut before we go any further, so there won't be any misunderstandings. You'll get a three-year pay-out, two hundred thousand the first year and one hundred thousand for the second and third years. After that, you'll get only token amounts, to keep things looking kosher."

Max didn't know how to respond to such numbers. He was suspicious and shocked at the same time. No wonder Johnny was working hard to weasel his way in. "Well," Max said, "that definitely qualifies as good news."

"The first payment should get Caleb and Abe into the community of their choice. The second two payments should keep them comfortable, and there should be a solid percentage left for you. It will certainly be more than you would have made on the

Goulds. I was impressed, by the way, with how promptly you closed that down."

"It wasn't easy. They didn't want to be closed down. But here's a piece of not-so-good news. Someone bashed in my car window last night and left me a tennis ball as a message. Are you sure Johnny won't be a problem?"

"Not to us. I've got that chucklehead covered. Now, let's talk to the man who's waiting upstairs."

Max remembered Caleb telling him about Y. Y. and Ping. Was he about to meet another one of the Chinese connections? As they walked from the office to the stairs, Max followed up on something else Caleb had mentioned. "You and Abe must have been awfully close. My father said it had to do with open-heart surgery."

"That's one way I can explain it. You can also think of it like this. One morning you wake up to discover that you're falling from a great height, tumbling down toward the earth. You haven't got a prayer. The wind roars in your ears and your eyes fill with water. There are only seconds remaining. Suddenly, a man appears beside you, you're not alone, you're falling together, and there's some small comfort simply in that, but then this man wraps his arms around you, and you notice a cord with a handle on his chest, and he pulls that cord, and the parachute shoots out above his head, bursting like a thunderclap into the roaring wind. You're carried back up into the sky, you rise and rise, and when at last you begin to fall earthward again, you're drifting down slowly, you can enjoy the view, the world is spread out below you, and you know it will be easy to land."

Though Max couldn't imagine his uncle as a skydiver, it wasn't hard to imagine Spiller and Abe thoroughly enjoying each other's company. They both knew how to talk, that was for sure. That fact alone didn't make it easier to have faith in Spiller, but put it alongside the photograph, the Viva Deluxe, and those outrageous numbers, and the lingering doubts faded further away.

Max found himself wondering just how close Abe and Spiller had been. A story about open-heart surgery followed by a story of one man wrapping his arms around another? Max shook his head as they stepped into the lobby. "It's amazing how little I know about you," he said.

Spiller stopped in front of the rabbi's office and lowered his voice. "You know even less about the man we're about to meet. Fortunately, all you have to do in here is listen and be polite. I'll tell you when it's time for you to leave, and then I'll be in touch later. Okay?"

Max nodded and Spiller opened the door. A very white man, in khakis and a blue, short-sleeved oxford, stood up from one of the chairs in front of the desk. He had the body of an ex-line-backer and the face of a baby. The hand he offered Max was as large as a substantial animal—a possum, maybe.

"Clive Powell," the man said, with a serious drawl. "No relation."

Max was glad to get his hand back unharmed. "To whom?" he asked.

"To the founder, you know, old Lord Robert S. S. Baden-Powell. I do wish I could claim a connection."

"Well," Spiller said, taking the rabbi's chair, "you certainly have his love of scouting."

"I can't accept a comparison like that," Powell said, sitting back down. He kept his attention on Max as he spoke. "Old B.-P. was a saint, but I *do* love scouting and I *am* glad to see this troop of Jews. It warms my heart. I'm all for internationalizing.

Globalize the scout code; it's what this country needs. The whole world would be a better place. Mervyn and I are in full agreement about that, and we're not alone, even if it looks different in the media. I mean, that debacle with the gays! What a mess! Let me ask you something, Max. Out in the wilderness, do you think any of the animals tell a full-grown, swooping eagle who to sleep with?"

It took a moment for Max to realize that Powell was waiting for him to answer. "No," he said.

"You better believe they don't. Why? Because it would be a stupid thing to do, that's why. But try explaining that to those bean counters I have to work with. They spend their lives in their corporate bunkers in the middle of Texas striving to keep the Mormons happy. B.-P. went out like Washington and Ike, you know. He left his warning behind, clear as a clarion call. You remember what he said?"

Max answered faster this time. "No," he said again. He glanced over at Spiller, who was smiling, leaning back in his chair.

"This is a quote, from just before old B.-P. passed away: 'Don't let Scouting become a salaried organization: keep it a voluntary movement of patriotic service.' Now, last time I checked, we had well over five thousand paid employees, and we're still hiring." When Powell made his hands into fists, they looked like sledgehammers. He took a breath, relaxed, and went on. "You can see it's a mistake to get me started about this. Were you a scout?"

"No."

"And yet your son is gung-ho. Mervyn told me all about him. It's stupendous. It shows the power of the vision. It's one thing that hasn't changed. I'll tell you a secret. Ever since I was a Tenderfoot, I've known that the best, most real scouting is covert scouting."

Spiller cleared his throat and tapped his watch. "I wish we had more time. Still, I'm glad this meeting finally happened. Abe's stroke was tragic, but you can see that we'll be in good hands with Max. He and his father are doing an excellent job of caring for the family business."

Powell stood up and gave Max the three-fingered salute. "I'm grateful for the support of your firm and for your long tradition of service. I'll look forward to seeing you over in Ephrata soon."

Max didn't know how a nonscout was supposed to reply to a formal scout salute, so he stood and kept it simple, as polite as possible. "Thank you," he said. "It's an honor and a pleasure to work with you." Then he nodded, waved, and walked out the door.

As HE DROVE back to the apartment, Max decided that Powell, in his odd way, explained a lot. That big-handed man must be the contact inside the national organization, and to get anywhere with him, Spiller would have to be a scoutmaster, and anyone involved would have to be connected to scouting, which is why Abe and then Caleb had urged Nathan into the troop. Max himself was clearly the younger face of Wolinsky Brothers and Associates, proof that the deal wouldn't be handled by a pair of all-too-fragile older men. Still, there were questions. If he was indeed that younger face, would he have to move back to Philly? What exactly would he have to do in Ephrata? Was the money for real? Which led, of course, to the never-ending question: how far could he trust Spiller?

Max's cell phone rang, but he could see it wouldn't be offering any answers. The Goulds were calling again.

"I hope I'm not bothering you," Gail said. "But we've been

doing some thinking and we've been talking with a few people we know."

Max tried not to assume the worst. He realized it might be time to get a new phone number. "No bother at all," he said. "What can I do for you?"

"David told me about how you weren't seeking any new investors. He said it sounded as if you were giving up. So I started thinking, What would happen if we found some new investors for you? Several friends are already interested, but I don't know what to tell them. I don't know how much you'd need to become—what do you call it?—recapitalized."

Max couldn't believe he'd thought the Goulds were good for only twenty-five grand. He considered starting a bidding war. There's four hundred thousand on the table, do I hear five? Tempting, but he was going to keep his word. "It's a nice thought, Gail," he said, "and I appreciate it. I know you must be disappointed. Believe me, if there were any hope, I might take you up on your offer, but I'm afraid it's one of those things that simply isn't going to happen. At this point, I think your best bet is to look around some more. I'm sure you and David will find a place that's better than Oceanview Gardens could ever have been."

Gail didn't say anything for a moment, as if she were waiting for him to mention one last possibility. "Are you absolutely sure?" she asked.

"I'm sorry, Gail. If I hear of any other new communities, I'll let you know right away. In the meantime, please give my best to David."

Max ended the call there, wishing his father and Spiller could have heard how much he'd just turned down.

. . .

THE NEXT TIME his phone rang, much later in the day, he heard a voice he'd been missing. "My mother told me to call," Estelle said. "She believes I should at least find out what your good news is. So, what is it?"

"I'd love to share it with you, but it's not something I can discuss on the phone."

"Really?"

"I could probably tell you about it over dinner."

Max felt guilty when he bought a bunch of tulips on his way to Estelle's apartment, but then he remembered that new professor's connection with Grier. Maybe that whole relationship would prove to be another example of Spiller's vision: maybe Grier was too young for him.

What would Spiller say about the fact that Estelle herself looked very young when she saw the flowers? At first she was trying to act tough, but she blushed as she took the tulips in her hands and held them close to her face. Max liked how wide her eyes opened, how happy she seemed in the kitchen, trimming the stems and then searching for the right vase. It reminded him of how he'd felt when he'd seen that photograph of Nathan. Not the same feeling, of course, but somewhere in the ballpark— there was relief and a sense that things might be working out for the best.

After carefully arranging the tulips in the rectangular glass vase she'd chosen, Estelle opened her liquor cabinet. "Do you need food before you tell me the good news, or will drinks be enough?"

"Let me take a look," Max said. He stepped closer to the cabinet, and to her. Then he pulled out a bottle of Maker's Mark. "This should be all right."

She poured the bourbon into two tumblers. He added a cube

of ice to his, carried it into the living room, and sat on the couch. She brought the flowers in with her and set them on the coffee table right in front of him. Then she sat down on the other side of the table, in her rocking chair.

"Okay," she said, "let's hear the news we're drinking to."

"Those nice people in their nice house are going to be fine. I called off everything I'd arranged."

She reached her tumbler across the table and touched it against his. "Cheers," she said. "But why?"

In the kitchen, her eyes had been the green he remembered, but something about the light in the living room made them look almost blue. Whatever color they were, those eyes were watching him, waiting for his answer. The bourbon warmed his chest and made him shiver. "It just felt like the right thing," he said.

"Good for you, Max. And good for them, too, I guess."

"There's more."

"More good news?"

"I think so, in a way. I told my father what I told you about him."

She sipped the bourbon and did a shiver of her own. "About his being dead, you mean?"

Max nodded.

"That couldn't have made him happy."

"He's not happy that often, but you're right. Anyhow, I did it because I'm hoping you'll get to meet him and I figured I'd try to make it less awkward if possible."

"Still optimistic, aren't you?"

"Maybe," he said, "but let's hear about yours."

"Hear about my what?"

"Your good news. I'm hoping you have some for me."

Estelle smiled. "Well," she said, "I quit smoking."

"Congratulations," Max said, remembering how she'd looked with her ashtray balanced on her belly. "How does that affect your before and after?"

Estelle finished her drink and changed the subject. "I wouldn't mind another splash," she said, "but I shouldn't drink too much of this stuff on an empty stomach."

When she stood up, Max wondered if it was time to go out for dinner. He'd been thinking about a new Italian place in Jenkintown. A small table for two. Candlelight. A bottle of chianti. But she didn't seem to expect him to get up. Instead, she went back to the kitchen, rummaged around in the refrigerator, and returned with the Maker's Mark as well as a plate of cheese and crackers. After she set the bottle and the plate on the coffee table, she stayed standing and adjusted the flowers in the vase. She blushed again, just slightly, and Max thought she was making a decision. "They're beautiful," she said. Then she sat down next to him.

IT WASN'T LONG before hand in hand they hurried into the bedroom, where they quickly stripped off each other's clothes. "It's hot in here," Estelle said. She turned on a fan, opened a window, and tossed the comforter on a chair.

When Max followed her onto the bed, she laughed. "I don't know if this is such a brilliant idea," she said. "You're lucky my mother likes you."

"I like her, too, especially if she convinced you to call me back."

"And you're sure you're not going to rob me?"

"There are a lot of things I want to do to you, but robbing isn't on my list."

She rolled onto her side and ran a hand down his chest to his stomach. "Do you want to start with another story? You could tell me a real one tonight, about your father, or your son."

Max pushed her onto her back. "I talked enough already. It's your turn to tell me something."

"What do you want to hear about?"

"Your mother, your dreams, your last relationship. Whatever you choose."

"What will you do while I talk?"

"Don't worry about that. You gave me some inspiration last time."

He followed her example, working his way down. He lingered on her breasts. He wasn't going to compare, but her skin was softer than Grier's. Hadn't spent so much time in the sun.

"I can see how this might be difficult," she said.

Max thought smoking was bad for the skin, but maybe she'd never smoked that much. Or maybe quitting had an instantaneous effect. She smelled more like the tulips than a cigarette. "You're not talking," he said.

"Mother, dreams, relationship," she said. "My mother continues to surprise me. I hope I can be as strong as she is. That's a dream. And about relationships, I don't think I've had any lately. I've been having affairs. Or lovers, but they haven't really felt like lovers. A handful of older married men."

"Now who's the devious one?" Max asked.

"Shh," she said. "That's nice, what you were doing."

"Tell me more."

"All right," she said. "Okay. The last guy was actually a younger married man. A lawyer at the office where I work, on his way up. He had two daughters, liked to bring them by, told me he wanted me to get to know them. They were cute enough, four and seven. I took them to lunch a few times when he was busy. I fussed over them. I wondered what it would be like to be their mother. I admit it. The guy would pull in piles of money, and in my mind I pictured the house, the cars, traveling out of this city, a kid or two that would really be mine. Something lasting, permanent. Not like your Jersey guy, though. Nothing concrete."

"Do you like slower or faster?"

"A little slower."

"What else?"

"That's good."

"What else?"

"Well, he started talking about moving to the southwest, smack in the middle of a desert. Albuquerque or Phoenix. Suddenly it stopped feeling right to me. What kind of person wants to live in a desert? I kept seeing cactuses and sand. I looked at him and I felt parched."

"Not like now."

"No."

"Then what happened?"

"I can tell you later."

"Tell me now, please."

"I started feeling like a bad person for days at a time instead of just every now and then. He never asked me where I thought we should go. And I couldn't tell what he cared about. I found myself tempted to hurt his daughters—to tell them things, you know. I had no desire to be like that. I decided it really wasn't what I wanted."

"Hmm," Max said, reaching beneath her to lift her closer to him. "Why don't you tell me what you want?"

"I want you to keep doing what you're doing."

"Okay."

"But there's something else I want you to do, too."

MAX HOPED HE would sleep peacefully in her bed this time, but he was awake at two in the morning, and he was hungry. He wandered to the bathroom and then he went out into the living room and ate more of the cheese and crackers. The blossoms of the tulips seemed to have opened wider. Looking at them made him thirsty.

He carried a glass of water back to bed. He'd been worried that he'd have some sort of dream about Grier, but as he stretched out alongside Estelle again he found himself picturing Sandy and Hiram, frolicking on a Hawaiian island. He stared up at the ceiling and tried to think about what he and Estelle might do in the morning. He wanted to drown out Sandy's voice, but after sailing across the Pacific and sweeping across the entire continent, that voice had momentum behind it.

It drew him back to the night he'd brought his cab home for the first time. It was well after dinner, close to nine, and Sandy was standing at the door, watching and waiting. "What is that?" she asked, even though, as was often the case, she knew the answer.

"It's temporary," he said. "I'm using it to make a few connections."

"It's a taxicab, isn't it?"

"I pick people up downtown. I drive them around and talk to them, and when I've got them interested I slip them my card and tell them more about the wholesale appliances currently in stock."

She sat on the stoop and leaned forward, elbows on her knees, chin in her hands. "So you're driving this cab around downtown, picking up stranger after stranger?"

Max was standing in front of her. "It's part of something

else," he said. "I won't need the cab for long. It's a way to spread the word and earn some extra money while I develop this new thing."

"Do you know how this sounds, Max?"

"No, but you're going to tell me."

"It sounds worse than the vacuum cleaners. Worse than the siding. And it's definitely worse than the telescopes."

Max sat beside her and rubbed her back with his open hand. The front yard needed attention, but he was bringing in a gardener to look it over. He still believed everything would work out. He was supporting a wife and a son, keeping up with his house payments. He didn't see any major problems looming. If this venture didn't fly, he had other ideas. Most days, he was confident.

"I liked the telescopes," Sandy said, gazing up for a moment at the overcast spring sky. "I would have bought one of those. I liked looking up at the moon and the stars."

"I thought they were good, too, but people didn't go for them."

She reached across and took his free hand in hers. She spread it open, massaged each one of his fingers, and then pressed her thumbs into his palm. It wasn't something she'd done before and it felt nice. "I don't know," she said. "Sometimes I'm surprised you ever proposed to me."

"Why would you be surprised about that?"

She pressed down harder, answered his question with a question. "You'll always believe that something's going to be taken away from you, won't you?"

Max could see where she was going. He'd heard it before. Sandy resorted to psychology whenever she wanted to tell him he was afraid. He had to have a bunch of things running all the time because he didn't want to be vulnerable. In other words, he'd lost his mother, so he had to make sure he wasn't ever in a position to lose everything again. This was her familiar logic. He didn't remember her ever mentioning the proposal before, though. "But I did propose to you," he said.

"I must have bullied you into it."

"That's not true," he said. "I didn't need to be bullied. You're confusing me with my sad father. He could use some bullying these days."

She balled her hand into a fist and twisted it back and forth in his palm. "I wasn't thinking of him," she said. "Besides, your father's not sad, he's depressed. It's clinical. And maybe you're not far behind."

Her knuckles were starting to hurt the base of his thumb, so he took his hand away. Then he stood up. "Come on," he said. "It's not that bad."

She didn't move from her step. She was staring at the cab. "I don't know," she said. "Maybe you and I don't see the same things anymore. Or maybe you don't want as much as I do."

Max opened the screen door. He wasn't trying to cut off the conversation, but he was tired and he was ready to be in the house. They could talk more over a drink, or in bed. "Come on inside," he said.

"You go ahead," she said. "I'll look at your yellow taxi a little longer."

In the weeks and months that followed that night, Max often blamed himself for not staying outside on the stoop with her. He could have parked the cab around the corner, out of sight, where it wouldn't have bothered her, and if it had still bothered her he could have promised to get rid of it in the morning. They could have talked for hours about how much more they both wanted from life. They could have been specific, listing all that she wanted and all that he wanted. Together, they could have planned a way to get everything.

But, instead, Max was lying next to a woman he'd met at a bowling alley and his ex-wife's voice wouldn't stop blowing in from Hawaii, whispering in his ear.

"Tell me what I need to know," she'd said at the bar mitzvah, taunting him.

He closed his eyes as tightly as he could. He told himself that when he slept, he'd be able to push her voice away. In his dreams, his own voice could overpower hers and then it would travel far, covering five thousand miles in a heartbeat. It would be louder than a whisper, more than strong enough to get Sandy's attention out on her island paradise. *Here's what you need to know,* he'd begin. *You made a mistake. You were wrong about me.*

Still awake, he shook his head. *No,* he thought, *I'll dream bigger than that.*

The last thing he remembered, before he finally slipped off to sleep, was the feel of a cool breeze coming in through the open window. He stood up to get the comforter from the chair. Then he covered Estelle and climbed back in beside her.

22

AS THE TREK wore on, Nathan settled into Troop 158's unconventional summer schedule. The mornings were for selling. They showered in the temple's basement and ate an early oatmeal breakfast. Then they put on their uniforms, split up into Cobras and Owls, and went out to various locations prearranged by Spiller. They were stationed at shopping malls, flea markets, parks, cafeterias, and retirement communities. At twelve-thirty, they were driven back to the temple for lunch and a pep talk. Afternoons were for local hikes, museums, historic sites, and the more traditional scouting lessons, with fire and ax, first aid, rope, compasses, and maps. Then there was dinner to cook, eat, and clean up, followed by a campfire meeting and taps.

The kosherness made their backpacks heavier on the weekends, when they ventured out on trips to Valley Forge, Gettysburg, and the Pine Barrens. Those weekends started with a rush because they traveled on Fridays and they were strict about the

Sabbath, so camp had to be completely set up before sundown. From sundown to sundown there could be no cooking, no working at all. You were permitted to keep a fire going, but you couldn't start a new one if yours went out.

Rabbi Weinberg often appeared just before sunset on those Friday nights. "Nothing like Sabbath in the wilderness," he'd say, and then he'd lead a service after an early dinner. He kept the ceremonies brief. The longest prayer he read was always for the woman of valor, whose price was far above rubies. *Strength and dignity are her clothing, and she laugheth at the time to come.* Nathan paid attention; he liked hearing about her, how fully she cared for her husband, herself, and her household. *She looketh well to the ways of her household, and eateth not the bread of idleness. Her children rise up and call her blessed, her husband, also, and he praiseth her.* The other scouts were less interested, and most of them couldn't keep straight faces when the rabbi recited the lines about how the woman of valor *worketh willingly with her hands,* how *she layeth her hands to the distaff,* how *she openeth her mouth with wisdom, and the law of kindness is on her tongue.*

Rabbi Weinberg let their snickering pass, but he was not always so easygoing. One night, back at the temple, when he learned from Spiller that the Owls had accidentally cooked spaghetti and meatballs in the dairy pots, he was livid. The Cobras were spared the tirade, but Nathan heard the rabbi shout about uncleanliness. The Owls had to bury their dishes and utensils overnight, and then they had to fast for twenty-four hours to purify themselves.

Nathan wasn't the best salesman of the group—that was Ricky—but he wasn't the worst, either. He'd made an advancement plan and he was staying with it. He liked the rest of the patrol, and he even managed to organize a few stickball games between the Cobras and the Owls. One way or another, he was busy from dawn until well past dusk. His mother and Hiram were gone from his days, and for a while at least they were almost completely gone from his thoughts.

His father crossed his mind more often, especially when he was selling. He tried to get trust by not seeking it, but that was tricky, and he did better when he decided that he could sell some knives or not, it didn't really matter one way or the other.

What really mattered, it turned out, were the parties that started to fill his summer. During those early trek weeks, he attended parties in backyards and basements, swimming parties, a roller-skating party, a party at a miniature golf course, and a party at Vic's Famous Roast Beef Restaurant, just to name a few.

However, it was the very first party—the one for Sharon Kutnack—that made his summer suddenly seem like it might have potential after all.

NATHAN HAD NEVER been to see a lacrosse game, but he knew Sharon was the captain of the team and the leading scorer. He'd seen her run a few times during phys ed and she looked strong and fast, like a real athlete. So it made sense that she'd want to do something athletic on the day she was turning fifteen. Still, Nathan was surprised when he found out she'd chosen to have a bowling party.

In the back of the van, driven over by one of Ricky's friends, Nathan had felt nervous. He was sitting next to Felix, hoping they weren't heading for trouble. No matter how nice Ricky had seemed lately, Nathan didn't think it would be wise to trust him. "You've done this before?" he asked Felix.

"Sure."

"Does Spiller know?"

"I think so. Ricky says that as long as we're back by midnight, and as long as everyone works well during the days, it's all right. If we don't make our quotas, then it will probably change."

"What about the rabbi?"

"Don't worry about it," Felix said. "Hey, do you know Cindy?" Nathan shook his head.

"She plays clarinet in the band. I really like her. She's friends with Jennifer and they'll both be there tonight." Felix paused for a moment, then pushed his glasses up and leaned in closer, whispering. "I can tell you something else, too."

"What?"

"Cindy said Jennifer smiled when she heard you were coming."

All at once, Nathan felt a different kind of nervousness, but he tried not to let it show. He was glad he had his lighter with him, just in case. "Was it a big smile?" he asked.

The party was already well under way by the time they pulled up at Del Ennis. Inside, there were about twenty-five people gathered near the first six lanes. It seemed like an odd place to celebrate, but someone had done a good job of making those lanes look festive. Bright HAPPY BIRTHDAY! banners hung down from the ceiling, the scorer's tables were decorated with enlarged photos of a smiling Sharon, and behind the chairs there was a large dessert buffet with a colorful spread of cake, cookies, and pie.

The contrast between those lanes and the rest of the alley was severe. A handful of bowlers were quietly practicing. There were groups of two or three but no other parties. Those distant lanes looked darker, and the people out there looked small and lonely. But Nathan didn't have time to think about them too much because as soon as he picked up his shoes, he noticed that Rich was sitting at one of the scorer's tables. Nathan rushed over and sat beside his friend.

"It's scout-man," said Rich. "They let you out of your tents at night?"

"I guess so," Nathan said. "How's Team Sunoco starting off?"

"You're not missing anything at all."

"What do you mean?"

Rich kept an eye on the bowlers in front of him, marking the scores down on the sheet as he talked. "I mean," he said, "our coach is an asshole. He wants us to understand that baseball is not a game. He insists that it's a science. 'There's no room for fun in baseball'— that's an actual quote. I'm thinking of switching over to bowling camp."

"You're lucky, trust me. Where's Jeff and Eric?"

"Speaking of lucky," said Rich. "You didn't see them on your way in?"

"No."

"Jeff was chasing after Sally again. Looked like they were holding hands. And Eric walked out there with Donna Rheinheimer."

"Out where?"

"A bunch of people have been wandering outside. Spinning the bottle or whatever, where Mr. Kutnack can't see."

"Where's Mr. Kutnack?"

Rich pointed over to the small bar by the cashier. A man sat alone on a stool, shoulders hunched, sipping a beer.

"You want to take this turn for me?" Rich asked. "It can be your practice. Maybe the four of us can bowl a game later, if those guys come back inside. You can tell us campfire stories."

"This is the first story," Nathan said. "Troop 158 gets to party at night." He felt as if he hadn't been with any of his friends for so long, even though it had only been a few days. No matter how much time had passed, it felt great to be back. He found a ball that fit and then tightened his shoelaces. For a moment, he thought of his father. They bowled together every now and then. His father always crouched low on his way to the line, as if he were somehow sneaking up on the pins. Nathan tried to do it like that, creeping forward. He rolled the ball too far right but still knocked down seven.

He looked around to see if Jennifer was anywhere nearby, wondering if she'd noticed his arrival, but he didn't see her. Instead, he saw Felix, who waved and called his way, "Nathan, come over here for a second. Somebody wants to talk to you."

"Let me clean this up," he said. It wouldn't be a tough spare. He concentrated on it, reached out for the pins, like his father had taught him to do. He hit it perfectly, then gave Rich a high-five and said, "I'll be right back."

Rich smiled. "That's what Jeff and Eric said."

JENNIFER WAS WAITING by the front entrance, standing beneath a wall of bronze plaques that commemorated some of the high scores rolled at Del Ennis. Nathan wondered what she was doing for the summer. He had no idea, which made him realize that he'd hardly ever spoken to her. The last time they'd talked was when he'd asked her if she was coming to his bar mitzvah and she'd said yes and then never appeared. She was a tennis player, and maybe she'd been doing that at a camp. She was tan, and he thought her right shoulder looked stronger than her left from so much serving.

"Hi, Nathan," she said, "I'm sorry I missed your bar mitzvah."

Nathan shrugged, not wanting to give away too much by saying he was sorry, too.

"I heard you did a good job," she said.

"I don't know."

It was her turn to shrug her shoulders. "That's what I heard," she said. "I'm not much of a bowler. You want to take a walk?"

"I was just about to ask you the same thing."

Outside, a group from the party had gathered near the van. Nathan turned to go in the opposite direction, toward Logan's Garden Center, which was just past Murray's Market and Don's Hair Salon. They walked quietly across the empty parking lot. Jennifer had excellent posture, and there was a determined look on her face. Nathan kept glancing over at her to make sure she was really there. This whole evening seemed too good to be true. Not that long ago, he'd been abandoned at the temple, and an awful summer was all that awaited him. He never would have guessed that by the end of the night he'd be walking in the dark with Jennifer.

There were a few pieces of wrought-iron patio furniture out on display in front of Logan's and that's where they sat down. With one hand, Nathan traced the floral pattern in the small round table that separated him from her. His other hand fiddled with the lighter in his pocket. "Are you going to smoke?" he asked.

"No," she said. "I've given it up. I don't want to stunt my growth. You don't smoke, do you?"

"No."

"Good," Jennifer said, sitting up straighter in her chair. "Now," she went on, "I hear you have a crush on me. Is that true?"

Nathan could feel himself blushing. He hadn't expected such direct questioning. "I won't lie to you," he managed to say. "It's the truth."

"That's what I thought, but I can't figure out why. You don't even know me. I guess that's how crushes work, but I'd still like you to explain it to me."

He didn't want to sound mushy or stupid, and yet he felt like talking about the sweet, clear sound of her voice. How he liked hearing it coming right at him. It had always been heading somewhere else before. He also wanted to say something about how he liked looking at her, face to face. The closeness of it. How it made him feel older, in a good way. "Well," he began, but she cut him off.

"Not right now," she said. "You probably need to think about it. I've been thinking about it ever since Cindy told me. I can remember you asking me to your bar mitzvah and I think I can remember you saying something that made me laugh in English class a few months ago, but I don't know what it was and I can't remember anything else. I don't see how that adds up to a crush."

He thought of his mother and father and then the appearance of Hiram. "Maybe crushes aren't logical," he said.

"They definitely aren't," she said. "I mean, why should I start thinking about you just because my friends tell me you're thinking about me? That's not logical, but here we are."

"Yup," Nathan said, "here we are." He looked briefly at her, then looked out over the parking lot. He noticed the straight white lines drawn for all the absent cars. There was nothing hopeful about asphalt and so many empty spots, but he was thinking about how much room there was. Earlier in the day, the place was probably packed. Now there was space for anything.

Jennifer stood up quickly. "Before this gets more awkward than it already is," she said, "I want you to know that I'm not going to let you kiss me tonight."

He hadn't really thought that was a possibility. Maybe he was a fool, but he'd been wondering if he might get to hold her hand.

Now he wondered if he'd somehow made a mistake. If he'd said the right thing, if he'd had his reasons ready, maybe they'd be kissing at this very moment. Once again, he didn't know what to say next. "Okay," was what came out.

"But there's another thing I want to tell you," she said. "I said I was sorry for missing your bar mitzvah and I meant it, so I have a present for you. Close your eyes, put your hands at your sides, and I'll give it to you."

He wasn't going to argue with her. He didn't want to argue with her ever. "Okay," he repeated, and he did as he'd been told.

Nothing happened right away. He wondered if this had all been a cruel joke, if a bunch of people were about to appear and start laughing at him. He almost opened his eyes, but then he felt a hand on each of his shoulders. The hands were small and they made his shoulders feel large. He smelled spearmint gum; he felt her breath against his face and then her lips pressed against his. They were soft lips, but they seemed to press hard. He could feel the teeth behind them.

He didn't know what he was supposed to do. He thought he should part his lips, but hers were gone before he could try that. He wanted to wrap his arms around her, but her hands had moved from his shoulders to his upper arms, and though they were small hands, they were strong enough to hold down his arms. When she stepped away, the spearmint lingered.

"We should go back inside," she said.

"Okay," he said. "Thanks for the present."

"You're welcome."

"I just remembered," he said, "I have a present for you, too."

"Not tonight," she said, and then she laughed and he was glad to hear the sound. It echoed out across the parking lot and returned to them, softer, like something that had happened before and might happen again.

WOULD EVERYONE BE able to tell what they'd done? Would people be able to see it all over his face? He tried to look casual when they walked back inside Del Ennis. He hoped to find Rich, Eric, and Jeff at one of the lanes. He'd bowl a game with them and they could talk. But before he'd taken two steps past the door, Ricky was pointing at him and saying, "There he is."

Ricky was the only scout who'd been brave enough to wear his Troop 158 baseball cap. He was standing next to an older woman and the two of them were talking. Nathan wondered if now he really was in trouble. He didn't know the woman. Was it Mrs. Kutnack? Or was it Jennifer's mother? And why was Ricky turning him in?

Nathan said good-bye to Jennifer and then went over to face the woman. When he stepped closer, he was relieved to see that she didn't look upset. She had bowling shoes on, so Nathan figured she'd been one of the lonely people practicing on those far off lanes. Ricky didn't hang around. "Catch you later," he said, and then he headed outside.

"So," the woman said, "you're Nathan Wolinsky?"

"Yes."

She smiled and they shook hands. "I heard you were in Troop 158," she said, "and when I saw that boy's hat, I thought it wouldn't hurt to see if you were here."

For what felt like the millionth time that night, Nathan didn't know what to say. Maybe a danger of the silent treatment is that you forget how to talk to people. A scout should be prepared, but he was a new scout, and no one had talked to him about kiss-gifts and random introductions.

"My name's Estelle," the woman said. "I'm a friend of your father's."

"It's nice to meet you."

"Maybe we'll meet again sometime," Estelle said. She seemed happy and a little nervous, and then she was walking away.

As he watched her go, Nathan tried to figure out what had just happened. He decided he had a lot to learn about women.

23

ESTELLE STARTED SPENDING more and more time with Max. She wasn't sure where they were going; all she knew was that they'd had four surprisingly great nights in a row. As she bustled around her apartment, showering, cleaning up, getting ready for a Friday of work, she was also asking herself questions. When would they switch from surprising to predictable? Did she even want a switch like that?

Max was still in her bed and he flirted from there. "Maybe I should become a lawyer," he said. "Then I could be with you all day."

She was buttoning a light green blouse over her bra. "You'd also be able to defend yourself," she said. "If necessary."

"Did I ever tell you how my parents met?" he asked.

When she said no, he went into a long, slightly confusing story about John Wanamaker's. As she listened, she tried to choose the right pair of slacks for the day. Max's father was pretending to be a salesman, or he was one kind of salesman mistaken for another kind of salesman, and he managed to pick out the perfect colors for the woman who became his wife. "Basically," Max said, "it was like this: my mother couldn't wait to take her clothes off for my father."

She held up two pairs of khaki linen pants, one with pleats, the other without. "Channel your dad for a second. Which of these should I wear?"

He chose the flat front and she agreed with him. Then she watched him get out of bed. He walked naked toward the bathroom, stopping by her side to kiss her cheek. There was something nice about being dressed while he was naked. A turn-on, yes, but it also made her feel as if she might be able to trust him. She liked having him in the apartment, liked hearing him in the shower as she put the coffee on.

He came back from the bathroom, one of her red towels wrapped around his waist. "I wonder what kind of story we'll wind up telling about how we met," he said.

"It's a little early for that, don't you think?"

"Maybe, but I'd love to go out for breakfast with you. We could talk it over."

She glanced at her watch. "Not possible. Woman's got to make a living, as you know."

"Come here for a second," he said, and when she did he pressed the back of his hand against her forehead. "You could have a fever."

"I don't think so, Max."

He pulled her closer and kissed her. She didn't want to get her blouse wet, so she leaned away, but not too far. He was wearing some of the new aftershave she'd bought him. It smelled like clean sheets and it was drawing her in.

"You feel pretty hot," he said, "and you look extremely hot."

"So much bullshit, so little time."

"Forget breakfast then," he said, stepping over to get his clothes. "Let's spend the whole day together. I have to take a road trip and you can come with me. You'll be able to learn more about my latest project. It's a gorgeous day for a drive."

"Are you serious?"

"I bet you've got plenty of vacation days stored up. Probably weeks of sick leave. The firm will make it to the weekend without you, I promise. A trip would be good for us."

If she lingered any longer, she'd be running late. But the idea was appealing and he was right, she did have some vacation coming to her. It was also true that just the other morning she'd been talking to her mother about wanting to spend more time with Max, wanting to see what it would be like to have a full day with him instead of just the nights. "Where do you have to go?" she asked.

"Ephrata, out in Lancaster County."

"Not the most exotic destination."

"You might be surprised."

It only took one phone call and then, before she knew it, they were eating breakfast at Max's favorite diner, and he was staring at her from across the table, grinning. "I figured out the story we can tell about how we met," he said. "Here it is: I saw you one night and you bowled me over."

He could make her smile, there was no denying that. She stirred more cream into her coffee and said, "Spare me."

ESTELLE DIDN'T WANT to go overboard with Max and she wasn't about to get her hopes up. The guy was some kind of a con man, after all, no matter what her mother thought about his potential. Still, she was having a good time. And, in a way, it was refreshing to be with someone she knew she shouldn't trust. It kept her on her toes, made her mind run a few laps, from doubtful to hopeful and back to doubtful again. She did a quick circuit while they passed through the tollbooth for the Pennsylvania Turnpike: it took years to get to know anybody, and even then you didn't know them. At least Max seemed to listen to what she said; he concealed things, but he didn't seem to conceal too much from her, as far as she could tell. She liked asking him questions and hearing his answers, and even if she couldn't completely trust him yet, maybe he was changing, or maybe that was just what he wanted her to believe.

She looked over at him as they headed west. He was talking a lot and there was something singsongy in his voice, an infectious, childlike excitement. It reminded her of her chance meeting with his son. Seeing Nathan could have made Max seem older, but, instead, it made him seem younger. He and his son resembled each other so closely, the same oval face and wide forehead, the same thick, bite-sized lower lip. She studied Max's mouth, watched it move from word to word. In all her years in Pennsylvania, she'd never thought about Ephrata for a second, but it clearly meant something to him. It filled him with family stories.

"What kind of name is Ephrata?" she asked.

"It's biblical, linked to Bethlehem. I guess the settlers named the town hoping Jesus would join them here in America." And then he was off again, telling her about his uncle. "Abe was the one who opened up this whole Lancaster County territory. Imagine this stylish young Jew driving out west to sell to the Pennsylvania Dutch. It's another world, the black suits, the horses and the buggies, the closed communities, but he figures they'll be interested in a good deal. My father thought he was crazy."

"Was he crazy?"

"The first factory he visits—it might have been Atlas Overalls or the Singing Needles Company—he's trying extra hard to be friendly; there's a little girl in the office, visiting her parents or something, so he opens his wallet and pulls out a photograph of his baby nephew—"

"Of you?"

"Right, it's me, and he wants to show this baby picture of me to the little girl. He's hoping to get a smile, a nice way to start, but the buyer sees what he's doing and hustles him out of the office. 'We don't believe in graven images,' the buyer says. Abe might have felt pretty crazy at that point."

"You sure that reaction didn't have anything to do with your face?"

"Pretty sure," Max said, turning her way. "I'm talking too much, aren't I?"

She swiveled the sun visor over to block the rays that were streaming down through her window. Then she reclined her seat a few notches. "I like listening to your stories," she said. "They bring back fond memories. Let's hear what else happened to Uncle Abe in his foreign territory."

"Well, he didn't give up. He needed to prove something to my father. Abe's no early riser, but he decided to schedule appointments as early in the day as possible. He's driving through the dark to meet buyers at six thirty or seven. He wants to get them while they're fresh. One of those mornings, he walks into Dutchmaker. It's a factory run by Dr. Conrad, who was given an interest in it when someone couldn't pay their medical bills. Anyhow, Abe puts his samples on the conference table and starts to speak. There are a few details he wants to highlight, but the doctor tells him to be quiet. The doctor has a cane and he uses it to point to a floral, polyester double-knit from Uprich Mills, a company that was, at the time, close to bankruptcy. Abe carries the sample over and gently lays it in the doctor's hands. Again he tries to say something and again he is told to be quiet. Dr. Conrad sniffs the fabric, then rubs it against his forehead, and then he places a three million dollar order."

Estelle was slow to respond. She had closed her eyes and sleep was tugging at her. Her mind couldn't quite accept that she wasn't at work. She was picturing a man like Max in her law office trying to sell polyester to the senior partner, a guy who wore fifteen-hundred-dollar Italian suits. "Three million dollars," she said.

"His commission was only 2 percent, but that was a giant order back then, the largest order he or my father had ever written. It saved Uprich. My father couldn't believe it."

Estelle heard what Max said, but she also heard the senior partner shouting for her, asking where she was, demanding to know who had let this salesman into the conference room. She readjusted her seat and rubbed her eyes. "That's a good ending," she said.

"There's more. Uprich was very grateful. Guess what they did?"

"I don't know."

"It would be hard to guess, actually. The next time Abe and my father went to New York City, they came off the train and found a twelve-piece marching band waiting for them. Everyone in the band, from the piccolo player to the tuba player, was wearing an Uprich hat and they followed Abe all the way through Penn Station, out onto the street, blaring one John

Philip Sousa march after another. Abe said it was one of the best days of his life. He loved seeing my father so surprised and so happy and neither one of them could stop laughing."

"So your uncle wasn't crazy after all."

"That's right," Max said. "He wasn't crazy."

ESTELLE DIDN'T SLIP into a nap, but she was slipping into something. Max was reminding her about what he needed to do. He'd have to leave her alone while he went to a meeting. It shouldn't take too long and he'd try to find a good place for her to wait. Though she didn't know exactly what he'd be doing, it had to be better than what he'd planned to do with those old people. He was working on a deal that involved Boy Scout uniforms, tied somehow to his father and uncle's business.

Then Max was reminiscing again, talking about the sights his uncle loved. There was a sign by a market in the shape of an enormous green dragon. There was a cloisters from the 1700s. There was a former Miss America who'd been born and raised in Ephrata. She'd won back in the fifties and her name was Evelyn Ay and she used to walk around town with her high school sweetheart and her champion Great Danes. "Abe was always on the lookout for her," Max said. "He wanted to make her the next Mrs. Wolinsky. 'What do you think, Maxie,' he'd say. 'Wouldn't you like to have a Miss America for an aunt?' He was going to convert her to Judaism. It would be like Arthur Miller and Marilyn Monroe, except they'd stay married, and Evelyn would be completely happy."

Max lapsed into quiet for a while, and the countryside opened up as they drove, blue sky above them, rolling green hills on the horizon, and in between the towns the strip malls and gas stations gradually gave way to more and more farmland. Red and white barns stood off in the distance. Estelle knew most of them were probably being used every day by people who were working hard to get by, but at first glance they looked like weathered monuments to a different, long-gone way of life. They made her feel as if she were traveling back in time. She didn't have any uncles to think about, but her dad drifted toward her, bringing along his own distinctive memories. She started to talk him away.

"I haven't told you much about my father," she said. "He used to dream of living in the country."

"Where in the country?" asked Max.

"I don't know if he ever really decided. He kept saying he had to leave the city. That was around the bicentennial. He went away for a while and then he came back and then he went away again."

"What did he have against Philadelphia?"

How much did she want to explain? How much could she explain if she tried? *Crazy* was a word she'd used to describe him in the past, and she wasn't the only one. How quickly he could disappear, how hopeful he could be, and how distant. But she wasn't ready to get into that. She wasn't after sympathy from Max. They were on a road trip, in the middle of a good day. "I don't think Philly had much to do with it," she said. "He was another confused and restless man. One of the last times I saw him, he picked me up from high school and asked me how I'd feel about having a brother or sister. He knew that was something I'd always wanted."

"I wanted both," Max said. "A brother and a sister."

Estelle smiled. It was all too easy to see Max as another version of her father and her ex-husband, but she preferred thinking that he was, instead, another version of herself. She was glad to get more evidence. "I'd already chosen names for mine," she said. "Elinor and Emil. We were going to be the three *E*s."

"You were ahead of me. I didn't have any names, but I knew what we'd do together."

"What was that?"

"It's predictable," he said. "We'd join the family business. Wolinsky Brothers, Sons, and Daughter. We'd make a fortune."

Estelle wondered what that vision meant for Nathan— would he be included in that business? would he ever get his own siblings?—but she shied away from those questions. It seemed far too early to talk about whether or not Max wanted more kids.

The Dutchmaker factory was on the far side of Ephrata, part of an industrial park at the bottom of a squat hill. Max pointed it out as they drove by. "I want to show you something else first," he said.

As they kept driving, Estelle hoped she wasn't about to see the house of some unsuspecting new victims. A few miles later, they drove into a town called Lititz.

"Is that a biblical name, too?" she asked.

"I think it was a village in Europe, a place these settlers wanted to honor," Max said, and then he turned into the driveway of the Moravian Cemetery and pulled into the parking lot. "My uncle used to like to stop here."

It felt good to step out of the car and stretch her legs. She didn't know what she was doing in a cemetery on such a beautiful afternoon, but it wasn't much stranger than the rest of the day. Skipping work for a spontaneous trip to Lancaster County? Looking at a con man and thinking about kids? She took Max's hand and they walked up a path toward the graves.

It seemed like a small cemetery to her, though there were still plenty of tombstones, and some of them were extremely old. At first, Estelle thought she and Max had the place to themselves, but then she saw a group of people kneeling near a few of the graves on a hillside. She was surprised to see a whole section of soldiers' graves from the Revolutionary War. Max explained that the wounded from the Battle of Brandywine had been brought to a makeshift hospital in the town, where most of them had died. Many of the inscriptions were in German and many of the words had been washed away to nothing over the years. Those blank headstones looked eerie to her.

"Did your uncle know someone here?" she asked.

"We're almost there," Max said, leading her away from the kneeling people, down a path to a solitary marker, a large marble slab, next to a tall pine tree, a miniature American flag, and a bronze plaque. It was the grave for General John A. Sutter, born in 1803 at Kandern, Baden, died in 1880 at Washington, D.C. His wife, Anna, was buried with him. The plaque offered more information: IN MEMORY OF JOHN AUGUSTUS SUTTER, WHO FOUNDED CALIFORNIA'S CAPITAL, THE CITY OF SACRAMENTO, AUGUST 12, 1839.

Estelle remembered Sutter and the gold rush from high school, but what exactly was Max's uncle's connection? And what was the grave doing here? She looked over at Max for an explanation and he put an arm around her as they studied the marble tombstone. "It's another story that my uncle would tell me," he said. "Like James Lake Young, except Sutter didn't do nearly as well in the end. He left his family's drapery business in Switzerland and traveled halfway around the world to build his own town out on the California frontier. There, for a while, everything was beyond perfect. He had thousands of acres of gorgeous, fertile riverfront property. He had herds of horses, a famous fort, and he played host to all the men who hoped to make their fortunes in California. Then, to top it off, gold was found on his land and it seemed that everything would some-how get even better."

Estelle stayed beside Max as he walked around the tomb-stone. It was a well-tended grave, surrounded by pachysandra, pine needles, and a handful of yellow daylilies. Max sat on a bench behind the flag and leaned forward, resting his chin on his hands. "This Swiss nobody could have become one of the wealthiest men ever," he said, "but his land was overrun by those gold rushers and, in a few short years, he lost it all. His claims were denied in court after court. He wound up almost penniless, begging for money from Congress, dead and buried here in the middle of nowhere."

Estelle sat down next to him. "And why did your uncle like that story so much?"

"It has to do with the dreaming," he said. "The possibilities, and how failure is just a breath away." He took his cell phone out of his pocket. "Do you mind if I call my father?"

"No," she said, and then she stood up to give him some privacy.

"Stay here," he said. "I want you to hear his voice."

Estelle was curious, so she sat back down and listened as Max spoke into the phone. From the little she could hear, Max's fa-ther sounded like Max, just older and sleepier. Her own father had spoken with a booming voice. After he left for the last time, he didn't call often, but when he did, she had to hold the phone away from her ear. It was as if he needed to shout about his new life. He always said he was working hard and he always talked about the spectacular view from his window. He was in St. Louis. He said he could smell the big, muddy Mississippi.

Max asked his father to put Abe on the phone. She couldn't hear that voice at all, though she strained to catch it. Max started talking about where he was, reminding his uncle about trips from years ago. Meanwhile, Estelle looked up at the hill, where the kneeling people were still kneeling. This time she noticed they weren't particularly dressed up and she thought she could see buckets by their sides. They were cleaning the tombstones. She watched them and remembered traveling by herself to St. Louis for her father's funeral. She'd gone straight from the airport to his apartment. It was a three-room shotgun flat above a pizza parlor on a road named Skinker Boulevard. All she could smell was pizza dough and tomato sauce. A few blocks away, there was a university and an enormous park, with man-made lakes, paddleboats, an art museum, a zoo, and an amphitheater, but she couldn't see any of that from either one of his windows.

Max reached over and massaged the back of her neck. "I'm going to finish what you started, Abe," he was saying. "And, guess what, that woman I mentioned the other night is here with me. We're having a peaceful day. We're taking our time, but we seem to be liking each other more and more. I've told her all about you. Maybe I'll bring her by later tonight when we get home. We'll hit the diner together, celebrate a bit. Until then, listen to your brother. Cut him a break or two for a change. And remember that I'm missing you out here."

Estelle leaned in closer, and just before Max switched off the phone she heard his uncle's voice, a sudden, hoarse whisper. "Maxie!"

They sat in silence for several minutes after that. The flag fluttered in the breeze. The pine tree rustled behind them, dropping more of its needles to the ground. A few distant dandelions spread some of their seeds. She let Max kiss her, and it felt good, soft and a little rough. She tried to keep all her thoughts on that warm sensation, but she was also wondering how she could possibly trust her mother's judgment about men. And she suspected that her own judgment was no better.

24

LISTENING TO MAX talk to him on the phone, Abe feels tears and maybe he's crying. He wishes more people would call to say where they are and what they're doing.

On good days, he can hear the voices he misses. He never married, but he had his style and it didn't go unnoticed. There were women on the road. One by one, they settled down with other men. Sometimes that stopped their trysts with Abe and sometimes it didn't. When those women whisper to him, they say, *Oh, Abraham, it could have been you.*

Most of his colleagues like to laugh. *Cat got your tongue?* they ask. They have appointments, places they need to be. *Only got a minute,* they say, *but it's good to see you. Maybe there's time for a drink. Just one. Before it gets too dark.*

Abe longs to hear more from Caleb. He wants to move past the back and forth of their terse commands. The bickering that lasts a lifetime: *Sit down, don't bother me, stand up, quit it, hold still.* Will this be their final conversation?

They sit in the dank apartment, they drive the neighborhood streets in the Taurus. There are hours at the community center, hours in bed, hours sleeping, hours waiting to sleep, and the Viva Deluxe doesn't change a thing.

Abe's not upset with his brother, but he's begging for more. *Come on, Caleb. You've done everything else for me, now let's really talk. Tell me what you're thinking.*

For some reason, it's Mervyn who answers, shouting and running over. They shake hands and walk side by side through the vast waiting room downtown at Thirtieth Street Station. They're each rushing to make a train, heading for different staircases, on their way out of the city again. There are hundreds, maybe thousands, of people, everyone sharply dressed, stepping forward with purpose, saying what they need to say. For a moment, Abe and Mervyn stand still amid the hustling crowd. Above their heads, the destinations and times shift and change on the big board, the sound like someone shuffling deck after deck of enormous cards.

"You saved my life," Mervyn says. "I'm grateful."

Abe's heard Spiller say this before. Was it during a visit or a dream? He's not certain. It's so hard to know the difference. Either way, the fact is he can't remember saving anyone's life. He tries to think back. How could he have forgotten something like that? They've been close friends for years. There were good days and bad, plenty of ups and downs, occasional successes to go with the spectacular failures. Because of the failures, Abe didn't bring Caleb and Mervyn together until it was too late. That's a shame; it was a mistake, but no one's life was in danger. No one was going to die.

Mervyn checks his platinum watch. "Got to run," he says.

"Wait," Abe says. "I can't remember. How did I save you?"

"You were there, Abraham. After my heart attack. After

my divorce. Whenever I needed you. Now tell me what you need."

Abe doesn't know what to say. "I want to talk more. It's so good to see you. Let's sit down for a minute. We'll grab a cup of coffee."

Mervyn glances at his watch again and shakes his head. "I wish I could, but you know how it is. Hurry up now, tell me what I can do."

"Look out for my nephew," Abe says. "Look out for my brother."

Mervyn nods, smiles, takes one step forward, and disappears back into the crowd. Alone, Abe makes his way to his staircase. He seems to have it all to himself. Then he discovers that these stairs lead right into the old Ellsworth Street apartment. Though Caleb has again become a baby, dreaming deeply in his crib, Abe is not a child. In fact, he's far older than he ever was in that apartment. He has somehow become the exact same age as his father and now the two of them stand in the living room, looking like twins. It's strange, but nothing could feel more natural. Solomon strides to the front door, hat in hand, as confident as ever, ready for another day of work. He turns to Abe. "Let's go, son," he says. "It's time. No rest for the middlemen."

Abe doesn't hesitate. He follows his father.

25

LESS THAN AN HOUR after Max called in from Sutter's grave, Caleb woke up from another Barcalounger nap and glanced over at his brother. Abe was there, parked in the Viva Deluxe, but his body was rigid and his face looked frozen, the eyes wide and unblinking. Caleb nudged then shook his brother's shoulders. He checked Abe's wrist and neck for a pulse. Caleb's heart raced, his hands quivered, he was sweating, but Abe felt only cold and gone. "Say something!" Caleb shouted. "Abe!"

What happened next blurred together and Caleb lost track of what he was doing. How many times did he slap Abe's face? Was he the one who dragged Abe down onto the carpet? When did he finally reach for the phone?

The police came, an ambulance came, the police told the ambulance to leave, and then someone from Belasco's Funeral Parlor arrived with a hearse. Shocked, Caleb watched as his brother's body was taken away. In a daze, he spoke with the man from Belasco's. The man wanted to know if Caleb would be all right by himself. The police wanted to know the same thing. Caleb told them he'd be fine. "My son will be here soon," he said.

He must have been convincing because suddenly he was alone in the apartment. He sat on the couch across from the empty Viva Deluxe. No matter where he looked, no matter whether his eyes were open or closed, he saw Abe's stiffened fingers dangling off the scooter's padded armrests. "My brother," Caleb said, over and over again.

HE CALLED MAX as soon as he could, but the voice mail kept picking up. He couldn't bring himself to leave a message. He thought of other people he could call, other people he needed to call. The rabbi, his friends, Spiller. He wasn't ready for that, though, and he was tired, so he lay down on his bed. He felt like he was in a coffin, deep underground. He kept the lights on, but he could still hear the scrape of the shovels, the patter and then the thud of the dirt against the wood.

He'd seen plenty of people lose plenty of people and he knew the standard rituals too well. He'd be expected to tear his shirt over his heart, sit shivah, spend a week crouched on a low stool, unshaven, his clothes unwashed. Recite the Kaddish three times a day and hope to help elevate Abe's soul. Then thirty days of *sheloshim*—no shaving, no hair cutting at all, more prayer. *Yit-gadal ve-yitkadash, Shmei rabbah.* May his name be magnified and made holy.

But those Jewish laws, the whole Shulchan Arukh, seemed arbitrary to Caleb. Mourning took as long as it took, and the necessary rites depended on the person gone as well as the person left behind. Where to begin with his brother? How to begin to end? They had been ending for years, loss by loss, and still he had no idea what to do.

He took a shower, thinking the steam and hot water would feel good, but as soon as he was in the bathroom he wanted to hurry out. Abe's complaining seemed to echo off the pink-and-black tiled walls. How fragile he'd become after those strokes, and how difficult it had been to get him clean! "I'll do it," Abe would say in the shower, but he used too much soap or not enough, and either way, with suds all over his legs or without ever even wetting his head and neck, he'd start saying, "I'm done, I'm done." Alone, washing himself, the water hitting his face, Caleb was ashamed to feel what felt like relief. Then waves of guilt. Then he wondered who would help him, and that was something else he didn't want to think about.

It grew later—seven, then eight—and he still couldn't reach Max. He was exhausted, but he also felt restless. He stretched out on the couch instead of the bed and he tried to will himself calm. He stared at the scooter for almost an hour. Then he got up and went to work on the annoying bumper sticker. His fingernails were useless against it. When he tried a knife and spatula, he damaged the Durathane paint without obscuring the words at all. He found a roll of silver duct tape, tore off a piece, and covered every letter.

He stretched out on the couch again and went back to his staring. What did he expect to see? He didn't know and, as he tried to figure it out, he slipped into another nap. When he awoke, it was almost ten. He stood up and circled the scooter. Then he walked into the kitchen and grabbed a can of seltzer, which fit perfectly into one of the cup holders. "What the hell," he said.

He sank into the contoured cushions of the Viva Deluxe. It was a CEO's seat. Extremely comfortable. He adjusted the headrest, inserted the key, and switched the scooter on. The throttle lever was a narrow strip of metal just beneath the handlebar—pushing on the right side made it go forward, on the left made it back up. There were no brakes—releasing the throttle stopped the scooter, gently. For a moment, Caleb hunched over the handlebars, like a bike racer, streamlining. He got off, went to the closet, zipped on a windbreaker. Then he climbed on again, leaned back, inhaled, and throttled forward.

He heard something break beneath the wheel of the scooter. When he looked down, he saw that he'd crushed that eerie sculpture Spiller's wife had made. That was fine with him and he kept going.

Motoring outside was tricky. He had to climb on and off the scooter to open and close the doors. But once he was on the ramp up to the sidewalk, the Viva Deluxe hummed along. In no time, he was rumbling down Cheltenham Avenue. He didn't feel younger. He didn't feel on his way to a more active and rewarding lifestyle. He felt silly and heartbroken.

He thought he'd just take it around the block. A few cars raced by. He stayed alert, not wanting the rhythm of the ride to lull him to sleep. He could smash into a telephone pole or a parking meter. He could tumble off a curb into traffic and that would be the end. He might not die quietly like Abe. The scooter had no seat belt.

Still, he felt safer than he did when he drove the old Taurus at night, and before too long the sensation of silliness gave way to a sort of thrill. He was chugging through the dark, the scooter was easy to handle, and he liked the breeze against his face. Parts of the sidewalk were uneven, but the halogen headlamp illuminated the bumps. It was warmer than he thought, so he stopped to shove his windbreaker into the basket. He didn't want to be a quick convert or a prospective advertisement, but he was glad to be outside and he slowly turned the speed knob higher.

He hadn't gone far when he decided to conduct a more extensive road test. The Viva Deluxe had a twenty-mile range on each charge. He checked the battery gauge. It glowed bright green. He was suddenly hungry and Lee's called out to him. He remembered walking with Abe and Max, not that long ago. He also remembered how angry he'd been with Abe for turning around. He told himself to think about something else.

The neighborhood after dark was not what it once had been. Up and down the streets, nearly everything was closed. The dimly lit places still open for business were called various things—he passed a bar, a dance club, a lounge, and a café—but they all looked the same. A few smokers milled around the doorways. Waiting for a red light to change at Old York Road, he popped open his can of seltzer and took a sip.

He didn't see anyone else out on the street until, at the edge of a gas station, he passed a group of baggy-clothed kids. They were sweatshirted and hooded. Caleb couldn't get a good look at their faces, just eyes that seemed flecked with red. He considered a U-turn. As he rolled closer, one of the kids called to him. "What are you doing out here, old man?"

Caleb didn't slow down, but he answered. "I'm picking up a cheesesteak."

The group laughed and Caleb relaxed, leaving them behind. He told himself that the neighborhood hadn't changed that much. It had always been a little dangerous, full of people trying to make their way at someone else's expense. Now it was more run-down. More empty. Still, it was all about confidence. Move with purpose, like you know where you're heading.

He smelled Lee's long before he pulled up to the door. Fresh rolls from D'Ambrosia Bakery, warming in the oven. Thin steaks sizzling on the grill, right beside piles of chopped sweet onions, browned for hours. Homemade tomato sauce bubbling away in a pot on the stove. It was a bright, fragrant oasis, purple neon buzzing in the window.

A tall Italian guy in a double-breasted blazer and wool slacks walked over from the counter and opened the door for Caleb. "Come on in, Pops," he said. "I wouldn't be driving that thing alone in the dark around here."

"Thanks," Caleb said, rolling in. "I've been doing all right so far."

He motored up to the counter and ordered a Supreme with onions, peppers, and sauce. It felt good to be surrounded by people. The cashier, a young black man with a shaved head, peered at the Viva Deluxe and said, "Nice vehicle." As he maneuvered around the handful of crowded tables, Caleb thought those glossy pamphlets might have been truer than he'd imagined. He could become an urban version of those improbable fishermen, finding pleasure in the great outdoors. He thought about that promise of comfort and ease. How seductive and how impossible.

He savored his Supreme, the sting of the peppers, the sugary onions, the richness of the tomato sauce. He took small bites, wanting to make it last. He'd bought a bottle of vanilla cream soda, too, and he drank from it as he ate.

Eventually, the plate was clean and the bottle was empty. Others needed his table and he needed to move on. He knew he should go straight home, keep trying to reach Max, but when he rolled back outside, he went the other way, venturing out onto the roads they used to take, years ago.

He veered off the main streets in the general direction of Federman's Coats. Caleb saw no lounges, bars, or clubs on this route. He knew he was doing something stupid. Still, he kept going. First there were boarded-up old stone row houses, condemned, leaning into each other, their foundations slipping. When he crossed over a cobblestone street, the scooter rocked from side to side. He gripped the handlebars tighter. What might have been a family of rats scurried across the road and dove down into a sewer. Then he turned a corner and came to the empty factories and warehouses. They covered whole blocks. When he tried to get closer to them he found imposing gates locked and chained shut, concrete walls topped with barbed wire and shards of thick glass. An enormous German shepherd followed him from behind a hurricane fence. The dog barked ferociously, but Caleb was glad to see it. *Company,* he thought. In his mind, he could hear the sewing machines pounding away.

Years ago, when they weren't out of town selling in New York City or Baltimore or Trenton or somewhere else, Caleb and Abe would do their Philly rounds and they'd meet for lunch. On days they didn't have time for the diner, they'd grab sandwiches near Federman's and look for a place to sit outside. There were benches then, but they were full of factory workers. Sometimes Caleb and Abe would see space on a stoop. They'd pause for a moment to consider it. Then they'd keep going, eating and strolling through the bustle, talking about what they'd sold that morning, how many yards, who was stringing them along, which lines they needed to start carrying, where they had to go next.

Abe was always more hopeful, willing to take risks that Caleb shunned. They lost bundles in most of Abe's fiascoes—the woolens from Nepal that were confiscated, the corduroy from Odessa that was far too flammable, the ridiculous investment in the Swedish hat factory, and so on. But who wasn't a fool from time to time, and always in the end?

Caleb wondered if Abe had woken up before dying and tried to speak. He pictured his brother slapping at Death's hand, shouting, *Quit it. Don't touch me.*

When he decided that he'd gone far enough, he turned the scooter back toward the apartment. The dog was way behind him, curled up and alone by now, and the streets grew quieter, as if someone were slowly turning the city off. In the distance, trucks roared by on the expressway, one after another, like waves rushing up the shore. The tires of the Viva Deluxe rolled over the sidewalk, keeping time with the hushed roar of that far off traffic. Caleb thought of Max, driving back from Ephrata with his new woman. Maybe that was something hopeful.

He shouldn't have closed his eyes, but he did, just for a few seconds, to rest, though he didn't stop moving. He was so full and so tired, and he found he could hear his heartbeat, somewhere beneath the other sounds, steady, still strong. He kept listening, and then, through it all, up rose Abe's voice, almost exactly like his own: *Max is better than you think. He'll make good. He's better than you think. He'll make good. Make good. Make good.*

"I don't know, Abe," whispered Caleb. "What am I supposed to do now?"

No answer came and he kept riding, all the way back to the apartment. Then, as he prepared to handle the doors again, someone spoke to him from beyond his lights. "Stop. Stop it right there."

Caleb heard footsteps. He spun the speed knob, but something had grabbed on to the back of his seat and the scooter barely moved. The voice was at his ear. The breath was warm and smelled of smoke. "You want me to roll you off this fucking thing?"

Caleb released the throttle. "What do you want?" he asked. He turned around to face the person behind him, but a hand gripped the back of his head and held him still.

"What is this shit you're driving? You can't walk or what?"

"I can walk," Caleb said. "It's a scooter. It was my brother's."

"Don't you know little old men shouldn't be out so late at night?"

Caleb said nothing.

"That's good. You keep quiet. This'll be easier. Don't move and I won't have to use my knife. You live in this building, right?"

"Yes," Caleb said.

"I was waiting for Max, but you'll do. Let's get inside."

Caleb wanted to stay calm. He tried to be tough and he fought off fear. He considered screaming, but the hand resting on his head felt strong enough to snap his neck in a second. On Cheltenham Avenue, a few cars raced by without stopping. *It's what I deserve*, Caleb told himself. *You put a bad son out there, you get a bad son back.*

He stayed in the Viva Deluxe and, in front of his door, he handed his keys to the man, who asked, "Are we going to find anybody else in here?"

"I live alone now," said Caleb. "Do you work for Johnny Sklarman? Is that what this is about?"

"I'll ask the questions, old man. I'll tell you this, though. Johnny's not doing too well this evening."

Inside, the first thing the man picked up was the roll of duct tape. He used it to wrap Caleb into the scooter. Caleb watched as his legs were bound together, his wrists bound to the armrests. "Don't make me do anything worse," the man said. "I want this to be over quickly. Just tell me who else is working with Max and Spiller."

Before he could answer, the phone started to ring. "That's probably Max calling," Caleb said.

"Too bad he's not here with you. He could have spared you this. But he didn't and I need you to start talking now. Who else is involved in this thing?"

Caleb looked at the man. He had blond, crew-cut hair, a bony face, blue eyes. He was short but as wide as a steam fitter. Caleb didn't know what to say. He wondered if the tape was cutting off his blood flow. Where was Max calling from? Why wasn't he back yet?

Caleb saw bright silver dust when the man slapped his face. "Answer my question," the man said. "And don't stare at me."

"Don't hurt me."

"You're hurt already, old man. I can see that. But you're lucky, I won't hurt you too much more."

The man slapped the other side of Caleb's face. The phone stopped ringing, started again, and stopped. Caleb wanted to touch his face where he'd been hit, but he couldn't move his arms. His hands flapped uselessly. He thought he was sweating. "Max doesn't tell me anything," he said. "He does his work. He won't let me get involved."

The man raised his hand again and Caleb flinched, but no slap came this time. "You can make this easier on everyone. Just tell me what you know. Nothing bad will happen. I'll do some renegotiating and everything will be fine."

"Max was down in Florida and then he came up here for his son's bar mitzvah. That's all I know about his plans."

The man shook his head and pushed his stubby fingers through his hair. "Have it your way, old man. Just remember that whatever happens to Max is something you could have stopped. Now it's out of your hands and into mine. You'll have to live with that."

When the man walked back to the door and reached for the doorknob, Caleb wanted to shout out something about Ephrata and Dutchmaker, but he didn't. He started to sob, tears filling his eyes.

The phone began to ring again. The man smirked, glanced over his shoulder, and said, "You won't forget to give Max my message, will you?"

Caleb wondered if he'd missed something. "What's the message?"

The man's face broke into a full-blown smile, as if the question had actually made him happy. "You are," he said, "sitting in your wheelchair, looking so miserable, like your best friend just died." Then, instead of leaving, he stepped away from the door, grabbed a dish towel off the kitchen counter, and taped it into Caleb's mouth.

26

MAX COULDN'T GET over the simplicity of the meeting. It had been old school, from start to finish. All he'd had to do was walk into the conference room and show his face to the five people sitting around the table. They saw him and remembered Wolinsky Brothers and Associates and that gave them confidence in the transaction. The whole preapproved deal became just another chapter in a long history of buying and selling. He didn't have to put on an act. He was his father's son, he was his uncle's nephew, and that was more than enough. It was the kind of business he could get used to. Maybe his father had been right about old school all along.

Of course, he was also benefiting from his connection to Spiller and Powell. Spiller wasn't in the room, but Powell was there, beaming his smile, boosting everyone's spirits. He talked about his "personal patrol" of forward-thinking colleagues in Texas. He said they were thrilled with what was finally happening. Then, near the end of the short meeting, Powell stood up and declared, "This venture is bound to succeed. It combines the best of the East and the West; it has a view of the old and the new. We are definitely prepared for the future."

Dr. Conrad's son, who'd been presiding from the head of the table, rose to his feet and gave the closing benediction. "I speak for everyone at Dutchmaker when I say that we are very pleased. I predict this will be a profitable association for all of us. Let us prosper together."

"Here, here!" Powell shouted, starting off a round of applause with his possum-sized hands.

Max wouldn't really believe any of it until he got paid, but it did feel good and it seemed smooth. Trust the man, Abe had said. Well, he was doing more than that. He was trusting and he was admiring. He didn't want to jinx anything, but he saw no harm in a little celebration, so he took Estelle out to dinner at Ephrata's oldest inn, a place that dated back to the 1760s. The original building was a small stone cottage that had once hosted Lafayette and Baron von Steuben. Estelle chose a quiet outside table, across a lawn from that cottage. Max ordered a bottle of cabernet, and while he waited for it to arrive he called his father. He couldn't wait to tell him how well everything had gone, but no one answered.

He and Estelle lingered over the wine, the rack of lamb, and the raspberry-glazed chocolate torte. After each course, he called his father again, but the voice mail kept picking up. He didn't want to worry. Maybe they were asleep, or maybe Caleb had at last managed to get Abe out on the Viva Deluxe.

Since Max would be driving, he ordered coffee with the dessert. Estelle chose brandy. He asked for a sip and then said, "Where should we go tomorrow?"

Estelle pushed her chair back from the table and crossed her legs. "We could keep heading west," she said, "stop off in Harrisburg. I hear they've got some excellent graveyards there."

Max laughed and held on to her drink. The snifter fit snugly in his hand. It made him feel like a man of privilege and fine fortune. He breathed in the sweet smell of the brandy and wondered if he'd ever really gained anything worthwhile from all his scams. Did the conning ever get him what he wanted? He looked across the table at Estelle and realized that he might be celebrating more than an easy afternoon at Dutchmaker.

It had been such a pleasure to pick Estelle up after the meeting. She'd chosen to wait at the cemetery, saying it was a good place to think some more about her father. When Max came back to find her, she was in the middle of a group of people, helping them wash some of the newer tombstones. He'd watched her for a minute or two before walking over and it surprised him that the first thing he felt was proud. Proud of what she was doing? Proud of his connection to her? He wasn't sure, but he didn't dwell on it because that wasn't the only thing he felt. He noticed her strong back, the way her hair caught the late afternoon sun, the smooth skin of her neck. He quietly knelt down beside her. He didn't want to disturb her if she was grieving, but as soon as she saw him she took his hand and kissed his cheek. He couldn't tell who was happier to see whom.

Of course, there was no mistaking Ephrata for the tropical paradise of Hawaii or the safe haven of the Keys. He could still picture Sandy frolicking with Hiram out on a pristine beach, and by this time Grier and her new professor were probably connecting nightly on one of the research boats, snorkeling hand in hand at sunset and sunrise. It wasn't that those images didn't bother him. He couldn't say that. But they didn't bother him too much, and gazing across the table at Estelle he could imagine them one day not bothering him at all.

IT WAS ALMOST midnight when they reached Philly. Max was tempted to drive straight to Estelle's place and hurry into bed with her, but he wanted to stop at the basement apartment first. He could make sure everything was all right, and if Caleb and Abe happened to be awake Estelle could meet them, say a quick hello.

He walked in looking down, wondering why the door was unlocked, so it was Estelle who saw Caleb first. She ran over to him, shouting, "Oh my God!" Max went for the tape by his father's mouth. He knew he had to be careful, but how could he not rush? He'd never seen his father's eyes so wide open. He smelled sweat and urine, he heard his father trying to speak, and it sounded like someone sinking underwater. Caleb's head felt clammy and hot. His cheeks were wet. Where was Abe? While Max peeled away the tape, Estelle rushed to the kitchen and came back with a pair of scissors. She worked on freeing Caleb's wrists and legs. "It's okay, Dad," Max said. "I'm here."

Max gently took the towel out of his father's mouth. The room seemed suddenly silent, and then a moment later it seemed Caleb was the only one breathing, wheezing and wheezing, as if he'd just run as far and fast as he could. Estelle rushed into the kitchen again and came back with a glass of water. Caleb could barely hold it in his hands, but he brought it to his mouth, took a long drink, coughed, and spit up most of what he'd managed to get down.

When Caleb started to speak, Max couldn't understand a word and this terrified him. He listened closer, but it was nonsense slurred together. His father was having a stroke, or he'd already had one. It was worse than Abe had ever been. "What are you saying, Dad?" he asked. He turned to Estelle. "What's he saying?"

Estelle put a hand on his back. "He's crying, Max."

Max nodded. He reached for the tissues on the coffee table and used them to wipe away the tears. How long had his father been trapped here like this? Once the questions started coming, they didn't stop. Had Johnny done this? Where was Abe? Where was Johnny right now? Where was Spiller?

"Let's get him out of this thing," he said to Estelle, and then he reached under Caleb's arm.

"Abe," Caleb said.

It was the first word that Max could understand and he was relieved to hear it. "Where is he?"

"He's dead," Caleb whispered. "Abe is dead."

As CALEB MOVED from room to room, he talked about what had happened. Max listened carefully. He sat on the closed toilet while his father showered, he stood by the bed while his father put on jeans and a sweatshirt, he leaned against the kitchen counter while his father boiled water. He thought his father would collapse any second, but instead Caleb seemed to grow stronger. "I was sleeping all day," he said, pouring the water into a teapot. "I can't sleep now. What are we going to do?"

Max knew what he needed to do first. He called Spiller to make sure Nathan was safe. No one answered, so he left a message, and then, even though it was after one and during the Sabbath, he tried Rabbi Weinberg. He wound up talking to another answering machine, saying again that Abe was dead, that Caleb had run into trouble, and that they were all worried about Nathan. He was still talking when Weinberg picked up the phone. "Max," he said, "I'm so sorry. I'll come right over. And don't worry about Nathan. He's fine. The troop is camping in Pennypack Park this weekend. I had dinner with them."

Max thanked the rabbi, apologized for calling so late, and said, "Why don't you come over tomorrow, if you can. I don't think we'll be up much longer tonight."

Estelle wanted him to call the police next, but Max wasn't ready to do that. "That's not what we need at this point," he said. She didn't like that answer and the way she glared at him made it clear they'd have to talk more about it later. In the meantime, he wasn't going to discuss what had to happen next. He couldn't leave his father alone just yet, but as soon as he could he would find Johnny and Dexter and figure out a way to hurt them.

For now, he, Estelle, and Caleb sat side by side on the living-room couch, their mugs of decaf Lipton steaming on the coffee table. Despite everything he'd been through, Caleb was trying to be a charming host for Estelle.

"I'm so sorry," she said. "I can't imagine what it's like to lose a brother. And then to have this—"

Caleb patted her knee and interrupted. "It's okay," he said. "Abe was at the end of his rope. He lived a full life." Tears came into his eyes again. He rubbed at them with his palms. "Let's talk about something else, okay?"

Estelle took his hand. "We can talk about whatever you want," she said.

"Or we don't have to talk at all, Dad," said Max. "You can lie down and get some rest. In the morning, we'll go see your doctor."

"I'm awake, Max, and I'm fine. Things are bad, it's true, but I'm still alive."

Caleb started asking where Estelle worked, where she lived, where she was born. The chitchat was a way to repress what had happened, Max understood that, but he didn't want to hear it, so he stood up. The Viva Deluxe was bothering him. Every time he looked at it, he saw his father strapped in, unable to move. Then he pictured his uncle dying in the same seat, hours earlier, Caleb finding him there, already gone. Why had Abe badgered them for months about buying one of these? It seemed like an absurd and terrible kind of death wish now.

Standing next to it, Max thought he could smell his father and his uncle, their sweat full of age and fear. He wiped off the seat. Then he tried to push it, but it was heavy and awkward. It would be easier to move if he drove it, so he climbed on. He wanted to ride the goddamn thing outside and ditch it by the curb, but that would have caused a fuss. Instead, he steered toward Abe's room. He had trouble maneuvering out of the kitchen and when he tried to back up, he banged into the refrigerator.

"Careful, Max," Caleb said.

Max banged into the refrigerator again, harder this time. He slammed his two hands against the armrests. "Come on, you piece of shit!" he shouted. Then he managed to turn the corner.

He drove in through Abe's open door, parked by the bed, and climbed off the scooter. The room was dark and musty. He opened one of the windows and thought about switching the light on, but he didn't feel ready to see everything he and his father would have to face in there. What would they do with it all? He hustled from the room and slammed the door behind him.

He was out of breath when he returned to the couch. Estelle stood up as he was sitting down. "I'll get some more hot water," she said.

Max knew he had to take her home, but it felt too soon to leave his father by himself. Plus he was grateful for the way she was helping him through this impossible evening. Maybe they could call a cab once Caleb was asleep. He leaned closer to his father. "How are you doing, Dad?"

"I'm okay, son," he said, and then, raising his voice to make sure Estelle would hear, he added, "She's a very nice woman. You were right. I do like her."

Max sipped his tea. It was cold and he wanted something stronger.

Caleb started to whisper. "I didn't tell the guy anything. He seemed pretty angry at Johnny. I don't think they're getting along too well."

Max whispered, too. "I'm sorry for all this."

Caleb's eyes were closed now, and he was leaning back further, resting his head near the top of the couch. He was far beyond exhaustion, but he kept whispering. "The guy hit me twice. I was scared, Max. He wanted to know who you and Spiller were working with. I told him you didn't tell me. I told him you never told me."

Max's lips were almost touching his father's ear. "I'll take care of it, Dad. I promise. You get some sleep."

"It's not your fault," Caleb said, speaking more slowly. "I want to talk to Abe. I want to dream about him."

AFTER HE CARRIED his father to bed, Max looked through the liquor cabinet and found some Wild Turkey. He brought the bottle, two glasses, and the phone back to the couch. "I'll call a cab," he said. "We can have one more drink while we wait for it to get here."

Estelle yawned and Max joined in. "I'd rather stay put," she said. "I can go back in the morning, if that's all right."

Max patted the couch. "I'm afraid we don't have the greatest accommodations."

"That won't matter," she said, stretching out and using his thigh as a pillow. "I think I'll have to pass on that drink."

Max didn't try to change her mind, about drinking or staying. She was practically asleep already and he had to work to get her standing up so he could pull out the bed and put the sheets on. The two of them padded back and forth to the bathroom, he stripped down to his underwear, she borrowed one of his T-shirts, and they climbed onto the thin mattress. Max switched off the light and hugged Estelle close. "Thanks for being here," he said.

She didn't say anything and then he felt her leg twitch against his and he heard her breathing become steady as she slipped deeper into sleep. He tried to clear his mind and follow her.

27

ESTELLE WOKE UP just after three o'clock. Her
throat was dry, she had a dull headache, she wanted a cigarette,
and she wasn't sure where she was until she looked over at Max
and got her bearings. She walked quietly to the bathroom, and
then, as she washed down two aspirin, she remembered what
had startled her awake. In her dream, she'd opened the door to
her apartment and found her mother bound and gagged in the
rocking chair, struggling desperately to speak. The moment
Estelle removed the gag, her mother started shouting. "What
are you doing with your life! What are you doing with your life!"

That vision was too unoriginal to be truly disturbing, and yet
when she returned to bed, she stared at Max, wondering why
she was still with him. He was on his stomach, hugging his pillow to his head. His broad back rose and fell, and she watched
the side of his face for a few minutes. Then she put her lips to
the stubble on his cheek. She didn't really want to wake him up,

so she rolled onto her back, let her head sink into her pillow, and looked up at the unfamiliar ceiling. During her affair with that young lawyer, she'd fantasized about spending the night downtown in his Rittenhouse Square condominium. That would be the first step, she'd thought. She'd move in and the wife would finally have to move out. Nothing like that had ever happened, though. They went to her apartment or to a hotel. She met the kids, but she never saw where they lived.

So when was the last time she'd actually slept with a man in his own house? Before the lawyer, there'd been, briefly, an older cardiologist named Cliff. He was married to an emergency-room doctor and the two of them had busy medical schedules that didn't seem to coincide. Cliff was only too happy to have Estelle stop by their house at the appropriate times. But she never felt comfortable there; it was so sleek and modern and empty, and the appropriate times were always lunch hours or weekend mornings, so she never really slept there anyhow. The first and only time she did, Cliff shook her awake suddenly and rushed her out the back door as the wife walked up the driveway with a man of her own.

Before that, there was an architect who barely had time for sleep, let alone sex—but she was too tired to go through them all right now. It basically boiled down to this: so many impressive, upstanding professions, so many cads. And she herself was far from blameless. Her marriage had failed, but that didn't mean she needed to go out and see firsthand how many other marriages were failing, too. Despite the way it sometimes seemed, she knew there were eligible, unmarried men in Philadelphia. Like Max, in whose house—if you could call it "his" or "a house"—she was at this moment trying to sleep.

She turned onto her side and studied him again. Should she

go through the pros and cons, so to speak? She was attracted to him and he seemed to have a good heart. She liked that he had a nice son and she liked that he'd always wanted siblings. She liked that he was taking care of his father, even though that was clearly a struggle. She also liked that he was still trying hard to figure out what to do with his life. They had that in common. She didn't want to be simpleminded or schmaltzy, but she was beginning to believe there were all sorts of ways they could help each other.

And yet, as peaceful and innocent as he looked in his sleep, he was obviously ethically challenged. She wasn't about to deny that. He finds his father strapped to a chair and he doesn't want to call the police? That was far more disturbing than her dream had been.

If she gave him the benefit of the doubt and assumed he was genuinely trying to change for the better, she still wouldn't know if it was something he could do. He might try and fail.

She guessed the same could be said of her. "Hey, Max," she whispered, inching closer to him. "Tell me this. Will we be good together?"

He didn't stir, which was fine. It was probably far too soon to say. They were in the middle of too much. So, as she watched his back rise and fall, she decided he was thinking it over. She'd do likewise.

28

WHEN MAX OPENED his eyes, it was almost six. He'd had close to five hours of good sleep, free, for the most part, of dreams or nightmares. He could remember only one image: four women in wide-brimmed hats sitting around a conference table, speaking Chinese to each other. They were in mourning, their faces hidden, but he still thought he could guess who they were. Sandy, Grier, and Estelle. He had to wonder at the fourth one for a moment, until he realized that she was, of course, his mother. What would she think of all this? She'd want him to go back and do a million things differently. Start over. That would be fine with him. They could time-travel together, back to when he was five or six. She could be young and alive, dreaming about getting pregnant again. If that was too much to ask, maybe he could travel just one day back. Then he could be at the apartment in time to say good-bye to his uncle and save his father from Dexter.

He quietly washed and dressed, forcing himself to think about the hours ahead of him, think about what was actually possible. The best thing he could do was take better care of Caleb. He had to make sure nothing like last night ever happened again. He didn't have a plan yet, but he wanted to get a jump on the day, see if he could flush out some information. Before he left, he looked in on his father and kissed Estelle. He thought he'd be back before they woke up. Still, just in case, he wrote them a short note: *I'll be back for breakfast. Don't go to the diner without me.*

As he walked to his car, he was remembering what Caleb had said about Johnny and Dexter not getting along well. That made sense to him. Johnny might have lost control of his thug. Max could imagine that much more easily than he could imagine Johnny telling someone to strap Caleb into a chair. Spiller had probably thought Johnny was in charge, and then Dexter stepped around them both. Which meant that Johnny might be in trouble. Again. Max didn't see himself having much sympathy this time.

He drove over to the tennis club, figuring that was a good place to start, and it felt like an excellent guess when he saw that one of the two cars in the parking lot was Johnny's minivan. Inside the club, the main floor was brightly lit, but the court lights hadn't been turned on yet. Max peered into the office and saw that the kid who'd been stringing racquets before was stringing racquets again. It made Max wonder what Nathan was up to at Pennypack Park. Was he already awake, preparing breakfast, or was he still in his tent, dreaming in his sleeping bag? When would he find out about Abe? Max wanted to be there to help him handle the news. That's where he'd go next. He nodded hello to the kid and said, "You're working early."

"I've got a match at seven."

"Are you having a good summer?"

"I've had worse," the kid said, then he finally looked up from his work. "How's your summer going?"

It was an obvious, polite question, but it took Max by surprise. "My summer so far," he said. "It's been action packed. Not what I expected, that's for sure. Thanks for asking, though. You seen Johnny this morning?"

"Saw his van," the kid said, "but not him."

Max had a lousy hunch. It seemed like a continuation of the way he'd felt when he'd walked into the apartment and found the door unlocked. He'd known something was wrong. He was still finding out how wrong. He went down to the tennis court where he'd woken up not that long ago. The court was empty this time, no old women staring at him, asking him questions, just the hum of the air conditioner and the sound of his footsteps, echoing in that cavernous space. He walked past the net, listening carefully, but the only breathing he heard was his own. He stared at the green curtain as he approached. It was absolutely still. And yet, when he pulled it back, his heart was pounding. He was ready to see what he must have looked like when he'd been sprawled out on the asphalt. But he saw nothing except a few stray tennis balls.

Well, it was just his first theory of the morning. He couldn't really expect to drive directly to the right place. Johnny had other cars. Besides the minivan, there was that Explorer and who knew what else. After waiting a moment for his heart to relax, Max let go of the curtain and turned around. Then, as he started to walk toward the net, he heard what sounded like a moan and it seemed to come from one of the other courts. He hurried back behind the curtain and ran forward, kicking the tennis balls out of his way as he went.

Johnny was behind court 4. Dexter had apparently used more than his blackjack this time. There was a broken racquet near Johnny's feet. Max looked at the racquet because he could barely look at the body. Johnny was wearing his tight tennis outfit and everywhere Max saw skin, he also saw dried blood and cuts and bruises. If it hadn't been for that moan, Max would have assumed this was the body of a dead man. Johnny's head was battered and his eyes were swollen almost completely shut. Max had never seen anything like this. His hands were shaking as he took out his cell phone.

Johnny moaned again.

"Hang in there," Max said, dialing 911. "I'm calling for an ambulance."

"Hospital," said Johnny. He struggled to move.

Max knelt down and rested a hand on Johnny's bony shoulder. "They'll be here in a few minutes. You better stay put for now. We don't know what's broken yet."

"Water."

"I'll get you some." Max ran to the water cooler and filled an empty tennis ball can. By the time he ducked back behind the curtain, Johnny was sitting up, leaning against the wall. Max handed him the can of water. "Just take a sip or two."

Johnny took a long drink and then coughed most of it out onto the asphalt. "How bad do I look?" he asked.

Max paused, not knowing what to say. An ambulance siren was getting closer and Max remembered how his father spoke during those hospital rounds. "You'll be fine," he said. "I'd hate to see the other guy."

Johnny started to laugh, but it was clearly painful. He drank more water, slowly this time. "It wasn't supposed to go this way," he said.

Max looked away from Johnny's battered body and thought

back to what it had been like to find Caleb in the Viva Deluxe. "How was it supposed to go?" he asked.

Johnny didn't answer.

"I guess it was supposed to go better, right?"

Johnny hawked up a mixture of phleghm and blood. He spit it off to his side. "I convinced Spiller to give me a little cut. That's all I needed, but Dexter wants more. He wants to figure out a way to take your place."

Max heard the ambulance come to a stop outside. He looked back at Johnny and tried to remember those university days, when he and Johnny were friends, when he would have been happy to take Johnny's place. It made him want to ask a few questions. Why hadn't Johnny done more with his gifts? Why had he kept doing the wrong thing, over and over? Why had he wasted so much potential? But Johnny was in no condition to answer—he was coughing again, wincing with each cough, probably from a broken rib or two. Besides, Max didn't really need answers. He already knew how mistakes like that happened.

When the paramedics rushed onto the court, Max held the curtain open for them. Johnny was wiping his mouth with the back of his hand. "Watch out for Dexter, Max," he said. "Tell Spiller to watch out, too."

The paramedics lifted Johnny onto the stretcher and Max started to step away. "If I were you," he said, "I'd just worry about myself for now."

29

CALEB HAD NO desire to get out of bed. He couldn't
stop remembering the day before. It had been far worse than any
nightmare. He wanted to go back to sleep and dream of better
times, but he heard voices in the kitchen. Rabbi Weinberg had
come much earlier than expected and Max's new girlfriend must
have spent the night. She was saying something about "another
note." Then there was a third voice. He didn't recognize it. An
older woman, he guessed. Plenty of women he'd never met before would probably show up to mourn Abe. Whoever this particular woman was, she spoke louder than Estelle or Weinberg.
"At least he's not lazy," she said.

Caleb didn't think they were talking about him, but he sat up
and told himself he had to face the day. The smell of food made
the decision easier. They were warming bagels out there, they'd
unwrapped some lox, onions had been sliced, and the coffee was
on. He took a set of dark clothes from the closet and shuffled to
the bathroom.

A few minutes later, showered and unshaven, Caleb walked into the kitchen. He was thinking about how quiet Abe had become after the strokes. He remembered that day in the hospital, Abe's real voice returning for a few hours and then disappearing forever, replaced by fragments and commands. Caleb knew the people standing in front of him were hoping to offer comfort, but he didn't know what to say to them. Maybe his own power of speech was slipping away.

Weinberg stepped forward and hugged him. Estelle hugged him next, and she introduced her mother, Janet, who hugged him, too. They said they were sorry and he nodded. He was about to say *Thank you,* but that didn't seem right, so he kept quiet a little longer, glad to have a crowd in the kitchen, glad to be able to lose himself in the simple task of pouring a cup of coffee. He tried to remember what he'd said during those days after Naomi's accident. Abe had done much of the talking for him then. Suddenly, he had to sit down. He went over to the couch, wondering what, over the years, Abe *hadn't* done for him.

Ever since the strokes, it had been easy to think of Abe as a burden, someone he needed to care for, someone who was completely dependent upon him, and yet, looking back, Caleb couldn't stop seeing that it was always Abe who'd been giving and giving, trying to give more.

Caleb told himself to stay calm. He set his coffee mug on the table and leaned forward, holding his head in his hands.

The rabbi came over and sat down beside him. "Caleb," he said, "tell me what you're thinking."

Caleb was rocking slowly back and forth. He had just remembered what he'd said after Naomi died. Back then, he'd been haunted by the feeling that he hadn't told her he loved her nearly enough. That's what he'd spoken about all through the mourning. How he wanted more time to talk with her, how there was so much more he wanted to tell her. And now, even though he'd had months and months with Abe, even though they'd been trapped together in a cramped, underground apartment, he'd somehow managed to make the same awful mistake. How could he have been so foolish?

Rabbi Weinberg moved closer and put an arm around Caleb's shoulder. "It's okay," he said. "It's going to be hard. It's almost impossible. I know. You can tell me."

Caleb wanted to say something. At first, "Ah" was all he could manage. Then, finally, a few words came to him: *Where's my son?* That's what he needed to know, that's what he was about to ask, but, before he could speak, the door opened and Max walked in, Nathan by his side.

30

MAX HAD WORRIED that Dexter would get back to the apartment before he did, so he was relieved to see the living room crowded with people. He was also relieved to see that Estelle hadn't left yet, and he liked that she'd invited Janet over. He didn't talk with either one of them right away because his father had him and Nathan in a bear hug. "I love you both so much," Caleb kept saying. "I'm so glad you're here."

"Come on, Dad," Max said. "We love you, too. Let's sit down."

The rabbi walked up and leaned into the hug, one hand on Caleb's back, the other on Nathan's shoulder. "I have to go to the temple now, but I want you to know it's good to see the three of you together. It gives me hope."

Max wanted to check in with Estelle, but the rabbi tugged on his arm and said, "Walk me outside." Max hesitated, watching until Caleb and Nathan were sitting next to each other on the couch. Then he caught Estelle's eye, smiled, and followed the rabbi.

Once they were out of the apartment, they stood on the sidewalk. Max noticed that the rabbi looked tired, dark half circles under his eyes. Probably hadn't been able to sleep after that late-night phone call. "Thanks for coming by," Max said.

"I wish it were for a different occasion. I preferred the bar mitzvah."

Max thought back to that day, two weeks ago. He remembered Caleb and Abe up in that front row, ecstatic, then all of them up in Nathan's room, going through gift after gift.

The rabbi glanced down Cheltenham Avenue. "My cab should be here in a few minutes," he said. He took a pack of cinnamon gum out of his pocket, unwrapped a stick for himself, and offered one to Max. "You're going to have to stay here now. You know that, right?"

Max waved off the gum and said, "Well, actually, that's the way things were leaning, even before this whole—"

The rabbi cut in. "I'll be glad to have you back in town. And I won't be the only one. I don't know if it has anything to do with anything, but I spent some time with Estelle in the kitchen this morning. She seems like a nice woman."

Max thought he was too old to blush, but his face felt warm. "I'm not going to disagree with you, Rabbi."

"Even her mother seems like a sweetheart."

"Okay, okay," Max said. "It's still early. There's no rush."

Weinberg grinned. "I won't say another word about it. For now. I'll tell you this instead. I heard things went well in Ephrata."

"How much do you know about that?"

"I know enough, Max. The temple and I have an interest in this venture. It was Abe's final mitzvah."

A yellow cab pulled up in front of them. Max was wondering just how many people Abe's "final mitzvah" would help. Could it really lead him into a better life and the rabbi into a better temple?

Weinberg stepped toward the cab. "Here's one more thing I've heard," he said. "Spiller will be stopping by."

"When?"

Weinberg took his hand off the car door and checked his watch. "Any minute now," he said. Then he climbed into the backseat and waved good-bye as the cab drove off.

Max was looking forward to seeing Spiller. He'd hoped to find him when he picked up Nathan at the Pennypack Park campground, but an assistant scoutmaster named Gottlieb had been in charge. Spiller, Gottlieb had said, was away, "taking care of some business."

Max started to pace the sidewalk, waiting to see if the rabbi was right. Before he took his tenth step, two black BMWs pulled up to the curb. The first one was the familiar convertible, top down, with Anna driving and Spiller in the passenger seat. It wasn't yet nine o'clock, but those two could have been on their way to an elegant night on the town. They had on their matching black slacks, and she had on a red blouse while he was wearing a shiny shark-colored polo shirt. It was hard to imagine them out camping.

They gave Max their condolences and then Spiller kissed Anna's cheek and said, "Why don't you go on in? I need to talk to Max. I'll be there soon."

Once she was inside, Spiller led Max to the second BMW, which was a sedan with tinted windows. The front passenger window went down, and Max could see two thin Chinese men, most of their faces hidden by sunglasses. "This is Y. Y. and Ping," Spiller said. "Your father probably told you about them."

"We're sorry for your loss," said Ping.

"Now," Spiller went on, "in the backseat we have a man who's leaving town. I thought you might want to say good-bye to him."

The rear tinted window descended and Max saw Dexter sitting there, duct tape across his mouth, his hands behind his back. A much larger Chinese man was right beside him. "Charles is another of my cousins-in-law," Spiller explained. "He's Dexter's escort for the day."

"I'm sorry for your loss, too," Charles said. "I'm also sorry about what happened to your father. If you'd like to do something to this moron here, I'd be happy to turn the other way."

Max thought it over, but what could he do? A punch or two wouldn't change anything. He'd wind up hurting his hand. Besides, when he looked into Dexter's eyes, he could tell the guy was already scared of whatever punishment he had coming. Max stepped back from the window. "Thanks for the offer," he said, "but I'll let you take care of it."

Spiller slapped the roof of the car. The window rose up and the sedan pulled out onto the street, heading downtown.

"What will happen to him?" Max asked.

Spiller walked to his convertible and leaned against it. "That's not something I get to decide. Some people I've been talking to in Atlantic City will figure it out. I'm just sorry he slipped around me last night. Weinberg told me how you found Caleb in that scooter. It must have been awful."

Max nodded. "I'm glad Dexter's off the streets. And I can't tell you how grateful I am for all you've done."

Spiller seemed to be bracing himself against the car. "But?"

Max almost didn't go on. Maybe it would be better just to wait and see what happened next, but before he could make up his mind he was saying more. "I'll look after my father and I'll help finish what you and Abe started, but I want to stay out of Johnny and Dexter's world. I want to try to be legitimate again."

Spiller appeared to relax. He stretched his hands up toward the sky, twisting his back one way and then the other until it cracked. "So," he said, "you're wondering how you can be legitimate and work with me?"

"Yes."

"I do good business, Max. It's Johnny and Dexter who work in less admirable ways, and they'll have to deal with their own bosses. I take precautions, it's true, and I hire people like Charles to protect me and my work. That's what good, legitimate businessmen have to do. And I probably don't need to remind you that Johnny was connected to you, not me."

Max hadn't been thinking of it that way. "I'm sorry," he said. "I never thought he'd wind up causing so much trouble."

"It's all right. It's in the past now. Let's hear what else you're worried about."

Again Max wasn't sure if he should go on, but this was his chance. Who knew when he'd get another? "Even before this whole mess with Johnny and Dexter, I was thinking about all the people we'll be putting out of work. Isn't that worse than separating a few old folks from some of their savings?"

"People lose their jobs. And factories move offshore. These things are unavoidable, with or without what we're doing. But if it's any consolation, we'll be creating jobs, too, and not sweatshop jobs, either. Anna's family runs a good, fair mill. Plus, who knows, our competitors might not resort to layoffs. They could make other adjustments, find new clients, new products. They've lost business before."

Max knew he was being sold. That's what Spiller did. It came down, once again, to the question of trust. How much could he believe?

Spiller was cracking his knuckles now. "What else is bothering you?" he asked. "Come on. Let's get everything out."

"Will you tell me what really happened between you and Abe?"

"What do you think happened?"

Max had no good guesses. "I'm not sure," he said. "You're doing so much for my family. You tell these stories about parachutes, about Abe and your open-heart surgery, but I still don't know the truth."

Spiller laughed. "You're right, you don't. But now I'll give it to you straight. Are you ready?"

"Yes."

"We were just good friends, Max. People seem to like fancier stories, but it's as simple and complicated as that. I could always count on him. We made mistakes together, maybe more than our fair share, but we didn't lose faith. We didn't stop looking out for each other. That's what we did and that's what I'm doing, for you, your father, and your son."

To Max, this sounded like the latest of his old-school lessons. It also sounded true. He stood there on the sidewalk, staring at a sixty-some-year-old guy, a guy who was a scoutmaster and a businessman, a guy who was his uncle's friend. Max kept staring and it wasn't hard to picture Abe and Spiller meeting at a diner out on the road, laughing after a hard day's work, making plans for something better, dreaming together of an easier future. It was a vision Max could believe in. It was time, once and for all, to trust the man.

"Well?" asked Spiller.

"I don't know what to say."

"Try 'Thank you.'"

"Thank you."

"You're welcome," Spiller said. Then he slapped Max on

the back, walked toward the building, and stepped into the apartment.

MAX DIDN'T GO inside right away. He paced the sidewalk again, studying the neighborhood, thinking he wouldn't be spending too many more nights at this address. He also wouldn't be going back to Florida anytime soon, so he took out his cell phone and called Grier. When she answered, he told her about Abe, and he told her that he'd be staying in Philadelphia much longer than he'd expected. She offered her condolences and said, "I think you saved us a difficult reunion."

"Things with the young professor are going well?"

"They are," she said.

"I guess we hopped on different trains."

"I guess so."

She sounded relieved, and he imagined that he did, too. "How's the sea grass doing?"

"I'm finally getting good results."

"That's great," he said, but he wasn't really listening. He was thinking about how quickly people moved from one person to another. How easy it was not to be loyal. Was he any different? Could he be?

"I have to run," Grier said. "Give me a call if you're ever passing through town, all right?"

He wasn't certain if she meant it or not, but he said, "All right," and put the phone back in his pocket.

He still wasn't ready to go inside, so he walked up Cheltenham Avenue to the corner of Fifth Street. He didn't want to kid himself. There would be tough times ahead. Who knew when—or if—Caleb would recover from this terrible new loss? But Max pushed those thoughts aside for a moment and looked out toward the city. Maybe they could find a great retirement community for Caleb downtown. Max imagined setting up a small office nearby, calling it Wolinsky Brothers and Son. And Caleb could come in whenever he felt like it, work the phones, see the clients he wanted to see. Max would sign up for night classes back at Temple. He pictured a nice condo for himself, in a pet-friendly building, where he could take Harrison up on his offer, get another puppy for this new beginning. Maybe there'd be a big enough place right around the art museum or over in Manayunk. No matter where it was, there'd be an extra bedroom for Nathan and plenty of space for Caleb, too.

And then there was Estelle. It was far too soon to say what would happen with her, but as he hurried back to the apartment he was looking forward to finding out.

31

ON THE MORNING of the funeral, the Wolinskys drove to Belasco's and were shown into a ready room, right behind the chapel. The only brightness in the small space came from the white and green mints in a glass bowl by the telephone. It wasn't that different from a hospital room — fluorescent lights, linoleum tile, antiseptic, with nothing on the walls — but instead of a bed there were a handful of black, plastic chairs. Before anyone could sit down, Bernie Belasco walked in. He looked like a well-dressed baker, with pudgy hands, short hair as white as flour, and a body that was doughy from head to toe. "My condolences to all of you," he said.

"Thank you," Caleb said. "We appreciate your help."

Bernie nodded, put a hand on Caleb's shoulder, and pinned a button with a black ribbon to his lapel. Then he said a short prayer and ripped the ribbon. "It will be a closed-casket ceremony, as you wished," he said, "but the casket is open now, and we'll leave it open for a few minutes before the rest of the mourners begin to arrive. If you'd like a moment or two with Abraham, you can come with me."

"I'll see him," said Caleb.

Nathan started to follow his grandfather. "You don't have to go, son," Max said. "It's fine if you just want to remember how he looked."

"I'll go," Nathan said. "I can go."

Only when he heard that determined voice did Max realize Nathan was wearing his bar mitzvah suit. Now it would also be the suit he wore to his first funeral. "All right," Max said, and he walked next to his son.

Bernie opened the door to the chapel. "I'll wait here," he said, "in case you need anything."

Max and Nathan were a step behind Caleb, but Max was watching his father closely. Caleb, his arms by his side, his back straight, walked up steadily, the same way he moved through all those hospital corridors during his many rounds. Max wondered if those visits had been some kind of preparation for this, a way to build up endurance for yet another awful, impossible test. Then, as soon as Caleb reached the coffin, his legs seemed to give out, and his head dropped down. Max rushed forward and wrapped an arm around his father, but Caleb had already grabbed on to the casket. He was holding himself up. He slapped the wood twice with his open hand and looked down at his brother. "Abe," he said. "Oh, Abraham."

MAX WASN'T SURE how long they stood together by the coffin. At first, he couldn't bear to look. He focused on Caleb and Nathan instead. Nathan took his grandfather's hand and Max felt proud. He closed his eyes, to brace himself, and then he looked at the body.

Through the strokes and silences, a spark had always lit Abe's eyes, his whole face. Even after he'd ceased making sense, you knew that Abe, or at least a part of him, lived on somewhere beyond the damaged neurons. You could see it in his gestures and his gait, hear it in the words he struggled to say. Now, with a glance, Max could tell that the life was gone. This wasn't Abe. Abe was elsewhere. Max had been right to look at his father and son holding hands. That's where the life was.

When he heard footsteps, Max figured it was Bernie coming to tell them to take their seats, but there were too many footsteps for one person. Then he heard his son shout, "Mom!" Max turned to see Rabbi Weinberg leading Sandy into the chapel.

Max hadn't called her, but Weinberg must have. That was the rabbi, always trying to make bygones be bygones. This time, though, Max had to give the two of them credit. It couldn't have been easy for her to fly in from Hawaii. Yes, he noticed her tan and how slim she was in her black dress, but it didn't seem to hurt him, it was just part of seeing her at her best again, stunning and thoughtful and brave.

She hugged Nathan first. "It's good to hear your voice," she said. Nathan didn't say anything else right away, but Max had a feeling the silent treatment had just ended.

His hug came next. He didn't want to get lost in it and he made sure not to hold her too long or too tightly.

"I'm so sorry," she said.

"Thank you for coming," he said, and then he let go, easing her toward Caleb.

That hug went on for a while. Caleb wiped tears from his eyes, and Sandy was crying, saying, again, how sorry she was.

"I can't believe you came from so far away," Caleb said. "I can't believe you did that."

"Of course I did that," she said.

"Thank you," he said.

Between the time the casket was closed and the service began, Caleb thanked dozens of people. He sat in the front row with his son and his grandson beside him. He'd asked Sandy to sit with them, too, but she wouldn't do that, and he understood.

Although Sandy had covered the greatest distance, she wasn't the only one who had traveled far to attend the funeral. Caleb couldn't get over it. So many people. People they used to sell to and people they used to represent. He saw the Nathansons, the Evanses, the Seldises, Patty Gay, Lester Beckman. A few of the old secretaries from Dutchmaker and Easternland and Tritex. They kissed his cheek, took his hand, hugged him too hard, told him what a wonderful brother he'd had, and then they moved on. There were the locals as well, his friends from the suburbs and from downtown, from Spring Garden, Chestnut Circle, and Breyer's Run. Caleb stayed in his seat because he was tired, but also because he was shocked by the faces that kept appearing before him. The line seemed to go on and on, a solemn yet uplifting parade.

Who had called them all? It hadn't been him. He wanted to make sure someone was making a list. He needed everyone to sign in. Then he remembered Bernie would take care of that. There would be a guest book, just as there had been a guest book for Naomi. Yes, he was back in the same room, sitting in the same place, and Bernie—who used to be a thin assistant, a son working for a father—was standing at the chapel entrance, greeting the mourners, guiding them in.

It occurred to Caleb that he really shouldn't have been so

surprised to see this line of people. They were, after all, the same people who'd been in the line before. Maybe the surprise was how different everyone looked, even though they remained the same. Like Bernie, like himself, they'd once been thinner, younger, hairier. On that long-ago day, when it had been Naomi's smashed body in the casket, they'd been stunned by the loss, but most of them were still able to look ahead, think about the future. What futures did they look ahead to now? That was a tough question to face, and yet they'd all have to face it, if not today, then tomorrow, or the day after that. In the meantime, they'd keep making their rounds, doing their best to stand by each other.

Caleb reached out to take the hand of the next person in line, but there was no hand offered. He looked up to see a man balancing himself on a walker, his whole body trembling. This man wore a tight-fitting knit cap, and he was bundled up as if for winter. Caleb stared into the pale white face, and he understood the man was shivering, and then he realized it was Joe Lonzinger, somehow miles from his hospital bed.

"Hello, young man," Caleb said. "Hold on a second and I'll stand up for you."

"Don't go to any trouble," Joe said, his voice shaking almost as much as his body.

There had been noise before, the sounds of Max talking to the mourners as they passed by, the sound of people finding their seats, chatting softly to each other, but now the chapel seemed quiet and still. Caleb pushed himself up. He slid the walker aside and took Joe's two hands. Then he moved in closer and hugged Joe, gently.

"I brought you another moneymaker," Joe whispered into his ear. "It's something Abe would have loved."

"Don't tell me now. I'd never remember. Wait until I come see you."

"I might forget it," Joe said. "My memory's not what it used to be."

"I'll take my chances."

"Truth is, I thought you'd be bringing him over to say good-bye to me. I thought I'd beat him into the box."

Caleb stepped back and helped Joe place his hands on the walker. "You look fine," he said. "It's good to see you up and around."

"Spoken like a real salesman," said Joe. "I'll tell you this. I missed Abe a lot already. Now I miss him more."

Caleb nodded. "Me too," he said. Then he watched as Joe leaned into the walker and pushed forward.

NATHAN DIDN'T KNOW who many of these people were, but they all seemed to know him. They told him how sorry they were, how proud Abe was of him, how sometimes every other sentence out of his mouth began with "Nathan this" or "Nathan that." He wasn't sure how to respond, and his father was busy talking, so he moved away from the line for a while and went over to see his mother. Ever since she'd walked in, he'd been wondering where Hiram was. What did it mean that she had come home without him?

She was standing by herself on the other side of the room, right next to the wall. They hugged again and sat down at the end of a still empty row. "I don't like funerals," she said.

"Me neither."

"At least the silent treatment's over," she said. "It's nice to have a little good news in the middle of all this."

It was time for him to apologize, he felt that, but he wasn't ready. Instead, he asked, "How's Hawaii?"

She looked around for a moment, as if she wanted to make certain no one was eavesdropping. "It's an incredibly beautiful place. We're learning more every day. You wouldn't believe the flowers there."

He wanted to talk about her and Hiram, but he didn't know if that was the right thing to do. Lately, he'd been thinking about the divorce a lot. He'd met Estelle and he liked her and he could tell that his father did, too. But it was more than that. Ever since he'd started spending time with Jennifer, he felt he could appreciate how a person might be thrilling and irresistible. They'd still only kissed six times, and he couldn't really describe what it meant, but it made him feel differently. It made him think that maybe now he and his mother would get along better. Maybe his experience would make it easier for his mother to talk about who she loved and didn't love and why.

But that conversation would have to wait. They both saw the rabbi move to the front of the room. "You need to get back to your seat," she said, adjusting the black *kippah* on his head. She took a handkerchief from her purse and started talking faster as she wiped at her eyes. "You should be with your grandfather and your father now. We'll talk more later."

He thought he should stay with her because she was crying and alone, but she hugged him and then pushed him away, so he left.

SITTING BETWEEN HIS father and his grandfather, Nathan tried to pay attention to the rabbi. He heard the words and the prayers, and he joined in when he was supposed to, but his mind wasn't really on the service until he watched his father stand up and walk to the front of the chapel. He held onto the lectern, gazed out over the crowd for a long moment, and then started to speak.

"A few months after my mother died, my uncle Abe took me

away to Florida for a vacation. He wanted to get me out of the house for a while. He wanted to take me someplace where I could be happy, where I could begin to have some hope again. Well, he gave me hope, all right, maybe even too much. What I mean is, I began to hope that Abe would make my mother reappear. You all know how stylish and charming and inspiring he was. I was seven years old at the time and I believed he could do absolutely anything. I thought he'd arranged a surprise. I thought we'd go away, find my mother, and bring her back to my father. Simple as that."

The people in the crowd seemed glad to have a reason to laugh, however briefly. Nathan noticed that his father was suddenly smiling, looking toward the back of the chapel. Troop 158 was filing into the room. Spiller came in right behind the Cobras and the Owls, all of them in uniform. Nathan made eye contact with Felix. Felix waved, then quickly dropped his hand.

The eulogy continued and Nathan found himself leaning forward, listening carefully, but he was also trying to imagine his father at seven. It wasn't easy. He'd seen only a few photographs. There was one he remembered of his four-year-old father on a tire swing behind the old house. His hair was long, in some sort of bowl cut, like the Beatles, and his mouth was wide open, as if he were belting out a song. Nathan could also remember a wild picture from elementary school, his father dressed in a plaid, purple leisure suit. He couldn't have worn that in Florida. Abe would never have let it happen.

After Naomi died, no one was taking many photographs, so it was even harder for Nathan to imagine his father at eight or ten or thirteen. He'd asked about it once and all his father had said was, "I was shorter than you and not nearly as handsome."

Now his father was saying that Abe had been an excellent

salesman, even though some ventures had failed. He mentioned attempts to make money on hats, sweaters, pajamas, stuffed animals, and car upholstery. While the crowd laughed a little more, Nathan thought of how many family stories he hadn't heard yet. He watched his father pause, smile, dab his eyes with a tissue. His father, whom he'd known all his life. His father, who was still a mystery.

Nathan wondered why he wasn't crying, too. He would miss Uncle Abe, and each time he glanced at his exhausted grandfather he felt sadder, but maybe he didn't feel sad enough and that made him feel guilty, and then his father said his name.

"My son, Nathan, was bar mitzvahed not that long ago. He gave a much better speech than I'm giving, and toward the end he posed a bunch of questions. I can't remember them all right now, but I remember one. It had to do with what we inherit. He wanted to know why punishments were passed down from one generation to the next. Why does a son so often suffer for the sins of the father?"

Whenever his father paused, Nathan could feel the hush in the room. His father claimed not to have any answers, but he wanted to point out that sins, punishments, failures, and mistakes weren't the only things that got passed down. "Goodness and hope and dreams are also passed down," he said, "from older brother to younger brother, from uncle to nephew, from grandfather to father to son. The good and bad are there, given to us, and we hold on to what we choose. I want to say that Abe has inspired me to choose more wisely from this day forward."

Nathan looked around the chapel again. He saw the Ten Commandments on the wall behind the lectern. He stared at the polished wood of the closed casket. He glanced at his mother, at the rabbi, at Spiller, the scouts, and the rows and rows of people, and everyone's eyes were on his father. How could he possibly doubt his father in a setting like this, at a time like this? And yet he knew his father was at least as good a salesman as Uncle Abe, and like a good salesman he would say what he needed to say, speak whatever words the situation required. Nathan wanted some assurance. A guarantee. He wanted to know what would happen next. He moved closer to his grandfather and whispered, "Do you think he's really going to change?"

Caleb didn't answer right away, and Nathan thought he hadn't whispered loudly enough, but then his grandfather leaned over and kissed his cheek. "I think so," he said. "I hope so."

AT THAT MOMENT, Nathan began to figure out why he hadn't been crying. Despite all the sadness and doubt that surrounded him, he was, like his grandfather, feeling hopeful.

Yes, in the middle of the funeral, he felt hope, and he felt it more and more powerfully as the summer went along. He felt it all through July as he camped out in the shadow of Beth Israel. Caleb came to visit him there a few times, as did his father and Estelle. In August, while the troop camped in the Poconos and at Treasure Island Scout Camp, Nathan received three postcards a week from his father, each one mailed from Philadelphia, each one giving him more hope that Florida was a thing of the past. Then, when he came back at the end of the trek, the first place his father took him was a retirement community downtown, right near Society Hill. Caleb had moved into a sunny apartment on the eleventh floor with a view of the Delaware River, and he looked happy there, happier than Nathan had seen him in a long time.

That first night back, the hope seemed almost overwhelming. The three of them drove out to Del Ennis, where Estelle and

Janet were waiting with two bags of cheesesteaks from Lee's. Before they started to bowl, Max gave Nathan a big gift-wrapped box. "You can't play baseball with this," he said, "but it might come in handy here."

The box weighed about fourteen pounds. It didn't take a genius to know what it was. A bowling ball, engraved with his name. Shiny silver blue. "It goes well with your eyes," Estelle said.

Nathan followed his father over to the pro shop to have the holes drilled and, while they waited, Max talked about the condominium he was bidding on, how many rooms it had, how he thought it would be perfect. Nathan just listened, wanting to believe his family was due for some good luck, wanting to believe it would last.

When he got back to the lane, everyone was ready to get started and they told him he had to go first. "Looks like you're batting lead-off," Max said.

Nathan put the ball down on the ball return and wiped his hands on his jeans. He felt like he had so much to say about what had been happening to him during the trek, and he wanted to hear more about what had been going on while he was away, but he knew there would be time for that later. Right now, his father, his grandfather, Estelle, and Janet were all standing around the scorer's table, watching and waiting.

He picked up the ball and gave himself room for his five-step approach. He was almost set, but he turned to look back at everyone again, wishing that Abe were there, too, alive, stroke-free, his power of speech returned. Nathan wanted to tell him all about the summer, how he joined a strange troop of kosher Boy Scouts and kissed a girl and became a man and had a much better time than he'd expected. How would Abe respond? What would he say? Nathan stood still, trying to remember his great-uncle's voice, and for a moment he thought he could hear Abe whispering down to him, telling him to keep dreaming, telling him to take advantage of everything he'd been given.

Then Caleb was calling out to him. "Come on," he said. "Let's see what that ball can do."

"Boom, boom," said Janet. "Knock 'em down."

Nathan stepped forward, focusing on the spot between the second and third arrows, reminding himself to follow through. He felt the weight of that new ball and then he was releasing it, rolling it down the alley, and he lifted his arm up and reached out for the headpin and he could hear his father close behind him, saying, "Looks good, looks *real* good," and they all watched that silver-blue gift begin to hook, nice and smooth, right into the pocket.

Acknowledgments

THIS BOOK WAS a long time coming and it required a lot of help and I am indebted to many great people. The Creative Writing Program at Boston University and the Wallace Stegner Fellowship at Stanford were extremely generous with their support and guidance, and the same can be said of my fantastic teachers over the years: Dan McCall and James McConkey at Cornell; Leslie Epstein, Ralph Lombreglia, and Allegra Goodman at BU; and Elizabeth Tallent, John L'Heureux, and Tobias Wolff at Stanford.

The University at Albany, SUNY, continues to be an excellent, exciting place to teach, and my colleagues from the English department, the New York State Writers Institute, and the rest of the university have been consistently encouraging and inspiring. I'm very glad to be working with them, and it's a pleasure to especially thank Donald Faulkner, William Kennedy, Suzanne Lance, Mark Koplik, Judy Axenson, Randall Craig, Gareth Griffiths, Michael Hill, Bret Benjamin, Lisa Thompson, Joel Berkowitz, and Lee Franklin.

I have been blessed with incredible readers — readers who have become my best friends and who have taught me an enormous amount not only about how to write but also about how to live in this world. I am deeply grateful to Debra Gitterman, Elizabeth Graver, David Blake, John Gregory Brown, Carrie Brown, Eric Korsh, Richard Wurman, Michelle Chalfoun, Christopher Castellani, Tamara Guirado, Adam Johnson, ZZ Packer, Angela Pneuman, and Julie Orringer.

I'd also like to offer my heartfelt thanks to a few people who were willing to take a chance on the Wolinskys and me: the wonderful Marie Hayes at *StoryQuarterly;* the kind staff at *Moment* magazine, especially Harvey Grossinger and Rebecca Frankel; my insightful, ideal agent, Dorian Karchmar at Lowenstein-Yost Associates; and my extraordinarily wise editor, Antonia Fusco. Thanks as well to Jude Grant, Anne Winslow, Brunson Hoole, Kelly Clark, and everyone else at Algonquin for their hard work on this book.

Finally, my love and thanks to my amazing family, without whom nothing would be possible: to my parents, William and Carol Schwarzschild, who taught me to read and gave me books and stood by me every step of the way; to my uncle and aunt, Mark Merin and Cathleen Williams, who shared their California life with me and never stopped encouraging me to do what I wanted to do; to my brothers, Arthur and Jeffrey, who are my two favorite people in the world; and to Charles and Mildred Merin, my bubba and zayde, who made us all.